MISPLACED
LIVES

Also by Barbara Victor

ABSENCE OF PAIN

B A R B A R A
V I C T O R

A NOVEL

MISPLACED
LIVES

1817

HARPER & ROW, PUBLISHERS, New York

Grand Rapids, Philadelphia, St. Louis, San Francisco
London, Singapore, Sydney, Tokyo, Toronto

Grateful acknowledgment is made for permission to reprint the excerpt from *High Windows* by Philip Larkin, which appears on page 102. © 1974 by Philip Larkin. Reprinted by permission of Farrar, Straus & Giroux, Inc.

FIRST EDITION

Designed by Alma Orenstein

Library of Congress Cataloging-in-Publication Data

Victor, Barbara.
  Misplaced lives / Barbara Victor.—1st ed.
    p. cm.
  ISBN 0-06-016373-9
  I. Title.
PS3572.I26M57   1990
813'.54—dc20   89-46127

90 91 92 93 94 CG/RRD 10 9 8 7 6 5 4 3 2 1

This book is dedicated
with love and gratitude to
Larry Ashmead and Elaine Markson

ACKNOWLEDGMENTS

FOR THOSE PEOPLE who knew that the headaches weren't terminal but signs of doubt, that the momentary lapses in speech or the inability to listen weren't acute signs of narcissism but merely fatigue and for those same people who also understood that all those months and months of agony that is sometimes called the creative process made their friend less than human, I give my love and gratitude.

Robert Jones
Brigitte Jessen
Michel Alexandre
Eveline Trawidlo
Robert Solomon

And for my editors who made this a better book I also give my love and gratitude.

Susan Watt
Eamon Dolan

Special thanks to Nicholas Tabbal, Beth Tedesco, Alain Carrière, Lennart Sane, and Brenda Segel.

MISPLACED
LIVES

PROLOGUE

"DOUBLE FAULT!" Adrienne calls the ball right before it crashes into the green netting behind her. Taking a position on the other side of her court, she hunches over her racket in preparation for his next serve. "Love–thirty," she adds.

"Damn it," Pete explodes, "I don't need the score, thank you very much!"

"Lighten up, it's only a game!"

"Only a game when you're winning. When you're not, it's World War Three with the original cast!" He swings his arm around in a circular motion.

"Got a kink?" She wipes the sweat from her face with one corner of her T-shirt.

"More like shooting pains."

"Quit finding excuses just because you're out of shape!"

"Like hell I am!"

"So play ball, sweetheart," she teases. Rocking on her heels once more, she leans forward to receive the ball.

Pete Molloy does his usual two-step shuffle, a quick movement at the baseline at the same instant that he tosses up the ball, his right arm slicing the air in an upward motion before it comes down hard on its target. "Nice shot," Adrienne yells as she dives for it and misses. "Good one!"

It happens without any warning so that it takes Adrienne Fast fully several seconds to comprehend and to react.

Had she been totally logical right then it might have occurred to her that the quickest way to reach him was to walk around the side of the court. Instead she rushes forward to jump over the net. "Pete," she shrieks. "Oh, my God, Pete!"

The couple who had been volleying next to them appears to be frozen, watching in horror as the scene unfolds. "Please, someone help," Adrienne cries as she collapses over Pete's crumpled figure. Her hand reaches out to touch him but instead ends up over her mouth to stifle another scream. "It was your point," she sobs irrationally. "Please get up, it's still your serve."

Now the couple has rushed over, and while the woman hangs back, the man bends down next to Adrienne. "Please," she whimpers as she watches this stranger press his fingers against Pete's neck, "please help him, he's sick!" The man's response is to snap at his companion, who is still hanging back. "Call 911 and make it fast!" Horrified, Adrienne watches as the woman bolts across the court, almost crashing into a group of people who are heading in their direction.

Pete lies motionless, flat on his face, his damp tennis shirt hiked up at his waist to expose a patch of bare flesh, his arms to his sides, racket near his left knee, one tennis ball still bulging from a hip pocket, another rolling toward the net. Somehow Adrienne has been edged aside, crying softly by herself, while the man and several others attend to Pete. But when they manage to turn him over on his back Adrienne lets out a piercing scream. Blood covers his entire face where his nose was smashed against the floor in his fall.

Someone kneels down to breathe for him while someone else begins pressing in and out on his chest. The man from the neighboring court puts a comforting arm around Adrienne's shoulders to steady her while the woman, after seeing all the blood, issues her own warning. "Jack, be careful, just don't touch him, you never know!" But she needn't have worried since someone else, with obvious expertise, is giving Pete mouth-to-mouth resuscitation while the tennis pro takes over massaging his heart.

"Do it slower," the man named Jack advises. "You're doing it too fast!" Tears continue to stream down Adrienne's cheeks and into the corners of her mouth.

"Are you a doctor?" she asks desperately, clutching at his arm.

"No, I'm an accountant," he answers, standing firm as Adrienne tries to push him forward to volunteer him for the job. But the woman is upon them again, yanking at his sleeve.

"Don't you dare!" she yells. "He's all covered with blood, are you crazy?" Then she adds in a hoarse whisper that can be heard clear across the tennis bubble, "You don't know where he's been."

At that moment Adrienne loses what little control she has left. "He's been with me," she cries before collapsing in a heap on the court, "only with me." But nobody pays attention. Still they all try to breathe life back into Pete Molloy.

Still Pete Molloy doesn't breathe back.

Several minutes later the paramedics finally arrive only to push everyone out of the way and start from the beginning, this time aided by tubes, dozens of vials of medicine, needles, oxygen, electric wires, suction cups, and a complicated computerized heart monitor.

It is too late. Clearly all the life has seeped out of his body, even from his eyes, which stare blindly into space. Adrienne has managed somehow to crawl over to him when she sees that the others have given up, after the paramedics disconnect all the wires and the tubes and other equipment. Now she is in charge. Gently wiping the blood from his face with the bottom of her tennis skirt, she weeps softly, smoothing his face tenderly, leaning her cheek against his chest. "My whole life," she moans, "you were my whole life."

— 3 —

"Were you here when it happened?" one of the para-medics asks her, but she doesn't respond.

"I was," Jack, the accountant, offers, "and he just fell over."

"Well, it's apparently a heart attack, but no one will know for sure until they do an autopsy," the other para-medic says.

"Jesus, just like that," Jack says, "and the guy was in really terrific shape." He shakes his head in bewilder-ment. "Go figure, he played tennis three times a week, a real health nut, too. I used to watch him in the locker room downing a handful of vitamins, mixing up wheat germ, a real clean liver!"

"You never know about cholesterol," his companion whines.

"Anyone know who he was?" one of the paramedics asks, motioning to Adrienne. "She's in shock!"

"He's the Nassau County district attorney," the ten-nis pro answers.

Adrienne raises her head then from Pete's chest and in a small voice filled with grief asks, "He's dead, isn't he?"

"I'm afraid so," someone says gently, bending down to comfort her.

She draws back from the body suddenly, her lips pressed together in anguish.

"Are you his wife?" Jack inquires, kneeling on the other side of her.

Adrienne's eyes appear as lifeless as Pete's now. "I would have been," she answers softly, "maybe someday."

CHAPTER ONE

The News

IT IS SPRING IN PARIS, that spectacular season when the chestnut trees are in bloom again along the Avenue Foch and the chestnut vendors, if they're Algerian, are paying fines for illegal peddling somewhere near the Mairie. Paris-in-the-spring, those brief several months a year when the *bateaux mouches* list precariously to one side under the weight of the hordes of German tourists, and the boutiques along the Faubourg St. Honoré are mobbed with myopic Japanese peering into display cases for one more whiff of the latest designer scent. May in Paris, when Scandinavian families wearing clumsy leather sandals and drab cotton socks sift through piles of souvenir T-shirts and gaudy key chains while their tour buses block traffic on the Rue de Rivoli. Spring—that special time of the year when artists venture out of their Left Bank garrets (now more costly than SoHo lofts) to exhibit their paintings on the narrow streets that border the Boulevard St. Germain des Prés, and Portuguese laborers exit from their hovels (now more delapidated than Harlem tenements) to hawk their gold-filled religious medals on the steps of Notre Dame.

This is the season of brilliant sun and flawless skies, when the air is filled with the smells of freshly baked pastry, diesel fuel being pumped into gaping holes in the sidewalks, and stale cigarette smoke; when the rancid odor of steak tartare left out too long in the sun and unbathed French dogs left in too long in the rain permeate those quaint, but filthy, outdoor cafés. Springtime—the season when terrorists of all persuasions, having met their bomb-throwing quota along the Champs Élysées, install themselves in well-guarded villas on the Riviera, making their Neuilly apartments available to deposed African leaders nervously waiting for a coup to end. Paris, the city Americans perceive as one exotic marathon, inspiring them to dress in jogging attire as they race from museum to museum in search of culture. It is spring in Paris—that exciting, stupendous, all-too-brief season that precedes the saddest months of the year—summer in Paris, when there are no French.

Gabriella Carlucci-Molloy would have known it was spring in Paris even if she wasn't walking in the soft evening breeze on her way home from work, her head buried in the pages of *Paris Actualité,* reading Pascal Bourget's regular social commentary, this week accompanied by the photographs that she shot all over the city. Gabriella would have known it was spring in Paris by the usual collection of derelicts who surface every year at this time to sprawl on benches along the Rond Point of the Champs Élysées.

She tucks the magazine underneath her arm as she walks past the smooth stone fountain, close to the neatly lettered signs in perfect French that the homeless have spread on the sidewalk. As she leans down to drop some change in their cups, it occurs to her that the homeless problem in Paris is another American import that is beginning to blend into the Champs as easily as McDonald's once did years before.

Crossing the street, she walks past the Yves St. Laurent boutique where the window arrangement is a nightmare of purple and orange polka-dot miniskirts, near the tax-free perfume shop where the display is a collection of melted lipsticks and one resident dachshund meticulously licking a mangy front paw. She turns the corner toward Avenue Matignon and is conscious of several admiring glances. For despite her too-curvy body—given the anorexic tastes of the French—and her too-healthy complexion that does nothing to capture that popular pale Parisian look, Gabriella is sought after constantly. Perhaps she touches something in the French male, a reminder of his Latin roots that he has forgotten after years of gazing northward across the channel—genetic links to pasta and bull fighting long since forgotten for hamburgers and table tennis. Or perhaps it is because she is considered an exotic bird in a jungle that has become less than paradise, a symbol of a country where it is still rumored that the streets are paved with gold. Yet Gabriella is not fooled by this flattery nor does she allow herself to be lulled into believing that she is anything more to them than an interesting foreigner. In France she will always remain a stranger, at best an expatriot who has landed in their midst for a short-lived French connection.

The Drugstore is just ahead, where the outdoor metal stands are already filled with an array of shellfish. Several policemen with machine guns slung across their chests pace aimlessly back and forth, turning around only when a siren begins in the distance—a two-note augmented fourth sing-song that conjurs up images from other times. And despite all the picturesque history that Paris offers, it is a city where Gabriella finds few distractions to interfere with her work. It is a place where every scene is a potential landscape to be photographed, every face on the street an interesting character study. There is nothing about its nature that tempts her, nothing about its essence that puts her at risk emotionally.

Since joining the staff of *Paris Actualité*, Gabriella's subjects have ranged from death-row inmates to Basque Separatists; from high-ranking political leaders to low-profile fashion designers; and who all, amazingly, allow her into their cells, bunkers, palaces, and showrooms where she captures their frailties on film. And how has she managed to succeed when others in her field have failed? Yankee ambition, they accuse, or perhaps it's because she's relentless, they add (either one a typically American trait), at tracking her subjects down and then not letting up until they give in to her requests. She is seductive, her almond-shaped amber eyes holding promises of friendship and more. She is shrewd, convincing them that hers is the only lens that will portray innocence, justice, power, and beauty, if any of those things really exists anyway. But if they don't, she can always go back to making a living shooting christenings, weddings, and First Holy Communions which was one of the reasons why she came to Paris in the first place—since taking on such jobs over here seemed more creative than taking them on in Freeport, Long Island, New York.

The white brick building where she lives is straight ahead. She climbs the three steps that lead to the cobblestone courtyard before pressing in the numbered code that releases the black wrought-iron door. The elevator is a glass and wood cage suspended by two worn and creaky cables that she rides to the fourth floor.

Pascal Bourget is waiting for her in the foyer, his hands crammed into the pockets of his crumpled jacket, an anxious expression on his narrow face.

"Gabriella," he says immediately when she enters. "I'm afraid there's some bad news."

"What happened?" she asks as she slips out of her coat.

His hands flutter in the air, thin Gallic fingers that flick a perfect ash from the tip of a Galloise onto the floor. "Your ex-husband died."

She looks at him in disbelief. "What are you talking about?"

"There's a message on your machine—I heard it."

Gabriella's head tilts in the direction of the bedroom before she races in, kneeling on the floor in front of her answering machine. Rewinding the tape, she waits anxiously for the message to play. Pascal is right behind her, standing in the doorway with his arms folded across his chest. "Gabriella," the nasal voice of her former sister-in-law, Claire, whines, "Pete had a heart attack." Pause. "On the tennis court, you know the one he always liked to play at in Freeport—the one with the green bubble." Cough. "Near the courthouse." Sob. "Gabriella, please come to the funeral, at Conroy's, you know, it's near the court-house, it wouldn't look good for him if you didn't mourn." The machine clicks off then, the time having run out even if it's all very clear. Stunned, Gabriella looks up at Pascal, her face registering disbelief.

"A heart attack." She barely is able to mouth the words. "It's just not possible, not Pete!"

"Life in America is too tense," Pascal observes, his eyes already filled with tears. And if Gabriella hadn't dis-covered the Pilo Carpine 4 percent drops in his jacket pocket recently and learned that he suffered from glaucoma, she might have assumed that his tears were caused by emotion.

"Dead," she repeats dully, her body seeming to sag under the enormity of the word.

"Will you go?" Pascal asks, clearly ill at ease.

"Where?" she asks, distracted for the moment as memories begin assaulting her.

"To the funeral," he explains. "Will you go to Amer-ica?"

"Yes, of course," she stammers. "Why yes, how could I not?"

He shrugs. "Then I suppose Bourgogne is off next week—at least for you?"

She wipes her eyes with the heels of her hands. "My child is going to need me. Can you imagine how Dina must feel right now?" And it doesn't escape her that her grief is largely focused on her daughter's grief.

"It seems to me she hasn't needed you since I've known you," Pascal reminds her.

As the tears run down her cheeks, Gabriella buries her face in her hands.

"Try to be calm," Pascal says.

— 9 —

But it is too late for calm. Calm ended when Gabriella decided to impose this geographic distance between herself and her child; when she reasoned or perhaps hoped that it was the only way to make Dina come to her senses and realize how impossible it was to cancel out a mother.

It seems like only yesterday that an adorable baby, a round-faced child with saucer blue eyes and silky blond hair that fell just above her brows and just below her tiny ears, lifted up pudgy arms in the air and whimpered, "Up, mommy, up." Gabriella can still smell the scent of baby powder and cod fish oil, that greasy white ointment that would soothe little Dina's stubborn diaper rash, even now—so many years and miles away. How could it happen that sixteen years later that same child would grow to be a young girl, blond hair cut stylishly to the shoulders, blue eyes rimmed in black kohl, and raise her arms in anger and shout, "Up yours, mother, up yours," before stomping out of Gabriella's house to live with Pete. Out of her life. Gone forever.

Gabriella stands, her hands clasped over her breast. "I'd never ask you ordinarily, Pascal, but could you forget about your plans for tonight and stay with me? I've got a ton of transparencies to go through and film to label from the shoot the other day, if I'm going to get to New York by Thursday." She pauses to calculate, "It's already the end of the day Monday, which only gives me tomorrow and Wednesday. I'll never make my deadline unless I get everything done."

He checks his watch. "It's too late now to change plans. There's a literary awards cocktail party at the Lutetia Hotel that I can't miss. I have to write it up for the next issue and you were supposed to take photographs of everyone arriving, in case you forgot."

"I can't," her voice breaks, "you'll have to go without me."

"You know, Gabriella, Pete won't be any deader if you go and you can still do all those other things later."

"It's not just that. I've got to call Claire and then I've got to call the editors to tell them I'll be away. And anyway, I'm in no mood for any cocktail parties. My hands are shaking so badly that I could hardly hold the camera steady."

"Perhaps you're being too emotional," he chides. "But then that's the Italian in you, *n'est-ce pas?*"

"He was part of my life for almost twenty years, since I was nineteen, the father of my child. So it's hard not to be emotional."

"Perhaps I'm being unfair but as I remember he would never speak to you lately." He smirks. "Or is that because American men only talk to their psychiatrists?"

Gabriella could spend weeks out of touch with Pascal lately even if she sees him every day. "He certainly wasn't much help when Dina stopped speaking to me," she admits sadly.

"Don't blame Pete," Pascal retorts, "after all, if you hadn't chosen to leave him this whole drama might not have happened."

"But I wasn't the one who left," she begins before turning to wander into the living room.

Magazines are piled high on the seats of two black canvas chairs, plastic-encased photographs of a recent fashion show are strewn all over the chintz sofas, boxes of unused film spill out from an open metal suitcase that is propped up against a plant. Gabriella walks around everything to stand in front of a table. One finger barely touches a picture of a young girl who smiles out from the frame. "She's sweet, isn't she?" she says wistfully, turning to look at Pascal. And as she does each angle of her face reveals a different expression. Her features are perfectly symmetrical with high cheekbones, generous mouth, straight nose, and tiny cleft in her rounded chin. "She's wholesome and fresh," he replies, "very American." Each tilt of her head betrays a different emotion as she turns away to sit cross-legged on the floor. "You know, *ma coquette*," Pascal tells her, "no one lives forever."

"There's a big difference between living forever and dropping dead on a tennis court at forty-six years old."

"His life was good."

"His life was short."

"You Americans are so into quantity instead of quality."

But it seems useless to defend once again even if his derisive view of life—especially life that isn't French—used to fascinate her. In the beginning. Until it became evident how lost he was without his props. Without a cigarette dangling from the corner of his mouth, Pascal was ordinary. With one, he looked the part of the craggy literary figure, the one who constantly criticized her intellect—or more accurately, her lack of it. And with his many props as he strolled along the Seine—the Louvre or Trocadero—she even believed him when he told her that moaning and groaning, thrashing and flashing for a woman of her age, almost forty, was no longer amusing or attractive. For in her naïve American way, she reasoned that nobody could have everything—an obstructed view of the Eiffel Tower from her kitchen window and a great sex life. "Why must you attack America all the time," she wants to know, forgetting that she vowed not to argue—not now.

"I'm not attacking, only trying to make you realize that death knows no boundaries or disparate cultures. It can happen to any of us at any time." A weak smile crosses his face. "So it's a pity not to go to these literary awards. *Il faut vivre*—you must live, *ma chérie*."

Looking at him in amazement for barely a moment, her response is unrelated to his advice. "Dina backed the wrong horse," she says more to herself than to him.

"What does that mean? This isn't exactly a race, it's life and death."

But it is so simple right now, so elemental that her insight into it is consoling somehow. "It's the same in a way," she answers, "since Pete made it to the finish line first and Dina lost her bet."

"She may have lost her bet but she won the prize."

"What prize?"

"The truth is that Dina is going to inherit everything Pete has which makes her one very rich eighteen-year-old girl."

"She didn't run off to live with him for the money," Gabriella says, the anguish clearly etched on her face. "How would she have known? He was the picture of health—young, athletic." She shakes her head. "This wasn't supposed to happen."

"Why did she go off with him?"

"To hurt me. To punish me for something I must have done to her. And what I don't know, because I've tried to figure it out for the past two years and couldn't."

"Haven't you suffered enough?"

"Apparently not," she says with a touch of irony.

"Well, then don't go to the funeral."

"I've got to go because right now Dina is suffering more than I am." Images flash before her eyes then, of Dina before the rupture, always before, as if time stopped on the day that she left her. Gabriella can still see the thirteen-year-old who woke up one morning to discover blood all over her sheets. They decided the day would be theirs, a self-proclaimed holiday where they skipped through Central Park and visited the zoo, balloons and intense discussions about life, ice cream and serious questions about growing up, a recognition of the child becoming a woman or perhaps it was the other way around that day. Neither was sure and neither cared. Or the Sunday afternoon when Dina was six and fell off her tricycle in Washington Square Park, her bottom lip split in two and Gabriella had to carry her all the way to St. Vincent's Emergency so the child could be stitched and the mother sedated. And it suddenly occurs to Gabriella that if she ever let go of any of these memories, if she allowed them to fade at all, the explosion inside her head would be so final that there would be nothing left.

"It's so typically American for a child to abuse her parents like that," Pascal observes. "Somehow there is a natural respect for authority over here that is missing over there."

Perhaps if Gabriella felt strong right now she would point out that this natural respect for authority was what made it so easy for the Nazis to walk right in and take over France. Instead she says, "It wasn't easy for Dina either to reject her mother. This isn't a one-sided story where only one of us has the pain—it's mutual."

"You Americans are simply too permissive with your children which is why they are so spoiled. Why, even during the Occupation our children behaved so well." He pauses to push a piece of dark hair from his bony brow. "But maybe that was because they watched how hard the adults worked in the Underground to save France." And perhaps if Gabriella felt less fragile right now she would point out that if those adults who claimed to have been in the Resistance really had been, then the Germans would never have had a chance. Pascal clears his throat. "I remember it so well, how we had to make do with so little." A cultural malady, she thinks, and the reason why the homeless are destined not to survive very well on the streets of Paris, since the French never throw anything away.

"I've got to leave, forgive me, but it is the Prix Femina."

She nods. "I understand," she says quietly, not understanding at all and hating herself for needing him so much right now.

He touches the tip of her nose after he helps her to her feet. "There's not much I could do anyway, *chérie*, except to assure you that this too shall pass as everything passes in life. We are all very ephemeral." He smiles then, that smile that ends up as a smirk, that perpetual smirk found on French faces that tries to cover centuries of emotional inadequacy, the one that begs to be swatted off each time that she notices it. "Perhaps someday under calmer conditions you'll explain why Americans get divorced for such silly reasons."

"It wasn't silly," she defends, walking him to the door.

"Infidelity is a silly reason, at least in Paris."

"That's because in France the decision to be unfaithful usually ends up in the bedroom while in America, that same decision usually ends up in a courtroom."

"But that is exactly what creates so much chaos."

"It's over now," she says sadly. "Pete is dead so it makes no sense to discuss all the mistakes we once made when we were married."

"Perhaps you would still have your daughter if you had overlooked those mistakes then."

"It was hard to overlook all of Pete's infidelities. It wasn't just one time or even one particular woman. It was a constant assault on our marriage, an impossible test of my understanding."

"Then you should have distracted yourself by taking a lover."

"I did."

His eyebrows rise in surprise. "And what happened?"

"He found out."

A breath expelled between pouty lips. "Americans simply don't understand sex," he complains. "You fool yourselves into believing that you will feel the same way about someone in five years or in five hours or even in five minutes after the moment has passed. The problem is you think too much of the future."

"I wouldn't exactly call five minutes after making love the future," she replies with cautious dignity.

He smiles tolerantly. "It is a part of what is a false expectation since a future based on making love is unrealistic."

This doesn't surprise her although lately she has grown weary of this separation between love and lovemaking, as weary as she has become of his insensitivity and cultural bigotry in rejecting any music that wasn't Baroque or any art that wasn't created at Giverny. And if she was unable to express her discontent at this lack of growth in their relationship or within him as well, it is only that it never occurred to her that she was entitled to more. At least it never occurred to her since her own daughter rejected her two years ago.

"Will you come back here tonight after the literary awards?"

"It will be very late," he says.

"Will you come here tomorrow?"

"Tomorrow my schedule is hell," he replies.

"Will I see you before I leave?"

"If you come to the office," he assures.

"I don't know if I can, I'm leaving for New York."

"Then I'll call you there," he decides.

Again Gabriella draws that comfortable curtain around her feelings as she waits for the elevator, aware that as time passes it becomes easier and easier to pretend not to care.

"How long do you think you'll be gone?" he asks, an afterthought.

"I'm not sure but maybe until I work things out with Dina."

"Death shouldn't grant her immunity for being so rude."

"Manners aren't exactly the issue here."

"They probably should have been." His expression now is Sixteenth Arrondissement judgmental, that look that can be found around the tables of some of the best restaurants in Paris; that mournful regard due to an unfortunate experience with the foul odor of spoiled Brie.

"Where will you stay?" he inquires almost as a matter of form.

"At my parents' house."

He leans over to plant a kiss on either cheek. "We'll talk—bon voyage!"

And it's not that she doesn't feel a certain loss, especially right now, since it's obviously not the best moment to include an affair on the list of things that died on this perfect spring day in Paris. But what is more disturbing right now is the thought of going back home, not unlike that recurring dream she has had lately, the one that forces her to remember the past, the lives she once created, possessed, and then somehow misplaced along the way.

□

The morning sun streams in through the floor-to-ceiling casement window that takes up almost one entire wall of the small room. Dina Marie Molloy opens one eye sleepily and turns over on her stomach as she removes his arm from around her shoulder. Cautiously, she edges over to the far end of the bed.

"Don't get up," he whispers. Dina doesn't respond, having decided when she was a child that the sound of her own voice in the morning should be reserved for a dire emergency. Instead she leans over to tuck the sheet snugly around his neck. He groans. "Come back to bed."

The sun streaks its light across the bleached wood floor, settles briefly on the brilliant colors of the American Indian scatter rug that Dina's father brought back from Arizona last summer. She stretches as she surveys the mess in her room—the pile of papers and several heavy textbooks that spill out of a tan canvas knapsack, the broken rocking chair that is propped up against one wall, a reminder that it needs to be repaired, and the clothes. Reaching over on the doorknob, she retrieves a pair of white cotton shorts and a red T-shirt.

Dina is sturdy, built more like her father than her mother. Tall and well-proportioned, with large bones and broad shoulders, she is a young woman who is most often described as handsome rather than pretty, statuesque but rarely voluptuous. Yet with her startling blue eyes, blond hair, pale skin, and her mother's perfect features, there is something almost ethereal about her.

"I've got a hard on, Dina," he murmurs from somewhere underneath a pile of bedclothes, "and it's got your name written on it." She glances over toward the bed but still doesn't respond, concentrating instead on tying her long hair back into a ponytail. Sitting down on the floor, she begins her morning exercise routine, something that began after she spent Spring vacation with her father in Naples and gained five pounds. She grasps the heel of her right foot and extends the leg out to the side. Replacing it, she takes the heel of her left foot and extends it out until it is perfectly straight, repeating the exercise several times more before lying down to do buttocks rolls.

Classes don't begin for Dina until noon, a schedule she carefully arranged when she first arrived at Brampton College in Connecticut. She is a night person, a trait she inherited from her father. But unlike her father who is able to function on practically no sleep at all and still make a brilliant early-morning court appearance, Dina has trouble waking up before ten or eleven.

"Come back to bed and I'll fuck you," the voice offers.

But the words insult her now where once they might have enticed her, once when making love with him held the promise of other possibilities. Or so she made herself believe. But that was in the beginning when she was still optimistic and naïve, before she realized that the price of having even a small part of him included being the recipient of his quixotic moods and occasional selfishness. Yet however miserable this affair makes her, however many regrets she may have for having chosen him, she is not unaware that he will always have a permanent place in her heart—if only because he was the first.

The sunlight bounces back through the prisms of the crystal wind chimes that hang from one corner of the ceiling, making streaks of faintly colored pinks and blues that settle on that pile of clothing that is strewn everywhere. Several pairs of jeans, one brown leather cowboy boot—the other kicked underneath the bed—a gold lamé slipper, its mate wedged beneath the closet door, and a pile of freshly washed laundry crammed into a red-and-white checkered sack are scattered around.

"I'm going to have deadly sperm buildup and a rotten headache if we don't do it," he says.

Dina turns around to watch him, fascinated as he slides up in the bed to kick off the covers. Touching his body from his chest down to his lower abdomen, his hand lingers on an enormous erection that seems to have just materialized out of nowhere. He is forbidden to Dina, a man who is old enough to be her father; with masses of gray-streaked hair, he is almost a certain lecherous character out of Nabokov with a broad forehead, heavy brows, black eyes, a malevolent figure in a white silk shirt dueling Pushkin in the St. Petersburg snow, stocky build.

Joshua Moskowitz is a Jew, the son of Russian immigrants, and, at Brampton College, a professor of Social Realism in the Soviet cinema. If they knew, Dina's father would undoubtedly call him a "perverted Commie bastard" and her Aunt Claire would simply refer to him as "that kike." But they don't.

"Let me do it with you," he coaxes her, and it's only because he uses the word *with* that she gives in, just as she gave in the first time—as if without her, it wouldn't be quite the same.

Removing her clothes, she covers her breasts modestly and without a word climbs on top of him. "Oh, my God," she gasps, breaking her vow of early-morning silence because, after all, being filled with an erection of that size certainly falls under the heading of dire emergency.

"Who does it better than me?" he murmurs.

"I don't know," she answers, and chances are if she did know she wouldn't be with him at all. Or perhaps he wouldn't be with her for fear of being discovered as a fraud.

— 19 —

But even if Dina doesn't know for sure right now, she does suspect that there could be more. Perhaps it's because of that stranger who lurks within her whenever they make love, that other woman who wants to moan from the pleasure of it all except that there isn't very much of that. And it's probably just as well, for the well-behaved Dina would have trouble allowing that other person to surface. Too shy to be anything but passive, too repressed to be anything but tame, she holds back, not daring to tell Joshua what's going on, which unfortunately for her isn't much. But that has to do with that other presence that invades the bed, someone or something that recites that familiar Catholic platitude in Dina's ear: "Fornication is a mortal sin."

"Fucking you is pure heaven," Joshua murmurs. And Dina holds her breath, waiting for it to end as suddenly and abruptly as it always ends.

"Stay with me for a while," she whispers when she feels him withdraw.

"Can't," he replies without any hesitation. "Now be a good girl and hop off."

She doesn't protest as she raises herself from him, tumbling over onto her side, her legs still slung across his chest. But she feels defeated, inadequate that she hasn't yet found the right combination that will keep him for a while after it's over. "Joshua," she tries again, "you don't have classes until three today, so please stay with me just for a little while."

He smiles patiently. "What's all this now?" he asks, his eyebrows raised in astonishment. "I thought we agreed, no possessiveness."

"Just a cup of coffee. That's not making a life commitment."

Moving her legs from him, he stands up and arranges his testicles within the crotch of his shorts that he has just stepped into.

"Maybe I don't want a cup of coffee, maybe you want one and just assume that I'd go along with the idea, which by the way is a kind of control. Remember, Dina, you start with a cup of coffee and end up with nuclear holocaust—controlling the whole world by destruction or destroying it by control.''

And perhaps if Dina didn't find his crotch so fascinating, the way it bulged when he casually propped one leg up on a chair during his lectures, she'd tell him how ridiculous he sounded when he got so pedantic.

''I don't need a lecture now, this isn't a classroom.''

''Life is a classroom.''

And despite her impatience, her emotions still tend to draw her back to the beginning of their story. ''Are you attracted to me, I mean, do you find me interesting and intelligent?''

''Dina, I don't see the connection.''

''It has to do with me, Joshua, and why we're together.''

''I'm with you because I enrich your life.''

''And what about you—what's in it for you?''

''It makes me feel good to do good.''

''And the others—do you feel that way about them too?''

''Equally. I try to give you all something different.'' The playpen is his oyster.

Dina begins pulling the laundry from the bag and folding it.

''So how come I get to do this,'' she asks, holding up a sock, ''while the others get to go to rock concerts?''

He shakes his head. ''Because I sense in you a need to share intimate chores with me. Perhaps it's your insecurity.''

She resumes the folding. ''Then why do I feel so empty after you leave?''

''Your expectations are too great.''

''I don't think so since I've got nothing to base them on.''

''Do you resent doing my laundry?''

She considers that. "No," she lies although gradually the laundry has become the symbol of everything that's wrong, the focal point of all her discontent. The Jockey shorts with the faded brown streaks on the seat, the white undershirts with the gray perspiration stains underneath the arms, the pretentious polyester ascots, the tasteless argyle socks, take on a life of their own, clouding her vision, blotting out her sense of sight, taste, and smell until every memory of his face, his tongue, his penis, is lost within the confines of that red-and-white checkered laundry bag. "Joshua," she says, with so much emotion that he visibly recoils, "I'm entitled to more from you or from someone else if you can't give it to me."

"Ah, that upper-class narcissistic entitlement that stems from an unhappy childhood."

"Shut up, Joshua, and leave my childhood out of this."

"Well, well, now we're getting someplace. Come on, Dina, the problem is that you never talk about your parents."

"My childhood and my parents have nothing to do with this. It's you and the way you treat me after it's over."

"After what's over?" he taunts her.

She squirms. "You know, it."

"That wonderful youthful it. When you stop calling it it, you'll lose all your charm."

"Why do you always want to leave so quickly afterward?" she presses.

"Because there's nothing left to say."

As if there was something to say before or during for that matter.

"Well, it doesn't make me feel very good about myself," she confesses.

"You must be premenstrual," he observes with a note of triumph. No small victory to be able still to inflict that oldie but goodie on yet another unsuspecting generation.

"No, I'm not," she protests innocently, for her generation has not yet learned to balk.

"Then you better start appreciating me because in answer to that other question you asked—no, you are not that interesting or intelligent. Not yet. Right now and especially right this minute, you're acting like a typically spoiled American brat—something that you wouldn't find in the Soviet Union."

The insult has found its mark for Dina's anger is escalating; the temper she tries so hard to control is beginning to get out of hand when the telephone rings.

The Private Line

Pete Molloy arranged to have a private line installed in Dina's room after he tried all night one night to get through on the dormitory phone and kept getting a busy signal. He decided right then never to subject himself to that long line of parents and friends who constantly try to get through to any one of fifty girls on the floor. The private line, he explained to Dina, was for his convenience only and not to be given out to anyone else, except Adrienne, who had to be able to contact her in case of an emergency.

Momentarily startled, Dina reaches past Joshua to pick up the phone.

"Hello, Daddy," she says automatically, her gaze still lingering on Joshua. But Joshua isn't paying any attention to her—he has cleverly seized this opportunity to make a hasty exit. Standing up, he steps into his jeans, pulls on his cowboy boots, grabs his shirt and a windbreaker, and starts for the door.

"Oh, my God," Dina suddenly screams, clutching her stomach. "Oh, no!"

Joshua whirls around, one hand still on the knob, a disgusted expression on his face.

"Temper tantrum or not, I'm outta here!" But his words are lost to her as she continues to sob uncontrollably into the telephone.

"Yes, yes," she says, weeping, "the train. No, now, yes, I can do it alone."

"Dina," he says cautiously, "what's going on?"

She has put down the receiver and is now reaching for a wad of Kleenex, the tears still streaming down her cheeks. "My father"—she chokes on the words—"had a heart attack."

"Well, in 1990 the good news is that heart attacks aren't always fatal."

She hiccups. "This one was!" she sobs before collapsing onto the bed. Joshua emits a low whistle.

"Dead?"

"Dead," she repeats, her face buried in the pillow. "Dead, dead, dead," she screams over and over until it begins to register, as if another person is pounding it into her head, forcing her to accept a reality that is too hideous to imagine.

"Hey, take it easy," Joshua cautions, rubbing his stubble, "just take deep breaths." He moves away from the door. "Makes you wonder," he mumbles more to himself than to Dina, "about making big bucks."

Dina moans softly, rocking back and forth with a pillow pressed against her chest. "What am I going to do now," she says over and over. "I have no one left."

He is confused. "Wait a minute, what happened to your mother? Is she dead too?"

"No," she whispers, flinging the pillow aside.

"So you've got someone."

"I have no one," she cries bitterly. But what confuses Dina, even in her current state, is this overwhelming feeling of loss for her mother when she should be feeling it for her father.

All of this is too much for Joshua Moskowitz, who prides himself on an uncanny ability to grasp the most convoluted relationship, to understand the most complicated scenario, who finds new meaning and hidden nuance in every Soviet film that he dissects for his classes, who can remember every character in a Dostoyevski novel without ever having to flip back over the pages. "If your mother's alive, then what's all this about not having a mother?"

"She lives in Paris," Dina answers tearfully, "and I haven't seen or spoken to her in two years."

"A jet-setter," he judges disdainfully. "Amazing how the rich fall in and out of love with their children!"

"She's not a jet-setter and she's not rich. She's a photographer, and it was my choice to cut off."

"Stand by your choices, Zen. But what was the reason?"

"I went to live with my father," she manages to reply before her voice breaks.

"I get it, he was into heavy control."

She glances at Joshua, determined not to let on that his assessment isn't entirely wrong. But suddenly she is back two years ago, on the night of her sixteenth birthday, when her father took her out for dinner and gave her the letter. And even as she read it then and learned things about her mother that shocked her, she knew that her father had written it less for her than for himself. He was just smart enough to play on all the resentment that Dina held for her mother anyway, during a tough adolescent period adjusting to the divorce and all the financial problems that went with it. Peter Molloy needed to get even. But Dina needed a father. "How could he be dead," she asks tearfully. "He was so healthy."

"Stress."

"He loved his work."

"Somewhere deep inside of him he was miserable."

She nearly loses hold of herself. "No," she cries, "he was happy, he loved his life."

"You'll never know now."

Picking up one of Joshua's hands, she holds it tightly

between hers. "Please stay with me until I leave for the station." And despite her grief, her mind is alert to any possibility. He glances at his watch.

"Can't," he says. "I've got a student coming for a conference in a little while." Uncomfortable, he shifts from one foot to the other. "I'm with you, Dina," he offers. "I'm thinking about you and I'll be back."

"Please," she begs, the tears beginning all over again, "don't leave me now." And she hates herself for sounding so weak and for not being as alert as she imagined.

"I'll see you later."

"I'll be gone."

"Call me tomorrow," he says, leaning over to kiss her cheek.

"I've never asked for anything," she pleads, blinded more by rage than grief at this point, "a cup of coffee after sex, and now, to stay with me when I just found out my father died."

"Don't mix things up," he argues, trying once again to kiss her.

"Get out," Dina suddenly cries, her hand up to create a barrier between his lips and her face, "just go away!"

Dina is running forward now, suddenly light years ahead of him, having already discarded thoughts and feelings that he will never know. She leans against the wall and watches as he opens the door and smiles weakly at her before bounding down the hall. But she hardly has time to take some clothes from her dresser to pack when there is a knock on the door. Flinging it open, a rush of hope fills her when she sees him standing there.

"Joshua," she says, her eyes wide.

He is flustered. "I forgot the laundry," he explains, a foolish grin spreading across his face.

And she keeps on running, backward now, her mind settling on a time when her father was alive, when she hated her mother, when she had a lover, only a few minutes ago it seems, when she was still a child.

CHAPTER TWO

The Funeral

THERE'S AN INCIDENT that happened in Gabriella's life that deeply affected her, something that she still conjures up from time to time to relive briefly during moments of idle reflection or to replay in excruciating detail throughout the occasional sleepless night. And it comes to mind now as she stands at the luggage carousel at Kennedy airport waiting for her bags on the way to Pete Molloy's funeral.

The memory always begins with Felicity Impelliteri losing her life at seventeen in the passenger seat of Kevin Doherty's 1968 white Chevrolet Impala. The rearview mirror pierced Felicity's brain when Kevin lost control of the car and drove it through the plate glass window of Pastrami Heaven. Perhaps it made such a big impression on Gabriella because Felicity was her first contemporary to make her aware of her own mortality, or perhaps because Kevin was the first to make her aware of something else.

Fate is strange, Gabriella muses as she watches the bags drop down onto the carousel. Just as Pete never could have imagined that he would have a fatal heart attack on a tennis court at forty-six years old, surely Felicity never gave it a thought when she climbed into Kevin's car that night that she would end up sprawled in that display case surrounded by salamis, a tub of shrimp salad, and a handful of red pimentos. But then Gabriella never considered that any grave consequences could ever happen to her either.

Before the accident Kevin was like any other good-looking greaseball who swaggered through the halls of Freeport High, a pocket knife clipped to his belt, one sleeve of a Sears polyester T-shirt rolled up over a pack of cigarettes, and a vacant expression on his face. Curiously he became more appealing after the accident, a boy touched by death, set apart from the others, and his expression suddenly changed to brooding while his T-shirt changed to cotton. Gabriella rediscovered him at about that time, having dated him briefly years before, when she found him to be dull. But she was into her hippie period then, intensely attracted to suffering for the sake of her art, taking black-and-white photographs of urban poverty, reading Jack Kerouac, and boycotting grapes.

Gabriella was seventeen and had just entered her freshman year at a community college on Long Island when they consummated their relationship after a dinner-dance at the Tiro el Segno gun club on MacDougal Street in Greenwich Village. And she had only dared to do it on her father's living room floor—on the avocado green rug, somewhere between a reproduction of an eighteenth-century Italian writing desk and a Lucite pedestal—because Sylvie and Rocco never got home from the restaurant before two in the morning, Audrey already had the embolism, and the maid was partially deaf.

By the time they were pulling into the driveway, Gabriella was already unfastening her taffeta sheath to make it easier for Kevin to hike it up over her thighs. But by the time they were on the floor, he was already suggesting an alternative to his having to rush back out to the car for the forgotten rubber, explaining that his way was also likely to make no noise. Gabriella adamantly refused, for the decision to lose her virginity was like an edict etched in stone and nothing was going to deter her. Yet as she stood at the door while Kevin rummaged around in the glove compartment, she couldn't help but think that had they done it years before when they first met, Felicity might have still been alive.

Gabriella sighs as she pushes the cart toward customs, remembering how Kevin had clamped his hand over her mouth in anticipation that she would cry out in pain. She never made a sound though, until the very end when the rubber broke and he pulled out so abruptly that her head slammed against the base of the Lucite pedestal. And after he left that night, she spent hours trying to clean the stain in the carpet, and then weeks after that agonizing over the possibility that she was pregnant. Soon after that, at nineteen, she met Pete Molloy, the John Kennedy of Nassau County politics, six years her senior, a charmer, a climber, and the best she could ever do, everyone told her.

The taxi stand is empty of people and the dispatcher quickly motions her to a cab, trunk already open while he lifts her suitcase inside. Gabriella looks rested this morning despite the fact that she didn't get much sleep last night. Her hair is parted off-center and hangs in loose waves to her shoulders, her cheeks are naturally flushed, her lips painted a pale peach. Yet she has made every effort not to overstep the boundaries of propriety. Dressed in a simple but well-tailored gray suit, a lighter gray silk shirt, and a single strand of pearls around her neck, she reasoned that showing up in black to Pete's funeral would have been hypocritical, improperly defining her role in his life and death. And as she sits back in the taxi on her way to the Long Island Railroad station in Jamaica for the trip to Freeport, she is aware that she once reasoned with similar logic when she chose to wear beige to their wedding.

A large crowd has already gathered outside Conroy's funeral parlor on Main Street when Gabriella arrives in a taxi from the train station. Several men wearing somber blue suits stand underneath the green awning. One consults a cheap stainless-steel watch strapped to his wrist while another, stomach hanging over a belt, gestures nervously toward the mortuary as he talks. And yet another, trousers flaring out over shiny black oxfords, takes a last deep drag of a cigarette before flicking the butt over the roof of a nearby parked car. They resemble aging choirboys, their once-cherubic faces having long disintegrated into red-blotched and bloated folds from dancing at too many weddings or mourning at too many wakes. And once again they find themselves huddled together, murmuring mindless platitudes with a kind of ease that comes from repeating the same thing over and over throughout the years.

Gabriella finds the suitcase too heavy to carry and so pushes it along the sidewalk toward the entrance. The men glance at her, attracted at first by the jarring and scraping sound, but then quickly averting their eyes as they exchange knowing looks, recognizing her yet unwilling to acknowledge who she is because of who they are. Pallbearers today, civil servants usually, they are the Irish Mafia who work within the confines of the Nassau County district attorney's office. These are the men who surrounded Pete Molloy with devotion, who were unconditionally loyal, the faithful entourage who were with him from the beginning until the end. And now they pretend not to notice Gabriella, for it goes against their peculiar code of ethics to greet their buddy's ex-wife on this the occasion of his funeral.

But Gabriella Carlucci-Molloy doesn't tolerate grudges, especially in times of crisis.

"Matt," she says warmly, dragging the suitcase behind her as she walks up to the tall heavy-set one in the group, "how are you?" Holding out her hand, she refuses to move until he finally raises his eyes from the tips of his shoes and meets her gaze.

"Hello, Gabriella," he replies, blushing. "I thought you were overseas."

"I was but I came back as soon as I heard."

"Damn shame," he mutters, shaking his bald head. "He was just getting all geared up to run for re-election in the fall."

"You're looking good, Gabriella," the one with the stainless-steel watch dares.

"Thanks, Jim," she responds with a slight smile. "I'm so very sorry."

"When'd you see him last?"

She pauses, caught in what she has dreaded most about coming here, when she would be forced to recall when she last saw Pete. The night of Dina's sixteenth birthday, when he brought her home from dinner and planted himself in the living room, arms folded across his chest like a bouncer in a nightclub, while Dina packed to leave.

"Two years ago," Gabriella answers, glancing from one to the other fearfully—as if they too remember the occasion.

"Never sick a day in his life," the smoker offers as he lights another cigarette.

"How'd you find out, Gabriella?" the watch wants to know.

"Claire called."

"Yeah," Matt says, shaking his head. "Just shouldn't have happened, but you know Pete—stubborn as hell. I bet he didn't feel good and just ignored it. Stubborn as a mule!"

"Autopsy said it was massive, ripped his heart right open."

"Dead before he hit the court, it said," the smoker adds.

"It's the job that got him, that's what did him in, worked long hours, took everything to heart like that."

"Yeah," Matt says with irony, "to heart."

They appear to have forgotten about her until one of them trips on the valise. "You see the kid lately?" he asks, rubbing his shin.

Again. All of those hours, days, months, and then

years of waiting for the time when she would have to account to strangers who already knew. To have failed to keep the problem within the confines of her home was painful enough, but to suffer the stigma was unbearable. "Not since she went to live with Pete," she says, bending down instead of looking at them.

"She's in there," one says, gesturing to the door. "I saw her go in with Claire a few minutes ago."

A sudden surge of terror fills her, more acute than having to view Pete lying in his coffin.

"Harry's in there too," another confirms.

"How is Harry?" Gabriella grasps at anything to avoid the other. Even Harry Bellin, a bailiff at the courthouse and a man that Claire Molloy pretends not to live with for the sake of propriety.

"Harry's the same, just had breakfast with him."

Tradition doesn't vary in Freeport, even when death has invaded the daily agenda. From bailiffs to judges, from clerks to attorneys, these are the men who turn Casey's, the diner on the corner of Main Street, between the courthouse and the funeral parlor, where the group meets every morning, into a private breakfast club to exchange opinions and gossip. Convicting and acquitting their own over rolls and coffee before they walk across the street and inside the courthouse to convict and acquit the others.

"I guess I'd better go inside," Gabriella says, faltering under their scrutiny. "Do you think there's somewhere I can leave my suitcase?"

"Sure."

"No problem."

"Ask someone." They answer in unison although not one makes the slightest effort to help, each suddenly is very busy lighting a cigarette or picking lint from a sleeve or conducting a study of the air around his head.

Biting her lip, she says, "Thanks" as she begins lugging the valise closer to the entrance. Her shoulder bag drops down and dangles from her arm, and as she stops to fix it, she notices more familiar faces.

They are the office workers who typed for Pete and lied for him, who filed for him or covered for him, who were also with him from the beginning. Loyal and perhaps even slightly enamored of their charismatic boss, they made themselves available to work over weekends or long into the evenings after everyone else had gone home. Motherly and good-intentioned, they were his confidantes as well, offering advice and consolation for anything that caused him distress. Now they stare at Gabriella, appearing surprised that she even knew to be here today.

"Hello, Gladys," says Gabriella, addressing Pete's frumpy longtime secretary. The response is a pair of shoulders that shrug beneath an ill-fitting black dress, one tattered and forlorn red fabric flower pinned on one breast.

"Hello, Gabriella," the woman answers meekly, glancing at the others for support.

"Helen," Gabriella says gently, taking a step closer, "how are you?" Helen taps one t-strap shoe in reply, its heel badly in need of repair. "This must be a terrible shock for you," Gabriella adds, the instinct to comfort overcoming the instinct to flee.

"Everyone who knew him is shocked," Louise, the file clerk, speaks up, her puffy blue eyes threatening to spill over with tears.

Unlike the men, the women's expressions are more fearful than mournful (grieving in these circles is a predominantly male activity) since they are justifiably concerned that they might be retired when the new district attorney takes over. "It's hard to believe," Gabriella blurts out.

"When did you get back?" Gladys asks, the emphasis on the *you*, which accomplishes exactly what it's meant to.

"Just this morning," Gabriella replies self-consciously, gesturing to the valise. "I came here right from the airport."

"Your daughter was at the viewing last night with Claire and Adrienne."

"Adrienne?" Gabriella says, glancing around.

"A saint," Louise replies.

"One of the staff," Gladys adds, "a lawyer."

"Pete would've been lost without her."

"In every way."

"Pity this happened just when he was thinking about settling down with her."

And Gabriella has barely digested that bit of information when the barrage intensifies. "Have you seen Dina lately?"

"Didn't you hear, she said she just arrived," Gladys answers for Gabriella, pointing to the suitcase.

"Poor Dina," Louise interrupts. "What's she going to do now without a father?"

"It's going to be really hard," Helen agrees, "having no one to depend on anymore. After all, they were so close."

Gabriella remains silent then, considering their comments to be sadistic, their questions rhetorical. Although it does baffle her how she managed, somehow, somewhere, along the way to lose her place in that particular biological trio. "It's going to take Dina a long time to get over it," Gladys predicts gloomily.

"If she ever does," Helen adds.

Still Gabriella remains silent even if it occurs to her that at least genetically Dina has the capability of overcoming this loss. After all, Gabriella managed to survive the loss of her own mother after Audrey became so ill, perhaps not quite as irrevocable a loss as Pete, but then there are different degrees of permanence.

"How come you live over there in Paris?" Gladys inquires.

"Married to a European," Louise asks, "or just living with someone?"

"No," Gabriella replies, aware of the knowing looks that pass among the women.

"No husband, no boyfriend, and no children," Helen concludes, twisting her wedding ring, "that's no life for a woman!"

But it doesn't surprise Gabriella to hear what she suspected to be true in these circles, that without a man, a woman is invalid, without a child, nonexistent.

"A woman gets into trouble when she has no one to take care of," Louise says, shaking her head. Or worse, Gabriella realizes suddenly, that a woman scorned by a man is on the prowl, scorned by her own child, clearly on the defensive.

"All we can hope for is that poor Dina doesn't forget who her father was and acts the way he would've wanted her to. All we can pray for is that she doesn't get involved with the wrong people," Helen says as she gives Gabriella a meaningful look.

"Now why would she do that?" Gabriella asks with feigned innocence although the point is well taken.

"It can happen," Louise agrees, nodding. "You just never know what grief can do."

A sudden current of strength surges through Gabriella. "Dina is going to be fine," she assures the women, or perhaps it's herself she is trying to convince, "because she's strong and too smart to do anything stupid!"

"How would you know what she is," the secretary accuses, the hostility finally unleashed, "you haven't been around for two years!"

As if Gabriella had abandoned Dina and Pete instead of having been banished by them. But she has already gone beyond the moment, well past these two years as she replies with amazing calm and dignity. "Well, I'm around now," she says before bending down once again to drag the suitcase toward the entrance.

"Is there somewhere I can leave this?" she asks a

muscular man who stands near the elevators in the entrance of the funeral parlor, a sorrowful expression fixed on his face, a plastic card pinned to his lapel that identifies him as a Conroy employee.

"Which funeral are you with today?"

"Molloy," she answers nervously. "Peter Daniel Molloy." And a sob gets caught in her throat. As if she was here yesterday for someone else and plans to be here tomorrow for yet another, as if there is a special on Molloys today.

"That would be on the second floor, viewing room to your right, common chapel down at the far end of the corridor. But I'm afraid you'll have to take your suitcase with you. We can't be responsible for personal property."

"Oh?" is all she can manage right then, although it does occur to her to inquire if a corpse doesn't exactly fall under the heading of personal property as well.

The first thing Gabriella notices as she looks around for a place to stash her valise is an arm that seems to be coming from somewhere behind her, reaching down, and swinging the suitcase up and then down to the side. Turning, she sees that the arm is attached to a person of medium height, trim, good shoulders, a face that seems neither hardened nor marred by time but rather with well-chiseled features, a courteous regard, and capped by dark wavy hair, bits of gray at the tips.

"Here, let me help get this out of the way for you," he says, the voice deep, the accent slightly Long Island. Which doesn't explain why she instantly lapses into a tone that is more Faubourg than Freeport when she replies primly, "Thank you, but there doesn't seem to be anywhere to put it." But he doesn't seem even to wonder why she happened to bring a suitcase to a funeral. "Why don't I check that for you?"

She gestures to the spot where the Conroy employee had been standing. "Someone just told me that Conroy's couldn't be responsible for it."

He reflects for a moment. "Then how about if I put it in the trunk of my car," he offers, "or I can put it in your car."

"I don't have a car."

"I guess I assumed that," he says and then holds out a hand. "I'm Nick Tressa."

She shakes it. "I'm Gabriella Carlucci-Molloy."

"You must be Pete's ex-wife."

"Yes."

"And you came here in a taxi," he adds, suddenly flustered.

"Yes, from Paris."

He grins.

"I mean that I came here in a taxi from the airport where my plane landed from—" She pauses to take a breath.

"Paris," he finishes.

She doesn't respond, concentrated right now on trying to define exactly what this attraction is all about.

"Why don't I begin by getting rid of this for you?" he asks.

"Thanks," she responds politely, relieved that she will have a moment to catch her breath.

"I'll look for you upstairs," he promises.

And she finds herself fascinated as she watches him move easily through the growing crowd of people, fascinated yet vaguely disturbed about something that she can't quite define.

The viewing room is long and narrow with tables of food and drink that line each of the bare walls, bare except for one that has three pastel sketches of Jesus Christ with Mary and Joseph gazing piously and pitiously over the casket. At its mahogany head are the same three pallbearers from earlier, who are now engaged in conversation with a small hunchbacked woman. Every few minutes one of them leans over the rim of the pink satin to peer inside the box, dabbing at his eyes as he does. At the foot of the brass-trimmed box are several of Pete's childhood friends who undoubtedly came more out of curiosity than grief since they had already grown apart over the years. Now they appear only frightened as they cast meager glances at their lifeless contemporary.

At the left and slightly toward the only wall bordered by light paneling are easels that hold wreaths, black ribbons tied across, words of comfort printed on the front. On either side of the wreaths are two vases that stand on the floor and are filled with white lilies of the valley, chrysanthemums, and red roses. And between them in front of the easels is a two-foot-high angel, its halo made of silver paper, its hands clasped in prayer, and a single tear-shaped pearl embedded halfway down one rosy plastic cheek.

At least forty or fifty people mill around, political acquaintances, lawyers, business associates, friends from law school, the gym, and the coffee shop, a handful of judges, many court employees, and about half a dozen faces that Gabriella doesn't immediately recognize. Moving cautiously forward, she searches only for Dina, until she finds herself with her back pressed right up against the coffin. People have turned to observe her now, some knowing who she is, others nodding greeting anyway. Yet not a soul in the room makes any effort actually to speak to her as she tentatively inches closer to the casket, peering over the side to gaze into the face of her ex-husband, Peter Daniel Molloy.

If she came here today with any doubt that Pete was really dead, it is swept away by the black eyebrow pencil that lines his lower lids. So simple. So hideous. That hits her first even before she begins talking silently to him, lingering there, repulsed and yet somehow fascinated. ''Our child is here too, somewhere in this room, only we didn't come together to mourn you, Pete, because you took her away from me.'' Yet it seems almost fitting that even in death he continues to separate them. How unbelievable to see him like this, his features unrecognizable, his hands familiar though with those prominent half moons on large nails, that one bent index finger from a volleyball that crashed into it on Jones Beach when they were newly married. How odd that the hands are clasped together like that over his breast in a gesture she never saw him use before. But what startles her the most is that she can picture this corpse naked, that she was once so intimately involved with every inch, every contour, every crevice of this body that is beneath the blue serge suit that he'll wear forever now. There's a smooth chest under that Brooks Brothers blue shirt, with a small patch of fine hair in the center, and tucked underneath the Mark Cross belt is a gut that was once hard and flat at the apex of their love before it became slightly paunchy as their marriage dwindled but then snapped back into shape after they were already apart. And that other thing that always made her feel vaguely ashamed for having known better, the thing she always considered to be on the thin side, long enough but not quite wide enough, hard enough but a touch crooked. Even though Pete Molloy had a perpetual erection. Even though he was a man who could make love after the most horrendous psychological turmoil, who was ready no matter what the emotional climate in the bedroom, and who could have a perfectly horrible screaming argument without any clothes on. In Gabriella's mind, any man who could do that was a man who lacked sensibilities, and any man who lacked those kinds of sensibilities wasn't capable of being a good lover. Strange that in all the years they were married she never really considered that to be a defect. Perhaps because there were so many others.

How outraged Pete would be today at this choice of an eternity outfit—how he hated it when others picked out his clothes, even when Gabriella would bring a change to the courthouse when he didn't have time to come home before racing off to one of those satirical political dinners. But suddenly rage fills her as the voice inside her head resumes all the bitterness. "You can't even tell me how Dina's doing in school, if she has a boyfriend, how her allergies are, and if she ever, by any chance, mentions me and why the hell this happened in the first place? Oh God, I hate you, you sonofabitch, for not taking all my phone calls, for ignoring me, for pretending I didn't exist!'' She has grasped the side of the coffin, her knuckles white from the pressure of her fingers, and it's almost too much of an effort not to reach down to slap him, to pummel him until he sits up and explains. Instead she leans down to touch his hair, tenderly, noticing that the gray is more evident at his temples, a nice shade considering how very fair he is and how it could have easily turned to yellow. ''Oh, Pete,''—the voice is weary now—''why was it so important to always be the good guy, to make me out to be the shrew, daddy to the rescue while mommy was the one to punish and discipline and spoil all the fun?'' Gabriella shakes her head. ''Why couldn't you have shared it with me and saved all the fighting, why when life's so damn short?''

But she stops, one hand over her mouth, shocked that she could have been so thoughtless for pointing out how tenuous life was to someone who knows better than she. Again she leans over to touch him, this man who gave her a child and then somehow managed to take that child away. Lightly she runs her finger along the side of his cheek, aware of the cotton inside that makes it appear full, mindful that if she applied the least pressure the entire side would cave in. And right then she begins to recite silently whatever it is that someone might recite to a corpse that didn't exactly end up being a best friend. And when she finally finishes and withdraws her hand from his face, her fingers feel moist from his skin. Yet if Gabriella really wanted to be objective, she would view this situation as nothing more than a tragedy of ordinary people who somehow got involved in circumstances that turned them into monsters. It was more a question of decent people's inability to cope with problems that just kept escalating because those same decent people simply didn't know how to extricate themselves from one another nicely once the trouble began. Those same kinds of ambitious people who live in apartment houses when they first start out where the corridors smell of corned beef and cabbage; whose dining alcoves have one wall lined with stereo equipment, paperbacks, bowling trophies, and photographs of family members beaming proudly at children's college graduations. People like Gabriella Carlucci and Pete Molloy. Before everything began to unravel, before he was unfaithful many times and she was unfaithful once, long after they turned that dining alcove into a nursery and spent every dinner sitting cross-legged on the floor, eating from a coffee table, jumping up every few minutes to see if their baby was still breathing.

Infidelities and divorce, alienated children and funerals. This wasn't the way things were supposed to end up.

"Were you one of my students too?" says the hunch-backed woman who had been chatting with the pallbearers, hobbling up to Gabriella.

Confused for an instant, her eyes dart back to Pete before she replies. "No, I don't think I was."

"I'm Miss Coveney," she prattles on, "Pete's third-grade teacher, and I've seen several of my old students here today." She half smiles then, which leaves one side of her mouth frozen while the other curls up in a grotesque grimace. A stroke survivor, this octogenarian has managed to outlive Pete. "You know, come to think of it, this is the second student I've lost from that class in two years."

"How awful!" Gabriella exclaims as she continues to scan the room for Dina. But when she turns her attention back to the teacher, she notices that Miss Coveney is talking with a couple.

"I'm Mike Jacomo," the man says moving slightly away from the old woman to address Gabriella, "and my Angela was in school with your Dina."

"Oh," Gabriella manages to say, glancing at the woman who stands next to him.

"This is my wife, Sara," Mike Jacomo says.

"I remember you," the woman states. "You always hated to sit in the playground when the children were small."

Stunned for the moment, Gabriella asks, "How is Angela? Is she in college?"

"Actually, our Angela had a little problem finding herself," the man replies, putting a protective arm around his wife's shoulders.

"She was confused about what to do after high school," Sara Jacomo explains, "so for the moment she's doing real well working in the appliance section of our hardware store. We're hoping she'll go back to school in the fall but in the meantime we enjoy having her around. What's Dina been up to?"

Slowly Gabriella begins to formulate the answer. "She's in school," she says cautiously, hoping they don't ask her anything more specific. For it is unbearable that she has been deprived of that phase of Dina's life, almost too brutal to endure that she has been forced to miss the applications to college, the agony of rejection, the elation of acceptance, and even the painful experience of missing her when she left to do her four-year stint. But at sixteen, seventeen, and eighteen years old, daughters somehow don't understand that certain things can never be repeated and sometimes once is all there is.

"I know she's in school," Sara Jacomo answers, looking at her strangely, "we saw her with Pete not too long ago."

"How did she look?" Gabriella blurts out, feeling like Stella Dallas peeking out from behind a garden hedge.

"Like you, except younger," Mike Jacomo replies. "In fact I said that to her and she got sore, insisted she looked just like her father." He scratches his head. "Funny, sometimes when I see Angela standing behind the counter, demonstrating the Crockpot or something, she looks just like

Sara to me, but then people waltz in the store and tell me she's the spitting image of me, so go figure!''

The old woman is upon her once again, a bony hand on her arm. ''Here comes the deceased's sister,'' she informs Gabriella almost at the same moment that she spots Claire. She moves quickly away, hurrying toward her former sister-in-law to hug her tightly, holding her for a bit longer than necessary perhaps, but then time ran out on all their past grievances anyway. Claire pats Gabriella's back with affection, with more warmth perhaps than when they were legally related and other things were still at risk.

''He would have been so relieved that you came here today,'' Claire tells her, stepping back to dab at her eyes with a white lace handkerchief.

Astounded, Gabriella replies, ''How could I have not come?''

''Who knows? Some women would've been bitter or even resentful, but you know what, Gabriella? I knew I could count on you to let bygones be bygones, what's done is done, he meant no harm.'' Claire's small hands flutter up to her plump face to push her glasses up underneath the veil, to pat a blond hair in place underneath the black hat.

''How do you know he meant no harm?'' Gabriella blurts out.

''Didn't have a mean bone in his body,'' Claire whispers, ''only the good die young.'' She puts a finger over her lips. ''Proof!''

''He certainly is the last person I would've thought would have a heart attack,'' Gabriella muses.

''He was so excitable, though,'' Claire contradicts, turning to Harry, the man who entered her life years before on the wings of a want ad.

''Say hello to Gabriella,'' she commands.

''How're you doing, Gabriella.'' Harry greets her warmly, his double-breasted suit making him look like the appropriate person to rush up to, press some cash in his palm, and whisper, "Twenty bucks on Wild Willy in the fourth!"

"I'm all right, Harry," Gabriella answers, "under the circumstances."

More people are pouring into the room, blocking the entrance, milling around the coffin, when Gabriella suddenly spots Dina. Dressed in black with her hair pulled back, she looks pale and fragile, dazed as she holds onto the arm of a woman that Gabriella doesn't recognize. Several mourners stop to kiss her, clutching her shoulder while they wipe lipstick from her cheek. Gabriella's eyes haven't left her, watching as she is accosted by the priest, who leads her to a corner of the room to talk quietly for several moments. And just as Gabriella decides to wander over to her, she notices that the person whose arm Dina was holding is waving to Claire and Harry as she heads in their direction.

A slightly worn-out version of a sixties folk singer, the woman is attractive in a natural homemade-bread kind of way. An anguished expression on her face, her features are prominent, skin tanned, dark hair flecked with bits of gray and frizzed in a moddish feminist halo around her head. Her hands, nails bluntly cut, look capable of strumming a guitar without a pick or of weaving a rug somewhere on an ashram. Now her hands rest lightly on Claire's arm while her eyes settle on Gabriella. "Hello," she says hesitantly, "I'm Adrienne Fast."

"Hello," Gabriella replies, even more hesitantly, "I'm Gabriella Carlucci-Molloy." It's hard to say which woman is more fascinated by the other. Gabriella right then is studying the three gold stars that are affixed to the woman's right ear, appearing to be heading north with the initial point of departure being the lobe. Adrienne is barely paying attention to something Claire is saying, seemingly more interested in Gabriella's gray sling-back pumps.

"Well, that's out of the way, at least the two of you met!" Harry blurts out.

— 44 —

"Don't start," Claire warns.

"And this," Miss Coveney barges in, addressing the group but mostly addressing Gabriella, "is the deceased's daugther, Tina."

"Dina," Dina corrects her, glaring at her mother.

The first mistake is that Gabriella instinctively reaches for her child because the child recoils on touch and for some reasons there aren't any allies in this group.

"We've met," Gabriella says more out of embarrassment than wit, "briefly—in the delivery room."

"Bonds are made and broken there, right, Mother?" Dina says sharply. But Gabriella doesn't hear the abuse.

"Just so there's no doubt," she says calmly, "I love you." But somehow Dina's shampoo no longer smells familiar.

"Please," she says formally, "don't do this, because it's not fair. You can't do this after everything that's happened. Not now." For some reason that stops Gabriella. Studying her daughter thoughtfully for a moment, she is aware that something very basic has changed, Dina is not the same, this child who was once so close, even if she was raised by her father to be second-generation fancy.

"Will you take a walk with me then?" Gabriella asks impulsively, hoping that by putting some distance between them and Pete (even dead) it might make a difference. But Dina shakes her head.

"Dina—" Adrienne begins, but the girl cuts her off.

"This isn't your business so don't get involved."

"Dina," Claire tries, an expression of dread on her face, although it's a wasted look since what she has been dreading has just occurred. "Be nice."

"Come on, Dina," Harry chimes in, "this is no time to fight." Dina's attention is directed at her mother.

"I want you to go away and leave me alone," she says without emotion. "Just because my father's dead"— her voice catches—"doesn't change how I feel."

Gabriella feels as if her heart will break until, for some

unexplainable reason, there is a realignment of her organs, a shift where every fiber of her body responds to a rage that overcomes her. And for the first time since hearing about Pete Molloy's death, she feels a material pain for so many reasons: for this vulnerable girl who masquerades as a tough woman, for her own heart that was up until recently only slightly broken, her vanity only slightly injured, and her life only slightly shattered. But this dying business is the last straw, this legacy of hatred that Pete left for his only child is the final blow.

"Dina," she says, gently guiding the girl away from the others, "come here for a minute, just a minute, it's not going to change anything, I know, but let me say something."

Instinctively, as if she knows that what will be said concerns only them, she allows herself to be led over toward the wall. A cease-fire of sorts until they are alone.

"It's not possible for you to forget how close we were," Gabriella hears herself saying, "how much we loved each other even though there has been some kind of misunderstanding. People fight, sweetheart, especially people who love each other, don't you know that?" Gabriella doesn't dare to stop to take a breath for fear that Dina won't allow her to finish this emotional filibuster. "So why can't we talk about it, and then if you still feel the way you do, after we both try to understand what happened, then I promise not to do anything to bother you again." Hands clasped in a pathetic gesture right beneath her chin, she pauses before her final plea. "Just once let's talk, and then you can stop speaking to me if we can't agree."

"I've already stopped speaking to you," Dina says cruelly, "so why go through it all over again?"

Gabriella takes a breath. "I know I've made mistakes," she continues, refusing to relinquish even one precious moment of contact, "I know I lacked patience sometimes, but there were so many problems and believe me I'm not trying to make excuses or blame anybody but if

I wasn't all that you wanted me to be it was never because I didn't love you or care about you or think about you." Her voice is choked and she pauses only to clear her throat. "I never stopped loving you, Dina, not even after what you told me." Her hand is almost on her daughter's arm. "I'm not dead," she says softly, "not even to you, not even after you told me I was. I'm alive." And the rest is better left unsaid for the effect is obvious. But Dina has turned her back and is already standing safely next to Claire.

"I wouldn't bother anymore," Claire advises Gabriella, "let it go."

"How can I not bother?" Gabriella asks, on the verge of losing all control. Harry then takes her arm, to lead her several feet away.

"Please, not here," he implores, "people are beginning to stare, it's not right." But the book hasn't yet been written on the proper etiquette between estranged mothers and daughters—especially on the occasion of the funeral of the person who estranged them.

"You're right," she admits, "I'm sorry."

"Just let it go."

"I can't let it go."

"Then give it time."

"How much time?"

"Who knows? But at least you're both young."

"So was Pete," she replies as she takes his arm to walk slowly back to the group. Depleted, she has finally resigned herself to not solving anything now, but apparently the other side is still swinging. "Why did you have to come?" Dina attacks, gathering momentum. "You didn't care about him so why're you here? You're nothing but a phony!"

Gabriella presses a Kleenex into Dina's hand. "Here, sweetheart, wipe your nose."

But Dina slaps it away. "Don't change the subject and just go away—we were doing fine without you."

"This is fine?"

"This wasn't supposed to happen," Dina cries softly.

"Neither was this, what happened between us—I'm your mother."

"Any cat can have kittens."

"I'm not a cat and you're no kitten."

"This has gotta stop!" Harry pleads. "It's just not right."

"Shut up, Harry," Claire snaps, "and let them have it out."

Adrienne turns her black batik-covered back then. "I'll meet you in the chapel." She casts a sympathetic glance in Gabriella's direction as she walks away.

"Dina, don't I have a right to defend myself?"

"No, because Daddy doesn't."

"But I've got no reason to attack your father, I came here for you," Gabriella says, her logic irrefutable, her tranquil expression belying her innermost thoughts of dismembering a corpse. "You're the only thing I care about, you and why this happened between us." But Dina's reaction is largely predictable for she is so obviously torn, torn between hurting the living parent and betraying the dead one. But right then there doesn't seem to be any choice.

"You pretended things were fine when they weren't, you pretended you were someone else, as if you were too good for Daddy's friends or family, as if the other kids weren't good enough for me to play with. You never joined in like the other mothers and then you made me really feel like a jerk when you got divorced." Dina holds back tears. "It was up to you to make sure nothing happened to our family, you're the mother, it was up to you." She takes a breath. "But you thought you were too good for everything, and so I had to suffer in other ways, not just emotionally but financially too."

Somewhere inside, Gabriella knows that what Dina says is true for in many ways she did pretend, to all of them. But what she did wasn't so terrible, even famous women throughout history pretended and fabricated pasts to raise themselves up from miserable childhoods, or altered less-than-perfect backgrounds to make themselves socially acceptable. Evading to protect Dina or refusing to be like the others wasn't wrong, shielding Dina was wrong. What Pete did was wrong. But Pete is dead.

"Dina, a lot of things are my fault, but why do you blame me for causing you to suffer financially? I had no money. Your father had the money. What did I have to do with his supporting you?" She holds out her hand. "Come on, take a five-minute walk with me." And how can she insist without sounding like some kind of an insane martyr that a five-minute walk doesn't even begin to compare to a nine-month pregnancy.

"I'm not taking a walk with you because there's nothing you can say that's going to change my mind"—she holds back more tears—"because that's not all of it—there's a lot of other reasons why I hate you!"

Considering the words, Gabriella decides that if she saw a body bag pass by right now she would bet that the bits and pieces inside of that body bag were her own bits and pieces. She visibly folds, staring at her child in disbelief until quite suddenly a curious metamorphosis seems to take place. Dina's entire demeanor changes, as if someone just turned on the lights—klieg lights. Gabriella turns to see who or what has evoked this incredible transformation and notices the same man who helped her with her suitcase.

"Hello, Mr. Tressa," Dina positively purrs, casting a boastful glance at her mother as only a female adolescent can who has already tasted power after seducing her first older man.

"Hello, Dina," the man replies matter-of-factly, apparently immune to her charms. He looks at Gabriella for a moment, eyebrows furrowed, a troubled expression on his face. "It's safe," he says, "in the trunk of my car."

"Thanks," she answers in a soft voice as she rummages around in her chic and impractical French purse. For an instant it appears as if he wants to say something more but Claire has come to life.

"Nick," she gushes, "it's so nice to see you." She glances at Gabriella. "Do you two know each other?"

"Not exactly," Gabriella responds, "except that . . ."

"Well"—Claire forges ahead before either can explain—"this is Nicholas Tressa, Pete's contractor on the beach house."

"Hi," he says, that same flicker of interest and concern visible.

"Gabriella is Pete's ex-wife, Dina's mother," Claire adds from somewhere on another planet. The man runs his hand through his hair and Gabriella instantly thinks "guinea," which makes her realize what it was about him that disturbed her in the first place. He is undoubtedly one of them and she's seen enough of them to know. Like one of those guys who used to come around to her father's calamari stand on the beach, eat for nothing, and then collect the money he had already decided was owed him. Or years later, the same ones who would hang out at the bar of the Villa Napoli with their bimbos, shoulder holsters, and chunky gold pinky rings. But as quickly as she dismisses Nicholas Tressa as one of them, she is aware that thinking of him as "them" is the genesis of her whole problem and why she always wanted to run away from where she came from. Had she thought of "them" as "us" she might not have been so ashamed of her father, Sylvie, and her uncle Rocco who were undoubtedly part of "them" also—however small-time.

Gabriella has managed to locate her sunglasses in one of her jacket pockets and retreats behind them while he continues talking to her.

"I'm really sorry," Nicholas Tressa says sincerely, "this can't be easy." And even though his eyes are intelligent and kind, she is not fooled because contracting is historically one of their professions. That and cement.

"Thanks," she says.

"Terrible thing," Harry comments, rubbing his chin.

"I just saw him last week," Nick answers, sneaking another look at Gabriella, "at the house and he seemed fine."

"Oh, look," Claire says. "Father Bonaparte is waving to us. We'd better get into the chapel." She hesitates then, flustered. "Gabriella," she hedges, "I don't know if there's a seat for you with the family." She looks desperately at Harry, who is in the process of conducting a profound study of one fingernail. But Gabriella is neither surprised nor offended, merely exhausted and warm, her head pounding from a combination of tension and fatigue. Holding her hair away from her face and neck, she smiles wearily.

"Don't worry about it, Claire, I'll find a seat, but first I've got to get some air."

"It's raining," Claire says, nudging Harry.

"I'll go with you," Nick offers, and before anybody else can protest, his hand is on the small of her back. "I'll walk Gabriella outside," he says solemnly to the others. "See you later." Gabriella looks briefly at her daughter but Dina's response is only another icy stare. Whatever it was that they happened to share for sixteen years seems to be over, at least for now. Claire and Dina watch in silence as the pair leave.

"Disgraceful," Claire whispers.

Dina remains quiet.

Claire yanks at Harry's sleeve. "Can you believe that, flirting over the dead body of an ex-husband?"

But Harry has nothing to lose anymore, the worst is over so there is no longer any reason for him to placate and cajole. "Better than flirting over the live body of a present husband," he says.

"And anyway," Dina adds, "she wasn't flirting with him, he was flirting with her."

The Walk

The rain had stopped and only the random puddle is a reminder of the nasty weather. The sun is shining brilliantly in a blue sky spotted with fluffy white clouds. But it somehow only makes everything even more depressing than if the funeral day were gray and dismal, as it usually is in the movies. Nicholas Tressa's hand is now firmly gripping Gabriella's elbow as they walk slowly in the direction of the courthouse.

"That must have been pretty rough on you in there," he says gently. She shakes her head a bit to get some of the hair out of her eyes.

"It was awful." But even that can't describe that she felt among the powerless of the powerless. "Do you have children?" she asks. And when he answers no, she notices that his face is studiously blank, an inwardly directed expression somehow.

"Did you expect that from Dina?"

"Not really, at least I hoped not, but I knew it wasn't going to be easy. We've had problems."

"If I can help you . . ." he begins, a sad fondness in his face, "I'd like to." But she shakes her head, this time as a response before he can go on because there's just no percentage in encouraging anything here. Even if avoiding some degree of intimacy isn't the easiest thing to do when there is a two-person stroll in progress.

They stop at the corner just as the light turns red, neither of them giving any verbal indication as to whether or not crossing the street is to be included on the route today. Gabriella is unmoving, staring straight ahead while he glances at her as if for some kind of clue.

"Would you like to walk a little more or should we turn back?"

Instead of answering she clears her throat, and when the light changes to green, steps daintily off the curb, still very much aware of his hand on her arm. They continue in silence for another half a block or so when she happens to look down and notices his Church's black loafers, black wool socks, and the narrow cuffs on his trousers. Ordinarily she might have been impressed by his good taste and style, maybe even willing to be more gracious since he was the only one who even bothered to help her, if she wasn't convinced that she already knew his story.

Not that it was so hard to know since she grew up around these types and their stories were pretty much the same. Except they usually had a bunch of kids who had the latest in electronic toys and he didn't. Nevertheless she judges him to be around forty-five, married to a spoiled Italian girl whose father has a descriptive phrase between his first and last names, visited Calabria as a graduation present, gets a daily massage after a daily workout so that his skin feels like vinyl, has a Jewish mistress in his collection, is leaner than he appears underneath his suit that's cut to accommodate those shoulders, and could do with a good night's sleep. But what is really astounding and what doesn't escape her is that she, Gabriella Carlucci-Molloy, harbors so deep a prejudice against her own.

"Sometimes it helps to talk to someone who's not so closely involved." And perhaps if she hadn't been caught by his concern, feeling an unexpected flurry, she wouldn't have responded so coldly. "Why would I tell you, a total stranger?"

He reacts with surprising good humor. "Because I happen to have known Pete and Dina, so I'm not exactly a total stranger." As they pass the courthouse, she is aware that he intends to speak again for he takes a short breath and turns his head to look at her. "I've been doing some renovation on Pete's beach house." A pause. "I've got a contracting business out in Sag Harbor, so it's pretty close to East Hampton. I used to go out there almost every weekend last summer to check on my crew, and then during the winter I'd stop by occasionally when Pete was out. I must have seen him at least half a dozen times since Easter."

She fully realizes that he is waiting for some kind of acknowledgment but does nothing to meet that expectation. Maybe it's because he has that absolute attraction which Gabriella and her kind recognize with a kind of inevitability.

"I live in Sag Harbor, near the water. It's really beautiful and quiet out there." He stops abruptly, his grip tightening, so she is forced to stop along with him. "Look, I don't know what to say to you except that maybe everybody was just in a state of shock." Gabriella looks blankly at him although her vision is beginning to blur from the tears, and suddenly she wishes that she hadn't stepped on this ride in the first place.

"You can't possibly understand because the story is too complicated and, quite frankly, I don't even understand it, but I know that you're the last person I'd want to confide in." There was no warning for that one.

"Why's that?"

"Just forget it."

They walk another half block in silence, the profile of his jaw set in a grim line, hers unyielding although her mouth trembles slightly.

"Should we turn around?" he asks.

When she pauses before telling him what else happens to be on her mind, she notices a light of rebellion in his eyes. "Look, Mr. Tressa—" she begins.

"Nick," he corrects.

"Look, Mr. Tressa," she repeats, "it's not that I don't appreciate your taking my suitcase and offering to take a walk with me, but now you're officially released from any more sympathy duty and actually I'd like to think that I was released from my obligation too." As if to underscore it, she gently but firmly removes his hand from her arm. Which is when she notices that his hands are strong, powerful, and without any pinky rings. The better to strangle you with, she catches herself, but not before the thought crosses her mind that it's a waste, a pity, that he is who he is. And married to that spoiled Italian girl with that mobster father too. He grins then and she is assaulted by the word *boyish*.

"I didn't do anything out of sympathy," he replies, still with that infuriating calm that certain men have when they know that they possess what amounts to the bottom line, the big equalizer, the only thing that can overcome logic, "and I'm sorry that you feel any obligation, so why don't we just enjoy the walk. Deal?"

"I'm not here to make deals, Mr. Tressa," she snaps.

He shakes his head in amazement. "Did anyone ever tell you, Miss Carlucci-Molloy, that you had a really terrific personality?"

She inhales sharply and resumes her pace but he is right next to her, seemingly undaunted. They continue to the next corner, past the coffee shop, along the plate glass window that used to be Pastrami Heaven and a couple of other now defunct stores before it became the Chrysler Dealership, several 1990 models in the window, and finally underneath a row of weeping willow trees that make an awning over the concrete. She turns then, fully intending to make her exit, to head back, when he takes her arm yet another time.

"I can manage myself," she says politely, "thank you."

A look of amusement crosses his face or perhaps it's pity, she can't be sure. What she does see so clearly, however, is a passion of spirit that apparently can't be crushed and hears a tone of voice that remains so sure. "Maybe your personality is so terrific," he continues with a touch of sarcasm, "because you've always gotten by on your looks."

Gabriella turns to glance at him, wondering briefly if Nicholas Tressa is really what he appears to be on the surface; the kind of guy who hangs out after work with the locals at Bonnickers or Bobby Van's, who rides around in his company pick-up truck on weekends, owns a 1740s farmhouse that he restored himself and prides himself on an uncomplicated character. Or if he possesses other colors and other souls. Doubtful, judging by every gesture he makes, his cadence of speech and his last name. Good-looking lightweight without a scintilla of culture or intellectual curiosity, so what difference does it make if he's involved with environmental issues or is one of them? He's Long Island. She's Paris.

"Forgive me, but I guess I'm a bit jet-lagged," she says, better able to be charming now that she has succeeded in filing him away under *N* for No Threat. "I just arrived from Paris this morning."

"How long have you been living there?"

She is surprised. "How did you know I lived there?"

"Pete mentioned it to me, but everybody knows everything about everybody and I do quite a lot of work in Freeport, too."

"That's exactly why I left—I can't stand that small-town camaraderie."

Another color appears. "I know your father and your uncle. I used to stop by the Villa Napoli for a drink or dinner."

"I didn't doubt for a minute that you knew my father and uncle," she says coldly, any thoughts of his belonging to an environmental group quickly evaporating.

"What exactly does that mean?" And for the first time she notices that his composure is faltering, that he is bordering on annoyance. But for some reason, instead of pulling back or feeling uneasy, Gabriella forges ahead, welcoming the opportunity to let the words spill out, to release all the hostility, to assuage the humiliation she has just endured at the hands of her own child.

"It means"—she enunciates every word—"that you may all be part of some kind of crowd or small-town clique or whatever else you call it these days, but it doesn't impress me—that you know my family or my ex-husband or anybody else for that matter. I've removed myself from that whole environment long ago, even before I left for Paris, I'm just not part of it anymore, none of it touches me."

He looks at her in positive disbelief. "There must be something I'm missing here so maybe you could explain it to me."

"I'm not here to explain anything, Mr. Tressa."

"What *are* you here for, Miss Carlucci-Molloy?" But there still remains a touch of compassion in his regard, a note of kindness in his tone. She looks at him now from deep inside her sunglasses and for the first time feels regret, although she's not quite sure for what.

"To bury a husband," she begins tentatively, "and—"

"Some of us did that for real," he cuts her off, his eyes never leaving her face.

"And what does that mean?" But she already knows.

"It means that I buried a wife, only she wasn't an ex-wife." He pauses. "Not that I'm minimizing your pain here, I'm just commenting on your attitude."

She lowers her gaze, trying to think of something that might explain while she tries to keep her voice steady so he doesn't realize that she is on the verge of tears. "I'm sorry" is the best she can do. He shrugs. Another color has emerged, another soul has surfaced, less tolerant perhaps than the others but understandably filled with pain.

"Maybe we'd better get back before we miss the eulogy," he suggests. And to Gabriella's confusion and grief is now added embarrassment.

"The truth is that I only came here for my child," she falters, her voice trembling, "and either I'm going to solve this problem or I'm not, but after I do one or the other I'm going to leave again—just as fast as I can." As if that might make it better. They stop to face each other under the very last tree in the row of weeping willows.

"So good-bye," he says gently, catching a tear on her cheek with one finger.

"So good-bye," she barely whispers.

□

Dina is seated beside Adrienne in the car, speeding along the Grand Central Parkway on the way to the cemetery. "Wasn't that a beautiful eulogy for your father?" Dina nods, too tortured to speak, and when she tries the only sound that escapes her lips is a sob. Adrienne turns. "I know, it's unbelievable, isn't it—talking eulogies when only the other day we were talking dinners, indictments, and tennis." But Dina's memory is blurred right now except for that sharp final image of him lying in his coffin right before it was closed. Everything began happening very quickly then—the casket was wheeled out to the waiting hearse, the funeral director waved on several cars so the procession could start, and Dina had stunned everybody by refusing at the last moment to ride in the lead limousine with Claire and Harry.

"Why didn't you want to ride with your aunt?" Adrienne asks, as if she reads the girl's mind.

"Isn't this bad enough without having to listen to all the dumb things they'd be saying to each other?" She gazes out the window, an image coming into focus of her mother standing outside of the funeral parlor next to a big suitcase. She looked so vulnerable and alone until Nicholas Tressa came up to her and gestured to the bag, as if he might have been offering to help. But when Dina looked again, as she was getting into Adrienne's car, her mother was still standing there and he was gone.

"This part's going to be even worse," Adrienne says softly, switching lanes to pass a panel truck.

"Nothing could be worse than what's already happened."

Adrienne looks pained as she takes a breath. "Do you want to talk about it?"

She shakes her head.

"I don't mean about the cemetery."

"I know what you mean."

"You shouldn't try to take everything on at once."

Dina doesn't answer right away and when she does her tone is more bitter than grieving. "It's a closed subject."

"It's impossible to close, Dina, she's your mother."

"And all this time I thought you were campaigning to be a substitute, or was that all an act for Daddy's benefit?"

Adrienne shifts slightly. "Of course not. But I only want you to try and get rid of some of that bitterness. It'll make everything easier."

"For whom?"

"For you, Dina, who else? The only way you'll ever be at peace with yourself is to make peace with her."

"So at least one of us can live happily ever after?"

"I never expected to," Adrienne says sadly.

But the girl expected more of a fight. "Why do you say that?"

"Because of a conversation you and I had long ago, right after your parents divorced when I visited you at the beach one weekend." She glances at Dina. "Before your father and I began to see each other," she stumbles over the words, "on a personal basis."

The Photograph

It began with a letter that arrived at the beach house two weeks into the summer vacation addressed simply to "The Molloys." But if Pete hadn't insisted that Gabriella not telephone Dina so "she could adjust," everybody might have known about the trip long before that white envelope with no return address appeared to ruin everybody's vacation.

Gabriella wrote that she had gone off to Peru to do a story for *Paris Actualité* on a revolutionary leader who was holed up in the mountains plotting a revolution. Nothing seemed to be happening after several days so that the magazine was considering ordering her back had she not gone on that excursion and enclosed that photograph. It was a picture of herself sitting on the steps of a train, her slender legs dangling over the side, skimming the top of the Uru Bamba River that ran next to the steep mountain track. Kneeling behind her and smiling into the lens was a darkly handsome man badly in need of a shave, aviator glasses concealing his eyes, several gold chains twisted around his neck, looking less like a revolutionary than a wealthy South American playboy. Dina studied the picture for several moments before handing it silently over to her father who also studied it for several moments before tossing it on a table. "Poor Mom," Dina said mischievously, "she didn't get her story."

Pete took a long sip of his drink. "I wouldn't feel too bad for her, obviously the trip wasn't a total bust." He was leaning against the railing of his sundeck, his back to the tranquil East Hampton Bay, one hand holding a sweating glass of gin and tonic.

"You're just jealous," Dina teased, "because you can't grow a beard like that."

He forced a smile. "I most certainly could," he joked and then added in a more serious tone, "but I'm not impressed that your mother hangs out with revolutionaries."

Dina cocked her head. "I don't know, Dad, I think it's pretty neat." She turned to look at Adrienne Fast, a colleague of her father's who was visiting for the weekend and who had been sitting on a chaise listening to the exchange. "And anyway, it's her job, right, Adrienne?" The woman didn't answer.

"It doesn't look like much of a job to me," Pete cut in, walking to the bar to refill his glass. "It looks like a lot of free time and a paid vacation." Dina ran up behind him, playfully wrapping her arms around his waist.

"Hey, careful!" he cautioned.

"I think you're jealous, Dad," Dina said with a grin,

"and it's not fair because you have tons of different girl-friends." Adrienne surprised them both then.

"She's right, Pete, it must be confusing for Dina to understand the double standard you've set."

Pete smiled tolerantly as he dropped an extra ice cube into his glass. "There's no double standard, except that my social life doesn't interfere with my responsibilities as a parent."

"Neither does Mom's," Dina defended.

"It does if she puts herself in jeopardy by hanging out with people like that."

"And what about some of the people you hang out with?"

"Who's that?"

"All those criminals and mobsters you put in jail."

"That's my job," he replied tersely.

"Double standard," Adrienne said, smiling.

"At least I don't delude myself into falling in love with everybody I take to dinner," Pete said, changing the subject.

"Does that mean you're never going to fall in love again?" Dina asked, a twinkle in her eye.

"That phrase, 'in love,' is so hackneyed that the best I can expect at my stage of the game is mutual respect and common interests."

"In that case," fourteen-year-old Dina suggested, "you and Adrienne make a perfect couple."

The woman blushed. "There're other things."

"Like what," Dina pressed, "passion?"

"I've had my fill of that," Pete said with a tight smile.

"Poor Dad, no more passion!"

Adrienne walked over to the edge of the deck to contemplate the horizon while Dina wandered over to the table, picked up the photograph, and with measured cruelty said, "So what do you think, do you suppose Mom and this guy have common interests and mutual respect?"

But Pete was halfway through the screen door then.

"I've got a brief to read," he muttered as he slammed into the house.

Dina collapsed into one of the low-slung canvas chairs, her head resting on her arms as she appraised Adrienne. The woman was nice even if she didn't seem to have a terrific sense of humor. Dina noticed that she hardly laughed and when she did, which was only when Pete said something funny, it was with such effort that she was possibly the only person in the world who could actually take the fun out of it.

"So what do you think?" Dina asked.

Adrienne was fading as rapidly as the setting sun. "About what?" She doled out her words carefully.

"About Dad not being into love and passion."

"Why should that affect me?"

"Because you've got a thing for my father."

"Why do you torture him like that?" Adrienne said suddenly.

"Like what?" Dina asked innocently, examining a fingernail.

"You know what I mean."

"No, I don't."

Adrienne's chin was trembling as she walked over to sit on a chair next to Dina's. "Look, I know you're hurt about the divorce but he's hurt too and tormenting him isn't going to get you what you want."

"I've got my whole life ahead of me and he's not tormented—it's you who isn't getting what she wants."

"I'd like to be your friend," Adrienne said quietly.

"What you'd like to be," Dina replied with perfect calm, "is my stepmother."

Adrienne appeared startled. "What I'm trying to say," she said, recovering, "is that everybody's floundering a little, trying to fit in as best they can under the circumstances, and it's tense. Everybody's testing their places."

"You're not exactly testing your place, you're trying to change it."

The sky was pink when they finally got up to head inside. Silently they walked into the kitchen and with a kind of practiced precision went through the routine of preparing dinner. Adrienne patted seasoning on a plump roasting chicken, her hands stained red from the paprika, while Dina carefully sliced tomatoes, onions, and cucumbers for the salad. "He still loves my mother, you know," Dina announced.

"They have a history," Adrienne hedged.

"And she still loves him."

"That's your fantasy."

"Then why was he so upset about that photograph?"

"You're too young to understand, but it's about something called territorial imperative."

Dina had a shrewd expression on her young face. "It's about that they both made a mistake when they split."

"One thing's for sure," Adrienne said, stepping to one side, "they both love you very much."

"Tell me about it," Dina said, savagely tearing apart the lettuce.

"Is that so bad?" Adrienne almost smiled as she put the chicken in the oven.

"Sometimes I feel like a wishbone."

"Then why don't you let me try to help? Why don't you let me be your friend?"

"He'll never marry you," Dina said instead, slamming shut the refrigerator door, "he'll never marry anyone."

Adrienne blanched. "Now what does that have to do with anything?" she said steadily as she untied her apron.

"Never," Dina repeated adamantly, "not as long as he lives!"

□

They have almost reached the exit on the parkway for the cemetery when Adrienne steers the car over to the right lane and into the service area. "It's almost on empty," she explains as she guides the car alongside of a pump. Rolling down the window after it has stopped, she instructs the attendant to fill it up. "Will you tell me the reason," she asks Dina, "why you stopped speaking to your mother?"

Surprisingly, in response Dina drops her face into her hands to weep. Adrienne strokes the girl's hair gently until her sobs subside enough for her to speak.

"So much happened," she begins, "that if I made up with her now it would be like everything Daddy tried to do for me would've been for nothing."

The gas station attendant approaches the car and Adrienne hands him her credit card. "He would have wanted you to make peace with her—especially now," she says, rolling up the window halfway. "He certainly never tried to turn you against her."

"Of course not," Dina says quickly, "all he did was try to be honest and treat me like a grown-up whenever I asked questions or wanted to know reasons. He never changed the subject like she did or refused to answer me."

"But that's not why you stopped speaking to her?"

But Dina is too aware of the woman's fragility to be put on the defensive. "How come he never told you why? Didn't you ever ask him?"

Adrienne glances away. "Many times, and he refused to discuss it with me."

"Then why should I?"

"Because you only have one parent left now, and you're not talking to her, and because I care about you." The attendant waits as Adrienne rolls down the window. He hands her a small metal tray and she signs the receipt, hands back the pen, and rolls up the window. Starting the engine, Adrienne drives the car out of the rest area, merging into the lanes of traffic on the expressway. When they reach cruising speed, Dina begins to talk.

"I stopped speaking to my mother because I lost respect for her, because it became impossible to trust her."

Adrienne accelerates slightly. "Did you tell her that?"

"She would've only denied it or blamed Daddy for turning me against her."

"So it was easier to cut off."

But even Dina knows the reason is more complicated that that, more complex than a simple breach of trust or an isolated misunderstanding. It's even more involved than making a correlation between the rift and Dina's development as a woman. But by the time it happened her breasts were fuller than her mother's, her feet several sizes larger, her suspicions more acute, and her need for a father overwhelming.

"Nothing was easy," she answers, bumping against her door as the car swerves out of the way of a dead animal that lies in the middle of the road, "including the divorce. But I needed to get on with my life and stop being consumed with her problems."

"What kind of problems?"

The memory rekindles the explosion inside Dina's head. "All she ever did was worry that Daddy wasn't supporting me because the checks were late, and every time I mentioned college she got this worried look on her face."

Adrienne reaches into her purse for a handkerchief. "But that was a reality."

"I didn't need realities, I had enough realities," Dina says bitterly. "What I needed were assurances. It wasn't my fault they got divorced so why did I have to pay?"

"Then why didn't you get angry at your father too?"

"I did until he explained why, and then I knew it wasn't his fault."

Adrienne takes her foot off the accelerator, allowing the car in front to gain distance. "There're two sides to every story."

"Do you know why they got divorced?"

"Maybe not."

"Do you think cheating is perfectly fine?"

"No, it's not perfectly fine, as you put it, but those things happen in a marriage and it's not always one person's fault. Your mother was probably hurt, that's why she left."

"My mother didn't leave, he did. She was the one who cheated."

Adrienne glances at Dina. "He told you that?"

The girl nods.

"Look, there were a lot of problems."

"That didn't give her the right to do that."

A sad smile crosses the woman's face. "People do things that they don't always think through until it's too late."

"She should have thought of me, she was the mother!"

"Mothers aren't always perfect either."

But where was Dina to have learned that mothers weren't always perfect, that they too were human and made mistakes? Certainly not in Catholic school, where the nuns taught her that the ultimate mother never interfered after giving birth to the ultimate child, that the sex organs of all good mothers retracted and disappeared between moments of conception. Definitely not on television, where those situation comedies portrayed mothers as all-forgiving, all-knowing, and all-sacrificing, strong without being aggressive, appealing without being sexy. Certainly not in those women's magazines where women were taught how to juggle successful careers, demanding husbands, and precocious children, without appearing too clever.

"You can say what you want, but he tried to keep the marriage together."

"How do you know that?"

"He told me."

"Did he ever tell you what was going on between them at the end?"

"Of course not," Dina replies with surprising hostility. "It had nothing to do with me."

"Of course it did," Adrienne says gently, "because it ended in a divorce."

"Which was her fault."

"Partly, but your father wasn't perfect either."

But where was Dina to have learned that fathers were anything less than perfect, that they were anything but strong and wise and protective of their children from all things hurtful and bad? Certainly not in Catholic school, where the nuns taught her that priests were one step removed from God, revered and respected by everyone from local politicos to faithful rectory housekeepers (those dedicated women who scurried between Father's study and Father's kitchen); that fathers were the ones who fought the wars and supported the children and wives (those dedicated women who scurried between father's study and father's kitchen). Definitely not on television, where those situation comedies portrayed fathers as the only ones who knew a muffler from a transmission, fusion from fission, and were never too tired to answer the most banal question, pitch a baseball, or write a check. And fathers were even allowed to look at other women (humorously ogling secretaries and barmaids on sitcoms) while mothers were only permitted to look at other men on public broadcasting documentaries that dealt with divorce.

"My father may not have been perfect," Dina says, shivering despite the warm temperature in the car, "but at least he never did that."

And in a tone that is barely audible and filled with regret, Adrienne replies, "You're wrong, Dina."

The urge to tumble out the door and roll down the embankment into the soft earth below seems suddenly so inviting. And it isn't that Dina didn't know about her father, it's that hearing it from someone else—a total stranger until very recently—cancels out all the pretense. Her mind wanders back to a night when she was seven and her mother left her with her father and went away with a small metal suitcase filled with boxes of film and a large canvas bag full of cameras and lenses. Gabriella walked out the door despite Dina's sulking, although Pete seemed delighted to have his child all to himself for a change.

He scooped Dina up in his arms, so high she could touch the very top of the wall, and told her what a special time this would be—a story from her big picture book before lights out and an extra dish of ice cream. Dina can still feel the soft texture of her father's blue terry cloth robe and smell the musky scent of his bay rum when she cuddled up against him on her bed. It took several minutes for her to make up her mind and choose the story, several more minutes for Pete to adjust the lamp, fluff up the pillows, light a cigarette, take a drag, inhale, cough; for Dina to stop wriggling her toes and find a comfortable position before Pete finally began to read. But the doorbell rang just as the mouse ran up the clock, which was when Pete leaned over to kiss the tip of Dina's nose before flinging aside the book to race to answer the door. Dina played a game with herself for a while, imagining that her father would come back when that wet spot on the tip of her nose where he had kissed her would disappear. And she can still recall hearing a woman laugh, hushed whispers, footsteps down the hall, a door clicking shut, music blaring from a radio, and how she waited and waited, humming and calling him softly, "Dah-dee," until he finally came back in to kiss her good night. And it wasn't really fair that Dina's fury should have been directed at her mother for leaving her that night, for putting her in a position where she felt so abandoned and humiliated, anymore than it was rational right now to blame her mother for something that her father had done as well.

□

"Please, Adrienne," Dina says, crying softly, "leave him alone. He's dead and it doesn't matter anymore." Once again she feels like lost luggage, just as she did after the divorce, unclaimed baggage that was improperly tagged. "There's other reasons," she adds, "other things that she did."

They exit the expressway several miles later and follow the service road for several yards until the entrance to the cemetery appears in the distance. The gates are carved out of stone, two massive lion heads balanced on pillars on either side of the road. It is the final resolution, the end of a series of blunders and joys that were part of Pete Molloy's life, a theatrical finish coming up so that the mourning process can begin, so that the mourners can be liberated from this awful grief.

"I'm not sure I can do this," Dina whimpers, so pathetic, so timid.

"It's almost over now," Adrienne comforts as she noses the car into an empty spot in the lot. A pat on the knee and a tentative smile through a haze of tears as she turns off the ignition. Dina opens the door and steps out, gathering around her an air of dignity that is so touching in all of its seriousness.

A silk scarf is loosely draped around Gabriella's head in defense against the light rain that has started to fall again. She arranges it and rearranges it as she stands slightly away from the others on the grassy hill, listening to the priest and trying to remember every detail about her life with Pete. But it remains inconceivable that she will never see him again—even if she still blamed him for driving her to that extreme act that ultimately ended their marriage. And though she tried to prepare for this moment on the flight over by reasoning that death is merely another state of life, that life is nothing more than a series of different containers, the gaping hole in the ground leaves her weak. The sleeping bag they once shared on a camping trip, the double bed when they first married, the king when they bought the house and began to have a little extra money, a crib for their baby and now this, a coffin. In the end it seems that

Gabriella never had any real sense of it anyway except to realize that coming home for him somehow reminds her of when she left. It has that same feeling of sadness and solitude.

It was all so trivial so long ago, but then what wasn't. A low-class Irish kid who worked his way through school.

"Eternal rest be granted unto him," the priest says.

Learned the right things to say to charm the world.

"Let perpetual light shine upon him," Father intones.

Who developed a repertoire of sexy tricks.

"May he rest in peace."

Who perfected that magic smile, the one that got her in the beginning.

"Dust to dust."

Before he began collecting all those pretty ladies.

"Ashes to ashes."

With the kind of face that didn't mark.

"The Lord giveth."

He was her lover once.

"And the Lord taketh away," the priest prays.

So how was it that he became her enemy, she wonders hopelessly.

"Amen."

Claire leans against Harry, Gladys against Louise, the pallbearers against one another, Sara against Mike, but Gabriella's vision is too blurred to notice the rest of them. She turns only after they pull out the ropes from underneath the coffin, when she hears the thud and then the sobs and sees her child. Had there been a light it might have drawn her, but it doesn't matter for in the instant that it takes Pete Molloy to disappear forever, she takes the leap from past fiction to present sorrow.

CHAPTER THREE

The Family

"COME ON, MAMA, OPEN WIDE," Gabriella coaxes as she gently nudges the spoon in between Audrey Carlucci's lips.

"If she don't wanna eat, don't force her," Sylvie advises, his head buried behind a newspaper.

"Maybe it's just too hot," said Gabriella, speaking directly to her mother, whose mouth remains clamped shut.

"Sometimes she don't eat so good in the mornings," Sylvie adds as he shakes the pages of the paper until the folds are evenly creased.

Gabriella blows on the spoonful of soft-boiled egg before offering it again. "There," she says, "it was just too hot, she's eating." Reaching over to unlock the brake on the wheelchair, she guides it closer to the table. And when Audrey finishes chewing her food, slowly and deliberately, Gabriella takes one of her limp hands and presses it to her lips, remembering how much it took to get her mother to learn to eat so the feeding tubes could be removed. Still that same sinking feeling in the pit of her stomach remains each time a memory of how she hovered between life and death comes to mind.

"So tell me about the funeral," Sylvie asks, putting down the paper. "I tried to call you from the restaurant but you musta been out cold because you didn't answer the phone and then by the time me and Rocco got home it was late. You was really waterlogged from the trip over!"

"Jet-lagged," she corrects affectionately, "and I was so tired that I literally fell asleep with my clothes on at about seven and then woke up at about eleven, just long enough to get undressed and get back into bed. I didn't even bother to unpack yet." And the clothes she wears now are things she found in a drawer upstairs—a pair of jeans and an old Freeport High School sweatshirt, which makes her look like a kid, especially with her face scrubbed clean and without any makeup and her hair tied back in a ponytail.

"The funeral was amazing," she begins, "everyone was there, and the priest gave a very moving eulogy about Pete as a poor kid who grew up to become this pillar of justice." She is aware of her father's expression.

"Sure, everyone loved Pete Molloy, even the guys he busted used to drink with him when they got out. That charm of his got 'em every time, terrific with the world except his wife, right, dolly?" But it doesn't make her feel good to hear it over and over, the same thing that Sylvie has been saying about Pete Molloy for years, even if it is as true now as it was then. Gabriella turns toward Audrey, whose eyes blink vacantly, staring beyond her and somewhere into space. Her hands are folded demurely on her lap, her legs unmoving and atrophied, pink socks rolled down to her pale ankles, white tennis shoes on her feet that never get soiled or worn.

"What's the difference, Papa," she replies, willing to argue for the first time in a long time, knowing that it's impossible to lose, "he's not here anymore to be charming or horrible—it's over! And you know what, Papa, he didn't do it on purpose, neither of us knew what was going on, we were so young. What did he know? What did any of us know?" And it strikes her then how death exonerates, excuses and forgives, even the most horrendous crimes, as long as the one who committed them is the one who is dead.

Sylvie looks pained. "I guess no matter what happened between the two of you, he was too young to go."

"At least he went quickly," she says and the words hardly are spoken when it strikes her how death reduces an ordinarily articulate person to a heap of banal clichés and trivial words.

"Quick ain't no consolation for dead even if he killed himself with all that ambition of his. You ain't got no idea what went down here the last coupla years since he was elected D.A. He went after every punk on the South Shore like they had hurt him personal. Like he was Batman or somethin' he used to call in the television when there was a drug bust or a murder or some kinda numbers scam or welfare scandal. There was Pete Molloy with that million-dollar smile of his, dressed up with them suspenders that always matched his tie, blond hair slicked back, lookin' like Robert Redford. He woulda hooked up the electric chair on the front steps of the courthouse if they let him." Sylvie runs his hand through his hair. "And you wanna know the real tragedy? The real tragedy is that all that crime stuff only hurt my business and other businesses in town because people got too scared to go out at night. But nothin' made no difference to those punks. They got out on bail and were right back on the street sellin' their dope or shootin' up and where's Pete? Six feet under and I can still hardly fill up the room at dinner!"

"He wouldn't have been happy living any other way," she says sadly, "he needed all that drama!" And that sadness is for herself as well, for all those wasted years when she believed what he told her; years of lonely nights, cold dinners, and frustration when she seemed to function only as the guardian of his clean shirts, house, and child. But if there was one ticket to a show, he went, enough money to buy one suit, it was for him, never for her, because he was building a career for them, he told her, always "for them," as if that should have been enough, as if she was dumb enough not to know that "for them" was a euphemism for "for him." And as far as Dina was concerned, he was the visiting hero, which made it even more difficult for Gabriella.

The Party

At a birthday party for Dina when she turned four, she decided to spend the entire time sitting under the table to pout. Perhaps Gabriella shouldn't have lost her temper and been so adamant that she come out and join the other children. Not that it did any good. Pete appeared after the party was over and the children had gone home, as usual, while Gabriella was busy cleaning up the mess, picking up the paper streamers, squashed birthday cake, and smashed chocolates.

"Where's my girl?" he called out.

"Under the table," Gabriella responded, as if it were the most normal place in the world for Dina to be. But then Pete hadn't been there for the party, so how was he to know?

"What's she doing there?" he asked, flinging his briefcase on the couch. "I thought my girl had a birthday party today."

"Ask her," Gabriella answered cryptically as she continued to clean up the mess.

"What's my little girl doing under the table?" Pete asked as he bent down to peer at Dina who, at that very instant, had decided to cry, clever enough to sense a sympathetic parent when she saw one. Which was exactly what Gabriella said to Pete, who was now lying flat on his belly on the floor, reaching under the table for his little girl.

"Pete, don't do that, please, don't make her feel more sorry for herself."

"Come on, pumpkin," Pete coaxed. "Daddy's home. You can come out now, everything's all right." As if everything hadn't been all right with Gabriella, as if it didn't matter how long or how intense the effort was, it was meaningless until the key turned in the door at the end of the day and Daddy came home. Which was exactly what Gabriella said to Pete, who was cuddling Dina on his lap.

"You always make me out to be the monster when you do that without even knowing what happened."

"What's the matter, sweetheart?" Pete cooed.

"I lost the game," Dina whimpered.

"What game?"

"Pin the Tail on the Donkey."

Pete glanced at Gabriella to inquire. "Why did she lose the game when it was her party?"

"Because Angela Fiorella's aim was better than hers."

"You should have seen to it that she won," Pete reprimanded. "After all it was her tail and her pin and her donkey."

"I don't agree," Gabriella argued. "She has to learn how to be a good loser."

"This isn't about winning or losing," Pete said coolly, "it's about loyalties."

Gabriella crawled over to the radiator to wipe up a glob of chocolate cake and then remained on her hands and knees to consider that maybe it was about loyalties. Or maybe it was about marriages. And that was exactly what Gabriella said after Dina was in bed.

"Why do you undermine me in front of Dina?"

"Because you have no idea how to raise a child."

"How would you know, you're never home."

"I know because I've watched and because you've got nothing to draw on. You never had a mother yourself."

"I certainly did until I was thirteen."

"Even before she got sick she was too intimidated by your father to do anything on her own. What she did best was smile and look gorgeous."

"Not true," Gabriella cried, retreating behind a sulk.

But it hadn't yet occurred to her to compare her father

and her husband and how they each treated their wives. Perhaps because by the time Gabriella was married Audrey was already paralyzed. Except so was Gabriella.

Silent and brooding, she sat on the couch, sneaking glances at Pete because to her, in spite of everything else, he was still the most attractive man she had ever seen. "Why do you stay married to me," she challenged suddenly, "if you think I'm such a lousy mother?" It hadn't yet occurred to her to realize that there might be other reasons for her appeal.

"Because I keep hoping that you're not too dumb to learn."

For perhaps had she realized those other reasons, Pete might have realized them as well. "Don't call me dumb," she warned.

"I'm not calling you dumb, Gabriella, I'm just waiting to see how you develop—if you end up like all the other dumb guinea women."

Jumping up, she swung at him but he grabbed her arm in mid-air, grappling with her until they both ended up on the floor. They were still for a moment or two while they caught their breath, she with her arms pinned above her head, he lying on top of her, his face close to hers.

"You still turn me on more than anybody else," he whispered, and he should have known because she knew that he was still conducting that same old survey on those evenings when he didn't come home from work. But nothing had changed since he had been doing that, since before she married him. And ironically she had married him for some of those very reasons. He was smooth and sexy, elusive and bawdy, everything that she wasn't. And he married her only because she was risky, the one girl he couldn't have even after he had her. His lips were inches from hers then as she made a pretense of twisting out of his grasp until he held her around the waist, until she linked her arms around his neck and drew him into her.

"We've both changed, I guess," she murmured, "but

it's dumb to fight.'' His head was buried in her breasts, one hand fumbling with the buttons of her shirt, a lazy smile on his handsome face.

"Tell me what you want, baby."

"More," she said in his ear.

"More than this?"

"Yes, more."

"A divorce?"

"Yes," she mumbled, "but after." His mouth was on hers, his pants unfastened, her blouse somewhere in the far corner of the room, her bra in his left hand.

"Never," he said fiercely, "you're too beautiful. I'll never let you go!" Her hand was on him, caressing him while her jeans were around her ankles, then kicked across the room, her shoes flung to the side.

"Why not?" she gasped as he entered her. "What're you afraid of?"

His breathing was more rapid, his movements more intense. "We'll be together forever," he whispered.

"Why?" she moaned.

"Because I'm a Catholic," he said breathlessly, propping himself up on his elbows so he could better see her, "an Irish Catholic." Her head was to one side, the back of her hand against her mouth.

"And me, what am I?" she whispered.

"Gabriella," he gasped.

"Oh, my God." She took a quick breath.

"Same church," he managed to say, a sob still lurking in his throat.

"Different pew," she corrected softly in his ear, holding him tightly against her, cradling his head in her arms.

□

"*Stronzo,*" Sylvie mutters, "he didn't need all that garbage with them fancy suits, flashy cars, hot and cold runnin' broads, he didn't need all that—specially after he had you!" A scowl then. "And that's what killed him in the end, livin' so hard that his heart couldn't take it no more! And for what, for *niente*, that's what!'' Yet his tone still holds that familiar note of admiration because he would never think of condemning Pete if what he had done he had done to someone else's daughter. For he resembles Pete in so many ways. Even at sixty-five, there are features that remain of that good-looking wild young man with the ruddy complexion.

Sylvie worked outdoors, physical work, when he had the calamari stand on the beach, and his hands still show signs of those calluses from cutting up fish and shucking oysters and clams. And with his full head of wavy hair, even gray now, and that fabulous smile with those spectacular perfect white teeth, women continue to show interest. Recently he has been staying in shape by rising every morning at six to meet the delivery trucks and unloading the daily food supplies at the restaurant.

''*Quanto ero addolorato,*'' he laments now with such passion that Gabriella actually has to contain a smile, ''and the kid, I wasn't gonna say nothin', I was gonna wait for you to say somethin'.''

''She's still very angry at me, Papa.''

''For what she's angry?''

''I'm not really sure.''

''So?''

''So, what can I say except right now that's the way it is.''

''No, wrong, what you gotta say is that now that the sonofabitch is dead, she's gonna straighten up.'' He holds up one hand. ''OK, OK, I'm upset, so I admit it, but I ain't never wished him dead, may he rest in peace, and anyway between you and me, nobody ever died from wishin'.'' He settles back in the chair. ''And don't think there weren't plenty of times I coulda killed him with my bare hands when I seen how miserable he made you!''

''It's all over now, Papa, forget it!''

''Funny though, I woulda thought Dina woulda

called, in the beginnin' specially when she first went to live with him, after you left for Paris, France, I woulda thought she woulda answered my messages that I left on his machine, but the kid never so much as picked up the phone.''

''It wasn't personal, Papa. She was confused.''

''Yeah, confused, my own grandchild.'' He shakes his head. ''You wanna know how I feel about that?'' he says angrily. But he doesn't wait for a response. ''I feel cheated, that's how I feel. First you cheated me outta walkin' you down the aisle—that *stronzo* took my baby and then he took my baby's baby!''

''Well, I'm back.''

''Yeah, yeah, you're back, but for how long you're back?''

She doesn't say, although his words are not lost on her.

''I warned you not to marry the bum, typical Irish I told you, you remember, Gabriella, I told you to dance with him, eat with him, watch a parade, but don't marry him because all them Irish guys have no friggin' conscience.''

''Papa,'' she protests, ''that's like saying all Italians are Mafia.'' For an instant that man from the funeral comes into her head, the one who made her feel so pretentious and judgmental and weak every time he looked at her. The man who actually made her blush when she heard her own words sounding like slogans of defiance against everything. If she does see him again, which is doubtful, perhaps she should apologize for being so rude, and perhaps if she does get to explain, which is also doubtful, she shouldn't make her thoughts so foreshortened.

''So now you're defendin' him?''

''Maybe I am,'' she says, amazed nonetheless at this new-found tolerance for this person who cheated on her, humiliated her, and took away her child.

''Yeah, well, if you wanna know, it's only 'cause he's dead.''

Gabriella blots her mother's chin gently with one corner of the napkin, ignoring her father while she has a word or two with her mother, silently, the way she usually communicates with her in front of other people. Oblivious, Sylvie keeps talking.

"You was wrong to take off for Paris, maybe you shoulda stayed even after she stormed off and kept on tryin', stayed right here so she knew you loved her. That's what I blame you for, Gabriella, I blame you for that!"

"You wanna blame someone," Rocco Carlucci says as he shuffles into the kitchen, his black eyes glittering in their sockets, his face more emaciated than before, his white hair slicked back with some kind of oil that smells of almonds, "blame me!"

Gabriella is up, out of the chair, and in her uncle's arms. "I'm so glad to see you," she cries. "I missed you!"

"Missed you too, dolly," the old man wheezes, his emphysema having gotten progressively worse over these past two years. "I'm so happy you come home, even if you hadda come home for this—*che pitia!*"

When she finally steps back to look at him, she is shocked to see how frail he has become. His baggy pants are hiked up around his bony concave chest; his arms are spindly, his fingertips cold. "Alive you coulda fixed it, maybe, dead makes everythin' *finito, es vero, cara?*" He turns to his brother then. "So you wanna blame, Sylvano, blame me 'cause if I hadda watched her closer"—he pauses to smooth her cheek—"she never woulda married the bum." For it was Rocco who became the surrogate mother after Audrey got sick. He was the one who was the curator of all decorum in the Carlucci house, the guardian of Gabriella's morals and manners, and the one who suffered the most when she eloped with Pete.

"Nah, Roc," Sylvie contradicts, "it was me. I shoulda watched her better!"

"Done is done, Sylvano!"

"So *basta!*"

"So *finito!*"

"So don't I have anything to say about it?" Gabriella asks as she reaches for the box of cereal to pour into her uncle's bowl.

"So *parla!*" the two men say in unison.

"I loved him," she says simply. And a feeling of relief sweeps over her, like a wave that cleanses, for she has finally found the moment to admit it, even if the confession turns almost instantly to despair, even if it somehow seems inappropriate at this stage just to sit back as her entire life unfolds before her eyes.

"Love," Sylvie says disdainfully. "What did you know about love at nineteen?"

Instinctively Gabriella reaches for her mother's hand. "As much as Mama knew at nineteen when she married you."

"Ah, Sylvano," Rocco says dreamily, "she's right, you know, the music, the party, you remember that Easter when the lightning struck in her heart, a clap of thunder when you and La Bella Audrey met?"

"Times was different then, Roc," Sylvie protests, his voice breaking slightly. "Life was different then!"

Freeport

Located on the South Shore of Long Island, approximately forty-five minutes from Manhattan, Freeport was once considered to be a luxurious beach resort—one of the most affluent suburbs. That was during the era when the town was a haven for all different kinds of celebrities: vaudeville stars who relaxed there between tours or retired there when tours were completed; Guy Lombardo, Mr. New Year's Eve; and Rocco "Bull's-Eye" Carlucci, the man who made headlines when he shot at Tony "Nine Lives" Bianci point blank and missed.

Carlucci was a bachelor, a small and dapper man who dressed with an Old World elegance in three-piece suits and gray suede gloves, a man who certainly didn't give the impression of ever having touched a gun, let alone having fired one. Actually, though, it was the house where Rocco lived that provided more grist for the gossip mill than Rocco himself. People were fascinated by the replica of the Sistine Chapel ceiling that was painted on the bottom of the pool, the driveway bordered by identical topiary bushes, and the Japanese garden with the large pagoda (rumored to have been shipped from Japan), which doubled as a cage for the two Dobermans that roamed the property at night. It was there one Easter Sunday, at an annual egg-rolling garden party that Rocco threw for all his friends and neighbors, that Sylvie met Audrey and fell immediately in love with the blond long-legged beauty. They were married a mere two months later in the same garden with the same people in attendance.

Some said it was because of Rocco and those like him, others said it was the beach, but a few years after Gabriella was born, in the mid-fifties, many low-level upwardly mobile Mafiosi moved into town. Claiming to seek privacy in this unpretentious beach resort, they managed also to gain instant roots and respectability in a county where the majority of public officials had names ending in vowels. Construction workers were soon seen swarming around the wide tree-lined streets, renovating the old rambling houses with their enormous front porches, the ones that had been occupied by those vaudeville stars, most of whom had died or were only existing in nursing homes. But in the sixties things began to change, both for the town and for the Carlucci family as well. An influx of city dwellers who worked mostly in Manhattan's garment industry and who had made fast money during the Korean War, fled deteriorating urban areas and headed for the tranquillity and charm of Freeport. More art deco houses were carved out of the last remaining fields of untended grass and pasture meadows where horses and cows once grazed.

It was the priceless topography of old trees and wide

streets that attracted them, new money in an old setting, that and the beach, miles and miles of as yet unspoiled white sand dotted with clubs that had names like Lido, Cippriani, or Gritti. But the irony came when hordes of welfare families from all over Long Island were discarded in Freeport, sheltered in sprawling homes that had been purchased by the county and turned into boardinghouses. Freeport had been selected as the sacrificial lamb, the place chosen to protect the rest of the South Shore from a similar fate, and those people who tried to escape the poor found themselves once again living among them.

In 1962 things got so bad on the beach with gangs of kids marauding the area that Sylvie and Rocco took down the pink pelican sign from the front of their calamari stand on Jones Beach and moved it to a new location on Sunrise Highway near the Freeport train station.

They named the restaurant the Villa Napoli, as a tribute to their origins.

Only six months after they opened, when the red, white, and blue flags were still up, signaling the restaurant's recent debut, when Audrey Carlucci still resembled those photographs taken of her when she was a Rockette at the Music Hall, Rocco was arrested for attempted murder.

The sentence could have been a lot worse had he actually succeeded in hitting Tony ''Nine Lives.'' Yet it was harsh for other reasons. One year into the two-year prison term, right after Gabriella celebrated her thirteenth birthday in the banquet room of the Villa Napoli, Audrey suffered an embolism which left her forever dependent upon others to perform the most basic chores and bodily functions.

Strangely, Freeport began to improve after that, with more middle-class people of all races moving in to live side by side, the poor somehow remaining in one area that was kept relatively clean and crime-free. Most of the original residents adjusted as well, staying on either because they hadn't the strength or the resources to leave, or as in Sylvie's case, where sickness in the family dictated continuity. But for Gabriella, Freeport became a nightmare, the place where everything bad happened to her and to her family. Once she had imagined that nothing could ever be as awful as that day when the FBI came to take away her uncle, and that she could never miss anyone as much as she missed him. Then she realized that she had been wrong, that maybe Rocco had been a test to prepare her for the most hideous pain there was yet to feel, when her mother got so sick.

□

"So how long you plannin' to stay over there in Paris, France?" Sylvie asks.

Gabriella holds a straw to her mother's lips, watching as she draws in some orange juice. She pinches it slightly so that Audrey doesn't suck in too much of the liquid at once and answers. "It's painful here, Papa," she begins. "I keep remembering Dina as a baby and then as a little girl and then when she ran out of the house and left. So right now I'm not thinking about leaving France, it just doesn't feel right to move back."

"You're makin' a big mistake, Gabriella, always thinkin' the grass is greener someplace else, and another thing, you're not gettin' any younger."

Rocco looks up to smile a toothless smile at his niece, his dentures not yet in place this morning. "My petunias are coming up in the garden, you want to see them after breakfast?" She touches his hand gently and nods.

"It's not a question of thinking one place is better than another," she tells her father, "it's just that life is about meeting new people and having different experiences, and Papa, this isn't Napoli where girls are old at twenty if they're not married."

"In my house it's Napoli," Sylvie answers, "and what you should be doin' is findin' a nice Italian boy—"

"So maybe she should live in Rome," Rocco interrupts, but Sylvie gives him a dirty look before continuing.

"Get your kid back, buy a dog, cut your hair maybe, or if you don't have no time to walk a dog, buy a bird, but stop runnin' around takin' pictures, *che desgrazia*, what kinda life's that for a decent Italian girl?" He leans forward. "You need money?"

"*Patienza*, Sylvano," Rocco cautions, "she's a good girl."

"You need money?" he repeats.

"No," she says, "I'm fine. I don't need any money."

"You know, Sylvano, she didn't do so good the last time she found someone to marry, so maybe she's right working like this."

"She ain't right," Sylvie says, clearly annoyed.

"Papa," she begins hesitantly, "if I thought you needed me here because of Mama, that would be different."

"Not for me and not for Mama," he says, "it's for you." And another lie has passed between them, told by him out of a sense of pride, accepted by her out of a sense of guilt. There is a strained silence. Sylvie resumes. "Where'd Dina go after?"

"Back to school."

"She didn't even call."

"Did you really think she would?"

He shrugs.

"Papa," she begins again, "could I borrow the car so I can drive up to Connecticut this weekend to see her?"

He looks at her suspiciously. "When you goin' back to Paris?" For the second time this morning the question to end all questions has been posed.

"I don't know yet," she answers honestly. "It depends on Dina, but I've got a problem staying here indefinitely because of my job. In fact I've got to go to the city and talk to them at the New York offices."

"Sure, sure, take the car," Sylvie says and then snaps his fingers. "Hey, you wanna job, a really good job? I can get you a job in two minutes, one phone call and you got a really good job!"

She starts to say something but thinks better of it.

"You remember Tony Spinozza, the guy with eight fingers who owned that photography studio on Main Street." She glances at Rocco who appears to be oblivious as he clanks his spoon against the side of his cereal bowl, shoveling the mush into his mouth. "Well, he got bigger, cut through the wall after the pizza parlor went bust, and now business is boomin'—he does all the weddings and communions and family stuff all over the South Shore." She nods, feigning interest.

"Really, Papa."

"No kiddin', and one call from me and you've got a job!"

"Papa," she says carefully, "that's not exactly the kind of work I do." But Sylvie is beyond listening.

"Come to think of it, this could work out better than I thought." He turns to Rocco. "Hey, pal, pay attention to this," he says before looking directly at Gabriella. "Tony's wife died and left him two motherless children, nice kids, to raise all alone." He concentrates on his hands now, which are folded on the table. Even Rocco looks embarrassed as he waits for the finale. "Maybe you shouldn't be so fast to say no, after all, you didn't do so great with your own kid, maybe you'd do better with someone else's."

Shaking her head, she turns to her mother. Audrey has a trapped look on her face, as if she wants to say something or do something and can't. "I've got to take Mama upstairs to wash and dress her," Gabriella says, aware that her father and uncle are watching her.

"We're not so bad, are we?" Sylvie asks, pinching her cheek.

"No," she says, standing to walk to the sink, "you're

not so bad. But right now, Papa, I've got more important things to think about—like Dina and"—she wrings out the sponge—"and the kitchen." She turns. "After breakfast I'm going to go to Fiorello's and buy some paint and then I'm going to paint the whole kitchen—even the ceiling!" As if the idea had been an idea that she'd carried inside for decades. But Rocco is beaming, a broad smile that goes from fleshless lobe to bloodless cheek, a look of pure joy on his face as if he has just finished twirling to a tarantella.

"That's my dolly," he exclaims, clapping his bony hands, "painting the kitchen."

Gabriella sponges off the table, smiling at her uncle when she asks, "So what do you think, Papa, wouldn't that brighten everything up a little around here?"

"You brighten everything around here," he answers with tenderness.

"Mama," she says, leaning over the wheelchair, "I'm going to take you upstairs right now." She kisses her forehead. "And while you take a nap, I'll start the kitchen."

Suddenly Rocco's hands flutter over his ears. "All them bells all at once," he cries. Sylvie laughs as he reaches over to rub his brother's neck.

"Everything all at once is right!" He turns to Gabriella as he heads out of the kitchen. "You get the phone and I'll get the door."

The Request

"I know it's a lot to ask, Gabriella, but there's no one else I trust enough to do it." Claire Molloy is talking to Gabriella, who is sitting on a straight-back chair near the staircase, the phone receiver cradled between her chin and shoulder.

"Why can't you do it yourself?"

Claire sighs. "Because I've got my hands full going

through all the stuff in the house in Freeport and also going through all the personal things from the office." She pauses. "And, anyway, I don't drive."

"Can't Harry take you?"

"No," Claire says wearily, "he won't." She pauses again. "When are you going back to Paris?"

As if that's the only question anybody wants answered this morning. "That's not the point," Gabriella evades, "it's just that I don't feel right going through Pete's things at the beach."

"You're the only one, Gabriella. I can't expect Dina to do it and Adrienne is a stranger. You're family."

Family except when it comes to sitting where the family sits during a funeral service. "Look, Claire," Gabriella says, "I've really got my hands full with Mama and I've just committed myself to painting the kitchen here and I'm planning to drive up to Connecticut this weekend to see Dina."

"Don't bother," Claire says without any expression.

"Why?"

"If I were you I wouldn't bother, that's all! Not after her little display at the funeral parlor."

"How can you say that I shouldn't bother? She's my child." But Claire can say that and through no fault of her own since she lacks wisdom and sensibility. She is simply typical of those women who have never had their birth canals invaded and who, along with losing a chunk of placenta, have also lost any notion of pride when it comes to their babies. And for some reason, right now, Gabriella swears that she smells pablum.

"Well, anyway," Claire replies lamely, "Dina won't be at school this weekend. She's going with her boyfriend to some kind of a seminar."

"Oh," Gabriella says, her pulse throbbing and the blood pounding in her ears. A boyfriend, someone who knows her child intimately, someone with whom she shares her time, confides her secrets and whom Gabriella doesn't even know, has never seen. Ironic how a physical relationship between a man and a woman produces a bond that surpasses that original physical bond between mother and child. Ironic how being inside of a body in the biological sense is short-lived and forgotten while being inside of a body in the sexual sense is remembered and recalled long after the moment has passed. But to lament that particular loss is like closing the barn door after the horse gets out, or in this case, perhaps more like closing the barn door after the horse gets in.

"Actually," Claire explains, "I think it's a seminar on grief."

"How will I get the keys to the house?" Gabriella asks, suddenly eager to conclude all the arrangements and get off the phone.

"There's a spare set over the window in the garage or at least that's where Pete used to leave it when the construction crew was working there."

Gabriella stands to lean against the banister, turning her body around so that she faces the entrance to the kitchen.

"What I should probably do," Claire says, "is call Nick Tressa and make sure the keys are there, and if they're not, then ask him to drop them off."

"Whatever," Gabriella answers, craning her neck toward the voices that seem to be coming from the back door.

"Thanks, Gabriella," Claire says. "it's mostly just the files and some stuff from the safe in his study that I need."

"I'll take care of it," Gabriella assures her before hanging up. Entering the kitchen noiselessly, she stands for several moments unobserved near the refrigerator until her father turns and notices her.

"Gabriella," he says in a voice filled with hope, "say hello to Nick Tressa, Frank Tressa's son, may he rest in peace, an old friend!"

She studies him with a cool regard before speaking and to her dismay sees a flicker of amusement cross his face.

"We've met," Nick says, and not the least bit self-consciously, "at Pete's funeral."

"Hey whaddaya know," Sylvie responds with such abandon that someone who didn't know might have assumed that the illegitimate son of the pope had just graced his kitchen. "Gabriella, you never told me you met Frank Tressa's son." One hand slaps his forehead as he says to Rocco, "Whaddya think, Roc, small world. Gabriella met Frank Tressa's son at the funeral."

It occurs to her right then that this one must have slipped her father's mind or he certainly wouldn't have dredged up Tony Spinozza with his eight fingers and two motherless children. There is no doubt that Nicholas Tressa is an attractive man, Gabriella saw that immediately at the funeral, and he happens to look even more attractive this morning. Dressed in a pair of khaki pants that do little to hide the outline of a muscular behind, a white cotton V-neck sweater, and Topsiders without socks, he looks perfectly relaxed and rested, as if he managed to get a good night's sleep. And from across the kitchen, Gabriella is relieved to notice that his range of facial expressions includes more than just concern and pity.

But there have been sanitation workers that she's seen on this very street who were also attractive, and she would be a liar not to admit that she didn't fantasize about them as well—at least for as long as it took her to walk past while they dumped the trash bins onto the backs of their trucks. And they too seemed unbothered as they followed her with their eyes, just as he does standing in the kitchen—uninvited and unannounced.

"We got so caught up talking about other things this morning," Gabriella explains, smiling graciously, "that I forgot to mention that we met at the funeral." As she speaks she moves slowly toward her mother until she stands behind the wheelchair, one hand resting on her mother's arm. "Have you met my mother, Mr. Tressa?" she asks or perhaps challenges. Before he can react Sylvie squeezes his shoulder.

"Hey, what's this mister business, it's Nick, right Nick, Gabriella can call you Nick."

But he is already bending down so he can meet Audrey's gaze, holding one of her hands in his. "Hello, Mrs. Carlucci," he says naturally, "I'm Nick Tressa." His eyes flicker up to Gabriella only when there is no response.

"She can't answer you," she says quietly, part of her astounded by his grace, another suspicious of his motive. "She's aphasic, although sometimes I can tell by her reaction that she understands what's going on."

"Wishful thinkin'," Sylvie says. "It's no use hopin' no more." Gabriella holds onto Audrey protectively.

"Of course there's use," she contradicts, "she's made enormous progress and there's no doubt that she'll make more."

Sylvie walks behind Nick to clutch a shoulder again. "Nick don't wanna hear our troubles, he's got his own, right, Nick?"

He is charming as he smiles warmly, still looking at Gabriella. "You've got to keep talking to her," he says, "that's the only way she remains a part of everything."

"Come, sit," Sylvie interrupts uncomfortably, "come have a cuppa coffee."

"Yes, please," Gabriella adds, motioning to a chair.

"Say hello to Rocco," Sylvie says.

"Hello, Rocco," Nick says, shaking the old man's hand.

"How many years now since your father passed away?"

"He died in 1980 so that makes just about ten years now."

"How'd he go?"

"Stroke."

"Same thing like Audrey here only she pulled through," Rocco says, a touch of remorse in his tone.

"Frank Tressa was mayor of Freeport," Sylvie tells Gabriella proudly, "when you was a little girl. Say, Nick, how old were you when your father was mayor?"

"Let's see," Nick figures, "it was 1958 so I was thirteen."

"Thirteen," Sylvie calculates, "and in 1958 my Gabriella was just makin' her First Communion, so she was eight."

Gabriella begins pushing the wheelchair toward the door, hoping that he doesn't add "perfect" to the difference in their ages. "I'm going to take Mama upstairs," she says, giving Sylvie a meaningful look. Perhaps she would have been amused by her father's apparent delight at having a red-blooded Italian male under sixty in his kitchen if she didn't somehow feel like a trussed-up chicken lying on a silver platter or like Cinderella waiting for Prince Charming to slip her foot into a glass slipper before she slipped it into her mouth. "You'll excuse me," she addresses Nick, "but I've got to get my mother dressed."

"First coffee for our guest," Sylvie insists. "And I'm gonna take care of Mama this morning."

"Don't bother," Nick says in haste. "I can help myself to some coffee." It doesn't escape Gabriella that this man has absolutely no intention of leaving so fast.

"No, no, you sit," Sylvie jumps in, "I do it every morning, wash her, dress her, when my Gabriella here is busy lookin' at that leanin' tower in Paris, France, right, honey?"

"Eiffel," she corrects but barely audibly, "the one that leans is in Italy."

"So how's business?" Rocco asks as Gabriella lapses into silence.

"It's growing so much that pretty soon I'm going to have to move out of my office at home." He walks over to the far counter and reaches for a mug from a hook above the dishrack. "I've been running it out of Sag Harbor, but it looks like I'm going to have to take some space in town. There doesn't seem to be an end in sight to all this renovation and new construction that's going on."

Rocco nods absently, his attention span wavering as Sylvie says, "Your father woulda been proud, he woulda been real happy to see what you done with the business. Now maybe all you gotta do is run for mayor, right, Nick?" He laughs. "Come on, Roc, let's get goin' before it gets late. You gotta put your teeth in and I gotta get Madame ready before Violet comes. We gotta go to work!"

"Actually, I can't stay too long," Nick says apologetically, glancing at Gabriella. "I've got to walk to a job at the other end of town, but I just wanted to stop in because it's been so long."

"Too long," Rocco agrees, holding onto the table as he rises, "you never know when it's gonna be the last time for any of us."

Helping Rocco to balance, Sylvie places one of the old man's hands on the wall. "Nothing to do with age neither," he says, "look at what happened to poor Pete."

"Papa, wait," Gabriella rushes, "why don't the two of you catch up and let me take care of Mama this morning? After all, it's not very often you get to see . . ." And now she's caught. "Nick." She practically chokes on the name. But Sylvie's only response is to look at her as if she's out of her mind before laughing.

"Ten minutes and you're all caught up in this town, same people over and over sayin' nothin'." He laughs again. "You know what I'm talkin' about, they come into the joint, have a coupla drinks, dinner, and leave. There ain't nothin' I can say that's earth shatterin'. Right, Nick? It's Freeport!" He slaps him affectionately on the back. "Sit, I'll come back down before I leave." He beams, surveying the scene before he shakes his head in wonderment. "Frank

Tressa's son, whaddya know, *piccolo mondo!*" And almost as an afterthought he adds, "You ask Nick about the paint before you rush off to Fiorello's, you hear, Gabriella?"

She shuts her eyes a moment. "Yes, I hear, Papa."

Strangely, from the instant they are alone, Nick appears to be even more ill at ease than she is. Coffee mug in hand, he wanders over to the table to set it down. "I didn't mean to upset the routine around here," he says tentatively.

"Not at all," Gabriella the perfect hostess replies as she slips into a chair. "Won't you sit down?" Courtesy comes automatically, a genuine desire to be in his company is something else. Not that it would be so terrible if someone could coax her or lull her out of this hostile mode. "Milk?" she asks too seriously.

"Thanks," he answers too solemnly for a question that has only to do with a cup of coffee.

"Sugar?" she offers dourly.

"No thanks," he replies, his brow furrowed as he stirs the coffee. "When did your mother get sick?"

Gabriella slings an arm over the back of the chair in an effort to appear nonchalant. "When I was thirteen," she says and then falls silent, which makes her even more uncomfortable than if she could just recount it matter-of-factly. But it's the same thing every time someone asks, the temptation to say, "When I was thirteen years old, six months, four days, and it happened on a Thursday, by the way, at one-fifteen in the afternoon," but no one would be interested.

"She's beautiful," he comments.

"She was a dancer," she adds.

"A showgirl?" he makes the mistake of assuming.

"Certainly not," she corrects indignantly, "she was a Rockette at the Music Hall." As if that were the haute couture of hoofers.

"Sorry," Nick answers with a disarming grin.

Odd that he affects her enough not to belabor the

point or recount maudlin and depressing details about Audrey's illness and recovery. She is too concerned right now about a conflict that is going on in her head, something about either sending this man away or taking him in. Unfortunately the choice is not so clear since some men have an expiration date stamped on their foreheads and some don't. "What did your father do when he wasn't mayor?" she asks in an effort to dismiss her thoughts.

"He ran the family construction business, which was how he met your father and uncle. He never knew them when he was mayor. After they bought the restaurant and Dad was already in business, they hired him to do the renovations."

"I've got a feeling that your father was in the construction business the way my uncle was in the restaurant business." An impish look, an observation said only to amuse, although she watches his reaction with measured restraint. But he is noncommittal, impossible to read, in control, infuriating. "Do you know about my uncle?" she asks in her most elegant speech before the notion that he knew everything there was to know about her and her life occurs to her. Pete. Dina. Rocco. And all the rest. Every last detail before whatever happens between them begins. But that's just another fantasy, as unrealistic as stopping at the confessional on the way down the aisle to the altar. Or as ridiculous as going out on a date and during the entrée imagining herself married to the man, during dessert imagining having his children, even though she usually knew by coffee that the chances of her wanting to see him again were remote.

"I'm not going to get trapped into the argument that every Italian isn't a mobster or that it's dumb to believe everything you read in the papers since journalists have about as much integrity as politicians." He smiles wisely. "So, which is worse? My father the mayor, your uncle the mobster, or the guys that write about them?"

"You probably already know my answer."

"You really have a thing about Italians, don't you?"

"No," she replies evenly, "actually I've got a thing about the French. Italians leave me cold!"

Surprisingly, his expression is nothing less than surprise before he breaks into laughter, which stays with her long after everything else passes. "Is that why you live in Paris?"

"No," she says, slightly embarrassed that the impression she sought to make has been lost. "It's mainly because of my job. I'm a photographer with *Paris Actualité.*" She takes a breath and can almost hear her inner mechanisms lurching into another gear where the *a*'s become broader and the words more halting, as if English isn't her native tongue. "And because Paris is such an incredibly beautiful city where the culture and history just envelop you. I mean, your culture and history are so young that it's unfair to compare." It's the *your* that gets even her, although she stumbles only for an instant before forging ahead. "In New York, it's all graffiti on the subways, junk food, modern art, and buildings made of glass and chrome with hardly any interesting lines or design. It's vulgar. But in Paris everywhere you look there's something from another time that you've either read about or studied, it's just so much more civilized than America." But the peak is a false one when she notices that he doesn't appear terribly impressed, curious perhaps, but definitely not impressed.

"So you're happy living over there?" he asks.

"What's happy?" she responds, horrified to hear herself dredging up something from another era before she glances down at her hands, searching for some breathing space to regroup.

"Are you remarried?" he asks and then rephrases the question, "Are you remarried to a Frenchman?"

"Why?" she says, seizing the chance at a touch of cynicism. "Does questioning happiness automatically bring marriage to mind?" And despite herself she is willing to test the strength of the thread she has just pulled. "Are you?"

"No," he says tightly, his shoulders lifting.

"Actually, I'm involved with a Frenchman but I would never marry him." He seems to pay more attention as she goes on. "Actually it's not just me, he'd never get married, but then the French don't find it necessary to make that commitment legal."

"Maybe it goes back to what Voltaire said, that marriage is the only adventure open to the cowardly."

If her mouth fell open from surprise it would be no surprise. "How did you know that?"

He shrugs. "I read."

"My friend is a writer," she says, almost as an offering of her own literary connections, "a well-known writer."

"What does he write?"

"Mostly commentaries on life and society for the magazine I work for and also a couple of very important books of poetry." Another silence that leaves her feeling empty, and in her head she warns him not to touch her, not to even try because she has been off sex since her daughter left, which is why her French writer with his commentaries and his poetry seemed so right. But things change and now she finds there is a quaint country inn in her head—where they might wander to have a drink or even some dinner—with rooms upstairs.

"You see, in France," she continues, "the commercial aspect of a book is less important than the literary value and my friend's books are very well received and reviewed." She takes out the elastic so her hair falls loosely around her shoulders. "He's taught me so much about literature and music, we sometimes read Proust instead of going out."

He's been listening, watching, and then listening. "And what do you do when you're not reading Proust?" he asks, half seriously.

She appears flustered. "Why, discuss him."

"Well," he says, his hands flat on the table, "I wish I had more time, this is fascinating, but my men are waiting for me."

She feels suddenly like a fool. "What about the paint?" He is already standing, pushing back his chair, all humor erased from his face.

"What paint?"

"The paint I've got to buy at Fiorello's so I can do the kitchen. What kind should I buy?"

He glances around to give an opinion. "High gloss," he offers and nothing more. Something has been lost here, either the upper hand or an admirer or another chance, she can't be sure.

"What brand?" she presses, watching his every move, standing to face him. "I mean, I've got no idea what to get or if I even need a primer, I just sort of blurted out this morning that I'd do the kitchen and now . . ." She shrugs helplessly. Nicholas Tressa is neither dumb nor insensitive and can recognize a crack in a façade when he sees one.

"Would you like me to go with you to Fiorello's?" But the question goes much deeper than a couple of cans of paint at the neighborhood hardware store. Blushing, one hand flutters up to her hair as she answers him.

"That would be really nice of you, but are you sure you've got the time?" They stand absolutely still, only the intermittent humming from the refrigerator breaks the silence.

"I'll make the time," he answers quietly.

"Thank you," she begins and then pauses.

"When did you want to get the paint?"

A breath first because nothing is clear. Or perhaps it is. "Well, my original plan was to drive up to Connecticut this weekend to see Dina and then start painting on Monday." She's rushing now. "But then Claire called and said that Dina wouldn't be there this weekend, that she was going to some kind of a seminar on grief." A disarming almost helpless expression, palms up as she shakes her head. "Actually she didn't call for that reason, she called to ask if I could go to Pete's house in East Hampton and clean out some of the files, which means that I could start the kitchen today, now, or maybe it would be better to start it on Saturday and then there's the problem with the keys . . ." A stream of consciousness winding down. "But who knows what'll happen by then anyway so what's the point of—"

"Do you want to have dinner with me tonight?"

"Yes," she answers without even thinking about it.

Neither has moved, their eyes locked, a slight smile playing on the corners of her mouth, for it makes no sense, a more tender look around his eyes but then she had a feeling. "And what about the paint?" she barely whispers.

He holds out his hand. "Let's go."

CHAPTER FOUR

Beginnings and Endings

DROP CLOTHS COVER most of the kitchen floor except for a spot in one corner where the coffee pot is plugged into a wall socket. The kitchen table and chairs are also draped in the plastic, and cans of paint, as yet unopened, are stacked up near the door with metal trays and clean rollers next to them.

Gabriella's embarrassment distances them somehow, especially right now as Nick attempts to make conversation, asking questions about her life. It doesn't help that her nervousness is making it difficult to hold the spatula steady in her hand as she tries to scrape the loose paint from the wall above the stove.

"Do you want me to do that?" Nick asks, turning around from his position on the ladder and knocking down a few loose chips from one ceiling beam as he does.

"No, it's all right, it's just that I don't function at my best on twenty minutes' sleep."

"Jet-lagged?"

"I guess," she says, hands on hips now as she surveys the mess, "but the painting is always more fun than all this messy preparation."

She brushes some plaster dust from the tip of her nose. "But the good stuff usually comes at the end, doesn't it?"

A peculiar look crosses his face before he turns to con-

eyes without warning and she hurriedly wipes them away. "It happened twice, first my mother got so sick but survived, only it was as if she was dead, and then Pete died but didn't get to go through that stage of being an old fool." Her bottom lip trembles. "I suppose that even though we hate to picture ourselves like that, it's something we wouldn't want to miss given the alternative." She tries again, this time with more control.

"I'm sorry, but it's harder sometimes to bury someone if the relationship's been lousy than if it's been good." There is a look of suspicion on her face as if it's his fault that she's let down another one of her façades, as if it's his fault that she let it down with hardly any fight. "But it's hard to feel bad about anything that has to do with Pete Molloy in this house." She turns her attention back to the cracked plaster. "No one is exactly mourning him around here."

A gloom has settled around them, and only the sounds of their labor fill the air. Nick is silent, thoughtful, she imagines, which makes her want to confront him about an unfinished phrase that seems to be hanging somewhere over his head. "Go on, say it," she challenges, "say what you're thinking."

He steps down from the ladder and walks over to where she stands. Taking her hand in one of his, he folds up her fingers within her palm. "Why are you so hurt? Who did that to you?"

"The coffee stopped perking," she replies by way of protest, "do you want some?" Reclaiming her hand, she walks over to a cupboard and reaches inside for two mugs. But her make-believe toughness only seems to spur him on. Glancing over her shoulder for an answer to her questions about milk and sugar, she feels the tears coming once again.

"Gabriella," he says, "come outside for a few minutes so we can talk." She follows him out the screen door, which he holds open, and toward a large weeping willow on the far side of the house. They sit down on the grass, facing the garage. "What's your best memory of Pete?" he asks without any buildup.

Leaning back on her elbows, she reflects for a moment until her face breaks into a melancholy smile. "The way he smelled." She laughs briefly. "It sounds ridiculous but for months after we separated I used to walk around smelling Pete everywhere, on my clothes, in my bed, in the air in my house, and he hadn't even ever been there."

Nick is watching her closely and she knows right then that if he leaned over to kiss her she wouldn't protest. "What did he smell of?"

"I don't know, the cologne he used, a bottle-a-day man," she says, joking now, "but it was everywhere, and my biggest expense the first month after we split was getting my clothes cleaned, rid of the smell, rid of him. You know, the most unbelievable thing is that yesterday I could've sworn I smelled it on him in the coffin."

Nick smiles. "How long were you married?"

"Seventeen years."

"And all you remember is the cologne?"

Her voice is a bit too steady then. "No, that's not all I remember," she replies, "but it's easier like this."

"Gabriella Carlucci-Molloy," he barely whispers, holding her chin with his hand, "how come nobody ever grabbed you up and made you happy after that?"

She shakes her head free. "Maybe I didn't want to be grabbed up and made happy, who knows?"

"Why's that?" he persists.

Rolling over onto her stomach to avoid his gaze, she answers, "Oh, I don't know, maybe it's because I've always made a mess of things, at least those kinds of things." And when she does glance back at him to notice that his eyes have never left her, she isn't certain that she can stand it without touching him. "How did your wife die?"

"Long and painfully."

"No children?"

"No children."

"And your best memory?"

"There isn't any one particular memory, it's more about our life together, everything we shared was special because it happened to us."

"And the worst memory?"

"It's interesting but it's nothing that happened while she was alive, it's more about how empty I felt afterward, almost as if I didn't want to remember all the good times."

"So you block things out to save yourself the pain of remembering the good stuff and I block it all out to save myself the pain of remembering the bad stuff." She sits up, squinting against the glare of the sun as she takes a sip of coffee. "So how come nobody grabbed you up and made you happy either?"

"How do you know they didn't?"

She stops, having never considered that possibility. "Did they?"

"No."

She changes course then, before they reach a point in their mutual loss that will scar this moment forever. "So how come you know Philip Larkin?" An impish expression crosses her face.

"How come you do?" He takes a sip of coffee.

"Because I happen to be a great intellect," she quips.

"Well, I'm just a sentimental idiot who can't get into the real classic poets and Larkin writes the way real people talk."

Her hand reaches out for his, on the grass, stretched across the blades innocently as a kind of offering. "Are you in the Mob?" she dares as she curls up her fingers.

He laughs out loud. "Why? Because I'm Italian?"

Sticking a thin weed between her lips, she replies almost instantly even though the blush on her cheeks belies the ease of defending her question. "Partly, and partly because you know my father and my uncle and partly because you're in construction."

"Did anyone ever tell you that you were a bigot?"

"As a matter of fact I've been told that many times."

But his smile concedes that he doesn't believe she is a bigot, confused and pretentious, but not ignorant.

"No," he begins quite seriously, "I'm not in the Mob and neither was my father or my father's father. It's too bad because everyone worked very hard and didn't get rich although we all managed to live decent lives and not want for anything."

As he talks she knows she is being educated into falling in love again or maybe for the first time, slowly and just a bit but without any preamble or premeditation, just like that, with a guy she met at a funeral who happened to drop by her house and was willing to help paint her father's shabby kitchen. But because Gabriella is a worrier by nature, she needs to get back on neutral territory, and that doesn't include a place for her heart since her excursions into this kind of thing are lately quite unfamiliar and unsettling.

"Maybe we should get back to the plaster so we can have some lunch."

Rising, he holds out a hand. "You're right, let's at least finish stage one before we end up skipping it entirely."

For an instant she is tempted to ask what he means just as she is tempted to reach up to kiss him, for the meaning of his words obviously transcends a paint job.

"What's the matter?" he asks when they have stepped inside the kitchen. She appears to be transfixed by a spot on the wall. "I was just thinking how much happened in this kitchen since the last time it was painted." She flicks off a chip of paint with the tip of a fingernail. "See that, green underneath the white and pink underneath the green."

"Do you remember when it was green?"

"When I was a child, before my mother got sick."

"How did it happen?" he asks suddenly.

She looks up. "A stroke. But how it happened seemed less important than why it happened. She was so young."

"Were you frightened?"

"In the beginning yes, and then it was as if she had always been like that. I suppose people get used to anything. But it began to scare me again when I got older, the closer I got to the age she was when it happened. And then I stopped being frightened the other day, when I heard what happened to Pete. That's when I realized that it has less to do with heredity than with numbers. If your number's up, it's up, and eating bran three times a day or exercising or not flying in DC 10's or avoiding lines at El Al counters in Athens isn't going to make a bit of difference."

Nick has been watching her intently, listening very closely to every word. "Does that philosophy carry over into other areas of your life—that no matter what you do, it's all been decided in advance?"

A small smile appears on her mouth, for he has read her fiction, as if everything she has said or done since meeting this man was designed to make him interested, lure him in, regardless of what has been written in some giant ledger in the sky. "Not everything," she says now, "just things about life and death."

"Oh, that's all, just life and death? So maybe you'll tell me what else is left that could be important."

Gabriella's reaction is only a speculative frown, although it is with a sense of relief that she assumes that is only the beginning and subject to change. "Everything that happens in between—or maybe I should have said birth and death so that that in between is clearer—like life." And her look now transmits only sadness.

"Why so unhappy all of a sudden?"

"I was thinking about Dina."

"What about Dina?"

How can she explain to him that she feels like a fool who has skulked away in disgrace, slinked out of the room without anyone noticing, without so much as a fight after Dina left her. It was an admission of guilt of sorts, as if she had done something wrong to warrant the neglect and abuse from a child she only loved. "I worry about her."

"What about, specifically?"

And it wasn't so much backing away from her responsibility in the matter as it was running from the pain of rejection. For how many times did she try, only to be rebuffed, and how many times did she beg, only to be humiliated and for what? She used to say that the only emotion she didn't have was guilt over Dina, but that too was a lie since she could only imagine misconstrued words and misunderstood actions and wonder that if she'd explained or articulated better none of it would have happened. "I worry that she's going to regret what's happened and not know how to get herself out of this mess."

"Then maybe it's up to you."

"Of course it's up to me—up to a certain point and then there's nothing I can do, or is there?"

"Is that a question you'd like answered?"

"Actually, no."

"Do I have time to persuade you that it should be answered?"

"Maybe, at least until I leave."

He grins. "That's a give and take if I've ever heard one."

Her expression reverts to sadness.

"You'd make a lousy poker player," he observes.

She forces a smile then. "I just thought about Pete and how he'll never be able to feel anything anymore—not even pain." And for an instant she almost expects Nick to save her all the trouble and just take her in his arms to comfort her. She holds her breath as he moves several steps closer and only breathes when he passes her to put her mug in the sink. "But there are living people who can't feel, you know, and that's worse."

He turns around. "Are you one of them?"

"I'm not sure."

"Maybe you should think about it."

A little rough around the edges perhaps, she considers as she picks up the spatula from the floor. But if she had to focus on one feature of his, it would definitely be his hands. Like the hands of a sculptor, or rather the hands that a sculptor might sculpt. But if she had to choose another feature, that choice wouldn't be difficult either for it would be his mouth. Or more precisely, how his mouth would feel on her mouth and why it hasn't already been there. Blushing slightly, she imagines his eyes kind and direct yet not about to mirror ridicule. "Why?" she asks.

"Why what?"

"Why should I think about it?"

"Why do you think?" he says softly.

There seems to be no point in acting anymore and that comes as a relief to her. She has only to look at him rather than bother to respond.

□

The screen goes blank at the same time the fluorescent lights flicker on like so many dominoes, beginning at the rear of the room and ending at the front where Joshua stands near the blackboard. He begins his pacing almost instantly, up and down, back and forth, silently padding on those typical academic beige Hush Puppies, his sloped shoulders hunched forward, a slim leather-bound book in one hand. Dina shifts in her seat and yawns as he begins his lecture.

"In the first scene of the film we just screened, we saw Marina sitting on a tractor, plowing the field in her collective, which we know is somewhere near Kostroma. In the distance Igor is busy drilling the earth with a brand-new pneumatic drill, throwing the switch on and off with a thrust of his stomach. So, the stage is set for what I call the workers' seduction scene. Marina and Igor are about to meet." Several girls in the front row exchange knowing glances and sigh. "So how do we know this is an example of pre-Glasnost cinema?'' His eyes scan the room, sweeping across a sea of eager female faces who are his for the asking. ''How do we know that, Miss Molloy?'' He zeros in on Dina who stirs, startled, before gathering her father's old tweed blazer around herself in a protective gesture. Joshua crosses his arms, a bored expression visible while Dina reaches down to put on her glasses as if that will help her to remember. Her mind races to retrieve his words and then the gist of the film, which she barely watched.

''I'm sorry,'' she finally says, ''but I guess I wasn't paying attention.''

''Are you aware, Miss Molloy,'' he inquires, ''that there is a waiting list to get into this course?''

''Yes,'' she says again, ''I'm sorry.'' She is aware of the muted buzz that ripples through the class, not that she gives a damn what anybody thinks anyway. The thing that really stuns her is how Joshua could be so insensitive at a time like this, especially when he knows that she only came back to school because there was no other place for her to go, that she only came to class today because it was better than sitting in her room and answering the phone, listening to Claire or Adrienne complaining about their private pain.

Dina tried to explain everything to Joshua—her feelings of impotency and anger—when he showed up unexpectedly last night. But his only response was to unzip his fly under the pretense that making love would validate her existence and neutralize her morbid preoccupation with death. There was something almost menacing about his penis hanging out of his pants like that, so malevolent out of context, which only reminded her of a flasher she once saw on a subway platform.

To her credit, however, Dina was obviously not deterred, since she went on to explain how she had destroyed her mother but only in self-defense, metaphorically, of course, and only to eliminate her as the one obstacle that prevented her from living her own life. Yet it didn't make it any less demeaning to discuss such private thoughts with someone who was talking blow jobs while she was talking survival. It only took her a little while after that to stop denying what was real between them and what wasn't. But why had it taken so long? Perhaps because denial is such a comfortable and well-perfected female trait, whether denying a missed period or a lump in a breast or a philandering husband or the truth about a dead parent or a myth about a living one. And Dina had been an expert, so much so that when she finally snapped out of her infatuation with Joshua just this morning, he might have been in Kostroma, but she was already at the end of their relationship. Without regret.

The class seems to go on forever this morning or perhaps it's just that Joshua seems to drone on forever, but why hadn't she noticed that before? Why had it taken this monumental upheaval in her young life to make her see how she had picked a lover who was such a bore, such an inconsiderate bore, such an inconsiderate bore who really didn't care about her. But later she would learn that it is no coincidence that women who have difficulty cementing healthy relationships with men usually have less-than-perfect relationships with their fathers. Yet what a waste that Dina had to bury her father before she could extricate herself from an affair where her lover always seemed anxious to be with another woman—even while he was currently with her. Exactly the way both her mother and Adrienne complained her father behaved with them. Dina smiles sadly to herself as she reflects on why, perhaps, she chose Joshua in the first place. He never gave loyalty a second thought. "Like stopping for a drink on the way home from work," her mother once screamed at her father. "Like a greeting card," Adrienne once screamed at her father, " 'Get well soon, Happy Birthday, Let's fuck!' "

Concentrating on the lecture that is still going on, Dina listens as Joshua discusses the topic he knows best. "Let's talk about sexual equality on the collective," he says, heading up one aisle like a game-show host, "because don't forget in the last frame Marina is seducing Igor''—and down the other like an Evangelical preacher—''which is different than we're used to seeing in most uptight Western films''—and stops to wag a finger at several giggling girls in the back row—''since cinema depicts all the hangups and rules between the sexes.'' If he had a microphone cord, he would have surely whipped it around his legs as he bounds toward the back of the room once more. ''Women want to own the house and the car but they still want the man to hold open the doors and mow the lawn.''

He stops long enough for a hulking boy to call out, ''Yeah, Marina wanted it as much as Igor!''

''Yeah, she asked for it,'' another yells, his hand clenched in a fist and raised above his head.

''Go for it, Igor,'' a third adds in a booming voice.

Joshua is racing toward the front again. ''So-they-copulated-or-fornicated-or-whatever-else-you-want-to-call-it-but,'' he says, whirling around to face the class. ''Let's let the girls comment.'' With that he points to an unsuspecting redhead who sits slouched down in her chair. ''What do you think, Miss Lamay?''

''Does fidelity count on the collective?'' she blurts out.

Joshua throws back his head and laughs.

''Fidelity has no place in Kostroma. In fact, it has no place in Moscow or Kiev or Pittsburgh or Toronto or New York or anywhere that's culturally and intellectually growing.'' The bell rings then. ''So what I want to know,'' he rushes, ''is the impact that all of this has on the social and economic conditions. For Tuesday. Have a nice weekend, class!''

Yawning and stretching, Dina is sure she could get an A without even trying.

She gathers her things together, weary from all the memories that she conjures up of her parents before the divorce, before the rupture with her mother, before her father's death, always before something. Tossing everything into a large canvas boat bag, she prepares to leave the class. But as she walks down the aisle and toward the door, Joshua accosts her. "Where're you going?"

"To my room."

"Why so glum?"

"Not glum."

"I can't play favorites, you know."

But she doesn't bother to tell him that it doesn't matter anymore, that she has outgrown the games, the flirting, the conquest, even the disappointment. It is over. The end. "Are we still going to that seminar on grief?" she asks, looking him in the eye now.

"Absolutely," he replies. "I'll meet you at eight in front of my office."

□

At eight o'clock precisely Dina waits near the dining hall in front of the cottage that is Joshua's office, and at eight-ten precisely Joshua pulls up in his black Volvo, leaning over to open the door. "Hi," she says, sliding in.

"We're off," he says, accelerating, winding down the driveway and onto the road.

The last thing Dina remembers hearing is the radio and an announcer's voice predicting rain throughout the entire New England area with warnings of slippery road conditions, and then Joshua saying, quite calmly actually, "Shit!"

The car seemed to levitate, and Dina was amazed how she was able to look down and see the white line in the middle of the road from far above it. But the car didn't stay aloft for very long, as it seemed to soar toward a wooded embankment before it plunged down a thirty-foot ravine. Several bumps and crashes later, there was the sound of glass shattering and metal scraping against rock. When Dina finally came to, she was miraculously still seated in the same position with Joshua beside her. But the trees and sky were in the wrong place, upside down and turned around, and it took several minutes for her to realize that the car had flipped over. "Joshua," she muttered.

"Holy shit!" was his only reply.

They climbed out through the rear window and trudged up the side of the hill until they managed to reach the road. "Cemetery curve," Dina pointed to the sign. But she felt suddenly too dizzy and nauseated to say anything more. She waited there, hanging onto a tree for what seemed to be an awfully long time before two headlights appeared in the distance and coasted to a stop. Dina had the vague impression of being lifted inside of a car and placed flat on the backseat. But she passed out again almost immediately and didn't regain consciousness until she found herself lying in a hospital bed, hooked up to tubes and bottles, aware that she had been calling for her mother. Before she slipped back into a deep sleep again.

CHAPTER FIVE

The Date

GABRIELLA SAID IMMEDIATELY how delighted she was to be having dinner at The American Hotel in Sag Harbor when the truth was that she would rather have been dining in that reconverted church near Notre Dame, the one that had been turned into a bistro where people could spend the entire evening discussing its transformation from sacred to seductive. Or at Lipp on St. Germain where all the literary figures who wandered in and out provided sufficient distraction so that two at a table would never have to exchange a single word. Or anywhere else that would take the onus off her from having to reach down and come up with real feelings and truthful replies. A brief walk between a funeral service and the actual burial was one thing, a cup of coffee on the grass between plastering and painting was another, but this was beginning to get a bit too close, which is why she is dodging questions that are increasingly difficult to ignore. For Gabriella has hidden out so long behind a mask of sophistication that being with Nick Tressa is like coming home. And that is exactly what she has been avoiding for so long.

"Half our life together was the unspoken word," Gabriella says in answer to Nick's question about her marriage to Pete. "We went around holding things back because it seemed easier than confronting problems and ending up in a brawl."

She plays with an ashtray, stares at the flame of the candle, fiddles with the salt shaker. "I was only nineteen when we got married, so what did I know? And even though Pete was six years older, he didn't know much more. He'd been passed from one mentor to the other all his life, so how was he supposed to know about loyalty? He was raised never to question authority, so how was he supposed to have any imagination except when it came to lying and making things up because he was always so scared.

"His parents used to walk around wondering where they went wrong because they had a son who had this driving ambition to be everything they weren't. And he'd tell them all the time that he wasn't going to work in a factory or drink beer or eat Ritz crackers in front of the television at night. Pete had pretensions. Even when he worked out, he never just sweated in some gym in Freeport, not Pete. He had to go to some fancy health club in the next town, in Rockville Centre, for example, with thick carpeting and pink lights, one of those places that looked more like a psychiatric hospital." She glances up to notice Nick's look of amusement. "But Pete never stopped being charming or wily or tough," she concludes.

"It's funny, but he always struck me as someone who was so secure and confident," Nick says. "He always dressed so perfectly and played sports with all the best equipment. He just moved with such ease."

"Not if you looked closely," Gabriella says, "because if you did, you'd see that everything was on the surface. Pete was flashy and there was nothing easy about anything he wore or did. His clothes screamed poor-kid-made-good because he had to show everybody he'd made it. The French have an expression"—she thinks for a moment— "*Bien dans sa peau,* good in his skin, and Pete was never good in his skin. He never got over where he came from."

Nick considers thoughtfully. "So he moved like City College instead of Yale."

She nods, again surprised at his choice of an analogy. "And what about your marriage? I confessed," she says, grinning. "So now it's your turn."

He hesitates for only several instants before giving voice to what she might have already suspected if she had dared to imagine. "We married young and Bonnie died young, but we had a great marriage because she was the most giving person in the world. She cared about everybody, always putting herself last, she was genuinely kind." He shrugs, his expression almost reverent. "She sewed, she cooked, and she still had time to be a good friend to all her friends, and she had tons, and godmother to most of their children. In fact, every Christmas she'd make vats of jam for all the kids and put them in these antique jars she'd find at country fairs all over the Island."

"Was she pretty?" Gabriella asks and practically gags on her words, for women have been playing that comparison game since hair rollers were made of dinosaur bones.

"She wasn't what you'd call pretty, but she had a smile that could light up a room."

Too bad that men never knew when they were well off, Gabriella thinks sadly, but then it's tough to get it up for a saint. Actually what it's all about is that smiles that light up rooms, loving so selflessly, sewing, cooking, making jam, always the godmother never the mother, doesn't guarantee a lot of heavy breathing. With a man, it's more a question of who gets up in the morning to make the coffee and who gets up at night to bring the glass of water that sets the level of his desire, or perhaps it's the other way around. For if the level's on high, he'd gladly go to Bogotá for the coffee and Niagara Falls for the water.

"How long were you married?" she asks.

"For about eighteen years, but we grew up together."

"Did you have a crush on her as a kid?"

"Actually, we met for the first time in the third grade, and the reason I remember is because I kept getting the seat behind her. We were together in fourth grade and then we got separated until seventh when the school started this special class for intellectually gifted children, IGC they called it.'' He smiles vaguely. ''Except I was transferred out at the end of the first semester.''

Gabriella looks shocked. ''What a terrible thing to do to a kid.''

''Not really, since all I cared about was sports.''

''Did you keep track of her?''

''Not until ninth grade when there was a junior high school production of *Peter Pan* and someone conned me into auditioning. Somehow I got the part of Captain Hook and Bonnie was Wendy.''

''So she was your first real girlfriend,'' Gabriella says.

''My first date,'' he replies, relaxing a bit. ''We went to a movie that weekend, something called *The Untouchables*, starring Robert Stack, and I'll never forget it.'' He smiles fondly at the memory. ''I didn't know whether to put my arm around her shoulders or just sling it over the back of the chair or keep it on my lap.''

''So what did you do with it?''

''What a jerk,'' he says, laughing now, ''I sat on it.'' He looks serious as he continues. ''We went to Friendly's for an ice cream after the movie and then right before I took her home I got up the nerve to ask her out for the following weekend to a football game. We were in love. On our third date I gave her my ID bracelet, which was a real big deal in those days.'' His eyes are wide and innocent, the expression going back about twenty years or so. ''Everything was great until this new girl moved into town and I fell in love again, pretty dumb.''

''How long did that last?''

''Only long enough for me to lose my virginity, flunk my chemistry final, and realize that I wanted Bonnie back.''

''And did she come back?''

''Nope, in fact she wouldn't even speak to me again until we were both sophomores at Adelphi.''

"Good for her!" Gabriella says and finds she really means it.

"I guess I deserved it, but finally we started dating again, on an entirely different basis though. She wasn't that wide-eyed innocent girl anymore and I had calmed down enough to know what I had this time."

"She must have been very much in love with you to take you back and try again. She must have been hurt."

"She was hurt and she was in love with me, but I was in love with her too. Oh, maybe in the beginning she needed me more, or at least that's what I thought, but in the end it turned out that she taught me a helluva lot more than I taught her. She changed my tastes in music from Montovani and Ferante & Teicher, can you believe that, to Jefferson Airplane and the Beatles." He laughs. "From that semiclassical crap I used to listen to to Beethoven and Bach."

Gabriella laughs also. "Did you read?"

"Yeah, I read—Jack Higgins and Herman Wouk." He makes a face. "So Bonnie started giving me *Playboy*, only she told me to try reading the fiction they published in between the nudes. And then she gave me Conrad and Greene, and before I knew it, I was falling in love with her—more than just a crush or something that was based on the wrong thing. Even back then it wasn't because she was beautiful or sexy or anything like that, it was because she was warm and loving and charming and terrific." He studies his hands. "But the irony is that she got better looking after we got married." Looking up at Gabriella, he smiles an embarrassed smile. "She started wearing contact lenses and got braces and began to dress better. I mean, she really looked good!"

But what Gabriella feels and what Nick won't say is that sometimes in marriages where the woman perceives herself as intellectually superior and her husband as physically more attractive, she will take the lead as Bonnie did, set the tone, as she did as well, and become the mother.

"So you really had it all," Gabriella comments warmly.

"Not really," he replies, "nobody has it all."

"What was missing?" she asks, although she could probably predict the response. Any wife who worships her husband, adores him, caters to his every need, also numbs his sex drive by her flawless efficiency.

"There was a certain distance between us, I guess," he begins, "not that it was all bad. We had this mutual respect for each other and this unwritten and unspoken policy never to intrude on our space but . . ." And then he hesitates.

"But what?" she presses.

"But I suppose that included the bed."

"Don't ask me why, but sometimes it's hard to make love to someone you really care about."

He considers what she says a moment before speaking and when he does he seems more sure of himself. "It was as if there was an imaginary line that ran down the center of our bed." He pauses. "Do you think it's terrible to talk like this about someone who's . . ." Another hesitation.

"About someone who's dead?" Gabriella finishes. "No, I don't think it's terrible at all because you loved her and still love her. No, I don't think it's terrible."

"There wasn't any time then to think about details. I was too busy grieving for her." He touches Gabriella's hand. "Do you mind?"

"No, I don't mind at all," she assures, vaguely disturbed that she doesn't, although not particularly surprised either. Nick leans back in his chair and takes a breath.

"Maybe the way we slept together, I mean actually slept together, was significant of something we had that went deeper than just a physical thing. I can't really remember when either of us touched the other by accident during the night, you know, a leg getting slung over a leg or a blanket yanked too far over. Nothing like that ever went on, and it was like some kind of incredible consideration. She slept huddled on her side, I slept on mine. But we never went to sleep without first kissing each other good night and then talking about things in the dark. Sometimes Bonnie would have this one last thing to tell me, about an article she read or tickets she got for a concert and maybe forgot to clear the date with me. You know, just the kinds of everyday things people talk about.''

Gabriella nods. Topics that didn't arouse, she thinks, merely contributed to the continuity of their lives.

''It's not as if we didn't make love because we did,'' he continues. ''We fell into this pattern of once every two or three weeks, but there wasn't any mystery left for some reason.'' He shakes his head. ''It wasn't that way with Pete, was it?''

''No, it wasn't that way with Pete,'' she says softly, ''but maybe that goes back to what I said before. Maybe it's tough making love with someone you really care about.''

A realization when he states, ''There was a lot of passion between you and Pete,'' and then a question when he asks, as if he wants it contradicted, ''wasn't there?''

She nods slowly. ''Yes, there was passion but not a lot of intimacy.''

''You mean the kind of intimacy that kills passion.''

She smiles slightly. ''In either case it's deadly—passion without intimacy or intimacy without passion.''

''Why do you suppose it was that way with Bonnie and me?''

''Probably because you shared too many childhood memories, or maybe for all the reasons that most people who live together grow apart. You see someone having a bad intestinal flu or a heavy period or all the other flaws that strangers don't see, and it's just not romantic.'' She holds his gaze. ''Did you keep trying or give up?''

''I suppose we stopped trying to recapture whatever it was we lost or maybe we never had it and were too naïve to know. But whenever I thought about anything passionate and then thought about Bonnie, it always struck me as incestuous.''

''You had other things.''

''That's true. We had a kind of peace that I never had before.'' He grins. ''You see, I grew up in a house where harmony was defined as ending the day with everybody on speaking terms without any broken bones.'' He studies her a moment. ''Why do you look so puzzled?''

''I guess I was just wondering why you never had any children.''

He sighs, a pained expression replacing the one of fondness he had when describing his marriage. ''We tried for a long time, and by the time we'd been married for ten years we'd already been to see every specialist in New York. We even went to some kind of experimental fertility clinic and tried some off-the-wall homeopathic method, but Bonnie just couldn't conceive.''

''Did you ever find out why?''

''Yeah, we found out all right.'' He rubs his eyes wearily. ''Things were really going great that summer of eighty-five, for a lot of reasons. My company got its first big contracting job—to renovate the Freeport City Hall—and that meant more to me than just a big fee. It was like the kid made good, you know, I was going back to this big deal job. So I bought a couple of new trucks and put on five new construction guys to work the job.''

He pauses and what he doesn't say just then is that it was supposed to be a great summer for Bonnie too, at least it started out that way. She had streaked her hair, bought a brand-new Chrysler Le Baron, passed her real estate brokers' license. And discovered she had ovarian cancer.

''Maybe if we had tried to have kids before, Bonnie would still be alive,'' he says bitterly, but when he sees the confusion on Gabriella's face, he explains. ''We were so into our own routines up until then that having babies was the farthest thing from our minds. We had loads of friends, weekends skiing or going up to the Cape that we were just being selfish.'' He lowers his voice.

''All those doctor's examinations to find out that she had a year to live,'' he says, his voice carrying all the pain and misery of having had to watch her go through it, ''and those last six months were something I wouldn't wish on my worst enemy.''

''I'm so sorry,'' she says uselessly.

''In the beginning I couldn't believe she was really dead. I used to pick up the phone during the day to call her or worse, I used to reach for her in the middle of the night—something I never did when she was alive. It was a nightmare, until somehow all the pain turned to rage, and I used to walk around with this urge to punch everyone out—like if they looked at me wrong, I was at them. So maybe to protect myself from myself, I refused to go out or talk to anybody or see anybody.''

''How long did that last?''

''About a year, but when I did start going out again, it was only early in the morning and then I would drive out to Montauk to watch the sun come up.'' He looks uncomfortable. ''I realized something then, just sitting on the beach all alone, that Bonnie's death made me deal with a lot of other stuff too, all the anger and frustration I was carrying around.'' He shakes his head. ''But Bonnie was the clincher, the one thing I thought was always going to be there for me no matter what happened.''

''Did you talk to anyone?''

''Yeah, a few really close friends, people who had known Bonnie and could talk about her since that was all I was capable of talking about. Bonnie when she was well, Bonnie when she was sick, Bonnie when she was alive and Bonnie when she was dead.''

''Did it help?''

''At the time I thought it did, except that I couldn't feel anything—I was numb.'' Running his hand through his hair, he reflects for a moment before sighing. "So I did what any immature idiot would do under the same circumstances. I went on a binge of nameless and faceless women—as if that was going to make me feel something again."

Gabriella shrugs, not prepared to judge, unwilling to condemn.

"Except, guess what? It made me feel, it made me feel worse." This time it is Gabriella who reaches out to touch his hand. "So at least there's hope for you," she says, a tiny smile playing at the corners of her mouth.

He nods, holding the hand that she offered. "One night I wandered into a movie, something called *Terms of Endearment,* and would you believe I started crying until I thought there was nothing left of me. Sobbing like a kid when Debra Winger was busy dying on the screen."

"Yes, I can believe it," Gabriella barely whispers.

"So now it's four years that she's dead and finally it's becoming a memory. Finally, for the past year and a half I feel like a human being again." His smile reaches his eyes, people have remarked, his laugh seems to begin from somewhere deeper down inside of himself than his throat, others have commented. But what no one really knows is that all of that began happening to Nick at about the same time that he met Pete Molloy and did some work for him on the beach house, played a little tennis with him on the occasional weekend before he found himself at his funeral which was where he fell in love with Gabriella. On sight.

Gabriella's eyes don't waver for a moment as she studies his every expression to better understand his sorrow. "It's hard," she offers and then pauses under his gaze.

"You know," he says slowly, his eyes squinted in thought, "maybe what doesn't kill you makes you stronger."

"Maybe," she replies, "and maybe it just makes you realize that anything can happen to anyone, that none of us is exempt."

"Listen, are you in love with this guy in Paris?"

Withdrawing, she considers the choice between being honest and being coy, being Gabriella or being Bonnie. And she realizes almost as quickly that there is no choice at all, which is why Gabriella will never be canonized or possess a smile that lights up a room. "Our relationship is very special," she lies, trying very hard to remember how she once felt about Pascal, "because he's taught me so much. I feel this incredible gratitude to him."

"So that's what you call being in love?"

"Not in love in the ordinary sense of the phrase," she concedes, wishing she hadn't created this impasse, "but enormously attached because he's done so much to help me in my craft." Not to be ignored that in Gabriella's Parisian world, craft is to film what job is to movie. "It would have taken me years to achieve what I've done in so short a time."

"But you still didn't answer my question," he presses.

His directness takes her aback. "At least do I get to order dinner before I answer that and totally incriminate myself?" she teases, and then smiles slightly as she considers how much easier it is to create an affair than to be actually involved in one. Nodding as she speaks, she goes on, "There's a complicity between us and maybe that lasts longer than love, since love is so temporary, isn't it?"

"No, not always. Sometimes it gets better with time and grows into something on another level. Why are you so cynical?"

"Not cynical," she answers, "just realisitic." What is left unsaid is her opinion that love on that other level is about the same as love on the rocks. Women almost always end up alone when that happens, while men end up in a strange bed trying to begin from the beginning to recapture the thrill of what was lost at home. Which makes it difficult for her to understand why sitting here in The American Hotel in Sag Harbor, her body seems to react to him despite all the good sense she has gained from all her bad experience. Even if she hasn't forgotten how useless it is to respond to pronouncements of love, flattery, and desire; even if she can still feel herself riding that wave to its crest before plunging down to wash ashore recklessly after the tide goes out. Undoubtedly this one is the same, nothing more than another time, which makes her instantly retreat behind a wall that this time she knows is made of sand.

"Why did you and Pete get divorced?" he asks, and it occurs to her that if she wants out before he gets in, she can always act unstably. That tends to frighten men away as efficiently as acting insane on the street deters muggers.

"I had a lover," she explains with no lack of dignity. But with surprising alacrity his hand covers hers.

"Did Pete?"

"Yes, many."

"Then why did your lover cause the divorce?"

"Because Pete couldn't stand the humiliation."

"Could you?"

"No, which was why I had a lover. I went around feeling like a plank of wood or an ironing board. But it was different for me. You see in those circles for a man to lose control of his wife was as serious as going bankrupt."

"Where did you meet?"

"At the office, when he came in to do a piece on some Wall Street scandal. They sent me along with him to shoot the story. He was married and, of course, I was married, but we spent weeks and weeks together on that story until finally we ended up in a hotel room."

"Did it last a long time?"

"Not really, just long enough for me to wonder what I was doing one morning brushing my teeth in Bloomingdale's." She smiles vaguely. "Or realizing that traipsing out of a hotel in broad daylight in evening clothes wasn't for me." She shakes her head. "If fear kills a man's desire then feeling like a bimbo kills it for a woman." She smiles only after he laughs.

"Were you in love with him?" Nick asks and then

shrugs. "It seems that's all I'm capable of asking you to-night, if you were in love with this one or that one."

"Which must say a lot for my life or about the impression I've made, some kind of a butterfly." Thoughtful for a moment, she begins. "Actually my life has been complicated. I'm not the typical Italian girl from Long Island who gets married, divorced, and then flings herself into some artsy-craftsy hobby that she fools herself into believing is her life's calling." She pauses to sip some wine.

"Do you want to be complicated?"

"I want to be honest, and the truth is that I am complicated." She knows enough to look adorable when delivering a piece of bad news. "There's a lot you don't know about me that makes it hard to prove my point about being complicated." She leans forward on the edge of her chair, removing her hand from where he has it pinned underneath his. "Would you like me to tell you something?" He nods as he takes her hand back, exploring her palm with the tip of one finger. "You asked me about being in love with this one or that one. Well, do you want to know how it really was?" She stalls as his speculative silence surrounds them both. "The truth is that I was only in love once and got badly bruised. So"—she tenses then, poised to run—"why should I ever take another chance?" As if by saying it, it makes a difference, as if someone had already asked.

"Because it's not necessarily going to end the same way every time," he says.

If she had to cite the exact instant when she felt that he wouldn't leave her life so quickly, when she sensed that this was the beginning of a major dilemma, it was now. "Was it Pete?" he asks, and she nods.

"Tell me what went on between the two of you," he coaxes, his eyes a road map to his heart.

The Affair

When it first began it was impossible to detect except that Gabriella seemed more relaxed, easier, less excitable, more willing to accept Pete's failings, give a little, take a little, she told herself, like using a drug or taking a soma holiday on weekends when there were too many hours to keep up the lie. And it was all up to her to keep it a secret forever; she had it within her power except that an extraordinary thing happened. Discretion took away from the pleasure of it all. It suddenly wasn't enough to know that she also had a lover, it was important that Pete knew it too. For the difference between them and their infidelities was that Pete loved being unfaithful while Gabriella loved Pete.

It didn't matter which of them started it, dared to throw the first punch, tell the first lie. What mattered was how steadfastly attached they were to their own version of the rules. Pete's affairs were neatly wrapped packages containing meaningless trinkets that could be disposed of after he had the pleasure of opening them to handle and admire them. He told all his women right in the beginning that he would never leave his wife because she was his best friend, and that was what he told Gabriella in the end. Gabriella's affair, on the other hand, by virtue of its exclusivity, was the reason for her prolonged silences at home, working long hours in the dark room, brooding, conflict, and for convincing herself that not only was she in love with this stranger but also that somehow he had become her best friend as well, which was what she told Pete in the end. But right before the end, she and Pete spent a lot of time making anxious and frantic love, in total darkness when neither was willing to focus on the other; needing only to quell their fear of this impending failure that was upon them. If Pete could have dressed and left afterward, he would have. But he lived there. And if Gabriella could have moved into another room afterward, she would have. But there was none available. As time passed and her affair waned, it somehow wasn't enough that Pete only harbored a doubt, she needed him to know it absolutely. In literature it's a tour de force, in bullfighting the moment of truth, in adultery that instant when fantasy becomes reality, when fly now pay later takes over from pay as you enter and all bets are off.

Sitting up in bed and watching television one night, she asked in a lulling tone, "What would you do if I had a lover?"

"Do you?"

"I didn't say that," she taunted, "I just asked what you'd do."

But he refused to take her seriously for the thought of her being unfaithful was ridiculous. He said. As ridiculous as the thought of his being faithful. She joked. But the seed was planted.

Sitting up in bed and watching television one night several weeks later, she asked in a lulling tone, "What would you do if I had a lover?"

"Do you?" But this time he seemed to pay more attention.

"And if I did?" she taunted before giving it all up, the initial meeting, indecision, dilemma, guilt, seduction, all in precise detail. Pete looked like a stricken man, his face went dangerously pale and his eyes brimmed over with tears as he got up to stagger to the bathroom. Gabriella heard the toilet seat slam against the tank and then the wretching. And all the while he was in there she stood at the window and watched the snow falling, her cheek pressed against the cold pane, wondering how she was going to manage alone with a child.

Men cheated, women didn't. She knew that because a cab driver once said so; men cheated on their wives but women rarely cheated on their husbands. How strange it was that men could really believe that, as if there was a handful of unenlightened women somewhere servicing all those men. Shortly after that realization she made the choice not to sulk off in that state of humiliation that she had been in for years. For not only did she know about Pete but he knew that she knew, not to mention that everybody else knew about him as well. At least like this she could salvage a shred of her dignity even after having admitted to this undignified act, even if it would cost her another kind of dignity in the end.

"How could you?" Pete asked when he finally exited from the bathroom.

"How could you?" she countered.

"I'm a man, for God's sake, it means nothing to me. I didn't lose my head."

Something to be filed away. "And I'm a woman."

"That's the trouble, Gabriella, you forgot that you were a wife and mother first and you can't be everything."

"But you were, a father and a lover and a husband, what about you?"

"This marriage would have lasted forever if you hadn't done that," he lamented, deflecting her argument. "I never would have left you, never. You were my best friend."

"And what were all of them?" she asked dully.

"Nothing, they were just nothing." A terrified pause. "And what was he?"

"He was my lover," she dared, "but more than that he was my best friend." She probably destroyed him more with that answer than if he had actually caught her in the middle of the act itself.

"How could you have been so unfaithful?" he wept.

Which was when she learned that it was all a question of degree.

"Would you have preferred that I did it with a casual acquaintance or an enemy?"

"Then you live with it now, live with the guilt that it was you who broke up this home," he attacked instead of answering.

She was invincible that night, imperious yet resigned

to whatever he would deal her, for in the end they both knew that it was all up to him. Still they talked and negotiated fault well into the dawn hours and the next day and throughout the following night, more than they had ever done before in their marriage when they were both so busy lying to each other.

It struck her as ironic that instead of locking her out, as he had threatened, he locked her in, forcing her to hear it all—names, dates, professions, times, reasons—which was when she knew that it wasn't even personal. It was just time for both of them to end that particular stage of their lives and move on. Strangely though, her voice carried an apologetic ring to it for months after they separated whenever she talked to him, as if she had ingested all the guilt and the blame and the sorrow for both of them.

□

"Do you want coffee?" Nick asks while a waiter lingers next to their table.

"A cappuccino," she decides.

"And I'll have an American coffee," he says with a certain amount of pride that is not lost on her. Then there seems to be a question hanging over them, something else just waiting to be asked. After they both hardly touch their coffees, after he pays the check, when they stroll outside, when he takes her hand to lead her to the car, before they even get inside, he asks it. Without asking.

It's the first kiss that gets her, she knows it even while it's happening in the parking lot of The American Hotel in Sag Harbor even if it would never have occurred to her to refuse, even if dinner took about ten years. Anyway, when was the last time that a guy grabbed her and kissed her like that and made her re-examine all of her basic assumptions about men.

At thirty-nine, Gabriella has just stopped being terrified of taking trains alone, of exploring new neighborhoods, of crowds in shopping centers, and of meeting new people. It was only recently that she developed that line of steel that runs down her spine, a stoicism that makes it possible for her to walk and talk and function all over again. After Dina. So while Nick is concentrating on getting them to his house and while she is concentrating on appearing to be perfectly at ease, she feels a certain sense of pride that she has come this far.

He stops the car in the middle of a private cul-de-sac and she offers no resistance when he gathers her in his arms to kiss her over and over, nor does she balk when he stops several feet from his garage door to embrace her again. And when the engine is off and they are standing in the gravel driveway, one of them fumbling with his keys, the other with her purse, their bodies are still pressed together even as they step inside the house. Leaning against him for balance, she slips out of her shoes, his mouth nibbling at her neck, her arms around him now before they both begin undressing hurriedly as if they had been waiting for this forever.

She feels his nearness like a sudden rise in temperature, the scent of him on her skin, that first tentative touch before she is drawn into him with an urgency she had almost forgotten could exist. Arching her body against his, she crams every bit of him into every empty and lonely space of her soul. More bare flesh on flesh as new sensations flutter across her neck, her breasts, her abdomen, and only for an instant right then does she resist, to catch her breath perhaps, or not to surrender the little that is left, or to wonder if this might just be a reward for all those months and months of grief and abstinence.

On a couch she hides from him now as she sinks deeper and deeper into cushions that are soft and yielding, until she feels the weight of him sinking deeper and deeper into her. And if he was the very last man on earth she couldn't possibly hold him any more defiantly. His mouth covers hers, a kiss that goes on for decades, her lips no longer hers, hands clasped together somewhere to the side of their bodies, fingers laced tightly. Until she feels that sudden surge and hears him, a sound coming from his throat or perhaps her throat, and then her name and then his. Impulsively she links her arms around his neck to pull him closer, but he is already holding her face between his hands, their legs entwined, his breath warm on her cheek. Until suddenly her body rises with his, a renewed swelling filling her again, and as if he reads her mind he promises it will happen many more times, he intends to make love to her all night, and somewhere in her head it registers that she could possibly die from this.

Hours later when the sun streams in through one glass wall, Gabriella stirs, nestling sleepily against him until she suddenly remembers. Eyes fluttering open, she awakes to find him staring at her.

"What time is it?" she whispers.

"Too early to get up," he says, smoothing some hair from her face, his relaxed tone so typically postcoital male. But before she succumbs to that typical postcoital female sensation of feeling like a take-out pizza, she studies him a moment to notice a tenderness around his mouth, an expression so filled with love that it actually frightens her. For, once she saw that same regard on her father's face when they all sat vigil around her mother's hospital bed. And before she can say or do anything, for her instinct is to protest and then to run, his lips are on hers, and to her utter astonishment she doesn't push him away. "Isn't this a better way to say good morning?"

"I don't know anymore," she answers softly, "I've never . . ."

She somehow can't manage to finish a sentence. And she somehow can't manage to quit trying even if caution warns her to get the hell out of there as fast as she can— run as far away as possible from this place. This place where there are no Marcel Carne movies at the corner cinema, or a highway called the Peripherique to get out of town and into the country, or a restaurant named Boeuf Sur le Toit from the days of Cocteau when a Cow on a Roof was a celebrated poem. Yet where she happens to be right now just happens to be the place where a man has managed to touch her on a level that no one else has before, not even on the other side of the ocean in Paris, France.

"Why did you make love with me?" Nick takes her by surprise.

"Why did you?" she recovers.

"Because I'm crazy about you," he says simply, "so what's your excuse?"

Gabriella has no intention of encouraging this man, however, and ending up as some miserable housewife in Sag Harbor, taking pictures of christenings, weddings, and communions, making all her life's struggle to escape that end, including that famous detour through Paris, all for nothing. Not that this man, the one whose mouth has been all over her body, asked her. Rather he just wanted to know why it was that she allowed him that.

"Why does there have to be a reason for everything?" she asks in her best Lady Chatterley-talking-to-the-game-keeper tone of voice. Nick takes a breath, his head propped up in one hand.

"Because usually things don't happen like this, at least not to me. I mean they don't go from hostile to more or less civilized to making love the way we did."

The mere mention of the way it was leaves her feeling weak in the knees. "Why do Americans always have to complicate everything," she laments, "it's just something that happened." But he doesn't appear to be amused.

"Do you really believe that?" Instead of answering right away, she runs her finger along his nose and over his lips. After one failed marriage and several passionate and not-so-passionate affairs, Gabriella Carlucci-Molloy is clever enough to know that his question is not to be taken lightly, that it is the kind of query whose response will be assessed as a generality. And on the off chance that they are together another time, several times, many times, or not at all, he might judge her morality as an example of all female morality on the strength of her emotions this morning.

"No," she says softly, "I don't really believe that, but I also believe that we each have our lives and it's pointless to make it more important than it actually is." But all she wants to do is take him in her arms, for just then he seems to bring out a kind of maternal instinct in her that has evidently gone astray.

"I want to help with Dina, if I can," he offers unexpectedly.

"Please," she says firmly, although the look on her face is anything but strong, "there's nothing you can do, it's something I've got to work out by myself. With her. Or I've got to learn to live with my failure."

A look passes between them that transcends Dina. "I'm here if you ever need me," he begins, "because I don't intend to take what happened at the funeral lightly, nor do I intend to take lightly what happened with us last night. I guess what I'm trying to tell you, Gaby, is that I want to be involved in your life and I just want you to know that."

But the only thing she knows for sure is that no one calls her Gaby, and that if anyone told her she would have to come to New York for Pete Molloy's funeral and while there would meet a man with whom she would end up she never would have believed it. Except that she hasn't ended up with anybody thank you very much nor does she intend to. Even if she has never made love like that in her life. To anyone. But she certainly isn't going to tell him that for perhaps she was just long overdue for an affair that was purely physical.

Yet somehow this man seems more than just an unconnected organ, she feels something for him. In fact, she feels a lot for him already, which is why she makes the instant decision not to see him again. Then she recalls that Kevin Doherty used to call her Gaby and wonders briefly if that holds any significance—since Kevin was the first—about this man being the last. But that's as ridiculous as vowing never to see him again, even if Gabriella has always been a woman of extremes, even if this is an extreme situation given that she has a ticket back to Paris.

"Did you design your house?" she asks, feeling somewhat relieved that not only has she figured it all out but also has managed to dismiss him so neatly.

"Designed it and built it myself," he answers and then asks, "Do you like it?"

"It's beautiful," she says, looking up and around. And she is impressed by the tasteful furnishings in beiges and browns, and especially by the triangular space above her head made of unfinished wooden beams that surround the cathedral ceiling. An aluminum chimney soars the entire height of the house with cone-shaped fireplaces cut out on each of the two levels, a balcony wrapped around both floors. "Did you live here with your wife?"

"No, I built it after she died." He considers a moment. "I suppose it was less for needing to live somewhere else than it was to get busy. I needed a project." He touches her mouth lightly, bending over to plant a kiss on the tip of her nose. "But you still haven't answered my question. Why did you make love with me?"

"I can't answer it except that everything seemed to fit, it was a moment and now the moment is over." She turns her face away. "And anyway," she adds, her chin trembling slightly, "I've got to go to Pete's house to sort things out for Claire."

She takes a breath. "And my father thinks I'm already there, he thinks I slept there last night, which was what I intended to do until . . ." She stops to look at him. "Until plans changed."

"Do you want me to go with you?"

"Oh no, thanks," she says quickly, "there's too much to do, it'll probably take me all day. And anyway, East Hampton is so near here that it's nothing for me to drive by myself. It's just going to be a lot of boring busywork, you know, sifting through papers to see what Claire might need." Sitting up, she surveys the room and notices with dismay that her clothes are strewn all over the floor. But he senses her dilemma immediately and reaches behind him to hand her his shirt which she puts on before standing up.

"Will you drive back here and have dinner with me tonight?"

She hesitates. "Thank you, but no."

"Then how about if I drive to East Hampton and take you to dinner there?" he asks as he steps into a pair of jeans.

"Please," she implores miserably, "don't."

His expression is grim as he announces, "I'm going to make some coffee," before adding, "Do you want to shower?"

And she finds it fascinating that she hasn't even seen his bathroom, bedroom or any other room in the house, for that matter, although now the idea of using the shower, brushing her teeth and performing all those little mundane tasks will only make this episode seem even more real and more confusing. But a shower is a shower under the worst of circumstances.

"Thanks," she says, gathering up her clothes, "don't bother showing me the way. I'll find it."

She is almost to the foot of the wide circular staircase, practically standing on the first step, when he comes up behind her, gently turns her around and takes her in his arms.

"It's too late, Gabriella Carlucci," he says, as if she needs to be reminded of who she is, brought back to the beginning of the story.

"What's too late?" she can barely speak.

"It won't work," he adds softly, his lips against her hair.

"What won't work?" she asks miserably.

"Pretending that something like this happens every day." Arms against his shoulders, she holds him away from her to meet his gaze. "I live in Paris."

"So, you've got a lifetime lease or something?"

Drawing herself up to her full height, she replies very seriously, "The French don't give long leases to strangers."

"Oh, yeah," he says, drawing her close to him again, "well, I do."

CHAPTER SIX

The Confrontation

BUT GABRIELLA DOESN'T DRIVE from Sag Harbor to Pete Molloy's beach house in East Hampton this morning. Perhaps it's because she never really intended to all along, even if she did tell Sylvie that if she didn't come home to sleep that that was where she would be—cleaning out files and sorting through papers. Perhaps she just needed to prepare an alibi in the unlikely circumstance that dinner with Nick happened to last through breakfast. Except there was nothing unlikely about that possibility even from the beginning.

Driving on the Southern State Parkway toward Freeport, Gabriella considers how calculating a woman can sometimes be, not in the way that a man might perceive her, but rather when it comes to passion and so-called spontaneous sexual behavior. There is rarely anything impulsive about a woman's deciding to succumb to her desire, little that has to do with simply exploding at the spur of a frenzied moment after she has allegedly been driven to the point where she forgets who and what and where she is. It is more likely to be a decision that she has already made even before he realizes that he is the one she wants, and certainly long before he becomes aware that the erection he finds himself in possession of is specific rather than unfocused or urinary. It often takes her less time to make that decision than it does for her to clean her apartment, attend an important business meeting, buy lacy lingerie, suffer

through a last-minute bikini wax, and show up at the des-
ignated time and place appearing properly tentative and
uncertain, correctly fragile and confused.

□

But while some women achieve greater powers of duplicity
as they mature, a man tends to remain guileless throughout
his personal life, enough even to confess the moment of his
first desire and the instant when he had any inkling at all
that it would be satisfied. Those are the anniversaries he
loves to celebrate. But it's that other monumental yet touch-
ingly naïve error he makes that makes him so human; to
ask if ''it'' was ever that good with someone else as ''it''
has been with him.

Gabriella smiles slightly to herself as she changes lanes
to ease into the automatic toll lane, recalling how that question is usually asked when the perspiration is still trickling
down between her breasts, when her breath is still uneven,
and when the tingle of what has just transpired between
them is still lurking somewhere around her inner thighs.
As if it would ruin ''it'' for him to learn that yes she had it
like that with not just one other but with a series of others.
For without ''it'' she would have been unable to convince
herself than it was love, and if she couldn't do that, even
for the time the affair lasted, then she probably wouldn't
have been able to do it in the first place. What would have
been the point? Her foot slips off the accelerator then as
she considers what a phony she is—who is she kidding anyway to imagine that Nick Tressa is like any of the others?
As if he had even asked her such a dumb question. As if A
equals B equals Z. What is disturbing, though, is this desire she seems to have to tell him every last detail about
her life—reason enough never to see him again. Never
mind pinning it on the fact that she feels weak and vulnerable and longing for something other than going back
to Paris and shooting more rolls of film. She already made

that mistake once before when she forgot about everything else except a man. With Pete.

The Confession

Gabriella grew up believing that marriage should be the culmination of all her girlhood fantasies, a romantic connection between two strangers that developed into love, a relationship where intimacy knew no limits, a bond with a man where she could confess every secret passion or simply every secret. She was filled with just those fantasies and thoughts on the night she sat across from Pete Molloy at Emily Shaw's Pound Ridge Inn and bared her soul.

Gabriella held up her hand every few minutes during dinner that night, to admire the small engagement ring that Pete had just given her. "We've got to keep it a secret," she said very seriously, "we can't let my family know until after we've done it."

"Anything you want," he said. "I love you."

"I love you," she answered, overwhelmed by his love, "and I want to tell you something that nobody else knows—not even my family."

There was no stopping her, no chance of convincing her to heed those pithy advice columns found in the women's magazines that warned of that deadly condition called postcoital pillow talk—that mindless chatter that women were prone to utter when groans and grunts seemed no longer appropriate, idle talk that not only occurred when two heads were lying on one pillow but when they were tête-à-tête anywhere else as well.

In Gabriella's case there was a lull in the conversation that she must have felt was her God-given responsibility to fill, especially when memories of what had just gone on between them upstairs in bed were still so fresh in her mind. But there was something else too, the thought that it was only fair to offer up her past in return for his having offered the ultimate compliment—marriage. So she began, shyly at first, to divulge her deepest secret, growing more certain with each word that telling it would link her to that man who never stopped eating popovers as she talked.

Vigilance was not in Gabriella's ken, nor was suspicion or distrust. Only optimism and love filled her then, and had she been more sophisticated and cynical, she might have considered Pete's surprisingly calm reaction after hearing about the baby that she bore out of wedlock, the child she secretly gave up for adoption, the infant that resulted from that one night with Kevin Doherty on the floor of her father's living room.

"Did you love him?" Pete asked instead of a million other questions that she was ready to answer.

"I was young and probably more curious than anything else."

"Was it as good with him as it is with us?" came next, although she would have thought that a more pertinent question might have been one that concerned that horrible dilemma that she had been forced to face.

"Nothing could be as good as us," she replied, only by then her answer had slipped under the category of dutiful and by rote.

She must have looked slightly crestfallen, as if she had expected more from him (which she had) because he immediately went on to assure her that a new life was beginning, something else about forgetting about the past. She couldn't be exactly sure because feelings of gratitude kept wafting over her to distract her. He did make a rather off-handed inquiry, however, right before coffee, about whether or not Kevin knew, though he didn't press it when she hesitated, and certainly didn't follow it up by asking if either of them had seen the baby before it had been adopted. No accusations either that she had been less than honest when she had decided to tell all that night—at the twenty-fifth hour—right after they had gotten engaged.

All of those thoughts crossed her mind but she dismissed them, not for a moment willing to do anything that would spoil what was going to be a terrific life. Actually, it was pretty heady stuff for a girl of nineteen to be loved as unconditionally as Pete said he loved her. A pretty mature reaction for a guy of twenty-five, he added, even if he had to admit that it was a little surprising. But a barrage of questions followed, quietly and methodically and prefaced by Pete's sincere voice explaining, "The reason I want to know everything is so we'll never have to discuss it again. You'll never have to relive any of it ever." As if that was possible. Dates, places, names, times—every detail that Gabriella considered to be irrelevant to how she felt was discussed that night.

"You won't ever tell a soul," she implored when there was nothing left to disclose. Her hand with its sparkling diamond on the ring finger rested on his arm. "Our children will never know," she added.

He smiled. "Never, it's our secret. Till death do us part."

□

But it is not until the Freeport exit appears in the distance that it hits her. Pete told Dina. That's the only possible explanation for the sudden rift between them, the sole reason that Dina would act out of such sudden fury against her. What amazes Gabriella now is that she hadn't realized it before—Pete had obviously poisoned Dina's mind. That was the only possible reason that she would have been cut off so completely. How clever of him to have offered Dina the perfect excuse to run off and live with him, a million perks available as well, an easier life after a divorce that carried so many financial problems on the mother's side.

The justification—how shrewd of him to have found the right formula to make Dina believe that everything that happened had been Gabriella's fault. For how could a mother be worthy of raising one child when she had once discarded another. Knowing Pete, it all makes sense now. He did it to get back at her for humiliating him, for not begging him to return when he left, for rejecting him after the divorce when he wanted to come home. He'd never tell a soul, he promised, it was to be their secret. " 'Till death do us part,' " he vowed. Only he forgot to mention the deal was off if they didn't happen to make it together until then.

Driving past the rundown movie theater and the row of shabby stores on Main Street, all with OUT OF BUSINESS signs posted on broken windows, Gabriella is aware of a certain kind of justice. She should have known long ago that she could never get away with doing something like that without paying some kind of price. It was a miracle that her father and her uncle never found out. She left for a resort in the Pocono Mountains to work as a waitress. Still it was a fluke that she was able to hide it from everybody until almost the very end. When the time came to give birth she checked into a nearby home for unwed mothers.

The tires screech as Gabriella steers the car around a corner, slowing down when she approaches the beginning of the residential areas, turning first on New York Avenue, then New Jersey before heading for her street, which lies directly ahead. The Carlucci white frame and stucco house is the third on the left from the end of the block, but as she passes the first house she spots her father pacing anxiously up and down the sidewalk. Leaning her head out the window, she calls out to him.

"Papa, over here!" Whirling around, he notices her and races toward the car. "Where the hell you been?" Hands on the steering wheel, she inches the car up the driveway, its nose pointed toward the garage while she clicks open the automatic control to release the door. "At Pete's house, Papa," she lies. For a confrontation about where she has been is the last thing she needs right now, although it's absolutely impossible for him to know that she didn't sleep at Pete's. The phones were unplugged, she'd claim, so they never rang and she didn't even realize it until right before she left this morning, or she would have certainly hunted around for the jacks to hook them up. But she needn't have bothered for other things seem to be on his mind. "Pull it in more," he directs her, waving the car farther inside the garage. She obeys, wondering what else happened to make him so agitated this morning.

Sylvie stands at her side of the car and waits while she unfastens the seat belt. "So what's the matter with you?" she asks sweetly "you look like a caged tiger this morning." But when she finally steps out, to her utter astonishment, he gathers her in his arms and says tearfully, "The kid's been in an accident." Horrified, she pushes away from him, searching his face for a sign that it's a mistake or at least something minor, nothing but a scratch or two, anything but what she somehow knows he is about to tell her.

"What kind of an accident?" she manages to ask while he stops to blow his nose. As if it matters what kind of an accident. She can barely think or speak rationally.

"Car," he says, obviously trying very hard to remain calm. "Claire called and said she was drivin' up in Connecticut with some guy when the car went off the road." Gabriella hears someone else sobbing then, and doesn't even realize that it's herself until she feels her father's arms around her, holding her close, telling her not to cry, that everything was going to work out.

"She's alive, that's all that matters," Sylvie comforts. "She's alive."

"How bad is it, Papa?" she asks, her tone hushed, fearful that she has already asked for too much.

"According to Claire, she's pretty badly banged up."

"Where?" she says, better with one-word questions at this point to keep from screaming.

"I've got it all written down inside," he says miserably, "but I think it wasn't too far from her school, somewhere called Falls Village or somethin'." He takes her arm

— 145 —

before she can race into the house to look. "Gabriella, wait, I called Nick on account of you and him havin' dinner last night." He pauses, waiting for her to react. "On account of that I couldn't find you," he says when there is no reaction from her. He runs his hand through his hair. "I didn't mean to interfere or nothin'," he concludes, but she is already hugging him, crying and hugging him and assuring him that it doesn't matter. Nothing matters. Except Dina.

But right now the only word that comes to mind is *hovering*—the word everyone used to describe what her mother was doing those first few weeks after the stroke. "She's hovering," they'd whisper to one another until one day she apparently stopped hovering and pulled through to begin a new life of being completely helpless. And whatever Gabriella may have done in her life or believed she had done to deserve anything that was dealt her, she never considered the price would include her daughter. Not Dina. Not again.

"Gabriella," Sylvie says miserably, "I can't go with you because Violet ain't here this weekend and I've got no one to leave Mama with."

"I know," she comforts, her mind on a million other problems, "don't worry."

"But I can come up just as soon as Violet gets here on Monday morning or maybe even sooner if I can reach her today."

"It's all right, Papa," she assures him, wondering what trains leave what station for Falls Village, Connecticut.

"How you gonna get up there?"

"Probably the best way is to drive or try and find the train schedule up there, which is really complicated."

"Take the car," Sylvie advises, "you'll need it up there in the sticks." He looks troubled then. "Gabriella," he begins, "when I called Nick, I hadda tell why I was callin' and everything and he offered to drive here to take you."

"No, that's not necessary, it's better if I go alone." Her expression is firm. "I want to see Mama for a minute before I leave," she says. "I want to talk to her."

As is usually the case when Gabriella insists upon having a conversation with Audrey, Sylvie tries to stop her. "What're you gonna do that for, you only get upset and you upset her. Talk to me, I can hear and I can speak."

But she is not to be stopped as she races through the house calling her until she finds her sitting in her wheelchair in the dining room. Turned so she faces the bay window and the back lawn, Audrey appears to be dozing.

"Hi, Mama," Gabriella says softly, reaching down to hug her. Audrey's eyes flutter open. Kneeling, she continues in the same quiet tone although now her voice is more unsteady. "There was so much I wanted to tell you, but I can't now. Dina's been in a car accident." She takes a deep breath, trying not to cry. "So I'm going up to Connecticut." Silence for a moment before she explains, as if Audrey had asked. "I don't know how long I'll be there but I'll call to let you know how things are." But when she looks at her mother again, she notices that the woman's eyes are shut and her chin has dropped to her chest. "She's going to be fine, Mama," Gabriella says as she stands, "I know she will." She shakes her head sadly, the tears visible. "Because how much more can happen?"

The Hospital—Saturday Night

"When they first brought her in, the nurses reported that she was calling for her mother," the doctor says. "Interesting, but when she slipped into a light coma for several hours she began calling for her father." He pauses to suck on an unlit pipe. "So that's the reason we put her in intensive care, to monitor her more closely for any subdural hemorrhage. No need to panic about *that*, Mrs. Molloy, it's not because of the surgery.''

Gabriella's hands are shaking so visibly by now that the coffee from a container that someone handed her splashes over the rim as she brings it to her lips. ''Please start at the beginning because I think you're assuming I know more than I do. I've only just arrived, and no one really told me anything.''

The doctor looks at her peculiarly before reaching over to pick up the chart. He flips over several pages until he settles on one toward the end. ''Let's see, she suffered a concussion, several broken ribs, bruises, and contusions on the left buttock, lower back, and left shoulder, internal bleeding in the abdominal cavity, which is now controlled. The spleen was removed in an emergency procedure almost immediately, since it had ruptured.''

A wave of weakness sweeps over Gabriella and she's not entirely certain that she won't faint. ''Are you all right, Mrs. Molloy?'' he asks her, and once again she doesn't bother to correct the title he assumes she still carries. ''I'm all right,'' she says softly, ''please go on.''

''As I've just said, we're watching her very closely because of the head injury and because she's not altogether oriented all the time. In other words, she's been sleeping on and off, sometimes very deeply, for long periods of time and woke up only yesterday enough so that she recognized''—and then he hesitates.

''Yes,'' Gabriella says, anxiously, ''she recognized someone?''

He clears his throat. ''Well, the woman who arrived in the middle of the night last night. It seems your daughter gave her as the next-of-kin when she was first brought into Emergency, and so naturally I assumed, until just now . . .'' he pauses once again.

''You assumed that the woman was her mother,''

Gabriella finishes the sentence. "It's all right, doctor, I understand, it's only logical that you would."

He appears relieved, the casual and easygoing manner visible as he continues. "At any rate, all we can do now is wait." It occurs to Gabriella then that the woman who was summoned to Dina's side is not Claire, which was her first thought, but rather the woman she met at the funeral—Adrienne. But somehow she is not up to being curious just yet. "When will you know that Dina's passed the danger point?" she asks. Hovering. Like Audrey. Hovering.

"In another two or three days," he says. "Concussions tend to get worse before they get better." He pauses to rub a stubby hand through his gray crew cut. "May I ask you a question, Mrs. Molloy?"

"Of course," she responds instantly, wishing that he wouldn't.

"Who notified you of your daughter's accident?"

Gabriella answers a bit too quickly then. "My sister-in-law, Dina's aunt." And then asks a bit too defensively, "Why do you want to know?"

A boxer's nose, she notices, the doctor has a nose that looks like it's been punched across his square face. "Look," he says kindly, "you don't have to answer me, but I'm just curious about something."

Gabriella's regard is steady. "Please."

"Who's the woman your daughter called from the emergency room?"

"What's her name?" she replies, considering that if it is Adrienne, it would be better that she know now rather than running into her at the bedside. The doctor is already busy flipping to the very beginning of Dina's chart.

"Adrienne Fast," he says, glancing up. "Is she a relative?"

"No, she's a friend, a close family friend," she rushes to add, as if that will make it all the more understandable why Dina didn't call her mother.

"Well, at any rate," the doctor says suddenly, very seriously, "the next thirty-six hours will tell us something. Just as long as there's no turn for the worse, I'm very hopeful."

Up until then Gabriella has managed to maintain a calm façade but suddenly the smell of disinfectant mingled with urine wafts over her. Taking a deep breath to help her from passing out, she shoves any toughness that she still possesses up front. "Is the boy very badly hurt also?"

"What boy?" the doctor asks, but there is a sudden kindness in his eyes that wasn't there before.

"The boy who was driving the car," Gabriella explains. "I understood that Dina's boyfriend was driving when it happened."

"Mrs. Molloy," he says quietly, "may I ask you a personal question?"

"Certainly," she replies, although her initial impulse is to refuse.

"Is there a problem between you and your daughter?" She feels caught. "Ordinarily it's none of my business, except if it's going to upset her," he hastens to explain.

"If I upset her, I'll leave," Gabriella evades.

He doesn't seem eager to push it. "I really can't tell you the nature of your daughter's relationship with him, the driver, that is, whether or not he's a boyfriend, but I can assure you that he's in good condition—nothing more serious than a broken wrist and a couple of cuts and bruises. In fact, he'll probably go home first thing in the morning." The doctor shakes his head. "They were really both very lucky, lucky to be alive. The car plunged down a thirty-foot ravine and missed a cement piling by six inches."

"And the other car?" she whispers, nearly losing hold of herself.

"There was no other car. According to the police report, they were going forty in a twenty-mile zone when the car skidded around a curve the locals call 'cemetery curve.' In fact, the police are considering charging the driver with reckless driving.''

It's impossible to hear any more without first seeing for herself that her child is whole. ''Please,'' she asks, her voice trembling, ''could I see her now?''

''Yes, but just for five minutes—no longer.''

''Thank you very much,'' Gabriella says, remembering to be polite as she gets up, putting the coffee container in a large standing ashtray.

''Intensive care is at the very end of the hall,'' he says as he also stands. ''Oh, and by the way, Mrs. Molloy''—he adds before she begins walking down the corridor—''just so you're not too surprised, he's no boy.''

''Who?''

''The driver of the car. He's no boy.''

□

Gabriella enters the unit reluctantly, less for the sight of the other three patients whose ailments appear to range from cardiac to orthopedic, one of them hooked up to a heart and lung machine, the other two suspended from several lethal-looking contraptions that dangle from metal bars. She wastes about two of her five-minute visit lingering near the door, but she can't seem to do anything about it for she is physically unable to move. What jolts her is that her child lies so still, so pale, in that ominous hospital bed; a tube feeding liquid into one vein, lips so caked with dried blood, one eye with orange splashes of iodine covering an unsightly clump of black thread. Daring not to even breathe, she takes several small steps closer, feeling as if it has all happened once before. Dina stirs, a moan escaping her lips, and only then does Gabriella go the final distance to stand next to the bed. Gently touching her child's arm, so delicate on the stiff white sheet, she bites down on her lip so as not to burst into tears.

''Dina,'' she barely utters, ''I love you.'' The words are more a prayer than anything else.

The battered face that turns to avoid the glare from the overhead light is so terribly swollen that it breaks Gabriella's heart, the lids so heavy and bruised that it tears at her gut. Dina opens her eyes then, slowly, one at a time, shutting them one at a time before she seems to be able to focus.

"Hi, Mom," she murmurs weakly. Two words, yet enough to give Gabriella the courage to continue.

"How do you feel, darling? Not so great, I bet."

Dina runs her tongue across her parched lips. "They took out my spleen."

"You don't need it."

"Daddy would've said he'd buy me another one." She winces in pain. "Daddy," she sobs softly, "daddy."

Gabriella runs one finger tenderly down each cheek, catching the tears as they fall. "You're going to be fine," she says softly.

Dina nods, her eyes shut again.

"Excuse me," a nurse interrupts, appearing from behind a curtained partition across the room, "but it's been five minutes."

But what it has been is forever, Gabriella thinks.

"Ice," Dina whispers, seemingly forgetting her sadness. And as Gabriella bends over to kiss her brow, Dina opens her eyes and nods, a gesture of consent or perhaps dismissal. It doesn't matter. For somehow Gabriella feels that whatever else happens from now on, short of a catastrophe, she has made the transition from intruder to visitor to next-of-kin without incident.

Leaning against the wall right outside of the unit, she sighs a deep sigh of relief. How carefully she measured each word, restrained her every gesture, tried not to touch Dina too much, or too little, made every effort not to sound too proprietary or too casual. Too close and Dina would remember why she is so angry, too distant and she might forget why she is not.

□

In the waiting room, the ashtrays spill over with cigarette butts, the trash bin overflows with crushed soda cans and crumpled McDonald's wrappers. A boy lies stretched out on the only sofa, a ragged and shabby affair with stuffing protruding from the arms. The stench of stale air and cramped space make it almost impossible for Gabriella not to bolt, not to go tearing out into the corridor just to be able to breathe. Standing, she begins to pace, up and down, back and forth, stopping to struggle with a window that upon closer inspection appears to have been painted shut. Turning then, she catches a glimpse of herself in a mirror and is shocked to see how drawn she looks, the tension and fatigue so evident on her face, her eyes like two shards of yellow glass, her hair uncombed and tangled.

A walk to the end of the corridor, to the window on the far side of the hall from the intensive-care unit. She wanders aimlessly, almost to the stairway, when the medicinal odor that surrounds everything suddenly drives her back in her head about twenty-six years.

The Hospital—1964

Gabriella was in class that day, a Thursday, at Our Lady of Divine Redemption girls school when Audrey suffered an embolism in the foyer of her Freeport, Long Island, home. Mother Superior lumbered through the door of the home-room, one hand clutching a heavy gold chain and a garnet-studded crucifix, the other waving at Sister Miriam to be seated. Scanning the forty-eight plaid uniforms and starched white shirts, her gaze finally settled on Gabriella Carlucci. "Will you step outside with me, dear?" she asked.

Without a word, and with her eyes lowered modestly, Gabriella rose and followed Mother Superior's chalk-smudged black robes out of the room. "Gabriella," the elderly nun began, "I'm afraid I've got some bad news for you, but I know that with your steadfast belief in Jesus Christ Our Lord, that with His guidance, you'll find the strength you need to bear it." And then she crossed herself once for good measure, pausing afterward what seemed to Gabriella to be an eternity before clearing her throat, a mournful expression on her pink face, and continuing. "It's your mother, dear. I'm afraid she's taken ill."

Taken ill was putting it mildly for Audrey Carlucci had actually been taken for dead in the foyer of her Freeport, Long Island, home that morning, right in the middle of cleaning out the winter coat closets, at one-fifteen exactly, the time frozen on the face of her watch, which smashed in the fall. Fortunately she apparently had the good sense to kick open the front door of her house before collapsing in a coma. Obviously she had counted on a neighbor noticing a leg jutting out across the threshold and coming over to investigate. As it turned out, the mailman summoned the police, the only irony being the two letters he carried for Audrey. One was from a sweepstakes house announcing in big red print on the front of the envelope AUDREY CARLUCCI THIS IS YOUR LUCKY DAY, while the other piece of mail turned out to be a notice from Audrey's gynecologist advising that the results of her recent Pap smear were negative.

But perhaps it had been Audrey's lucky day, for if one of the ambulance drivers hadn't just seen an old Alfred Hitchcock movie and come up with the ingenious idea of putting a mirror to her lips, they probably wouldn't have worked so hard and so long to revive her and keep her breathing until they reached the hospital.

"She had a stroke, dear," Mother Superior continued. Even at thirteen, Gabriella thought how dumb that word sounded. Stroke. Stroke of what? she wanted to scream, certainly not good luck. But she didn't, remaining silent instead, staring numbly at her school principal while she waited to hear more, or if there wasn't any more to hear, then perhaps for a pat on the head or a handkerchief for her tears. "She's been taken to Holy Cross Hospital, dear, in the intensive-care unit, in God's hands now."

Somehow Gabriella wasn't particularly comforted by any of what she had heard about being in God's hands or having a lot of faith, as she ran the four blocks to the hospital. All she could picture was that bust of Jesus Christ (a religious kewpie doll, she always giggled to herself, when she saw it) that peered out from a small faux window frame right above the entrance to the hospital, a solidified glob of pigeon excrement underneath His crown of thorns, and what was she going to do without a mother?

Sunday Morning

Gabriella hears her name at the same time as she feels someone gently touching her arm. She starts before realizing that she must have dozed off. Sitting up slowly in the tattered chair in the waiting room, she recognizes Adrienne Fast.

"I must have fallen asleep," Gabriella mumbles, pushing up one sleeve to look at her watch.

"It's six in the morning," Adrienne says, sitting down wearily in another chair, one that faces Gabriella's. Shaking out her hair, Gabriella rubs her temples. "Did you sleep here too?"

"In the other waiting room."

There is a strained silence then.

"The doctor told me you arrived last night," Adrienne begins.

Gabriella looks up. "I saw Dina."

"I know."

"Have you seen her this morning?"

"No, it's too early," Adrienne replies. "We can see her at eight."

Another hush while Gabriella slides down in the chair to wiggle her toes into her shoes.

"I'm sorry that I woke you," the woman says self-consciously, "it was pretty dumb, but I found a motel."

Gabriella smiles. "Great, I'm glad you woke me. I couldn't stand another night in here."

"I thought maybe we'd check in, and between seeing Dina, we could rest."

Gabriella hesitates, and as she does, her eyes meet Adrienne's, holding her gaze for several seconds. Until she suddenly feels an enormous pressure in her chest, a bizarre combination of relief, resentment, and overwhelming sadness. "The doctor told me that Dina called you from the emergency room."

Adrienne throws her a miserable guilt-racked look. "Yes, but—"

"I didn't mean that," Gabriella cuts her off. "I didn't mean to put it so accusingly, to make you feel as if you had to explain anything. I'm sorry."

"No, don't apologize, I realize how difficult this must be for you," she says quickly, eager somehow to bridge the gap. But Gabriella's just as eager, too immune at this point to being excluded from Dina's life to get trapped in unreasonable judgments about who her daughter chose to call in a pinch.

"It's difficult but it certainly isn't your fault."

"Whether you believe it or not, I've tried to get her to make peace with you, if only for her sake. Even before Pete died I tried, which caused trouble sometimes." She pauses. "I wanted to talk to you, I intended to reach you before the accident, to talk to you."

"It's a mess, isn't it?" Gabriella says softly, "and it all didn't have to happen." She sits up straight in the chair. "I'm glad you woke me. I would've found you this morning anyway." Her expression is warm, her tone friendly. "I wanted to talk to you too."

"Should we get some coffee? I think there's a diner nearby."

Gabriella nods. "Sure." As she gathers her jacket around her before she prepares to stand, she has a thoughtful expression on her face. "It's incredible how angry Pete was."

Adrienne stands also, hiking her bag over her shoulder. "It wasn't anger," she corrects, "it was more like blind rage. And in the year and a half that I knew him, it seemed to get worse."

"I don't understand it." Gabriella shakes her head, stopping for a moment to face Adrienne in the corridor. "How could he have become so irrational?"

"You hurt him," she says simply.

"He hurt me too."

"I don't doubt it." She takes Gabriella's arm to walk toward the elevators. "So many men become overindulgent and concerned fathers to get back at their wives."

They stop their conversation for the time it takes to ride down in the elevator to the lobby, resuming when they are already standing outside of the hospital. "I rented a car," Adrienne says.

"I've got a car too," Gabriella replies.

"Mine or yours?"

Gabriella shrugs. "It doesn't matter."

"Come on, we'll use up my free mileage," Adrienne says with a tight smile.

Once they are seated in the parked car, Gabriella reflects, "You know, it's odd, but last night while I was talking to the doctor everything began coming back to me and I felt the way I used to feel in the very beginning when Dina first left. Somehow I haven't been put on the spot like that since I moved to Paris. No one questions me, or maybe it's because the French aren't so quick to give someone the third degree because they don't want to get it back. But last night the doctor began asking me if I knew this or if I was aware of that, and it reminded me of how it always used to be a test of my wits whenever anybody asked me anything about Dina or even if I had any children. I used to have to scramble to answer the most basic questions, like where she went to school or what she was studying or where she spent the summer. And it hit me last night that there's more I don't know about my own child than I do. All the information I've got is old, probably not even true anymore.''

Adrienne has been sitting hunched over the steering wheel, listening. ''What things can I tell you?'' she asks.

Gabriella smiles a sad smile. ''Oh, I don't know, maybe things about her boyfriend, the kid who was driving the car.''

''He's no boy.''

Gabriella looks at her strangely. ''That's funny, but those are the exact words the doctor used.''

Adrienne takes a breath. ''Look, the person who was driving the car was one of her professors.'' She pauses. ''He's married.''

''And he's Dina's boyfriend,'' Gabriella says and then shakes her head, ''I suppose I mean lover.''

Adrienne nods. ''Her first lover.''

''Not a great beginning.''

''No, not a great beginning,'' Adrienne agrees.

''But I suppose the emotional part would be as tough regardless of his marital status,'' Gabriella considers and then continues, ''So she lost her virginity with the wrong man.'' She looks at Adrienne. ''But you tell me, how many of us lost our virginity with the right man?''

Adrienne smiles. ''Not too many of us, since they usually got us before we had a chance to recover from our fathers.''

''If any of us ever really did recover, since we make the same mistakes again and again,'' Gabriella says, feeling something near embarrassment suddenly. ''I'm grateful that you told me.''

"You sound surprised."

"I am."

"Because of who you are and who I am?"

Gabriella nods.

"It's difficult, especially to be thrown together under one set of horrible circumstances after another."

"And because we're total strangers."

"We're not really strangers."

"No, I suppose not," Gabriella agrees, unsure whether to pursue the thought or drop it. She decides to change the subject. "Does Claire intend to come up here?"

"I don't know how you feel about it but personally I'm relieved that Claire hates hospitals. She told me she'll do her bit by praying for Dina at home."

"I feel exactly the same way," Gabriella says quietly. She looks at her watch. "I've got to call my father, but maybe I'll wait until after I see Dina this morning."

Shifting the car into drive, Adrienne says, "Why don't we get something to eat? When was the last time you ate anything?"

"Not since dinner," Gabriella answers and then reconsiders. "Dinner on Friday, that is. Since then I've been living on coffee and doughnuts." And for the first time in more than twenty-four hours she allows herself the luxury of thinking about Nick—even if it disturbs her in a way that she finds difficult to define. She finds herself missing him more than she can remember ever missing anybody before.

"Look, it's right up ahead," Adrienne says, "and look, there's the motel."

The diner is almost deserted—several truck drivers sitting at the counter discuss baseball scores, a waitress sitting on one of the stools ponders a crossword puzzle, calling out the clues to the chef through the open partition between the dining area and kitchen, and a woman huddles in a corner booth at the very back of the room. Gabriella and Adrienne slide into seats facing each other near a window. After the waitress takes their orders, they still don't resume their conversation for several moments, each seemingly transfixed by the sunrise.

"He was still in love with you," Adrienne says suddenly.

"Why do you say that?"

"Because I believe it."

"Well, I doubt it or else he had a funny way of showing love."

"Some men do."

"It wasn't love, it was his pride."

"That's all part of it, it's all wrapped up in the same organ."

"It's so sad."

"There are so many sad things. I'm not sure which one you're talking about."

"The ultimate sadness, that we could have gone from caring so much about each other to making things so ugly and horrible. Once I saw him walking near the station after the divorce. I was in a taxi and when it stopped at a traffic light, I leaned out the window and said, 'I love you.' He looked so shocked."

"What did he say?"

"Nothing, there was no time because the light changed. But I didn't do it to get a response, I did it because I wanted him to know that I loved him even if the rest of our lives together was over."

Adrienne shrugs. "For a man who wasn't exactly faithful or always so nice or particularly honest with his women, he certainly had us all crazy about him."

They are silent while the waitress serves them the coffee, muffins, and juice. After they have each taken sips and bites, Gabriella says softly, "I was prepared to dislike you."

"Because of Dina?"

"I'm not sure."

"Me too." Adrienne puts down the cup. "I kept thinking that you had it all and blew it—a husband and a child. Or more specifically, you had the husband and child I wanted and would never have.'' She thinks a moment. ''There's something almost cruel about falling in love when you're middle-aged, almost as cruel as when you finally get adjusted to not being in your twenties, your thirties are gone, and you find yourself in your forties.'' She snaps her fingers. ''Just like that.''

Gabriella smiles sadly. ''So maybe our fifties will be better even if there's certain things that are great now.''

''For instance?''

''When I was in my twenties, I went crazy trying to hide my Tampax boxes or any signs of having my period and now that I'm almost forty, I leave all those boxes and paraphernalia out for everyone to see.''

Adrienne laughs.

''And men,'' Gabriella says after a bit of reflection.

''What do you mean?''

''Well, now that we're older, we're supposed to appreciate a different type of man.''

Adrienne frowns. ''I know what you're getting at but somehow it didn't apply to me, did it?''

''Nor me,'' Gabriella says vaguely.

''That's not true. When you met Pete you were young.''

''But I still seem to run away from someone who's nice and honest and faithful, all the things sexy men like Pete aren't.''

''Maybe because there are no sexy men who are nice.''

It's Gabriella's turn to frown. ''I'm not sure that's true, only bad habits are tough to break.''

They lapse into silence for several moments while Gabriella thinks about Nick and then about Pete and then about Adrienne and Pete. ''Was it serious between the two of you?''

''In the beginning I used to believe that he'd break down and marry me because he'd get tired of running around.'' She sighs. ''And of lying to me all the time. Our relationship was so good sometimes, so peaceful that I thought he wouldn't want to risk losing me.'' She leans back, more relaxed. ''But I guess men don't marry for peace, do they, at least not for that kind of peace.''

''I don't know about most men,'' Gabriella considers, ''since Pete was the only one I married and he was completely unpredictable.''

''Which was part of his charm,'' Adrienne adds quickly, ''unless it was you hanging on by a thread or waiting for some kind of signal that you'd end up living happily ever after. But you know, he was nothing like that in his professional life. He was like two different men.''

''Did you work for him for a long time?'' Gabriella asks.

''No. As a matter of fact I started working for him almost right after your divorce. I went to law school late, just decided one day that I wanted to be a lawyer.''

''What did you do before that?''

''I was a guidance counselor, a fat unhappy guidance counselor who was supposed to help others be happy.'' She smiles. ''So I turned my whole life around, lost fifty-six pounds, took up running, even made it through one of the New York marathons. I passed the bar exam on my first try, and one of my law professors suggested that I interview for this job that had come up in Mineola—in the DA's office.'' Her expression is sad. ''Which was how I met Pete.'' She colors slightly. ''I fell in love with him on sight.''

Gabriella nods, the image of Pete at his best coming to mind, charming, energetic, affable. ''Were you married before?''

''No.''

''No children, then?''

''No, just a lot of stretch marks with nothing to show for them.''

''You've got a great deal to show,'' Gabriella says, ''you've done so much.''

"Sure," Adrienne says with surprising bitterness, "but you've experienced things that some of us will never know."

"I've had my share of good things, but I've also had my share of pain. I suppose it's all part of the memory I hold of him."

"All I seem to be left with are season tickets to the Met and a stack of unserved subpoenas."

"You know," Gabriella says calmly, touching Adrienne's hand, "you've had something that I've missed. You've shared things with my daughter these past two years that are gone forever now."

Adrienne glances up. "I guess it's some consolation to know that at least Dina and I are friends," she admits. "At least I've got something left of Pete's to enjoy."

It hadn't occurred to Gabriella that Dina was something of Pete's, not since she ceased wanting to be something of Gabriella's as well. "It's strange," Adrienne continues, "but for all of Pete's pulling back and evading issues, he could be so warm and giving." She blushes again, perhaps unaware that she is about to deliver a bomb. "He was really such an excellent lover."

Even though Gabriella knows Pete's entire operation from start to finish and several of his predictable variations, she recoils almost visibly, one hand over her heart, which begins to beat frantically within her chest. Not only does she find it difficult to breathe but also to comprehend that word. *Excellent.* An excellent tennis player perhaps or even a sentence using the word *excellent* as in "Pete was in excellent shape before he keeled over," which would have only proven the banality of the word anyway. But what, she wants to scream now, is an excellent lover? Confused, she wonders where this anger came from, especially since its focus seems to be centered on the companion of a corpse and especially since that corpse happens to be an exhusband. But death apparently does strange things to people, including making Gabriella guard her place in Pete's life with more ferocity than she would have believed possible.

But Adrienne is undaunted, absolutely unaware of Gabriella's inner turmoil. "I suppose I was naïve to take that as a sign that he loved me or that he would eventually make a commitment, but I did." She spreads her hands out on the table. "All it did was make me cling to some kind of false hope when what I probably should have done was to find someone else and make a life for myself. After all, he wasn't exactly faithful. But I loved him and kept fooling myself that he'd calm down and realize that he wanted the same thing that I wanted."

"What was that?" Gabriella asks gently, touched by the woman's innocence that might have been borne out of her prior state of overweight misery, a condition that denied her a basis for comparison or other choices. "A home, family, the same things you had, only time was running out for me."

"Would you have been willing to take that chance with Pete, having all of that and knowing that he'd never change?"

"Maybe," Adrienne says softly and then asks, "Did you ever find out why Dina left you?"

"No, not until recently." She considers confiding her suspicions but then decides against it.

"Do you think the two of you can mend it?"

"It's impossible for me to think that we can't mend it, except that I never would have believed that Dina could have actually cut off. We were so close."

"Maybe you were too close."

"I'm not sure what that means, being too close to your child."

"What I meant had more to do with a kid being too close to a mother."

Gabriella appears distracted for the moment. "It's not

as if I stopped her from doing things or growing, it wasn't a closeness like that.''

"Kids see things so differently than adults," Adrienne says gently, "and especially when it's a mother-daughter. Dina felt overpowered by you in a way and very competitive."

"But that's impossible," Gabriella rushes, "I encouraged her to do things for herself and have her own opinions."

Adrienne shakes her head. "It's not up to you to encourage or discourage, it's just something that she felt because she was thrashing around trying to find her own place." She pauses, her eyes squinted. "Let's face it, you didn't exactly look and act like a stereotypical mother."

Gabriella nods, aware that the woman is watching her closely. "Did Dina tell you this?" she asks. Her mouth quivers but she manages to catch the motion fast enough so that it becomes a good-natured smile.

"Yes."

A cautious look now. "What was I supposed to do?" Gabriella finally says softly. "How was I supposed to know that she felt this way if she never told me?"

"You weren't," Adrienne comforts, "which is why this isn't a question of blame or right and wrong. It's something that happens between mothers and daughters. I've seen enough of it to know from my days of working as a guidance counselor and it either works out or it doesn't or it does for a while and then doesn't for a while. There just isn't an ending to this story."

"So I should just do nothing and wait?"

"Look, Gabriella," Adrienne says, reaching forward to touch her arm, "I've seen much worse—kids who leave home and end up on the streets selling their bodies for drugs, kids who wind up getting stabbed or murdered or dying of AIDS. I've seen young girls pregnant and then willing to sell their babies for a meal. At least your kid ran away to her father—I mean, consider yourself one of the lucky ones!''

It was certainly a novel approach to the problem and one that Gabriella hadn't thought of before now—that she was one of the lucky ones. ''It might have been better if it hadn't happened at all,'' she says with a touch of irony, ''I mean, there *are* people who manage to go through life without having ruptures or scenes or emotional tirades.''

''Yes, that's true, but then they're not always as interesting as you are or as Dina is for that matter.'' She considers. ''Your daughter isn't ordinary, and maybe it's because she was exposed to a father like Pete, a maverick who swashbuckled through life.'' She smiles slightly at the memory. ''Don't think for a minute that what he was didn't make an impression on Dina.''

''Then why didn't she cut from him?''

''Because he's a man, because he's the father, or was, and because he had the good sense to drop dead so she could rewrite history and make him what she wanted him to be.''

Gabriella concentrates on the view from the window of the diner, flips through the tunes on the jukebox that is attached to the table before she turns her attention back to Adrienne.

''It's hard to see it so rationally when there's nothing rational about not seeing your own child for two years and then seeing her at your ex-husband's funeral and having her spill over with hatred. It just hurts too much.''

''It hurts me too,'' Adrienne says softly, ''I loved him.''

''How can you compare a lover with a child?'' And suddenly both of those words stick somewhere in her throat.

''Because when it comes to feelings there's no difference, especially when those feelings happen to be unresolved.''

Gabriella nods her head as she meets Adrienne's gaze. "You're right," she barely whispers, "you're right."

"It's too late for me to resolve anything except in my head but you've got it all in front of you. She's young and she's bright and she's hurt."

"And so are you, which is why you and my daughter have so much in common."

"Don't forget that you are too," Adrienne says, "and there's room in our club for another bright, miserable, and neurotic woman."

"Should I be insulted?" Gabriella says, laughing.

"Probably," Adrienne replies with a twinkle in her eye.

The Hospital, Sunday Night

It isn't until the evening that Gabriella is allowed to see Dina, who remains in intensive care. The day was spent waiting for the doctor to give the go-ahead based on certain X rays and tests that he ordered for Dina—tests that would show that the chances of subdural hemorrhaging were now finally ruled out.

When Gabriella wasn't hanging around the nurses' station or sitting in one of the waiting rooms, she was busy checking into the motel, napping, or speaking on the phone to an anxious Sylvie and Rocco. And in between doing that, she was chatting with Adrienne, sometimes about things that made a difference but usually about nothing in particular—just words and the occasional bit of humor to keep from losing her sanity.

Now as she enters the intensive-care unit, she notices that one of the beds has been stripped bare—not necessarily a sign that the patient was cured and left. But Gabriella pushes that thought from her mind, determined this visit not to waste any portion of the time allowed her. She pads softly up to Dina's bed and watches her child in silence for several moments. The temptation right then is almost too great not to shake her awake and explain that she believes she has it all figured out; the urge almost uncontrollable to condemn Pete for his cruelty while in the same breath to beg Dina to understand and forgive both her parents for their stupidity.

Although still swollen and bruised, Dina appears to have improved, some color has returned to her cheeks and her eyelids are less red. But all Gabriella thinks of as she leans over to plant a kiss on the girl's forehead is how to clear the clutter that seems to hang in the air above them. "Hi, sweetheart," she whispers.

Eyes flutter open. "Where's Adrienne?"

"Outside," Gabriella answers calmly, determined not to be hurt since the question is a sign that Dina is recovering.

She nods, apparently satisfied. "They took my spleen," she repeats.

"I know," Gabriella responds, smoothing her face tenderly. But the spleen falls in the same category of useless or extinct parts of the human anatomy such as the appendix or the coccyx bone. Or the hymen. Although the loss of that particular part jolts her as she considers that her child is no longer a child. Even if it also gives her a sense of optimism that now Dina is more likely to understand another woman's mistakes. For a woman who has had a lover, who no longer has a lover, who has suffered that loss or some other indignity related to that kind of experience, is part of every other woman who has ever gone through a similar encounter. A bond on another level, other than mother and daughter perhaps.

"Your doctor says you're getting out of intensive care tomorrow morning."

Dina grunts softly, concentrating on not crying. "I know."

"Do you also know that I love you?"

She appears to be on guard. "How did you find out about the accident?"

"The usual bearer of bad news called Sylvie. Claire."

Dina makes a face. "Figures." A pause. "Well, she certainly had a busy week with everything that's happened."

Gabriella hesitates, unsure if she can go a step more. "I think I understand a lot more now," she says cautiously.

"I doubt it," the girl replies, turning her face away.

Gabriella flinches. "I'm so sorry, Dina, if I did anything to hurt you."

"So simple."

"What is?"

"An apology, so simple."

"I don't mean to make it sound simple. I just don't know how else to begin."

"We're not beginning."

"We could if you'd let us."

"Don't put it all on me," Dina cautions, "as if everything is up to me. I've had a lot of pain because of you."

"All I want to do is understand all that pain so neither of us will have to keep reliving it." But it takes everything she has to ask, because her heart already feels as if it's been finely shredded.

"Maybe you should go now," Dina says, "there's no point."

Gabriella stands, a defeated slump to her shoulders as she touches Dina's arm. Her eyes linger on her daughter's face a moment more before she turns to walk slowly away.

"Wait," Dina calls after her.

Gabriella pauses, one hand on the wall to balance before she walks back to the bed.

Dina's body rouses then. "You're not going to make me feel guilty," she warns, "not this time because it's not my fault." Her eyes are narrowed. "It's been harder for me than for anybody else," she says, struggling to sit up, allowing Gabriella to help, "first the divorce and seeing Daddy so upset all the time, so depressed." She is crying now. "I didn't ask to be born, you know."

Again. A nickel for every time that Gabriella has heard that one and she'd be rich enough to have a chauffeur or a private jet to take her far away from here so she wouldn't have to hear it ever again. Until it suddenly hits her that the choice is hers. She can walk away right now or slug it out once and for all. Considering the alternatives, she rationalizes that perhaps she was only meant to have this child for sixteen years; to care for her, feed her, diaper her, raise her, love her, and then let her go when the child demanded it. Irrationally, it is likely that she was meant to have this child forever and be willing to take all the hurt, knowing that deep down the child really didn't mean any of it anyway.

It hardly takes any time at all for Gabriella to make the decision to assume that the child didn't mean it—to stick around in spite of all the words to the contrary. After all, if for no other reason than she had this child on purpose, this one was no accident or unwanted pregnancy, this one resulted from a premeditated visit to the doctor to remove the coil and a concentrated effort to make love with Pete morning, noon, and night for a solid month because Gabriella absolutely wanted a baby and Pete absolutely wanted Gabriella. Even if neither of them understood at the time what it was all about, that Gabriella needed a replacement baby and Pete needed to learn how to first be a husband.

Gabriella ended up nursing her own hurt feelings for many reasons, the most logical being that she was still so deeply steeped in the tradition that said mothers must bear their children's abuse, if only because the decision to bring them into the world to suffer the errors of others had been taken without their consent.

"Of course you didn't ask to be born," Gabriella soothes, prepared to admit her guilt for not having consulted with her. "And if I did anything to make your life unhappy, please let me make it up to you."

Dina seems at a loss. "It's too late now," she flounders.

"Why?"

"Maybe you'd better leave now," she replies weakly, retreating behind her hospital pallor.

Silently Gabriella rises. "Rest then," she whispers, kissing her brow once more.

"Wait," Dina says, eyes fluttering open. "Are you going to be here tomorrow?"

"Yes," Gabriella replies, "tomorrow and the day after and the day after that and every day until they release you."

But by now, Dina has backed away again. "You don't have to, Adrienne will be here."

"Then you'll have two of us," Gabriella says and when she turns to leave, the look on her child's face is more peaceful, more relaxed somehow.

The Visit . . .

Gabriella rushes down the corridor without stopping until she reaches the bank of elevators. A photography editor once taught her that after she got the shot there was no percentage in hanging around and risking second thoughts on the part of the subject or the possibility of exposed film or broken cameras. She paces briefly back and forth now until the elevator finally arrives, steps inside, and watches the green light flashing from floor to floor as the car descends toward the lobby. The doors slide open and a voice inside of her poses a question that even then strikes her as completely irrational. If she had to crawl over shards of glass or mounds of jagged rock just to have him hold her again, right now, would she do it? And it doesn't even strike her as peculiar or the slightest bit surprising when she spots Nicholas Tressa standing in front of the elevator bank and walks directly into his arms.

"I missed you," he whispers, his lips brushing against her hair. Taking a deep breath, she pulls back, taking his hands in both of hers, looking directly into his eyes.

"Look, this isn't feasible," she protests, although not at all convincingly.

"What are you—an architect?" he asks lightly. "What does feasibility have to do with anything?"

They walk arm in arm toward the parking lot. "Why did you come here?" she asks.

"Your father's on my side," he replies, still with a touch of humor. "Every time I called he kept telling me how terrible you sounded." He pulls her closer to him. "And it looks like I need all the help I can get!"

Silently she allows him to lead her to his car. Without the slightest protest, she permits him to help her inside. Without any hesitation she gives him the name of the motel when he asks, offering terse directions without even taking a breath, aware that something with a life of its own has already grown up around them.

They arrive at the motel and park the car in front of the main bungalow, then head for a row of small buildings that encircle the empty swimming pool, walking slowly as if the intention is only to take an aimless stroll. A cool breeze burns one side of Gabriella's face, and she holds tightly to Nick's arm, leaning into him as they approach the door to her room. When they first step inside, she has a flash that it is all too familiar, a setting and an incident that once happened before, long ago, but the thought passes as quickly as it takes her to consider the degree of her nervousness.

Nick watches as she stands seemingly lost in thought near the dresser, one hand on top of the television. When she does glance up, she understands enough to give it over to him with her eyes. He is her current lover, a temporary inhabitant of her body, the one who has unnumbed her heart, but then she always manages to have a ready explanation for everything—to put it all neatly in some kind of slot where everyone belongs to someone and there are reasons and excuses. Except for her. She's different. Although right now it occurs to her that if she forced her mind to white it all out, deliberately obliterating any memory that went further back than when they met or further forward than when they made love, she might learn to forget about some of that pessimism.

On the way to the shower she passes him and rubs up against him, a feline gesture that makes her clearly the aggressor. Pressing her body against his, she takes his arms in an upward motion to encircle her back, her tongue making lazy circles over his lips, withdrawing, teasing until she finally coaxes him out of his passivity. Her knees feel weak, lifting her and at the same time causing her to believe that she might collapse as she drifts somewhere else in his arms. Carried away by every sensation, she feels his hands all over her body, exploring, touching where the straps of her bra would have been if she wore a bra. Which is the instant when she withdraws, twisting out of his embrace, breathless and flushed as she makes a dash for the bathroom, shutting the door behind her before turning on the faucets.

When she comes back into the room she is stark naked, drops of water from her hair dripping over her face. "Will you hold me?" she asks almost as a child, taking small steps toward him. He is already on the bed, lying down, fully clothed except for his jacket and his shoes, his hands clasped together behind his head and a look on his face that she has never seen before.

"Come over here," he says gravely. And when she does, he envelops her, drawing her down against him, her back pressed into his stomach, the belt buckle digging into her flesh.

"Why are you dressed?" she asks.

He kisses her hair, his hands massaging her shoulders. "Because I want to talk to you."

"About what?" But she knows about what because she has known it since the first time she saw him.

"About you leaving and about me waving good-bye at an airport while you get on a plane to go to Paris."

There's a ready answer all prepared. "Don't you think that you'll have my address and phone number? We'll figure out when the rates are low so we can—"

"That doesn't exactly do it for me," he cuts her off.

And for an instant she wonders just how far she can go, how much reassurance he needs. But she feels herself being turned around then, still in his arms, and instinctively she reaches up to unbutton his shirt. Her hands pause only to touch his neck, his chest, before she takes his face to kiss him on the mouth. In an instant she senses him stiffen, pull away, and considers that it isn't the moment to ignore what else is going on.

"What do you want me to do, Nick," she says softly, "stay here and quit my job, forget about the life that I've made over there?"

He doesn't respond right away, but he doesn't avoid it either.

"I want you to let me know what this is all about for you. If I'm just the European holiday on the other side of the ocean, address and telephone number when the rates are low, a pickup at a funeral, which by the way is pretty unbelievable except that I fell in love with your photograph."

Her eyes are wide and unblinking. "What photograph?"

"The one Pete kept at the beach house."

"Where?"

"In his study, on his desk, right next to photographs of Dina and his parents and his sister—the family corner, he joked. Only I always suspected the others were a poor excuse to be able to keep your picture there without looking like some kind of an idiot, since he was in the process of hating you."

"He told you that?"

"He told me lots of things—how you lived in Paris, how you abandoned the kid, how you were an unfit mother, how you were unfaithful to him, the usual crap that a man says when he knows he really blew it."

"Most of it is true, you know," she says softly, prepared now to blow it herself. Either for him or for her, she can't be sure.

"Gabriella, I'm going to tell you something and maybe it's pretty stupid, but there's nothing you can tell me that's going to make me change my mind about you. The only thing that's going to do it is if you tell me you don't want me." He pauses. "And mean it, and you only have to say it once."

Her reaction is half-measured and half-desperate. Grasping his head between her hands once again, she kisses him with a kiss that lasts for years, tongue and then no tongue, body grinding into his and then no body. And when he still doesn't respond, she releases him, angry and baffled that she hasn't managed to do it.

"Why?" she whispers, shaking her head slowly from side to side. "What do you want from me?"

"You," he says simply, "just you."

"Isn't this enough, then?"

"No."

Again she responds without speaking, unfastening his belt, then the zipper, kneeling at the foot of the bed while she pulls off his trousers, his socks, flinging them at far corners of the room, at the head of the bed then, to remove his shirt, one arm and then the other, stopping only to undo the last button that is stuck. There isn't any resistance, but somehow it's no victory either.

"I love you," he says, his mouth devouring her, his body pressing into hers, "and it's not going to end at any airport!"

Looking into his eyes, she thinks incredibly that he is hers somehow. "No," she murmurs, not completely re-

sponsible for everything she is about to say, "no airports."
In the back of her mind she considers other places though.
She picks his hand from her breast to press it to her lips.

"I love you," he says again.

"I love you," she responds. And again and again, as
if neither of them can stop once the secret has escaped their
lips.

□

A wave of recognition passes over her when she holds him,
as if he is more familiar than the oldest friend or lover. And
even when she is no longer connected to him in any precise
fashion, merely entwined emotionally, there is barely an
escape. That moment of silence afterward holds demands
and unspoken promises that even now she doesn't know if
she can keep. It then flits in and out of her head that perhaps, finally, the abandoned child in her disappeared; first
her mother abandoned her and then her daughter—one
generation to the next—handed down like some kind of
cursed legacy.

"I haven't taken a chance since Bonnie died," he says
softly, his voice more beautiful in the dark than she remembers from before.

"Once you didn't want to get trapped into compar-
ing," she admonishes, uncomfortable with the intimacy.

"That was in the beginning."

"Nick," she says, kissing his eyes, his nose, his
cheeks, "this is the beginning, that's what's so crazy!"

"Then it was irresponsible of you to make love with
me."

"It's not even a week!"

"If you break my heart, I'll survive," he promises
with a wry smile, "but it would be a shame since you
haven't taken a chance either—not for a long time, and
don't tell me about the love of your life over in Paris,
France."

"I trusted Pete. Once I trusted Pete," she says in defense.

"This isn't the same kind of thing. We're older."

"I trusted Dina once too," she adds, although perhaps it's more to herself than to him but the point is made.

"When's Dina coming home?"

"Where's home?"

He touches her nose. "That's the point, neither of you know where that is."

She turns her face away. "I've got to go to the city tomorrow because if I don't show up at the magazine I won't have any decisions left to make because I won't have a job."

"I'll drive you in."

"I've got a car."

"I'll follow you in my car."

"First I've got to make sure that Adrienne can stay here until I get back. I'm hoping we can work out some kind of a shift arrangement for the next couple of days."

"Do you think Dina will be out of intensive care by tomorrow?"

"That's what the doctor says, and if she's not, I won't leave. But I'm optimistic."

"Will you have dinner with me in the city tomorrow night?"

She shakes her head. "I keep trying never to see you again."

"It's not working," he says softly, "so we'll have dinner and then I'll meet you back up here on the weekend."

Tears of despair threaten to spill from her eyes. "What am I going to do? I'm afraid."

"Me too," he says, his hands lightly touching her entire body before his mouth covers hers, before he releases her to cradle her in his arms. "But it's not forever, we'll get over it."

"What's forever?" she asks, still breathless from him.

"Nothing so far," he says, "but maybe things will change."

The Hospital, Monday Morning

They had decided that it would be best—right now—if Dina didn't know about them, which is why Nick waits in the lobby of the hospital while Gabriella goes upstairs alone to speak to the doctor. Adrienne is with her, also anxious to hear about Dina's prognosis.

"My plan is to come back up here on Wednesday," Gabriella begins, "because I've got to go to my office, and also I promised Claire that I'd go to Pete's to sort out some papers for her."

"Then what I'll do is leave here late Tuesday night so I can be at my office on Wednesday morning. That way I'll get at least three solid days in before I head back up for the weekend. When are you planning to go back to Paris?"

But that is a reality that she still is not prepared to confront and something she certainly doesn't want to discuss right now. "As soon as Dina is fully recovered and back at school," she says glibly, as if Nick Tressa doesn't even enter into it.

The sound of footsteps coming from around the corner can be heard before the doctor appears, a stethoscope dangling around his neck, a white coat, unbuttoned and billowing around him as he slams to a stop in front of them. "Good morning," he says cheerfully, "why don't we go into the lounge to have our chat."

They are barely seated in the shabby visitors' lounge when he begins his discourse, the chart in one hand, leaning against a wall to face the two women. "She's been moved out of intensive care this morning, I'm pleased to report, and she seems in good spirits, although I must say that she isn't one of the easiest patients we've run into here."

The women exchange glances. "But that's neither here nor there," the doctor hastily adds, "the point is that there's no more danger of any subdural hemorrhaging and the incision from the spleen removal seems to be healing nicely." He glances at the chart before continuing. "My inclination is to keep her here another two or three days or even until the weekend, and then if things keep progressing as well as they are, discharging her then." He looks from Adrienne to Gabriella. "Provided that she has a limited schedule and takes it easy for about a week."

"Can she go back to school?" Gabriella asks.

"Not if she has to climb any stairs."

"You know, I've got an idea," Adrienne begins, talking mostly to Gabriella. "Why don't you take Dina to the beach house for a few days? It'll do you both good."

The doctor holds up a hand. "I'm afraid you're going to have a little problem doing that," he says, frowning. "It seems that Miss Molloy requested that her mother not even be allowed in to see her."

Gabriella gasps. "Why?"

"I don't know why, I'm just conveying my patient's request," he says, getting up.

Gabriella stands as well. "When did she say that?"

"Last night," he answers, "to the nurse who was on duty."

"I'll talk to her," Adrienne assures her, "don't worry about it."

The doctor offers his hand first to Adrienne and then to Gabriella.

"Thank you, ladies," he says, "and I'm around if you've got any questions." He turns to leave and then turns back. "So D day is Saturday—everybody agreed?"

They nod, waiting until he exits the room before they glance at each other in disbelief. "Now I know she's on the road to recovery," Gabriella says. "She's back to her old self and her old feelings."

"She'll change her mind," Adrienne offers, "she's

confused." Her hand is on Gabriella's arm. "Look," she continues when there is little response from Gabriella, "I'm going to stop in at Brampton and pick up her books. That way if she takes my suggestion and recuperates at the beach, she won't fall behind and can finish the year." Gabriella only nods, still too numb to speak. "Don't worry about it," Adrienne assures her again, "it'll all work out."

But as Gabriella walks down the corridor then rides the elevator to the lobby to meet Nick, she can't help but wonder when her life became a series of either/or's. Either she was married or she had a career; either she was in love or she was happy; either she was a woman or she was a mother. Although somewhere in the back of her mind, this time she knows there is no choice.

CHAPTER SEVEN

Paris Actualité

GABRIELLA SITS IN one corner of an enormous brown suede modular sofa that takes up most of the main office at *Paris Actualité* in New York. There is no other furniture except for a large rectangular coffee table piled high with back issues of the magazine, beginning with the first copy ever printed in the States, and an array of architectural plants that are properly dry and drooping. Not a desk nor a chair, not a typewriter nor a FAX machine, nor a file cabinet or a stapler—nothing that might reveal that it was a business office. Designed in that typically pseudodemocratic French style to make employees believe there is no rank and they have a say in what ends up between the covers, the editors are convinced that this particular atmosphere of salon intimacy encourages creativity.

When Gabriella first arrived, several French women, still willing to be titled "secretary" rather than "assistant," rushed up to her to embrace her on either cheek, to propel her into the office where she now sits, and with high-pitched exclamations and a slew of superlatives, pushed the latest issue of the magazine at her. Now as she leafs through its pages and comes to her story, she feels a tremendous sadness instead of any exhilaration at seeing her photographs and reading her captions. The piece was hers; she had thought it up, researched it, and worked on it alone for months, becoming involved with the people and going further than usual with them and with herself before it all ended. From one minute to the next it was over, abruptly and tragically and without any good reason. Perhaps she feels so sad because it is one more thing to mourn or perhaps because the story touches a familiar chord somewhere deep within her that has something vaguely to do with her own loss.

The Story

The sequence was conceived originally to portray the subtle differences between French and American women, certain women, that is, who suffered from similar agonies. And it begins with a shot of a well-known French actress, kneeling on her lawn somewhere in the Bourgogne region of France, her chateau in the background (made properly surrealistic by using a 120 wide-angle lens). Two frisky hound dogs are held at bay, tucked underneath each of the actress's arms while her wheat-colored hair (flecked with several strands of silver) blows in the breeze. Her face is still lovely, the delicate bones visible, the wide mouth bare of any lipstick and the famous deep-set green eyes slightly puffy. The point was made, though, that women like this one were destined to end up in chateaus like that. Women who were once great and revered French movie stars obediently faded (with dignity) into the bucolic countryside (if they were lucky and saved their francs), content to lead unbothered, unglamorous, and tranquil lives, never bitter about the years that passed or their sex appeal that waned. It was as if they had been preparing for this final role all of their careers, the part that they knew they would eventually play from the beginning, as if everything else had been nothing more than a rehearsal for their retirement.

Turning the page, Gabriella studies the photograph of the husband (there could have been a bit more light, she notes), younger looking than his years, his chest thrust out, his stomach perfectly concave. His arm, the white silk fabric of his shirt billowing, is linked through the arm of a woman who is the youngest female scientist at the Pasteur Institute. (The caption is a pithy quote by a young woman who admits that she is indeed a "Nobel Prize aspirant.") In the next frame and slightly to the left, she is looking adoringly at the husband, who is looking like the perfect specimen of the French bourgeoisie. This caption explains that the young woman has temporarily set aside her career goals while awaiting the birth of her first child, which also happens to be the husband's first child.

Gabriella included in the next frame an old photograph of the actress/wife exiting a rather rundown clinic in a wheelchair. The explanation here was that she was never able to carry a child to full term, each miscarriage throughout her very public and very tumultuous stardom and marriage was reported with the same detail, drama, and pathos as was evidenced in most of her films.

The last frame of the sequence is of the husband as he steps from his Peugeot 405 convertible, hugging actress/wife before following her (at a respectable distance) into the chateau (purchased by her after the completion of her most famous film, when she first exposed her very famous breasts). And right below that is a picture of actress/wife as she sits at a very long and very formal dining table studying husband's perfect profile while he gazes out of the bay window—the hazy form of the very pregnant young woman standing next to a tree. The actress/wife died eight days later, dutifully succumbing to an overdose of sleeping pills, but not without proper consideration for her husband whom, she knew, so desperately wanted to have that baby without any scandal.

The story continues then with a photographic essay of the French actress/wife's American counterpart. Gabriella studies the first frame, which is one of a faded television personality as she sits in her living room surrounded by mementoes, awards, Emmys, and souvenirs that span her entire career. There is no dutiful husband there with her, however, bound by years of cultural propriety, customs that compel him to appear at the dinner table every evening regardless of any other extenuating circumstance in his life.

A shot next to that one shows the television personality's son before he drowned in a recent and tragic boating accident off the coast of New England, and next to that one, a photograph of her former husband as he cuddles a newborn baby in a hospital room, young wife propped up on pillows in a bed in a flower-strewn hospital room.

Turning the page, Gabriella takes a sharp breath, for the first frame of this next sequence is of the television personality as she moves mechanically up a flight of stairs leading to a courthouse; dark wraparound sunglasses hide her taut face, a kerchief is tied around her head. And she tries to maintain some shred of dignity as she ducks a myriad of popping flashbulbs that swoop down on her. She is hurrying into the building to plead not guilty to a charge of shoplifting (nothing more serious than several items of cheap makeup that she allegedly stole from the local five-and-dime store near her reconverted weekend farmhouse in Bucks County, Pennsylvania). The purported theft occurred on the day the husband's new baby was born, but perhaps never would have occurred at all had she succumbed to that overdose of sleeping pills as well. But the television personality had been saved by a committee of do-gooders whose mission had been to check on her. They arrived in time to shuffle her off to a famous addiction center run by another faded television personality. The television personality featured here had exited the center clean only to give in to another less acceptable symptom of her grief. The last two frames show television personality's former spouse engaged in various athletic activities with his young wife, proving that in America men like that usually disappear into a world where second wives are a generation younger and tiny new second-family sons help them to ignore their own mortality. While a faded television personality might end up getting arrested and then acquitted by a sympathetic judge and jury only to return to her plush farmhouse where a committee of do-gooders waits to receive her and care for her and doom her to a life of encounter groups and self-pity. And as Gabriella shuts the magazine, she still isn't sure which fate is worse on which side of the ocean.

□

"Paris tells us they have received a *très grand* reaction to the piece," Nicole Longet says as she sweeps into the room, stopping to give Gabriella a peck on each cheek, "but *vraiment, ma chérie,* where would you rather get dumped—in Paris or New York?"

"That's the point, isn't it?" Gabriella laughs. "And the answer is nowhere!" Hugging Nicole, she responds with equal warmth, "I've missed you and you look terrific—really great. New York is agreeing with you!"

"It's a woman's city," Nicole says, linking her arm through Gabriella's. "If I had to be alone in Paris, it would be mortal!"

"I know," Gabriella agrees. "At least here you're part of the majority." Curling up on the sofa once again, she says, "So tell me everything!"

Nicole sits, crossing her shapely legs before fishing in a glass box on the coffee table for a cigarette. "Let's see, the follow-up of the funeral comes out next week, and I feel so proud, as if I could take just a little of the credit!"

"You can," Gabriella says quickly, "because you helped me so much when I worked here."

"Well, if I had to be *tout à fait* honest," she continues in that particular way she has of mixing the two languages that Americans find so irresistible and the French find so insulting, "I would say that *je me suis trompé,* I was wrong, because I never thought you'd last over there. *Jamais!* I thought the chill would drive you out."

"Lasting is one thing and feeling comfortable is another."

"And do you feel comfortable? Should I be surprised to learn that *les Français* have made you feel *comme vous êtes chez vous?*"

"It depends on how you mean that."

"In every way—professionally and personally. Somehow I doubt it."

"As a matter of fact, right now I feel pretty happy but it's got nothing to do with living in Paris."

"Do you miss working in New York?"

"Part of me misses it but the worst thing for me would be to come back now."

"Why?"

"Because right now New York is the wrong place for me to be as far as my career is concerned. I'd be too complacent and forget about working."

"When a woman forgets about work and gets complacent it only means one thing."

"And what's that?"

"That she has a lover." Nicole smiles. "*Et alors,* so *oui ou non?*"

"*Oui,* only don't get too excited because it's not going to last."

"How optimistic of you, *ma chérie,*" Nicole says.

"It's just that he came along at the wrong time and certainly in the wrong place."

"It's never right unless it finishes right or doesn't finish at all," Nicole says, a touch of sadness in her voice.

"There were so many reasons to move back here before this, for my mother or my daughter, and I didn't. If I did it now, I'd feel like a fool, or worse than a fool, I'd feel so rotten I couldn't stand it. But I miss my mother so much and I miss Dina too, and the irony of both situations is that my being so far away has nothing to do with missing them. They each left when I was right there."

"How is Dina?" Nicole asks gently.

"Right now she's recuperating from a car accident."

"*Mais non*," Nicole exclaims, her hand over her mouth, "not serious?"

"It could have been, but it wasn't, at least she's going to be fine, no lasting injuries."

"But everything happened at once, the funeral and then this." She shakes her head. "And Gabriella, I was so sorry to hear about Pete, *si jeune!*"

"It was really terrible."

"And has this brought you and Dina together again?"

"No, and maybe I'm fooling myself that we ever will be fine again, if we ever were. But for the moment I'm hanging around and hoping that we can work it out."

"She's not a child anymore," Nicole says very seriously, "so perhaps the best you can expect is a truce so that when you are together, *de temps en temps*, it is at least *sans guerre*, without war. Not everybody is compatible, not even relations."

"I wanted more than that, I still want more than that."

"Things don't always work out the way we want them to or the way we think they are supposed to be."

"It's so strange, Nicole, but I wanted her so much before she was born, and maybe it was because I thought she'd fill the terrible void I had for my own mother." She stops to consider. "And somehow it just didn't work."

"You can kill someone's *esprit* by burdening them with your own unfinished business, *ma chérie*."

"Yet the break between us was all Pete's fault—he was the one who turned Dina against me."

"Nonsense," Nicole exclaims with surprising passion, "she was a grown girl when she left you, sixteen and old enough to make her own decisions and take the responsibility for her own actions."

Turning away, Gabriella clasps and unclasps her hands. "Then what should I do, give up?"

"Stop running away."

"I don't understand. I'm here now."

"Now you're here, but living over there makes it very easy for you to come back and fool yourself into believing that it's the geographic distance that makes you a stranger."

"Could we not talk about this," Gabriella says suddenly, her eyes welling up with tears, "at least not now."

"*Absolument,*" Nicole agrees. "Should we talk about Pascal?"

Gabriella smiles slightly through the tears, shaking her head. "A terrific choice, another really up subject!"

Nicole laughs. "Did you see his article, by the way?"

"The social commentary to my story? No, not yet. Is it good?"

"It's not the usual vintage Pascal, but I suppose that's because the subject is too personal for him to handle it from a distance."

"In what way?"

"He behaves as all men do in that position which is only *ridicule*. Any older man with a very young girl looks *ridicule* to everyone except his own mirror. Eventually he'll realize it, but in the meantime we try to show how we disapprove."

The fact that Pascal has someone else so soon surprises Gabriella, even if on a perfectly rational level they have both committed the same error in propriety. "Who is it?" she asks, trying not to act anything but normal.

"*Je ne la connais pas,*" Nicole says, "I don't know her. She's a new photographer the magazine hired for a *stage*—how do you call it?"

"An intern," Gabriella says, aware that the New York office obviously never heard she was having an affair with Pascal.

"An intern," Nicole repeats and then clasps her hands together. "Remember, Gabriella, there are only two lessons to be learned from this. An older woman with a younger man would look even more *ridicule* and secondly, the only thing that should matter to women like us, of our age, is work. In the end that's all there is that is faithful and that gives us pleasure.''

Nicole Longet didn't always think like that. Once she lived only for a man, to make him happy and be available to satisfy his every need by putting her own desires and interests aside until one day he unceremoniously dumped her for a young girl. But there was a positive side to an otherwise unbearably painful situation as this particular man happened to own a group of publications that included a magazine called *Paris Actualité*. Nicole was clever enough to demand a contract for life at a salary that worked out to be more than she was offered in a one-shot settlement and a title that made her editor-in-chief of the New York office. And she went away with her dignity at least not completely destroyed.

Self-taught in every way, Nicole learned and absorbed everything there was to know about running a weekly until everyone in the business forgot how she got her start. Now, at forty-five but looking a decade younger than her years, she is still as meticulous and intent about keeping up with every aspect of the business.

''*Peut-être* you should cut your hair a bit,'' Nicole advises, peering at Gabriella from over the rim of the bottle of water she is about to guzzle. ''It's a little long with those tendrils falling all over the place—too Bardot or Farrah!'' She swallows. ''Although you're certainly glowing, *ma chérie*, so this man must be making you a little bit happy, *n'est-ce pas?*''

Gabriella feels herself blush. ''I haven't had time to think about a haircut, let alone get one,'' she evades.

''You know, I shouldn't tell you this, because it doesn't serve my purposes, but Paris is FAXing us almost every day for news of you, they are very anxious to have you back. And *quel dommage pour moi, mais* they are *débordé* with story ideas and assignments for the fall and winter issues that have to be shot *toute de suite*. So what shall I do—when shall I FAX them of your return?''

Gabriella pauses, relieved to learn that she still has a job, that even so far away she is still remembered and still in demand. "I don't know yet, but I'll be able to tell you more after Dina gets out of the hospital. Can it wait another few days?"

"*Mais oui*, we'll make them wait!"

"The thing is," Gabriella says, almost as an after-thought, "that Dina has to take it easy for a week or two after she gets out and I'd really like to stay with her and take care of her."

"Will she want you there?"

Gabriella appears troubled. "Who knows?"

"But *voyons*, Gabriella," Nicole says, pressing, "talk to me." After several clucks of her tongue she is even more direct. "It's not good for the skin to keep everything inside."

"So typically French after all these years in America, aren't you?" Gabriella observes with warmth. "It's been a rough ten days and an extraordinary ten days and I don't know which feeling to hold as the real feeling of how it's been." She remains vaguely amused by what she had almost forgotten, how the French view the skin as the barometer of mental health. "Come, let's have a *coupe de champagne* to make us feel a little more gay," Nicole suggests, "even if I will pay for it tomorrow with my *foie*." For what is cure for the soul and good for the skin is bad for the liver.

"I'd better not," Gabriella says, declining, "your *foie* and my head not to mention that I've got a dinner date."

"Your lover?" Nicole chirps, her voice skipping up two octaves.

"My friend," Gabriella corrects, preferring to use the less graphic American term, "although it's beyond me why one can't be the other."

"Perhaps because in the end all our lovers turn out to be the enemy."

"You've been reading too many issues of your own

magazine,'' Gabriella says with levity just as Nicole's secretary pokes her head in the door. *"Monsieur Bourget est en ligne,''* she announces.

"Whom does he want to speak to?" Nicole asks.

"He asked for you," she replies, "but when I told him that you were in conference with Gabriella, he asked to speak to her."

"Vas y, ma chérie,'' Nicole says, shooing her out of the room. "Come with me into this empty office so you can be private." She turns to take Gabriella's hand a moment. "Just so you know, Pascal is doing another follow-up on your story in Bourgogne," she explains hurriedly. "Sasha, the mistress, had the baby last night."

"Oh, really," Gabriella says, surprised. "What was it?"

"Humiliating to Marianne's memory," she quips, "but don't quote me. After all, we're supposed to be beyond that kind of nonsense. We're French!"

The Conversation

"Pascal, can you hear me?" Gabriella says into the receiver, the crackle of international cable drowning out her words.

"Perfectly, as if you were right next door. How is everything?"

"Difficult."

"And the funeral?"

"Very sad."

"And your daughter?"

"Dina was in a car accident but she's going to be all right."

"Quelle horreur,'' he exclaims, "not serious?"

"Not serious," she replies, unwilling to discuss Dina and be subjected once more to his opinions.

"Très bien, very good," he says, a tone of relief in his

voice before getting to what was obviously the purpose of the call. "Did you see the piece?"

"I did and it looks really good."

"Well, the funeral for Marianne was unbelievable. Everybody was there from Madame Pompidou to Alain Delon, even the woman who sold her vegetables in Paris and the man who cut her flowers every day in the country. *Tout le monde!*"

"How wonderful," Gabriella says without expression.

Pascal clears his throat. "Did Nicole mention that the magazine is doing a follow-up piece on the baby—some photos for the front of next week's issue? Just enough so our readers can close the chapter on the whole incident."

"It's unbelievable that Henri would allow that since Marianne was just buried. It isn't even a month since she died."

"Don't be so silly, we can't leave our readers like that. They're entitled to see the beginning of a new life. After all, they suffered through the end of the other one."

So typically French, Gabriella reflects, this compulsion to tie up all the ends so neatly, the King Is Dead, Long Live the New Baby, or Mistress, or whatever, with all the details properly recorded. And this characteristic is not Pascal's fault, the blame rests more on the culture. He was raised in a country that suffers from a major absorption complex since medicines are dispensed in the form of suppositories and thermometers are rectal. "Who's going to shoot that segment?" she asks.

"Anne Marie Fontaine."

There is a part of Gabriella that is pleased that someone is finally giving Anne Marie a chance, a young woman just starting out, while another part of her is terrified that that chance will result in her taking her job. Especially since Anne Marie has exactly what it takes to launch a successful career in France. Tall and blond and twenty-five with cheekbones that taper into a well-defined jaw, and a body that is French-narrow with shoulders which are what Christian LaCroix models his shoulder pads after in all of his jackets destined for export. Anne Marie was a dog groomer who dressed in leather pants and silk shirts to clip poodles before she became Gabriella's assistant who dressed in leather pants and silk shirts to clip proofs. Another example of the French disregard for credentials, that on one hand gives everybody a chance to become something and on the other hand lowers the creative standards when compared to other countries. Anyone can become a writer if he writes books that are deemed unreadable and therefore literary, or a journalist if he reports stories that are right-wing critical, or a photographer if he shoots poverty and unrest anywhere else but in France.

"She's not very good yet," Pascal says. "You were much better in the beginning."

But there is no need for any consolation. "She'll learn," she answers, aware that the only loss she feels right now is for her own youth.

"She has no credits yet," he continues, blowing out some smoke into the receiver.

"Nobody does when they first begin." Gabriella comes to the girl's defense even if she suddenly craves something sweet to counteract the sour taste in her mouth. "Will you stay at the chateau?" she inquires and despises herself for actually asking.

"Yes, but only because Sasha gave birth there."

"How could she have given birth there when Marianne just died?"

"Where would you have Sasha give birth?" Pascal demands imperiously. "In a hospital?"

Amazing to her how he can make the most logical solution sound so absurd. But again it's not his fault, the blame rests on the culture, for he was raised in a country where dogs are allowed in restaurants, children are weaned on wine, and the last major scientific contribution that affected the entire world was pasteurization. "It's too late to

— 193 —

argue about one of our fundamental differences," she says wearily, proud of herself for sounding so terribly civilized.

"You're lapsing into your old ways, Gabriella," he observes, "American puritanical self-deception."

"Did you water my plants?" she asks, changing subjects.

He clears his throat. "Actually, I've been neglectful because there has been one thing after the other here. But when are you coming back?"

"I'm not sure yet, maybe in a couple of weeks, maybe sooner, but it won't matter to my plants because they'll be dead by then."

"Why so long?"

"There's a lot left to do here."

He inhales. "I'll try." He exhales. "But it's hard to jump from one end of Paris to the other—Left Bank to Right Bank to Neuilly to Île St. Louis."

And all around the town, she finishes the rhyme in her head, fully aware of the reason why her plants are dead and dying. "I'd appreciate it," she says. Only remembering things about him that are good and kind and decent and attractive. Easy now to do since it is over.

"Water twice a week for the ones in the sun and once a week for the others," he recites, "and, Gabriella, take care." Theirs was a relationship that perhaps wasn't the most fulfilling or passionate, but still they had shared a moment or two off guard, a shower once in Normandy and once in Paris, coffee and croissant more times than she could recall, and a year and a half of her life. And now it was reduced to a discussion about plants. She sits very still several minutes after hanging up the phone, baffled why she is so intent upon leaving everything here to go back to absolutely nothing over there. But if the reverse were true, she'd stay.

"Will I see you before you leave?" Nicole asks after Gabriella comes back into her office and is once again seated on the couch.

"Of course," Gabriella says immediately. "Would you

consider spending a few days at the beach, that is, if Dina lets me go there.''

''With pleasure.'' Her expression is hopeful now. ''So tell me, this man that you are having dinner with, is it serious?''

Gabriella nods. ''Which is why I've got to get back to Paris.''

''That's insane!'' she blurts out.

''Nicole, please, don't contradict yourself now, please whatever you do, stick with what you said before, I need that support. All that counts, you said, for us is work, the only thing that's, how did you put it . . .''

''Faithful and pleasurable,'' she says, and then adds, ''but that becomes all irrelevant if you find someone who is wonderful and kind and sexy and sincere.''

''He's American,'' Gabriella announces.

''Good,'' Nicole responds, rubbing her hands together gleefully, ''and what else?''

''I'm in love with him, and it's only been ten days.''

''It could take ten minutes or sometimes ten years and it never happens. Time is not the question.''

''Then what's the question?''

''Try dealing with answers first,'' Nicole says, laughing, ''but let me tell you something. It's so much better with an American, that much I've learned living over here, and since Jean Marc found his own personal fountain of youth.'' She smiles sadly.

''Are you over him?'' Gabriella asks quietly.

''Life goes on,'' Nicole replies with great resolve, ''even after so many years.''

''Why did it happen?''

''He turned sixty and blamed me for not making him feel younger, or maybe for not doing something magic to keep him from turning sixty.'' She laughs. ''I could have murdered him so he stayed fifty-nine, and had I known what he would do to me I would have gladly obliged!''

''Will you join us for dinner tonight?''

"Not a chance," Nicole says gaily, "and besides I have a *rendezvous* also."

"An American?" Gabriella teases.

"Only an American," she answers seriously, "and do you know why?"

Gabriella shakes her head. "No."

"Because *à mon avis*, at our age surprises are bad for our health."

"Not to mention our skin," Gabriella interrupts with a smile.

"And our skin. And even though American men may be unsophisticated and naïve, even though they are occasionally gauche and boring, they are so very very honest. If an American man can't, he doesn't blame you; if he doesn't want to, he tells you in such painful detail about the other woman; if he falls out of love with you, he doesn't wait until the whole world knows about it except you. With a Frenchman, it's impossible to know which stage he is in or how he feels because he guards everything inside. Deception is as French as a *baguette*, vanity as much a part of our history as the *guillotine*, and let me tell you that the end result is the same." She runs her finger across her neck. "As painful as having your head cut off!"

"When did you become such an expert on American men?"

"Not an expert, just an optimist." Nicole hesitates, taking a long drag on her cigarette. "It's easier to accuse the entire country of a cultural malady than to hold Jean Marc responsible for breaking my heart. At least it saves a small piece of my heart."

Then I mustn't have a heart, because I already know about Pascal and Anne Marie and somehow I'm not upset, Gabriella thinks to herself.

"Are you in love with *ce monsieur, l'Américain?*"

"If I am then why am I so anxious to get back to Paris?"

"Maybe there's a story here, *ma coquette*, about the

French lover or the great strength of the American career woman—both fables. The French lover is a finicky, frightened man, and the American career woman is terrified of being possessed."

"Well, don't assign it to me, because my intention is to leave just as soon as Dina is well and back at school."

"You're so sure, Gabriella, you've already made up your mind?"

"Yes."

"I could find a place for you back here with me, you know."

"No, Nicole, don't even tempt me."

"Why are you being so stubborn?"

"You shouldn't have to ask me that. If you've learned to be so American after your experience with Jean Marc, then maybe I'm learning how to be French after everything that's happened to me here. Maybe I'm learning that an affair is just that, an affair, and not something that has to last a lifetime."

"Or even longer than ten days?" Nicole asks with a wry smile, before adding, "and do you really believe I'm over Jean Marc?"

Gabriella hardly hesitates. "Not for a minute."

"Well, I don't believe you either."

The Decision

She neither waves nor smiles as she walks toward the table where he sits, hardly able, though, to keep from crying or laughing or throwing her arms around him because he looks so beautiful. But she has also made an effort to look beautiful for him, having read somewhere, perhaps even in her own magazine, that the last impression is as crucial as the first, the image he will guard for her forever when she finally exits his life. Except that each time that she sees him, her resolve crumbles just a little bit more.

She washed at the office before she left, combed her hair so the tendrils weren't quite so "Bardot" or "Farrah," reapplied her makeup so it looked as if she weren't wearing any at all, and was surprisingly uncritical of her reflection as she took a final glance in the mirror before rushing downstairs to hail a cab. Dressed in a black and blue silk skirt that falls midcalf, a sleeveless black silk blouse, and black ballerina slippers, she forces herself to break through the chaos inside of her as she presses her cheek against his in greeting.

"I'm sorry I'm late," she offers after she is seated.

He is even better than she recalls, each time she tells herself not to think about that, not to register the improvement that knowing him so intimately allows her. His eyes are darker, more glowing and intense than the last time, his chin more square, the mouth impossible to look at without remembering where it had been just hours before. A thousand possibilities fill her head: the image of the well-toned body, who else has loved him once, the sound of his breathing in her ear, why here and not there, simply one touch that creates such speculative excitement deep within her, why him and not someone less likely to make her forget. Nick Tressa seems to weigh his words before he speaks, as if he is looking for a way to head her off, or perhaps she's assuming too much or hoping or doing anything else that might make this easier for her to do. Or not to do.

"How'd it go today?" he asks genially.

"It was great to see everyone again and find out that Paris is anxious for me to come back."

"I don't blame them," he answers, taking her hand in his, pressing it to his lips. "If you were there and I was here, I'd be anxious for you to come back too."

"Which is what I wanted to talk to you about," she says quickly, wondering if he pushed her to this point on purpose.

"I had no doubt," he says easily, "but can it wait at

least until you catch your breath and let me look at you for a few minutes before you start to cry?''

With feigned indignance, she replies, ''What makes you think I'm going to cry?''

''Aren't you?''

And some questions are asked to elicit truthful answers while others are asked to elicit lies. ''Of course I'm going to cry because this is probably one of the hardest things, one of the worst things I could do to myself—''

''To us,'' he interrupts.

''To us, then,'' she agrees as if it is a toast, ''but it's something you'll thank me for someday when you're happily married and your wife is pregnant with your child . . .''

''And you're living with some very sensitive and very intellectual Frenchman who cuddles up with you at night to read Proust or sings the 'Marseillaise' in the shower—''

''And not stuck with me, someone you picked up at a funeral. You'll laugh about this someday, how you fooled yourself into believing you fell in love with some woman who brought a suitcase—''

''What if I only wanted your child?''

She is stunned: the question stops the barrage of self-deprecating scenarios if nothing else and shifts her to another level of reflection, which for the moment excludes him. She could have a baby at forty if they forgot about dinner and began right this minute and the child wouldn't have to be necessarily born an idiot. There were phenomenal medical advances, machines and sonar and new techniques and all kinds of other wonders that would inform the soon-to-be-middle-aged mother in advance if her unborn baby was flawed before facing one of those never-to-be-forgotten decisions. But all that is just a poor excuse for facing the real facts, since the problem here was not any of that. It is simply that she knows her history of leaving a trail of discarded babies and unhappy adolescent children that she has mothered and misplaced without even having the decency to sprinkle bread crumbs so that either might find her way back someday.

"I tend to be a little careless with my children," she says sadly.

"Children?"

"Child, children, what's the difference? The point is that I'm a bad risk."

His eyes bore into hers. "And what if I didn't care about children," he says, leaning across the table so his lips brush the side of her face, "what if it's only you I want?"

"Nick, you could do so much better than me."

"Probably," he replies not without humor.

She is momentarily flustered, again reduced to silence, felled by him. "Then why bother?"

He shrugs. "I've got no idea except there you were, standing in the lobby of the funeral parlor with this helpless expression on your face, looking so distraught about your suitcase and so frightened and so out of place, and something moved inside of me—like a chunk of a continent that shifted to the other side of the ocean with me standing on the edge. How can I explain something like that when it never happened before?"

"Do you think it's just some kind of inexplicable physical attraction that we've got for each other?"

He grins. "Of course that's what it is."

"Well, it's not the end of the world or something we've got to act on."

"I never said it was the end of the world. You're the one who keeps making it the end of something—the world or just us, and I don't understand why you've got to keep punishing yourself like that."

"I'm hungry," she says suddenly, burying her face behind the menu, convinced that if a morsel of food passed her lips she would be violently ill.

But she is no longer certain that she can rely on the excuse of a career or a life that she has made for herself so far away from here, or even the feeble apology having to do with motherhood and how it excludes all other commitments. Still, the possibilities remain and she takes them in orderly progression.

"Nicole made me aware of something I had almost forgotten," she edits prudently, "how all the shoots for fall and winter stories are being done now, in the next few months during the summer when things are quiet in Paris. I've got to get back over there to pull it all together or someone else will take all the prime assignments." Several pieces of shrimp are pushed to the side of her plate then, before she puts down her fork.

"Do you come up with the ideas or are the subjects already chosen?" he asks as he places his knife and fork at right angles to his chicken.

"Sometimes I come up with ideas, and sometimes when they've been assigned, I just plot the sequence."

"Does each issue have a theme?"

"Usually," she replies, surprised at the question, surprised that he can follow the conversation when her mind is on him, "except for the issues that appear during the Collections, which are naturally mostly fashion spreads."

He reaches over his plate to take her hand. "Could you do the same thing in New York?"

"Probably," she hedges. "But why should I?"

"I can't supply you with answers, Gaby," he says simply, withdrawing his hand, "that's something you have to figure out for yourself."

But she already feels herself falling, tumbling and spinning without any chance of landing on solid ground as long as he is around to present her with options. Or obstacles.

"I was a lousy wife and a lousy mother," she confesses suddenly, silencing his protest with her hand, her fingers on his mouth tenderly. "I married Pete because I thought he would get me away from that whole Italian thing and because he finished college and I didn't, because he went to law school and was going to be a professional. Because I didn't want to end up the way I started out.''

''People have married for worse reasons.''

''I loved him,'' she defends, as if he had accused.

''I'm sure you did, even if it's more to your credit than to his.''

''It wasn't all his fault.'' She carries it even further. ''I was a different person when I married him, and halfway through our life together I changed so drastically that he didn't know how to handle it. I began submissive and grateful because he seemed so superior to me. And it was understandable, actually, that I chose him because my life ended at thirteen, from hearing how great I was to hearing nothing because my mother stopped talking.''

''What about your father?''

''Poor Sylvie, he walked around in a fog for years. He couldn't believe what happened to Mama or to the family for that matter. It was as if he had let everybody down, that everything that happened was his fault. So when Pete came into my life it seemed so right that he just took over and controlled everything. I mean, I welcomed it after being ignored for so long. But then one day I realized there was more to life than watching television while he went off to work or reading magazines that I bought in the supermarket or experimenting with new recipes while Dina napped. I was capable of doing more, and that included making decisions about where we should live or what movie we would see on a Saturday night or working, you know, things that had to do with me and my life.''

She looks at him for a moment before continuing. ''It was so strange all of a sudden to discover that there really was a me, a separate person who had opinions and feelings. But that wasn't the only thing that broke up the marriage. The women, always someone in his life who lasted a week or a month or just a night.''

''But you would have changed even if Pete had been

faithful," Nick says. "You wouldn't have been happy doing nothing for yourself."

But the conflict that Gabriella lived with then still hasn't been resolved. "Maybe, except I went too far. Pete didn't count on my getting a job or hiring someone to take care of the house or having a lover. He had the right to expect that at least I'd be faithful and responsible to the bargain we made in the beginning when I married him. After all, Pete never changed, there were no surprises. He had always been unfaithful and inconsiderate from the very first day we met." She smiles. "So I guess in a way we both had the same problem—neither of us could take it anymore. Our defects became unbearable!"

"You know, Gaby, I don't think you even noticed your lover. I think it was the idea of being unfaithful and not the man himself."

"I suppose it was the notion that I could do it too since Pete had been doing it for so long. But then, I did everything for the wrong reasons, including getting pregnant." She stops to consider the implication of her words and then shrugs.

"Why did you get pregnant?" he asks.

"Probably because I thought it would fill all those empty and lonely places inside of myself."

"But why is that such a terrible reason to have a child?"

"But why?" she echoes with a kind of hopelessness, waiting for an explanation that has been eluding her for years. "Because you're supposed to have a baby because you want a baby, because you want to be a mother, because you want to give up everything to care for another human being."

"Who said that?"

"Everybody."

"And why does a man want a baby or at least why is a man supposed to want to want to have a baby?"

But she takes his question completely seriously and

answers with the utmost sincerity. "Usually because his wife wants one, or because he has a need to reproduce himself and live forever, or because he's a man and doesn't really have to know why since he's not really the one having it." She considers. "That's the difference—it's the actual carrying of it that makes women feel so responsible that they have to come up with reasons."

She pauses before concluding. "Men come up with tangible contributions—from conception right through to tuition."

"For an independent woman, you're very old-fashioned." He smiles slightly. "But you loved Dina for the right reasons?"

A look of sheer terror crosses her face. "I don't know if I did," she replies, "I thought I loved her for the right reasons, but how was I supposed to know what they were or what loving a child meant?"

"I suppose you did the best you knew how to do because that's what most people do—they're no guidelines in the beginning except whatever has been thrashed out and discarded and refitted for any given family. What I don't understand is why you feel so guilty."

"Why?" she echoes, barely above a whisper, "but why me," as if that is what she meant to say at the very beginning of this conversation. Her hands inch up to clutch at his wrists, wriggling out of his grasp as they do. "Isn't there someone better around," she repeats, "someone without all this baggage?"

"Better?" He takes back his hands and wrists. "Not better."

"But there is someone else?" she asks fearfully, one toe in at a time.

"There's someone, or at least there was someone until I happened to go to Pete's funeral and meet you."

A sheet of ice has fallen over her and it would have been so much easier then just to allow it to cover her entire body once and for all, numbing her with its cold until she feels nothing. "Are you in love with her?" she asks, willing him to default on the unseen enemy. But like all of those who survive on instinct, she senses she has allowed him an edge. Or would have had he been anything less than sincere.

"I thought about it before I met you."

"Then I don't feel so guilty," she responds, attempting a sigh of relief that lands somewhere like a piece of cold pizza in the pit of her stomach. "After all, you could think you love me and then meet someone else."

"Does it make leaving easier?"

She feels the tears and deliberately allows them to spill. "Yes," she lies.

By the time dessert is being served, she feels as if all she has endured, every last word she has ever suffered, each injury that was inflicted on her, has boiled to the surface. It is nine-thirty, and even for a weekday night in New York, the restaurant has already emptied out relatively early.

"Could we come to some kind of an agreement?" she dares when the silence has made them both sufficiently uncomfortable. But somehow she has managed to come up with a solution, and her tone appears to go much further than his.

"If Dina will agree, I'd like to take her out to the beach to recuperate, and then depending upon what she decides, either take her back up to school to finish out the year or take her with me to Paris and let her spend a year over there studying." She has reached the end of the line, the most logical conclusion to a problem that has little to do with logic. And his face, as he looks at her, seems resigned. She waits then, until the chill passes and her pulse rate drops back down from over one hundred to see if this feeling of wanting him so badly will just go away. "But nothing is sure," she stumbles. "She may refuse to go with me even to the beach." He moves beside her on the banquette and takes her face between his hands.

"Listen, I buy it all, the marriage, the kid, everything, I believe every last word of it. You were a lousy wife and a rotten mother and probably a terrible daughter too, and God knows what else you were. I buy it, but I didn't make you do all those terrible things and you weren't rotten or lousy to me, not yet at least, so it's up to me to run away, but I'm not running. I'm willing to take a chance for whatever reasons or whatever problems I've got to want a woman like you." He doesn't say another word because his lips are busy with her lips, and for the moment she forgets why she came here in the first place, what the point was that she was trying to make. "So why don't we come to some kind of an agreement?" he repeats, but once again the question is rhetorical.

"I love you," she offers in a tragic whisper.

"So?" he responds.

"So I'm not going back to the hospital tonight," she begins in a voice so meek that it makes him smile just to hear her. "I've got to go to Pete's house and get those things done for Claire, so?"

"So I'll get the check and we'll spend the night in Sag Harbor." She nods, although her expression is clearly not one of total accord.

□

Once again she is stunned by him as she watches him sleep, her eyes flickering from his features to the digital clock, listening to the sounds of his even breathing that is only interrupted by the numbers changing in proper succession, seconds into minutes into hours. On the dresser there is a photograph of Bonnie at the beach eating an ice cream cone, and next to that is a picture of Nick's parents, a pleasant-looking man with a mustache and a broad smile, a woman slightly taller with a more serious expression who stands with her arm draped across his shoulder, and above the dresser are two tickets to a concert at Tanglewood that is less than two weeks away. Somehow it is comforting to know that his past and future are accounted for, especially since his present is so uncertain.

He is a man who is always noticed, that much she saw when he walked into the room at the funeral parlor and then again when he entered her father's kitchen. He is a man who is not easily forgotten and who leaves in his wake residual feelings and dilemmas. She considers herself lucky enough to have had the chance to love him the way that she does, to have known something like what she has with him that she might have missed. For the memory and the experience are hers forever now. They are something that not all women have, a feeling that churns around inside long after everything else has left, a secret that is now embedded deep within her and that will make the loss of him easier to bear.

A flash of lightning followed by thunder followed by a moment of fear and she curls up against him, her back pressed against him, feeling him gather her even closer into him.

"What're you doing awake?" he whispers groggily.

"Thinking," she whispers back, turning around to kiss his nose.

"About what?" The eyes open, a troubled look crosses his handsome face, or perhaps the look she sees is searching as he tries to read her mind.

"About us."

"Don't," he almost pleads, his gaze so intent that she can feel it physically.

Tears fill her eyes. He has pushed a button that somehow must control the ducts. "Nick," she begins, the remorse so evident.

"It's only six-thirty," he protests.

"Nick," she begins again, and his name is uttered so haltingly that even she realizes the confusion.

"Maybe I should be wide awake for this one," he says slowly.

"I love you." So simple. "Where are you going?"

"To take a shower and make some coffee," he says.

She has rehearsed it several times during the night, composing the words so carefully so that in a very few sentences the whole gamut of her emotions would be understood and dispensed with. And forgiven.

It all happened so fast, she could say, and while they are sure it's love, why not use this time apart, this separation she is about to propose, to test their feelings. Then if they still feel the same way in several months, they could begin discussing a more permanent arrangement, since obviously one of them would have to make an enormous geographic sacrifice. Only they are both clever enough to know that it wouldn't be Nicholas Tressa who relocated his contracting business to Paris, France, renovating lofts along the Seine. Or, if his reaction was harsh, and he alluded to the fact that she had no intention all along of wanting to make a stable life with him, she would employ a more sophisticated tone. Millions of people have affairs where they meet several times a year and it makes things even more exciting since boredom doesn't ever have the chance of creeping into the relationship. Or the bed. But looking at him now as he stands at the foot of that bed, freshly showered, a towel wrapped around his waist, smelling of lemon or lime, with those creases on either side of his mouth when he smiles, his eyes so expressive and loving, Gabriella wants to buckle under and forget the whole idea.

"This isn't going to make your mother leap up from her wheelchair, you know," he argues with infuriating calm, "and it's not going to make your daughter suddenly decide to give you the mother-of-the-year award. Leaving me isn't going to accomplish anything more than making you delude yourself into believing you're paying some kind of price for all the terrible things you did and making me miserable. Is that what you want?"

She has already thought of all the answers and all the reasons. "No." Brilliant beginning.

"Then I don't get it," he says, already dressed in a

pair of jeans and a shirt, unbuttoned and billowing out as he slips on some loafers.

She begins to pace around the bedroom in circles then, half-dressed. "I'll be back for Christmas and New Year's and other holidays and then you could come over to visit me. It's really beautiful in Paris in the spring. And in the summer, it's practically deserted except for the tourists, and I could show you places that no one's heard about, restaurants or streets." A travelogue. A tour guide. A member of the French Chamber of Commerce.

He doesn't respond, merely turns to walk out of the bedroom, buttoning his shirt as he takes two steps at a time downstairs. She follows him, tripping occasionally. Exit one dumb broad, she thinks as she finds herself standing in the living room where it all began.

"Nick, please," she says, tears beginning again, "please understand. I owe this to Dina."

"How the hell is going back to Paris going to do anything for Dina?"

"She'll come," she says with surprising conviction. "After all, it's Paris. Who wouldn't?"

"And if she doesn't?"

"Then we'll work something else out." She falters only slightly. "But that's not likely. But that's only part of it. The main thing is that I can't trust this thing with us, I can't really believe that this time it's going to be different."

"Different than what?"

"Different than all the other times when things like this never worked out the way they were supposed to, when I actually believed that I would live happily ever after." One disappointment after another, one loss followed more loss, the most basic things taken from her without warning.

"I can't be responsible for all those other times."

"Apparently neither can I," she replies with a trace of irony.

"Will you try sticking to us and forgetting about the

past? Just try and explain why you're so intent upon leaving, because so far I haven't heard one logical or valid reason from you.''

But how to explain that she has changed without dredging up her mother and her daughter and her baby and her ex-husband. How can she simply tell him that perhaps he has the misfortune of knowing her a little too late in life. Except that the misfortune is also hers, and it isn't even necessarily a question of too late or too early for that matter. Perhaps it's only that he caught her off guard, for she never knew she was still capable of such intense feelings for another human being. Not since her mother and her daughter and her baby and her ex-husband all cost her a little bit of self-assurance that maybe she would live happily ever after. But so what if the dream collapsed, because there he is right this very moment, standing in front of a wing chair in his living room, arms crossed over his chest, and waiting.

''Well, are you going to come up with one good reason why you're going to wreck two perfectly good lives here?''

She looks up then, her face tortured. ''Please, why can't you understand?''

''Because I'm in love with you,'' he says simply.

''Then let me go and let's both see what happens.''

''I'm not stopping you.''

''Then tell me it's not over if I leave.''

''No.''

''But you're not being fair, Nick,'' she argues, ''you can't just walk into my life and expect me to turn everything upside down for you.''

''It's debatable who walked into whose life and turned it upside down. Don't you think my life's changed since I met you?''

''Of course, but why does it have to be me who changes jobs and homes and countries?''

''Because you don't belong there, Gabriella, you belong here. It's not like you're French and I was trying to rip you away from your culture."

"Nationality has little to do with it. I've got other reasons for being there."

"But don't you think you have more reasons for being here?"

"I'm not sure if I'm ready to make you a reason," she confesses, "I need time."

"Well, if it's not for me then how about making Dina a reason?"

"That's not fair!"

"You're right, it's not."

She is disarmed for the moment. "Maybe we should both try to be more tolerant," she reasons.

"Maybe it's hard to be tolerant right now."

"I love you, Nick," she offers once again as if it will make a difference when she's gone, "but I can't forget about what I need to do with my life because if I do forget, I'll end up resenting you. Just give me time."

"You've got all the time in the world, you don't need me to give it to you," he says, glancing off to the side. "I just don't know if I do."

She bites her lip thoughtfully. "I've done the sacrifice bit once and the victim bit lots of times. Now I've got to work it out so that loving you doesn't make me hate myself."

"Gabriella, I don't get it, I just don't get it. How the hell can you manage to make something that could be so simple so damn complicated?"

"Because I'm not simple," she says angrily, "and this whole situation isn't simple. In fact," she adds in a calmer tone, "there's no such thing as simple when it comes to two people involved in a relationship unless one of them is catatonic, and I don't intend that person to be me."

His tone is filled with sadness when he answers, "Come on, I'll drive you to East Hampton."

They ride in silence to Pete's house on Egypt Lane in

East Hampton where Nick stops the car several yards from the entrance to the driveway. There is something in Gabriella's throat, a lump, a regret, or a tear, so that when she speaks it is with a flatness of tone that is foreign even to her. "I'm not going back up to Connecticut until tomorrow morning," she says, her expression hopeful, "so we could see each other tonight."

Slowly then, without aggression, he leans across the seat to open the door. "No thanks, Gabriella," he replies not without rancor, "I don't need another memory, I've got enough to last me a lifetime."

CHAPTER EIGHT

The Discovery

THE HOUSE ON EGYPT LANE holds no special memories for Gabriella because Pete bought it only recently, right after the separation actually, as if to show her what she could have had, had she stuck it out, or what she would be missing, or what he could do without her. Not that she hadn't been out here before this, once when there was an oppressive heat wave in the city and Pete had to go out of town on business and Dina had insisted that they spend the weekend at the beach and Gabriella had agreed, less for the weather than to satisfy her own curiosity.

As she wanders through the house, she notes with a touch of amusement that it is as sterile and impersonal in its decor as an expensive suite in a midwestern motel. But more than for its almost fearfully sparse surroundings, Gabriella has no feelings of loss here, no nostalgic sentiments of regret. The house is merely a structure that for Gabriella holds no sign of any past or present. For nothing ever began or ended here for them, no history or distant echoes of laughter to remind her of happier times, when perhaps they had dreamed of building something together. It is with a sense of relief that she wanders through the rooms, because maybe if it had been another way it would have been unbearable to come here now, to overcome yet another regret.

There was nothing really specific about Claire's instructions, although she did mention that any files pertaining to the house and insurance were more likely to be found in the second floor study. Gabriella climbs the thickly carpeted steps to the landing, opens the door and stops to consider where the best place is to begin. There are no visible handles or knobs, no hinges or handles in the entire house, since it was purposely designed as a study in camouflage—everything was built-in. She runs her hand along each wall of the room and finally manages to find a place on two of the panels which, when pressed, causes a pair of double doors to spring open.

Two large filing cabinets are revealed, as well as a slide-out metal tray that holds Pete's computer underneath a large television set, compact disc player, and speakers. Another light touch on the opposite panel and another set of doors is released, disclosing a large walk-in closet containing rows of Pete's clothes. While Gabriella is surprised by the quantity of items in his wardrobe, she is almost drawn to the neatly labeled files in the adjoining cabinets. A quick glance through them confirms that they are indeed filled with insurance policies, the deed for the house, warranties for appliances, registration for the car, mortgage and banking information, paid bills, unpaid bills, and two additional files, one marked *photographs* and the other marked *personal.*

Gabriella reaches first for the manila folder with the snapshots, but she has no sooner picked it up than it slips through her fingers. An assortment of pictures tumbles to the floor; some black and white snaps that are clearly years old, and other more recent ones in color. Dina as a baby, Gabriella with Dina as a toddler, mother and daughter leaning into a birthday cake with three flickering candles, Pete with Dina in a playground, Pete's parents in their backyard, and then his father alone standing behind a smoldering barbecue, each of them lying in his and her respective caskets in different years but in the same state of lifelessness. A sequence in sepia then, of Pete and Gabriella's first apartment, their first car, their first house; a crack in the sidewalk in front of that house, how well she remembers that, where Pete fell off his bicycle and injured his knee and how determined he had been to sue the town of Freeport. More photographs of innocuous mountains and blue skies from several unidentifiable vacations until, at the bottom of the pile, are a couple of pictures of Claire and Harry in bathing suits—one of them waving into the camera, the other diving into a crowded swimming pool. Turning the folder over so the remaining photographs fall onto her lap, Gabriella looks at them quickly before picking up the folder marked *personal.*

Why she instinctively sits down in a chair before taking out the contents of that file is something she may never know. But as she begins to go through the letters and documents it's probably a good thing that she did. How typical of Pete to make copies of everything, letters written to him as well as correspondence that he wrote to others. Even notes to Dina's teachers or innocuous messages to the maid were photocopied and stuck somewhere among the household records. It was absolutely guileless of Claire to have asked her to sift through all of this, Pete's personal life, but it was naïve of Gabriella to imagine that she wouldn't stumble upon something that would completely shock her.

She knew it, yet there is something about actually seeing it, even though the letter she holds in her hand is a photocopy, that brings her closer to the brink of rage than it does to sorrow. Reading it now, it's as if an unseen hand keeps delivering blow after blow with each word. It is absolutely stupefying to learn just how far Pete had been prepared to go for revenge—this man whom she loved and married, who fathered Dina, who shared her life for seventeen years, and who still holds a permanent place in her memory. And the fact that he happens to be dead offers no consolation either, for it only deprives her of fulfilling this overwhelming fantasy of strangling him with her own bare hands.

He writes about someone named Daria Kelley, a twenty-one-year-old woman who lives on Woodland Place in Great Neck, Long Island, with her father, Timothy, a political consultant, and her mother, Marianne, an elementary school teacher. Gabriella's daughter. Pausing for a moment, she marvels at the seeming insignificance of the words to describe this decent yet quite ordinary family. Yet as she digests each piece of information that Pete so meticulously compiled, it's as if she has just discovered the definitive floor plan of heaven and hell.

Gabriella continues to read, learning that there is another adopted child, a brother named Timothy, Jr., who seems to have suffered some kind of genetic kidney ailment and who even received a donor organ, a boy Gabriella will never meet but whose illness undoubtedly affected his sister, Daria, as well as the other members of the Kelley family, people who are total strangers to Gabriella yet whose lives are suddenly intertwined with hers. More then about Daria's scholastic record. She's a good student, according to the reports, although it stuns her how Pete managed to obtain that information as well. It seems she attends Fordham University on a full scholarship, majoring in English, and is due to graduate this June. More information about summer jobs, a counselor at a camp in Maryland, an internship at a television station, and a change-of-address card from the post office when Daria moved out briefly from her parents' house to live with a couple of roommates near school. Gabriella's daughter. A human being she relinquished before knowing, a baby she signed out of her life even before it exited her body. But the more she thinks and considers the words and facts and revelations that appear page after page in the file, paper after paper, the one emotion that seems to cancel out the rest is rage. At Pete.

Throughout all the years, Gabriella's feelings never wavered whenever she allowed herself to think about what she had done. The same reactions always surfaced each time—fear and guilt—although not necessarily in that order.

In the beginning, when she first found herself pregnant, she experienced pangs of sheer terror that the nuns would find out or, worse, her father. Later on, after enough time had elapsed where any possibility of discovery became negligible, guilt set in, a deep-down gnawing at her conscience that she had made a terrible mistake and should have kept the baby to raise herself, that perhaps the adoptive parents were less than ideal.

Recently that same fear had returned in a different way. Gabriella began dreading that something terrible would happen to Dina almost as a kind of reprisal, as if by having given up one baby, the other would be snatched from her as well. So it was with a certain Solomonic relief that Gabriella accepted Dina's decision to leave her. Almost as if her worst fears of losing her had come true yet not in a more tragic way that she had envisioned.

Burying her face in her hands now, she allows herself to weep and mourn her loss even if still there is no one with whom she can share it. Not even with the only other living person who knows. Dina. But when she stops crying to wipe her face and blow her nose, it occurs to her that what is even more shocking than Pete's meticulous invasion of the Kelley family is that he wrote it all out in a letter to his own daughter. And as Gabriella rereads it line by line, over and over again until every last word is embedded in her head, she only feels one emotion. She is overwhelmed by the temptation to rush to the phone to call Nick for comfort; to say that she's changed her mind, to tell him that it's no good without him, to admit that she's made a mistake—perhaps all the wrong reasons for wanting him so desperately right now. All wrong if she didn't also happen to have this powerful urge to admit that she loves him too much to leave him.

Instead she walks slowly out of the study, down the stairs and into the living room where the sun streams through the window, busy making everything appear so bright and cheery. Clutched in her hand is a photograph of

Pete when he was young and not so cruel, before the pressures of life and love weighed on him to do something terrible to get back at her. Sitting down on the couch, she studies the snap more closely. It is still inconceivable that Pete is really gone, dead, far from her reach to berate him for having done to them what is unforgivable. Yet as the minutes pass Gabriella finds that she grieves for them more than she grieves for him, more than she might have grieved had they parted without incident, an uncontested divorce by mail without issue that had no venal potential. But in their case it had been more complicated, something that brought out the worst in each of them. Seventeen years of intimacy that in the end was reduced to repeated battles in family court until a sweep of a pen destroyed those last bonds and habit.

Yet Gabriella had been an accomplice, nurturing Pete's troubled spirit, encouraging his restlessness that carried with it so much danger and destruction, by allowing it to go on for all the years they were together. But she had no way of knowing back then that she was contributing to her own demise. And then he died, taking everyone by surprise, but most of all those who had a score to settle, emotional debtors of a bankrupt cause.

Perhaps it was unfair to blame Pete at all for having deprived her of the last word or any word at all, for that matter, on subjects that concerned them both. Throughout their entire life together she gave him the impression that she was content to grope her way with his rules, accept his excuses, bask in his brilliance and pleasure, and never dare to complain or even point out that she was in the process of building her own set of values. In the end she tried for a smattering of recognition or dignity, but by then it was too late for she had long since relinquished her right to audition for another part. And now all that was left, at least the one emotion that overpowered the others, was a reluctance to trust herself to make another choice that could end in as rotten a relationship.

She remains lost in thought about her life, events that are impossible to change, until her mind settles on Nick. Suddenly she needs to talk to him, to ask him to come to her. She walks slowly to the telephone and dials his number, gathering her courage as she waits for him to answer. But when he does and when she actually speaks into the receiver, her voice sounds so remote for she has already retreated behind that familiar wall of her own making, the one that hides all the pain and regret.

The vision of Nick's black Alpha Romeo Spider as it creeps up the gravel driveway is already embedded in her memory. She watches as he emerges, his legs on the ground before his body unfolds from behind the leather steering wheel. Khaki trousers, a light blue oxford shirt, loafers without socks, the entire package that is him has already educated her into what would be an enormous loss—one of a kind in her life—if she was dumb enough to let him go. Trapped by her own tension and distress, she hangs back and stares at him, the concern and desire so clear on his face, until a spark of energy propels her into his arms.

"What happened, Gaby?"

She takes a deep breath before plunging. "I need you," she says, and then adds for already she is in a negotiation, "at least for now but it doesn't matter, does it?" When he nods in agreement, she issues the first warning, "Don't do this because you feel sorry for me because it doesn't change anything." She leans against him, her instinct on high performance, and asks in a small voice, "Make love to me."

He hesitates only an instant before gathering her even closer to him. He is a man too smart to hawk his wares, yet he has been through their routine enough times to know their primary bond. Turning away, he unbuttons his shirt before casually tossing the pillows from the couch to the floor. "I must be pretty secure to be called up like this, don't you think?" But the expression isn't anything except loving and kind.

— 219 —

"I can't remember when I didn't love you," she begins, flooded suddenly with a thousand other thoughts that are hard to remember as well. She has never made love in this house although somehow it is a place that joins several of her lives.

He is familiar, every man she ever loved or made love to in her life; Kevin without the consequence, Pete without the ending, and all the others in between who briefly entered her body and even more briefly her heart. If she thought the excitement would diminish after all the pulling and pushing that kept their end constantly in sight, she was wrong. And even now it doesn't escape her that he knows exactly what it takes, that little trick of his of withdrawing just a bit whenever she rises to the occasion, just barely enough to make her want to crawl inside his skin to capture him completely. And when he allows her to go, she finds herself once more in that familiar open field taking in large gulps of air that reach somewhere she will never see. But now he climbs a series of steps, she can always tell, having politely waited for her to reach the top before he does. With fluttery fingers she counts the vertebrae on his back, considering he has never been second or third in her life, always first even from the beginning. Several damp strands of hair stick to her face as she piles the rest on top of her head, watching him closely before she hears herself saying, "I love you." But then, just as suddenly, it has all disappeared, without any possible distraction to forget about all the other pain, and she finds herself back to the beginning of the story.

"What's the matter?" he asks, aware of her change.

The whole rotten world, she wants to reply. "I found some papers upstairs in his files that explain a lot."

"About Dina?"

"About Dina."

"Do you want to tell me?"

She sighs. "No, not really, only that we had secrets that should have stayed secrets—things I told Pete before we got married that I believed he had a right to know." A pause. "Only I thought we were going to spend our whole lives together and I thought he would never tell anyone."

"So you were wrong on both counts."

"Will you wait for me?" she asks suddenly.

"While you do what?"

"While I get rid of all my wounded skin and try to grow another one so we can live happily ever after."

"Why do you have to be alone to do that?"

"Because I've got to finish what I've started."

"Dina?"

"Dina and Paris and my work and my own craziness adjusting to the fact that I may end up where I started out."

"Is that so bad?"

"Right now it's gone from unbearable to bad to scary. I'm waiting for it to pass through tolerable and then into no problem." She smiles vaguely. In her mind's eye, though, she sees herself in his arms being comforted while he asks for nothing in return—like a commitment. Such an eighties word, she considers as she sits up to study the lawn outside the window.

"Look, I'm easy when it comes to most things," he says not without a touch of humor, "but you're asking for something that makes me fundamentally miserable. You're asking me to keep loving you but let you go until you decide what you're going to do about us." He clasps his hands behind his head. "And that's crazy."

"And you're asking me to change my entire life for you. What about my job? Let's just consider that for a minute."

His tone changes to definite. "You can't do both as completely as you'd like to think. There can't be a total commitment to your work and a real desire to make this work because it's going to take its toll. One of the two is going to suffer."

"Just play at working to pass the time until you come home—is that it?"

— 221 —

"No, Gaby, that's not it. How about just finding a job that doesn't take you halfway across the world. How about making up your mind that you want to work this out with me, with us, so that when you call me to tell me which way my life is going, it'll be a local call." And there is no smile now.

"I should have known," she says. "I should have known it would boil down to this in the end."

But he isn't listening. "Because being with you takes up half my life—hours thinking about it before and then hours wondering after if I'm ever going to see you again or if you're going to announce that your flight is leaving to-night."

"Did it ever occur to you that you're behaving like a stereotypical male?" Traces of temper that she can't keep in check. "You take up half my life too, you know, because I'm always worried that being with you is going to cost me everything else. All you know how to do is give ultimatums or choices except they never seem to protect anyone but you."

He is relentless. "So why don't you use this time to figure it all out."

"And why don't you use it to read up on what's been happening this last decade or two between men and women."

"Gaby," he cautions, "this isn't a macro disagreement, this is very specific. But you're wrong anyway because nothing's changed when it comes to feelings between men and women and priorities."

Halfway to panic, she considers hightailing it into the bathroom, slamming the door, and hoping that by the time she exits, he will have disappeared. Left. Gone. Out of her life. Along with all those other memories buried upstairs in Pete Molloy's files. For suddenly Gabriella loves Nick without hope. "Something has changed in relationships if you add a feeling called respect, but you wouldn't know about that because you're Italian."

He shakes his head, his eyes soft. "Wrong, Gaby, it's just logical that one of us has to give in."

"So that person has to be me because I'm a woman?"

"No, because you don't know what's going to make you happy in the long run and I do." He reaches for her hand. "We've got this thing for each other though, don't we?" He presses it to his lips. "Where we can't seem to stay away from each other."

She can only nod. "Yes."

"So it's a shame that it doesn't begin and end there because it would make it easier for both of us," he adds gently.

Healthy about this and little else, she smiles slightly. "Maybe it'll wear off."

"Don't get your hopes up."

He is already dressed, but then so is she. "How about a walk in Greenwich Village?"

"What about work?"

"It'll wait," he says, his arms around her.

"This is like trying to kick a drug habit," she observes, sinking down into a chair, her eyes locked with his. But it's almost useless to point out that it would take courage for her to stay, more than she possesses right now, more than he has a right to expect. "Maybe a walk in the Village would raise your consciousness," she jokes.

"I'm willing to try," he says, joking back, "since I'm looking for answers."

"And I'm looking for reasons," she says, "to keep this thing going even though you're unbelievably selfish."

□

SoHo is crowded with locals, which is why they dress without interest or color, more Uptown than Downtown since tourists are usually the ones who deck themselves in what they perceive will fit into the surroundings. Gabriella and Nick wander, holding hands, down West Broadway, peering into windows, stopping at several jewelry stores to admire earrings sculpted by Ralph or Erica or someone else they apparently should have heard about but haven't. He offers to buy her a pair that are fashioned like fans, but she declines, a silver cuff perhaps, but she refuses, amber beads, but she is almost out the door before he insists upon a cappuccino, which she accepts happily, an arm linked through his as they head toward the café at the corner.

She once worried that Nick wouldn't travel well from one continent to another to fit in without making either of them look like hicks. That was back when she harbored fantasies about a long-distance affair, one that crossed the ocean from time to time. There would be romantic dinners in the Mairie, she envisioned, or walks along Trocadero, or hamburgers on the Upper West Side, or strolls along Jones Beach—all before love and marriage and real feelings got in the way to ruin everything.

Spooning the foam from the cappuccino into her mouth, she stalls before plunging. "When I was a kid I used to come down here. I had this fantasy that my mother was an artist and my father was a musician." She smiles. "And we lived in this loft overlooking Greene Street near where my father played the clarinet—never the drums, because Italians always played drums or at least that's what I thought. Anyway, that was my fantasy, my dream of the perfect family."

"How often did you come down here?"

"Every chance I had, which was mostly on weekends. I'd hang around MacDougal Street or Bleecker Street looking like a ghoul with my lips painted white and black lines around my eyes so I'd be a cross between a ghoul and a raccoon. And then I'd wear these copper bracelets with hammer marks all the way up my arm to my elbow, so at the end of the day my arm would be green. What I really looked like was pathetic, a kid from the suburbs who was looking for a bearded experience or an infusion of left-wing wisdom." They both laugh.

"Did your father approve?"

"He never knew because I'd have my Village outfit stuffed into a knapsack so I'd change on the train and then change back again before I got home."

"That must have been in the late sixties," Nick said, calculating, "so the Village was changing by then, wasn't it?"

"Maybe, but I didn't know it because I had no basis for comparison even though later on I found out that the Village I had read about was already gone, so you're right about that. I suppose I was ten years too late if you're talking about Joyce Johnson's Village or Jack Kerouac or Ginsberg's, or even Abby Hoffman's Village. It sort of went from that to Warhol to Bay Ridge within a matter of seconds." They laugh again even if by then there is more than amusement in his eyes. There is an incredible tenderness in his tone when he asks, "Did you make friends there?"

"Not really, it was pretty disappointing even if I did make one friend who in my limited world was sort of a celebrity. He was the guy who loaded Scavullo's cameras during shoots."

"Why was Freeport so terrible to you?"

"Not terrible, just nothing. There wasn't anything to do except hang out, except in the summer when everybody went to the beach. But nine months out of the year it was depressing, like the Riviera in January where all you see are a couple of tattered beach umbrellas blowing around on the sand or bits of garbage from an overturned trash bin or broken chairs flying around in the wind, and those same people who go to places like that off-season because it's cheap and walk around trying to imagine what it's like when the rates are high."

"So you moved to France to re-create what you missed in the Village?"

"I've never quite thought of it like that, but in a way you're right. France, or Paris, is ten years behind New York except when it comes to fashion, and then only a handful of Texans really care since they're the only ones who can afford to buy the clothes.'' She smiles. ''But I even got there too late, after Lena Horne and Lennie Hayton and Josephine Baker, later than Hemingway and Frankenthaler. I did it when it wasn't so chic.''

''So what happens next?''

Perhaps deliberately she chooses to misunderstand the question. ''So I graduated from high school with the usual traumas and went on to a junior college but only because my father forced me to. I didn't care about going. All I cared about was going back into the city and hanging out in the Village, only by then all the photographers moved their lofts to the East Twenties and Thirties. But it was too late anyway, because Pete came along and he was the most exciting person I'd ever met, so I married him.''

''That's not exactly what I meant,'' he says, smiling at her synopsis of a life. ''What I meant was what happens after Paris or do you just stay there and wait for the tide to turn back again so it's chic to live there again?''

''Each decade has something different and sometimes one is like the other. For instance, the eighties were like the fifties, so maybe the nineties will be more like the sixties. At least we can hope.''

''The biggest mistake you make is to obliterate your past instead of building on it, taking the positive parts to grow and the negative ones to learn from.''

''You don't grow by staying put and being blind or content. You've got to keep moving on and changing your life.''

''But you don't grow by running away.''

''What do you suggest I do?'' she asks, annoyance creeping into her tone. ''Go back to the beginning and just give up?''

''Why is that giving up if you live in a familiar place?''

She chooses her words prudently. ''Everything that happened here was a nightmare,'' she says slowly, ''beginning with my mother's illness and ending with my daughter's rejection.''

He reaches for her hand. "So, let me try to change all that."

Tears well up in her eyes. "You can't change anything, Nick, it's not up to you."

"Look, maybe I can't undo the damage that's already been done, but I can offer you a better life in the future, in the same place."

The tears run down her cheeks and several people turn to look while she blots her eyes with a paper napkin. "It's not fair to you," she protests.

"Why's that?" he asks, pressing her hand to his lips.

"Because there's so much you don't know."

"Like what?"

"Things that Pete told Dina about me that shattered her faith and ruined our relationship."

"Do you want to tell me about them?"

"Yes, but I can't. It would only continue this pattern where I live by someone else's mercy. I've learned my lesson."

"But you're allowing your past to destroy your future."

"Maybe it's the price."

"For what?"

"For being less than perfect," she answers with a touch of cynicism.

"Dina might have been looking for an excuse."

"Of course she was, but she didn't have to look very far." She presses his hand to her lips. "Things aren't supposed to be easy between a mother and an adolescent daughter, it goes with the territory, only Pete didn't help it. He probably should've been supportive of me and encouraged Dina not to rebel instead of encouraging her to defy me and then eventually leave me to live with him."

"He was probably very hurt."

"We were all very hurt, so why did that give him an excuse? And more than hurt, Dina and I were scared, for different reasons but we were scared. I doubt that Pete was scared—hurt, bruised, angry, but not scared.''

"I'm not exactly defending him," Nick begins, "but he was probably as scared as you—for other reasons. It's not easy being dependent on all the things that being married does to a man, all the things that women hate to hear about.''

"You can't compare losing a wife the way you did to separating or divorcing.''

"The end result is the same, the adjustment from a man's point of view is the same. There's a balance in either situation where one person is the caretaker and the other is the one who is being taken care of. There's a period where a man just flounders, trying to decide whether he needs to find someone to protect or someone who's going to nurse his wounds, and that's scary.''

"What—not knowing which role he's going to play or wondering who is going to control whom?''

"That's not fair.''

"But it's true. A woman is scared because she's alone with a child or she's hurt and confused about what she did wrong that her husband, boyfriend, or whatever walked out, or she's scared because he's been supporting her and she's not financially independent. It's a luxury sometimes to dwell on the emotional wounds—women don't always have that luxury until later.''

"Is that where you are now—knee deep in emotional wounds?''

"I'm complicated," she evades.

"Don't you think I already know that? I realized that the first minute I saw you at the funeral.''

"Well, you tend to make everything a black and white issue.''

"Would you marry me if I complicated everything?''

"You do," she says quietly, "the wrong things. Like my life.''

"Is that a yes?"

"It's more like an observation."

"What do you want," he says very seriously. "I mean, deep down when everything else is pushed aside."

The question is unsettling. Reluctantly, she replies. "I suppose just to get over all the sadness and the loss beginning with my mother and ending with Pete. I never knew how to allow myself to be sad, and now all I want to do is feel it and then get over it so I can change lanes."

"Let's do it together," he offers, a ticket out of this stalemate.

For a moment she wants to accept, to smile and agree and share it all with him. Can a girl from Freeport, Long Island, give it all up—career, glamour, excitement, in Paris— and find happiness with a decent and sexy guy back home? But that's not the issue. If she really had all that glamour and excitement and a career that was as important as she would have him believe, there would have been a major dilemma. The truth was that none of that was so great and maybe that was why she held on to ward off something worse than loneliness or boredom. Maybe that dull nagging pain that she carried around in her heart and that cast a pall over something called her life was too familiar and comfortable and safe to give up. Yet to be loved like he claimed to love her was damaging to her passion for self-pity.

"I can't pretend to know what to do about it right now. I'd make a lousy wife at this stage, or at least until the word means something that isn't so negative." And she wants to tell him to run away almost as much as she wants to elicit the promise that he'll wait forever. "I don't want to be rescued," she proclaims stubbornly.

Several people turn to watch them as they get up and leave the restaurant. They stop briefly in front of the plate glass window to kiss, a long and passionate kiss that looks as if it will last forever. A couple who had been seated next to them in the restaurant have also exited and now walk past on their way to their car. Gabriella hears the man assuring his companion, "Another happy ending!"

□

"What's goin' on in there?" Sylvie bellows, hands on his hips as he stands in the middle of his vegetable garden and gestures to the house. "You think you can waltz in and outta here just like that, don't even tell when you're leavin' so I gotta hear you on the phone like a thief?" Gabriella has just walked outside to talk to her father.

"Please," she says calmly, "don't get excited. I was just about to explain everything to you so you'd understand why I've made this decision."

"Comin' to tell me after ain't exactly the way I woulda done it," he retorts, his tone one that commands instant attention.

"Let's sit down, Papa, somewhere we can talk."

"Only if you don't begin by announcin' that you'd made up your mind," he bargains, his voice barely above a whisper now, fists clenching and unclenching at his sides, his bearing as cautious as a boxer's circling his opponent in the ring before throwing the first punch, "because I ain't sittin' back this time while you make another one of your fantastic mistakes, you hear me, Gabriella?"

"I hear you," she answers, biting down on one corner of her lip. "If you listen, you'll understand this isn't a mistake."

"You ain't thinkin' clear, if you ask me," he replies, "it's *completemento pazzo, capice?*" Linking her arm through his, she leads him over to a redwood table and a group of chairs. "And one more thing, Gabriella, if you don't like what I'm sayin', you ain't gonna leave and run off to talk to your mother, you hear that too?" She nods, wondering just exactly how she can put it to make it more palatable, more logical, or simply just not as crazy as it sounds—even to her.

— 230 —

She is dressed up this afternoon, in a taupe cotton suit that was obviously designed in Paris with the jacket broad at the shoulders and long at the hem so that it almost reaches the skirt, which barely hits her knees. Her hair is freshly washed and fluffed around her perfectly madeup face, and she has borrowed her mother's love-knot gold earrings and linked necklace. Under the oak tree not far from the vegetable garden she sits, demurely, while her father motions to her attire. "Whaddya all dressed up for anyway?"

"You see, Papa, Adrienne has been staying with Dina at Pete's beach house." She pauses to take a breath. "And she's convinced Dina—finally—to let me come and take care of her until she's well enough to go back to school. She's making good progress, so she'll probably be able to go back after the weekend, at least that's what she said when I spoke to her yesterday." Another pause. "So that's why I made the reservation to go back." She twists and untwists her hands. "I've got to get back to work—things are really piling up there."

He listens but refuses to comment, except about the clothes. "So you got all dressed up for the kid?"

"Not exactly," Gabriella hesitates. "I thought I'd stop off to see Nick on my way to Pete's."

"Oh, yeah," Sylvie comments, watching her closely. "Does he know about you leavin' next week?"

"He knows I'm going back, but not when."

"And what's he gonna think about that?" he says, exploding.

She flinches. "Not much."

"I coulda told you that." He nods his head slowly, eyes narrowed although the gesture has nothing to do with either his understanding or approval of the situation from start to what is now apparently the finish. "Why're you doin' this?" he asks, his tone suddenly conciliatory.

"Because I live there and my job isn't going to wait forever!"

"Neither is Nick!"

"I didn't ask him to."

"So why you gonna see him?"

She colors. "To ask him."

"He ain't gonna put up with it, not for one minute, and by the time you're good and sorry it's gonna be too late."

"Then that's the way it'll be," she says almost defiantly, except her sagging shoulders and sad expression belie any optimism and strength needed to recover from this self-inflicted wound. "At least let me handle it," she adds gently, reaching out to touch her father's arm, not prepared for his abrupt movement away from her.

"Because you're too dumb to know what's good for you!"

"Thanks," she says, taking the insult as an opportunity to retreat behind the hurt and confusion.

"And the kid," he then says in a softer tone, "what about the kid?"

She tries a brave smile. "I'd like Dina to come over after the term finishes. It's a wonderful opportunity. She can learn French and experience a different culture and we can patch things up with no interference from anyone else. She can spend the year abroad."

He stares at her in disbelief. "And what if she don't wanna come over, then what?"

"Then she can come over for holidays."

"And what if she don't wanna do that neither?"

Her voice is no longer steady. "Look, if she's not going to want to see me, if that's what you mean, then it's going to be a lot less painful for me to live over there than it'll be over here when I'm so close to her."

"Gabriella," he says with extraordinary patience, "I'm gonna tell you somethin' and you're gonna listen because maybe you're still in shock over Pete or Dina's accident, but you're thinkin' crazy!"

"Please," she warns, a tinge of hysteria creeping into

her tone, "this is the way it's going to be." But the ending falls flat somehow.

"I'm talkin'."

She loses control then, seemingly unable to catch her breath as the tears begin. "Don't do this, don't make it harder than it is. I've got to go home."

"This is home."

"Not anymore it isn't."

"You think over there with them frogs is home?"

"I've got a job over there," she says wearily.

"You do what I say," he orders, even though he knows he lost the right to order her around. It happened right before she left for Paris, nearly two years ago, when he awoke one morning to the startling realization that his only child was approaching forty, which made him aware that he was a lot closer to death than he was to birth. "All I'm talkin' is an obligation to yourself to make a life, that's all I ever talked, *es verro* or no?" A look that passes between them makes it clear that each understands what that "life" is all about.

"Papa, if you ever told me you needed me here for Mama, I'd stay."

He glances at her while he produces a cigar from his shirt pocket, clips one end of it, holds the piece between two fingers for a moment or two to examine it before tossing it away. "It ain't for Mama," he says slowly, "it's for you. You gotta stop runnin' around tryin' to be somethin' you ain't because you're no kid no more and most women your age don't get second and third chances, just remember that."

She smiles slightly. "You know, for someone who lives in another world and in another time, you certainly think you know a lot about women today!"

A lighter from another pocket appears in Sylvie's right hand. "Yeah, well nothin's changed, things are the same today like when I was your age, nothin's changed!" Settling back in his chair, he runs the flame from the metal

Zippo along the flat end of the cigar before putting it in his mouth to light it. "The most important thing now, whether you gonna believe it or not, is not Dina."

"How can you say that?"

"Because she's goin' through a stage, you read about it in book and what that *stronzo* put in her head didn't help none." He holds up his hand, the ashes from the cigar sprinkling over his pants leg. "But she's no rocket scientist neither or she wouldna bought all that crap he fed her!" He gestures again, this time knocking the ashes all over his shirt. "Nah, what's important right now, even for her, is somethin' else." He leans back in his chair. "So when you started shackin' up with Frank Tressa's son—"

"Papa," she cries, more embarrassed than outraged, "that's not exactly what happened."

But he waves her quiet. "Look, I ain't mad." He touches her cheek tenderly, "so just listen. I didn't say nothin' about you and him 'cause I knew you was a good girl and he was a decent guy and not some kinda creep that woulda used you and then tossed you out. We talked about it, me and Rocco, we knew what was happenin' these past few weeks, and I said, let it be, they're good kids and you watch, they're gonna have a big surprise for us soon." He tries a smile. "And it's kinda on account of my givin' my word to Rocco on account of his bein' the oldest and on account that we both knew Frank and all his cronies, and so help me they still come around the place to drink, that I let it go. But you know, Gabriella, they began askin', hey what's this about Nick and Gabriella—a weddin' they kept on hintin'."

Amazed, she blurts out. "How did they even know about us?"

"They know, that's all," he says. "It's a small town, Freeport, and even though Nick, he lives in Sag Harbor now, he's still one of us, you know, second generation like you."

"Now you know why I want to leave," she says sullenly.

"Look, Gabriella, it's the same all over, in all them fancy places, men gossip and they gossip about women and that's the point. A guy shafts a broad and he's gotta talk about it, and no matter what you gonna tell me about times changin', they ain't changin' when it comes to that, you hear. Women got the upper hand every time until they . . ." He turns red.

"Until what?" she presses, unbelieving that they have settled into a conversation about something that was never discussed. Sex.

"Until they sleep with a guy, so the point is you can't dump him, Gabriella, because then everybody's gonna think he dumped you and how's that gonna make me and Rocco look?"

"I'll get a note from him, how's that?"

He smiles then at the sarcasm, a beautiful smile that exposes his beautiful teeth. "Very funny, Gabriella, except it ain't gonna work."

"I can't believe this," she says, getting up to pace. "It's not that you're mad at me for coming home and having an . . ." And now she turns red. "An affair," she blurts out. "Oh, no, it's not that simple." She whirls around to face him before sinking down on her knees before his chair. "Now I'm responsible for your reputation with the guys at the restaurant."

"If you weren't gonna marry him you shouldn't have done it here."

"You're right, you know that, Papa, you're right."

"Listen, Gabriella," he says suddenly, his attitude changed as he waves his hand to dismiss the apology, "you love him?"

She is sitting on a chair facing him now when she replies without any hesitation. "Yes."

He slaps his forehead. "So what's to be sorry? What's

the problem? *No che problema.* You love him, he loves you, you ain't married, he ain't married, he's Italian, you're Italian—*perfecto.*''

''So simple, Papa,'' she says sadly as she gets up to lean against a tree, ''only it's not that simple. There're other things to consider.''

''Yeah, like what for instance?'' She opens her mouth to speak but he interrupts. ''And don't make Dina the reason because she's got her own life.''

''It's not just Dina,'' she says honestly.

''I know what it is.''

''What?''

He also stands, wearily, and shades his eyes as he waves to Rocco who pushes Audrey toward them. ''Here comes your mother and uncle but I'll tell you the reason.'' He takes several steps toward her to gather her in his arms. ''You're afraid of losin' again and, you know what, you gotta play the odds and after all that's happened around here, the odds gotta be in your favor!''

Rocco bends down to secure the brake on Audrey's wheelchair.

''Hi, Mama,'' Gabriella says, kissing her on the brow. ''Hi, Uncle Rocco.''

''*Bella,* you gotta date?''

''Go on,'' Sylvie commands suddenly, ''tell him.''

''I'm going out to the beach to stay with Dina for a while.''

''That's nice,'' he says absently. ''When're you comin' home?''

''After the weekend if she's all right.''

''Go on, tell,'' Sylvie repeats.

''And then I'm going back to Paris.''

''That's a lousy idea,'' Rocco judges. ''Paris is no place for you.''

''See that,'' Sylvie exclaims, ''what'd I tell you?''

''And I'm gonna tell you why,'' he wheezes, ''because you ain't gonna meet anyone there to marry and you wanna know why? Because you're an outsider, that's why. And I'll tell you somethin' else, Gabriella, that worries me—you livin' over there with all them bombs."

"What bombs?" she asks but knows only too well. Ten terrorist attacks in ten days, in movie theaters, restaurants, on the streets. She had the photographs of the women who walked into the boutiques on the Champs Élysées to buy shoes and were carried out without legs.

"Those bastards make the Cosa Nostra look like choirboys," Rocco says angrily, "only the Mafia never hurt innocent people, never used anyone outside to make the world pay attention to them. The way those creeps operate is nothin' but chicken, the worst kind of scum hits like that and then bolts." To Rocco Carlucci, putting a bomb in a shopping center is like farting in an elevator even if he refrains from explaining it exactly like that to his niece. "A coward," he adds contemptuously, "because the only person who knows who done is the person who done it." But a fart disintegrates while a bomb leaves a mound of rubble and broken bodies and scattered limbs. "I see pictures on television." He turns around to spit. "You just go back there Gabriella and pack up all your things and then turn right around and come home. You settle down and do it with a decent guy like Nick Tressa."

"*Ecco*, that's the point." Sylvie nods.

"Because if you don't, some bimbo's gonna grab him up and start knockin' out his babies before either of you knows what hit you."

"See, whadda I tell you?" Sylvie asks before he turns to Rocco. "You gonna go inside now 'cause I gotta prepare all the medicines for you and Audrey."

"You go ahead and begin, Papa," Gabriella rushes, "and I'll stay out here for a few minutes with Mama before I bring her inside." She kisses her father and uncle and then waits until they are out of earshot before she turns to her mother. "So, I don't have to tell you what Papa said because you've heard it before, about me staying here and settling down." Audrey looks especially lovely today in a yellow sundress, her hair pulled back, her eyes clear and alert, her mouth set so that the corners seem to turn up, as if she has just finished smiling. Gabriella looks at her a moment. "You'd want to know if I loved him, right? And would you believe me if I told you that I fell in love with him at Pete's funeral?" Audrey is watching her daughter very closely, her expression brighter than usual, or is it Gabriella's imagination? Taking one of her mother's hands, she holds it, sitting down on the grass once again. "But all I can think of is that I'm making a horrible mistake, because when was the last time I didn't make a horrible mistake, and then I think that something terrible will happen because it did to you and then to me when Dina left, so that's why I'm leaving." She rests her head on Audrey's lap. "It's not that I'm just a lousy mother, is it," she whispers. "It's just that I haven't gotten this daughter thing out of the way yet." Tears then. "So maybe all I learned was to be your mother and not how to be a mother to my own child." Wiping her eyes, she tries to smile a bit. "I love you," she says softly, "and it's always better after we talk."

They sit quietly, mother and daughter, for a while longer, Gabriella moving only to swat a fly that keeps buzzing around Audrey's head, Audrey shifting slightly in her chair as the sun moves in the sky, its rays shining in her eyes. Gabriella stands to position the wheelchair more in the shade. "I've got to go soon, Mama," she says. "I promised to be there before five, and it's almost two now." Audrey turns her head toward the sound of her daughter's voice. "I'm going to stop off to see Nick," she says, "if he'll see me." She begins to push her slowly toward the house, the next visit back home already on her mind. "Time goes by quickly," she comforts her, "so before you know it, it'll be Thanksgiving and we'll see each other again." But somehow, for the first time in all the years that Gabriella Carlucci and then Gabriella Carlucci-Molloy has been running away, it doesn't seem to help to imagine time passing quickly. Not now.

On One Hand

Even from a distance as he stands in the middle of the construction site, Nick Tressa looks more tense than he has in years, since Bonnie's illness to be precise. Hands on his hips, muscular arms bare and suntanned and protruding from a white short-sleeved cotton shirt, he appears to be surveying the progress of the job. Or lack of it, he thinks grimly, his dark eyes squinting in the direction of the church, which has already been partially demolished. Walking over to inspect a crane that now sits idle, listing precariously over the excavation pit, Nick looks determined to find something wrong, as if an external catastrophe might justify this inner turmoil that he carries around lately—since they broke up or at least since they said they were breaking up or at least since the last time he saw her.

This past week he has devoted totally to work, buried himself in work could be a more accurate description actually, since he invented reasons to stay at the office until well into the night.

From early morning, before his crew even surfaced, to long after they knocked off at the end of the day and even during lunch breaks when everybody would disappear into the local coffee shop or diner, Nick could be seen lingering behind to walk the job or calculate costs, carry on a phone conference with one of his subcontractors, or anything else he could think up that would take time away from brooding.

The Baptist Church on Main Street in Freeport, which previously had been the Methodist Church until the town changed its demographics, was recently purchased by a successful Long Island developer whose plan was to regentrify the town—to attract upwardly mobile young couples who couldn't yet afford city rents or houses on the more chic North Shore but who also didn't object to being a special kind of suburban pioneer for the right price. Nick's first reaction had been somewhat cynical when he learned that his bid had come in the lowest to win the job. Construct a fantasy, he thought, so everybody can pretend that the surrounding poverty, misery, and decay doesn't exist. Not unlike what he had been doing since that last time with Gabriella, constructing another fantasy, going through the motions of sleeping, eating, talking, and anything else that was vital to living.

Kicking a stone so that it bounces off the side of a truck, he considers the insanity of the situation. How many times had they ended it, one or the other of them, or threatened to end it. How many times had he issued an ultimatum, and how many times had she claimed that she needed time, even if in the end neither of them believed that the other was capable of acting upon his words.

But that was before she walked out that last time, right before she delivered that brutal blow to his groin, bull's-eye to his scrotum, when she refused to undo and redo her entire life. Well, maybe he deserved it. After all, hadn't he treated women so shabbily after Bonnie? Putting them off, evading, avoiding, making excuses, pretending that it was more than it was until he would lower the boom to let them know that it had been nothing at all. Yet Gabriella was different, just as he thought he was different for her—they loved each other—so how could either of them just walk out and forget about everything they had together? A history, he laughs somewhere inside of his head, he thought they had a history—for a couple of weeks, some history. Who was he kidding?

Nick glances at his watch and sees that it's almost three o'clock, the guys should be back from lunch pretty soon since they knocked off late today. He runs his hand through his hair and shakes his head. So many signs that they'd be together forever though, that she'd just go back to Paris to close up the apartment and quit her job. But now he'd like to know where he got that false sense of security, that unwavering confidence, that things would work out—as if just because he loved her so much she had to love him back. Or maybe it all boiled down to his inability to imagine that he would be forced to sustain yet another loss in his life.

He replayed the time they spent together in his head constantly, but always came up with that same feeling of bewilderment about why it always seemed to be falling apart. And this time wasn't any different.

Sitting down under the aluminum awning that serves as a lean-to where his work table, a couple of folding chairs, and a wooden sawhorse with some blueprints on it, are all crammed together in that small space, he stretches out his long legs. That guy in Paris couldn't be the reason she's leaving New York, that's clear, because he's either unconscious or he doesn't like girls. "Is sex great with Pascal?" Nick asked her one night and could have ripped out his tongue.

"Sex isn't really a big thing with us," she answered, "because Pascal believes it would make me forget about learning new things."

"Do you agree with him?"

"Absolutely—sex is just not important anymore."

She used to say that in the very beginning of their relationship, maybe day number two, before she started to laugh at how ridiculous it was. By day number six she was completely trapped since sex had obviously become as integral a part of them as breathing, even if it had nothing to do with loving each other, even if they managed to practice it with marathon regularity without either of them losing their sensibilities.

Nick stands up slowly and walks out from under the shading of the lean-to when he notices his foreman, Don D'Apello, heading toward him.

"Hey, Nick," the man calls out, "I've got a message for you."

Nick shades his eyes, unmoving, as he watches the heavy-set, balding foreman lumber up to him. "What's up?" he asks as D'Apello thrusts a crumpled piece of paper at him.

"I stopped by the office to pick up messages," he explains, "and you got a call from Sylvie Carlucci, wants you to call him back right away, says it's important!"

"Thanks," Nick says, already searching in his pockets for the car keys. "I'll take the car and try to reach him before the guys get back from lunch." He turns around then and almost as an afterthought adds, "Listen, if something happens and I don't make it back today, give me a ring at home tonight."

"Gotcha!" Don answers, waving him off.

Nick appears perfectly calm and unconcerned as he heads over to his car for the short drive to the temporary office set up on Grand Avenue. But the knot is back in the pit of his stomach, the one that's been there every time he thinks about her, the one that's been gnawing at him since she said good-bye the last time—presumably for the last time. Now seated in his convertible, he turns over the ignition, shifts into reverse, and with tires screeching, backs out and onto the road.

The screen door to the office slams shut as Nick bursts inside, startling his secretary who looks up from her typewriter. "There's a message from—" Millie begins, but Nick cuts her off.

"Yeah, I know," he says as he makes his way into the private office and closes the door.

The conversation is short and to the point, although Sylvie stalls for only a moment or two before blurting out what Nick has been dreading to hear.

"You ain't gonna like this one," Sylvie begins.

But after a while there's a kind of calm that settles in where the news is no longer a surprise, when he knows now that he can survive it. Still he thinks to himself, You bet your ass I'm not gonna want to hear it.

"She's leavin'," Sylvie announces.

"I know."

"No, I mean she's leavin' next week. She made the reservations already."

"Are you sure?"

"I heard her doin' it myself—that sure enough for you?"

"Yeah," Nick says softly, "that's sure enough!" He is sitting on the edge of the desk, the receiver cradled between his chin and shoulder, his eyes shut as he listens to Sylvie's voice, his familiar hoarse pitch sounding like a rock slide.

"Listen, Nick," he says with a trace of an apology, "I wouldn't say nothin' under different circumstances but seein' as how the two of you feel and everythin', you're the only one who can maybe get her to change her mind, whaddya say?"

"Where is she now?"

"On her way over to see you," he replies. "And what I had in mind was that if she's gotta go back there, to Paris, France, I mean, maybe you can make sure she just picks up her things and turns around to come back, even if you gotta go over there with her."

"Sylvie, I can't do that," Nick protests, although the idea had occurred to him many times before. "I can't force her to do something she obviously doesn't want to do."

"She loves you."

"Yeah, well," Nick says, clearly at a loss.

"And I told her what I thought, me and Rocco, we told her."

"What can I say, Sylvie?"

"There's nothin' to say, Nick, nothin' for me, but for her there's plenty to say. You tell her you ain't gonna put up with this."

"It doesn't work that way."

"Sure it does, that's the only way it works."

"Look, Sylvie, if you want my opinion, she's already made up her mind and there's no changing it."

"Listen," he pleads, "she's all confused, she don't know what she wants, and one of youse gotta be level, you hear? So I'm countin' on you, Nick, you're the one who's gotta put her straight."

"Terrific," Nick mumbles before hanging up, "I'll see what I can do."

When he puts down the receiver, he slams a fist into the palm of one hand and mutters, "Shit!" He bounds through the door of his office, causing it to reverberate on its hinge as it bangs repeatedly against the wall. Millie winces. "Sorry," he says, having made the decision to disappear rather than confront her if she does show up. "I'm taking the rest of the afternoon off," he announces, "and you don't know where I went if anybody wants me." But he pauses when he notices the peculiar expression on Millie's face.

"I want you," a voice says meekly.

Millie shrugs then as Nick turns around in the direction of the voice. "What are you doing here?" he feigns surprise. Gabriella gets up to walk over to where he stands. She smiles vaguely at Millie.

"I came here to talk to you," she says and then takes a breath, "do you think we could go somewhere for a few minutes?"

He appears flustered. "Sure," he says suddenly, taking her arm as he leads her toward the door. "I'll check in with you later," he tells the secretary. And as he guides Gabriella across the street, he realizes it had to happen sooner or later. The only thing was that he had hoped it would be later. Much later.

A clinch under one of Freeport's typical massive weeping willow trees, which only brings to mind endless possibilities and washes away some of the anxiety and doubt.

"I can't keep away, can I?" she says after catching her breath. He doesn't reply, merely pressing her against him. "Let's go somewhere," she whispers, her arms wrapped around his back.

"Don't do this."

Her head still on his chest, she asks, "You know, don't you?"

"Yes." He supports her as they walk slowly away from the office and down the street.

"How?"

"I could lie to you."

"Don't."

"Your father called me."

She stops, hands on his shoulders. "I can't believe it, or maybe I can believe it," she says with emotion, "but it's so Italian of him to do that, to interfere like that in my life, so," she fumbles now, "so woppy," she blurts out, "that it makes me sick."

"Gabriella," he says, looking directly into her eyes, "it's typically Italian because that's what we are, Italian, and so we interfere when it comes to family." He pauses. "And you know what? If he hadn't called me and I found you waiting for me in the office, you know what I would've thought?"

"Yes," she replies in a tiny voice.

"So it's better like this, at least for me. At least I know you didn't come here to tell me you changed your mind."

"Can we go somewhere and sit down?"

They are sitting at a table in the back of a dimly lit neighborhood bar that caters mostly to serious drinkers and ardent sports fans who watch the seasonal games on the gigantic color television set suspended over the bar. No one pays any attention to them. And anyway, except for one quiet drunk and the bartender, the bar is deserted. Nick touches Gabriella for the first time since they are together, putting his hands over hers on the table. "So what do you want me to say?" he asks.

"There's nothing you can say."

"Then why did you bother to come here?"

"I thought I owed you that."

"You don't owe me anything."

"Please don't hate me."

He makes a face. "Who said pity was sympathy's alternative to ridicule?"

She shakes her head.

"Well, hate is a poor substitute for hurt."

"I'm hurt too."

"Then why the hell are you doing this?"

She sighs. "The reasons are still the same and if we go through them again, they'll stay the same."

"That's because they're all wrong and won't get any better. You know, I walked around these past few days not getting it, going over it again and again until finally I got it. I figured out that being happy is something you'll never let yourself be, and it's got to do with feeling guilty."

"You sound like a psychiatrist."

He ignores her. "For some reason you think you have to pay the price for not having Dina's total love and devotion, and what I've failed to do is to get you to stop thinking that doing this to yourself is going to make a difference."

"Look, Nick, I came here to see if we could come to some kind of an agreement."

"Like what?"

"I need time."

He shrugs. "OK, then we'll play it like that while you're gone."

"Like what?"

"An affair," he says coolly, "we'll consider this an

affair and see each other from time to time with no questions asked and no expectations. How's that?"

"How can you turn it on and off like that?"

"The same way you can."

"But there's more to how we feel about each other than just an affair."

"It can't be both ways, Gabriella, and the way I wanted it obviously didn't work, so now we'll try it your way."

Be careful what you wish for, her mother used to say when she was small, because you might just get it. Once Gabriella could have done what Nick suggests, once when she didn't know better and didn't suffer from residual feelings—back in her youth. Those were the days when diaphanous lingerie took up space in her lingerie drawer, there to put on at the whim of a lover. Casual affairs might have worked once when she hadn't yet learned to care and when she only focused on sensation, when one man could have been any other without her noticing the difference.

Briefly, before she married Pete, she was oblivious to repercussions or regrets or anything that could happen afterward. Those were the days when she would occasionally dive naked into swimming pools, go to wild parties at the beach, smoke grass, and dance with strangers who quickly ceased being strangers. Briefly, after the divorce, she was oblivious in other ways, prone to suffer from bouts of jealous frenzies if she suspected a boyfriend of betraying her. Sitting by the telephone, she would wait for him to call, barely able to function if he didn't. Both phases of her single life had been unbearable when her every pleasure and happiness was contingent upon the opposite sex, when anything they did or didn't do had the potential to paralyze her mind and kill her ambition. It could have continued as well, had Gabriella not literally groped her way to the point in her life where she thrived instead on her own accomplishments. And now, it seems nothing less than a misfortune that just when she had liberated herself from a lover habit, Nicholas Tressa came along to subject her once again to the agony of sexual and emotional longing. Except that, if she was totally honest, she would have to admit that he didn't exactly force her to fall in love with him—even if she spent a good part of their time together thinking up ways to deny that condition.

"I can't have an affair with you," she says primly.

"Then what the hell do you want?"

"Understanding."

"To do what you want and not give a damn how it affects me? To want me when you want me and then expect me to turn it off at whim—your whim? Sorry, but it doesn't work that way. Maybe it'll work with one of your French lovers."

Her face registers fury. "This has been a great lesson for me and I want to thank you. It just makes me realize how right I was to leave here to avoid men like you." She waits only seconds before announcing as if they've only begun the conversation, "I'm leaving Monday."

"What can I say?"

But somehow then he is next to her on the banquette, his lips on hers, always the aggressor she thinks fleetingly, at least always when she tries to remove herself from his life. "I've got to go," he says abruptly. He gets up to study her a moment. "You're a fool."

"I know."

A smile of resignation perhaps, quite spectacular though, but then she would have responded with that same weak feeling and rush of sentiment had she stood before a marble bust of him.

"Don't call me and don't drop by to see me. I've got to get over you."

"I miss you already," she hears herself saying, almost as a morbid salutation. At least that's how it sounds to her as she watches him walk out the door.

When she finally is able to get up to head toward the exit and then walk down the street toward the parked car, his words keep rebounding in her head. She is filled with him and all the memories of their time spent together. Yet if she had to break each encounter down into mere moments, the time spent would become an eternity.

Standing at the car door, she finally musters up the energy to bend down to unlock it. She considers then, that perhaps she has finally made the ultimate sacrifice that will cancel out all those other losses that are her fault. But suddenly she begins to weep, for already every thought of him has made that curious transition into what is nothing more than nostalgia.

CHAPTER NINE

The Beach

THE SAND FEELS WET and sticky beneath Dina's bare feet, stretches of it as far as she can see running along the water's edge. Shading her eyes with her hands, she stands perfectly still as one finger traces the natural curve of the earth right up to the point where the ocean floor turns to fine sand, where the tide begins and ends. Thousands and millions of granules crunch as she skips toward the sea wall in front of the row of private houses—particles of colored glass, microscopic rock, a few random tops from soda bottles, and a used rubber that has washed up onshore. Briefly she considers how it got there before she resumes the tedious exercise of walking backward, long and deliberate steps that zigzag along the beach, turning only to observe the jagged line her footprints have made before she streaks forward toward the water once again. Hair flying wildly in the wind, arms outstretched to either side, she hears the word *free* reverberate in her head before it escapes her lips, over and over, leaving her vaguely troubled that something more original has eluded her.

She misses her father enormously, more each day it seems, so much so that her loss has somehow pushed all of the other agonies and resentments to the back of her brain, which is probably what gives her that sensation of freedom. For not only does she feel liberated from having to tackle other things, she also has this tremendous sense of relief that she survived the accident without any lasting damage. Yet occasionally, right this minute in fact, as she turns around to look at her mother sitting nearby with a book and a wicker basket of lunch, the word *lonely* comes to mind as another good adjective to describe her feelings. But how ridiculous would *lonely* sound if shouted into the wind while running Hollywood-style along this vast expanse of East Hampton beach.

Much to her surprise, the passing of Joshua from her life consumes almost as much of her thoughts as the passing of her father—at least consciously.

Upon awakening this morning, she decided that one incident makes her grow while the other forces her to regress and accept a transition that has stalled in time and can go no further. The relationship between sex and death is not so farfetched, she considered while showering, given how very finite life and love really are.

Mourning, Dina reasoned, was an extreme case of dwelling in the past, an unhealthy exercise of struggling to keep a memory alive of someone who would never be that same person again. Discarding a lover, however, offers the incentive to begin again. Yet both produce in Dina a wisdom concerning two crucial mysteries of life. Death gives her a more alluring and painful past, while having endured a bad affair allows her entry into that club of ex-wives and girlfriends who have developed a cynical appreciation of men. Strange, Dina thought while downing a cup of coffee, that even at eighteen, she already knows that losing a parent makes her more desirable if only for her new-found vulnerability, just as losing a lover makes her chances of attracting another much greater. Men are like dogs, she mused while strolling out onto the beach—they prefer to sniff a spot that has already been marked by one of them rather than seeking out virgin sidewalk on which to leave their trace.

"Lunch," Gabriella calls from the distance, standing up to wave, "and stop running!"

Dina teeters toward the sea wall as if walking an imaginary tightrope. Plunging over to one side, she whirls around in the direction of her mother's voice. Cupping her hands around her mouth, she yells, "Coming!"

Three days together at her father's house and still they haven't touched on anything more significant than exercise routines, weather, weight, and fiber. This morning, however, when Gabriella woke up with the idea of walking down to the beach for a picnic, Dina had already decided that the time had come for the confrontation, and the beach was as good a place as any to have it.

As Gabriella observes Dina, she realizes that at this point any understanding that she has of the girl is based largely on instinct and past patterns, since she hardly knows her any more. This is the child who always reminded her of a juicy, red, delicious apple—a wench beauty whose curves and cushions were unique among her anorexic peers, yet who constantly lamented her weight and resented her mother's trimmer frame. This same little girl who refused to relinquish one item of clothing when it no longer fit, or share her toys or candy with a playmate, was also not the least bit generous when it came to sacrifice or inconvenience. All reasons to believe that she left her mother on grounds that were less psychological than they were physical. But there was no reason for Dina to feel that same attachment or bond that Gabriella felt, since it is only the mother who has memories of those nine months of gestation before outside influences interfered.

"It worries me when you run," Gabriella admonishes. "The doctor said you should rest."

"I've been resting," Dina replies, poking around in the lunch basket. "What's there to eat?"

Gabriella's expression is hopeful. "Peanut butter or tuna fish sandwiches, apples or bananas—your choice."

"Boring," Dina judges, leaning back on her elbows, her words appearing to be measured somehow, giving a little only to withdraw it without warning.

Instantly on the defensive, Gabriella rushes, "Should I make you something else? Because it's really no problem, I'll just run back to the house."

"No, it's all right," Dina answers graciously. "I'll have what's here." She bites into half of a peanut butter sandwich. "Remember when I had braces and I couldn't eat this stuff?"

Gabriella smiles. "They used to drive you crazy."

"Not really."

She glances at her daughter in surprise, prepared to argue the point, grateful that their first disagreement has nothing to do with anything. "You complained about them constantly, we were forever running back to Doctor Lennert to loosen them or tighten them, don't you remember that?"

"Maybe," Dina casts a sideways look, "but I always remember that time in my life when I wore braces as being really happy."

"You were thirteen," Gabriella calculates out loud, "when they finally came off."

"I was so happy until then."

"And after that?"

"After that I was unhappy," Dina says simply.

"Why's that?"

"Because it was right before you and Daddy separated, and there was nothing but fighting and tension in the house."

Gabriella bites her lip thoughtfully. "It was horrible," she says softly, "all that fighting, and we were so stupid to kid ourselves into believing that we kept it from you. We used to drive around the block and scream at each other in the car and then shut up the minute we rounded the corner and pulled the car in the driveway. And I suppose that kind of truce we had, that forced silence, was worse in a way because that's what made you feel all the tension. If I could do it over, Dina, I'd find another way, we both would, so you wouldn't be so hurt by our problems."

"It wasn't Daddy, it was you," Dina lashes out.

Stunned that it has begun without warning, Gabriella sits up very straight. "Why me?"

Dina glances briefly at her mother before speaking, but when she does she avoids her, concentrating on her sandwich or on the cluster of sandpipers that dart around the beach near the water's edge. "You should have talked to me, told me what was going on so at least I would've been prepared for something horrible. The way it was all I could be was scared that something bad was going to happen to me." Dina's jaw is set in a tense line. "But all you cared about was getting away from him and keeping your job, you didn't even pay any attention to how I felt."

Gabriella threads her way cautiously through this first hurdle. "I suppose I was worried about keeping my job," she says honestly, "because we needed some kind of guarantee that at least the rent would be paid, we needed that steady income coming in. Don't forget that your father warned me in front of you, by the way, that there'd be no money if I left him."

"So why did you?"

Without seizing that very sore point and turning it to her advantage, Gabriella responds without guile. "We both tried very hard to work things out, not only because we didn't want a divorce but for you. It just wasn't possible and it's really no one's fault." And if it's correct to defend an ex-husband to his child, it is certainly easier to do it when that ex-husband is dead.

Nervously, Dina licks her lips. "If you really wanted to, you could've stayed with him."

"He used to say that long after it was over."

"So I take after him, and why shouldn't I," Dina defends, "he's my father." She takes a breath. "And don't start making statements about women having it worse than men after a split, because Daddy was the one in this family who suffered most when it was over. You just went along not doing anything different, business-as-usual kind of thing."

The barb hits the mark, for Gabriella winces. "How can you say that, when you just finished telling me how unhappy you were? How could I just go along as if nothing was wrong when you were so unhappy? We all suffered, not just your father, all of us!"

Dina holds back tears. "You were the one who left," she says very distinctly, the words separated from each other. "You were the one who walked out."

Gabriella barely moves her lips when finally she replies. "We both left."

"You left," Dina repeats.

"It's not necessarily the one who actually walks out who's the one who wants to end the relationship."

Dina turns toward her mother then, a funny expression beginning. "Oh, really," she answers, a note of sarcasm perhaps. "Then sometimes the one who leaves is actually pushed out?"

"Yes, sometimes," Gabriella blurts and then stops abruptly to consider where she has been led. Total silence for several moments while a thousand truths and untruths swirl around inside her head. Averting her eyes, she gestures out toward the water in an attempt to buy a little time and regain a little dignity. "Look at those birds cramming together on that buoy," she observes, her voice not quite steady. "Now how do you suppose they're going to untangle that rope?"

Dina shrugs. "Who cares. Do you really care about those birds?" And then resumes. "Don't ever blame me again for leaving you, Mother, don't ever blame me for abandoning you." That "Mother"—the most formal and distant appellation Dina has been known to use—and the chilling tone do not invite any discussion on this issue.

Timidly, Gabriella dares, "Are you talking about us now?"

"What do you think?"

"I think you are," she says in a voice that comes from nowhere before it slowly gathers strength. "And what I'm hearing is that I forced you to leave.'' Tears then, and for that she hates herself since right now logic is the only thing that will make an impression. ''Tell me how I drove you away from me,'' she asks. ''Please tell me.''

''I already told you,'' Dina says, evading. ''You should've kept the marriage together so I wouldn't have to grow up in a broken home.''

''But it didn't make it any less broken for you to live with your father, did it?''

''It was your fault, so at least he didn't have to be totally alone.''

''So you punished me because you considered me responsible?''

''He tried and you didn't!''

Again Gabriella flinches as if she has been struck in the face. Ill at ease and uncertain as to what to do, she considers constructing her own fantasy to obliterate the one Dina has created. After all, she's the adult and the one who evidently did something to drive away the child. And what makes it worse is that when she studies Dina now, she wants to die because her face has gone all knotted and damp. ''I love you,'' she says for lack of anything else more brilliant.

''You don't love me and you never loved me!''

Instead of crumbling then, Gabriella rallies suddenly, not knowing quite what to do with the anger that is rattling around inside, nor with the peanut butter sandwich that seems stranded in her hand. In an abrupt gesture of frustration she stuffs it back into the wicker basket as she prepares to climb down from the defensive to consider some truths.

''It's so easy to say that, isn't it?'' Gabriella replies, ''because then no one else has any responsibility in the relationship. So much more simple like that and so logical too, except for one small problem.'' She sighs deeply. ''It's not true.'' Dina turns her head away in response, but Gabriella continues. ''I loved your father and he loved me and

— 256 —

certainly we both loved you, both of us, and I wouldn't for a minute try to rewrite history and claim that he didn't, just as he wouldn't have done that to me.''

''Neither of you were in a position to judge how things felt to me. You weren't mind readers, you were only parents.''

At least now, Gabriella notes with relief, she is not alone on the receiving end of this review of her parenthood. Pete is with her. ''Then don't make us out to be anything more than human beings who made mistakes.''

''My father made mistakes because he had enormous pressure and responsibility with his work. It wasn't some kind of a flighty job, it was more like life and death.''

''Does that make him less responsible to his family than I was?''

''Yes, because all you had to do was make things peaceful at home.''

''I had a job,'' Gabriella protests.

''But that was your choice. He earned enough money to support us.''

''Dina!'' she cries, outraged.

''What are you so shocked about?'' the girl inquires politely. ''Maybe if you had paid more attention to us, all of this wouldn't have happened and we wouldn't have been at each other's throats all the time.''

But Gabriella is hardly paying attention, wondering instead who is really to blame for this preconceived notion of womanhood and motherhood. For who but women raise little girls and boys to think like that. ''Let's not get into a discussion about equality,'' Gabriella says lightly. ''We seem to have enough problems understanding each other without trying to make sense out of the feminist movement. But whatever you may think about my working or about the situation between your father and me, my feelings for you were always loving.''

''Feelings aren't everything.''

''What is, then?''

"Some kind of understanding, so that every time we had a conversation it didn't end up in a screaming match."

"Maybe that's what happens with mothers and daughters at a certain stage in their relationship." Another formula to consider, like a recipe cut from a woman's magazine. "That's what it was," Gabriella says with conviction, "it was a stage."

"It was a pretty long stage then," Dina says disgustedly, "since you always made me feel as if you wanted to get rid of me. Sort of like if I wasn't around, you could be doing all these wonderful things with your life." She takes a sip of soda. "Which is why it must have been a relief when I finally left."

"That's not true," Gabriella says softly.

"Either a relief," Dina says, maintaining the attack, "or an embarrassment, because you couldn't make yourself out to be this superwoman-single-parent-martyr who was trying to cope with this difficult teenager while juggling a glamorous job and recovering from this traumatic marriage." Her tone is sarcastic. "I mean, give me a break!"

"Where did you get these ideas?" Gabriella asks, horrified at her daughter's perception of what her life had been.

"It's insulting that you think I had to get my ideas from someone or someplace other than my own head. Why not give me any credit for figuring things out myself?"

"But why was everything my fault?" Gabriella asks in a moment of desperation. "Why wasn't your father responsible for some of your unhappiness after the divorce?"

"You can't have it both ways," Dina says cleverly, "claiming it was a stage that had nothing to do with the divorce and then trying to make Daddy responsible." She hesitates as tears spring to her eyes. "And anyway, he cared about me."

"So did I."

"But he did things with me after the divorce, took me places, to the movies and the beach, out to dinner and to the theater, even to museums."

"I can't compete," Gabriella says quietly, "because I had to take care of the everyday things, like the house and the laundry and whatever else happened to come up—like dinner when he wasn't taking you out."

"He made an effort."

"I said I can't compete."

"He's dead," Dina whispers.

"I certainly can't compete with that," Gabriella says and then regrets the sarcasm even if it's that death thing that really gets her more than anything else that Pete did to win the contest for best parent after a divorce. To die and therefore be exempt from any blame seems as predictable as dying and having all earthly defects turn into saintly attributes. Memory is absolutely selective when it comes to the pain of childbirth and the death of a parent. Unfortunately for Dina, Gabriella had long since become immune to those images of father and daughter romping happily together through some kind of postdivorce field of fantasy. Especially since Gabriella was usually left to catch up on household chores when they were gone.

It mustn't have been easy for him to maintain a continuity with his child as a visiting parent. But then it wasn't easy for Gabriella either, as a live-in parent, to maintain peace with her child when she functioned as the disciplinarian.

Yet they had their moments. Breakfast every morning with Dina after the separation, dinner at night even if Gabriella didn't eat but merely sat with her to keep her company. And some of their best times were spent hanging over a dishwasher or a laundry basket or a vacuum or a stove. Cleaning the apartment together on weekends, shopping at the supermarket as a duo, scouring Tower Records for tapes or newsstands for gossip magazines and then piling everything on the king-size bed to delve through. Confidences about trying pot and getting sick, memories of growing up without a mother, secret crushes on a delivery boy or a teacher, once cheating on an exam and getting caught, with please not to tell "my father" (funny, it wasn't "Daddy" during those instances), and at the end, confessions about how much better it was since the split. From Gabriella's point of view they were the ideal mother-daughter team, despite the frequent battles and tears and problems; it was the kind of one-parent home that is portrayed on those sitcoms where everything turns out fine in the end. Or maybe Gabriella's memories are as unrealistic as high school year-book predictions.

"You know," Gabriella says lovingly, "I have other memories, of the two of us when you were a baby and we used to take these walks up and down the streets before lunch, and then sometimes I'd bring along a jar of baby food and we'd sit under a tree to eat." Her tone is soft. "Or when you were older and we'd go shopping together and you'd let me help pick out your clothes." She smiles slightly. "*That* was a big deal since you were so sure of what you liked and didn't like."

"I've got memories too," Dina says.

"What kind?"

"Oh, like the time you slapped me across the face because I said something you didn't like about your mother."

"Your grandmother."

"No, your mother. They were always your parents, never my grandparents because you were the only one they cared about or paid any attention to." Dina's eyes filled with tears. "You actually slapped me because I refused to spend a Christmas vacation with them, because I didn't want to sit on the beach in Miami and watch her nod off. Actually now that I think of it, it would've been better than listening to you and Daddy fighting for two weeks!"

"I shouldn't have hit you," Gabriella says softly, remembering the incident, "but your father kept threatening to leave and I was under such horrible pressure, and you kept blaming me for the fighting, and probably I should've just begged your father to stay and not argued. Would you've been happy then?''

"Why did you always turn everything around so I ended up begging you for something?'' The ball bounces out of bounds.

"Then why did you blame me every time there was a problem?'' The advantage changes.

"Why was it always you?'' Dina moans. And changes back again.

"Did it ever occur to you that I had feelings too?'' The ball slams against the metal mesh fence.

"I didn't ask to be born, you know,'' Dina sulks. Weak backhand.

"Neither did I,'' Gabriella counters. Double fault.

"At least your mother and father loved you, even at my expense so I couldn't even run to them like other kids could.'' Love—zero.

"Sure, I had parents until my mother almost died when I was only thirteen and my father was too busy taking care of her to bother with me.'' Line ball.

"I always end up feeling sorry for you,'' Dina says bitterly.

"And I always end up feeling guilty,'' Gabriella concludes. Tie game.

A silence follows but not for long when Dina resumes. "So how come everything just sort of stopped between us when I wasn't dependent on you to feed me and dress me? How come you were such a failure at giving me emotional support?''

The question jolts Gabriella, but she doesn't rush to respond. She considers it. Now. Fifteen years too late perhaps but at least she's thinking about it. "Maybe I didn't know how,'' Gabriella replies with a touch of shame. "Can't you understand how frightened I must have been too?''

But the girl only shrugs, not prepared perhaps to give

away a point. "Dina," Gabriella says with the promise of tears to follow, "I loved you, I always loved you, but I wasn't born a healthy grown-up. There were ghosts in my head too."

Dina nods slowly, a judge assessing the evidence. "So how come Daddy didn't have a problem showing his feelings?"

She takes a breath then as if to change her entire person and speak for him. "He was different, Dina. Your father had this marvelous facility to make friends with total strangers, he was gregarious and open and loved to laugh." She shrugs vaguely. "That was the way he was." But what she doesn't add is that Pete's ability to relate to people was always the same, never adjusted to those who were closer than others.

"He cared," Dina says simply, "and you didn't, that's what I think."

"That's not true," Gabriella protests.

"You were a better daughter than you were a mother," Dina attacks, shifting to the grandparents she has barely acknowledged since this beach reunion began. But Gabriella had expected that tack.

"You refused to see my parents," she begins evenly, "and I understood in a way because kids hate to be around sick people. So if I seemed to be a better daughter than a mother it was only because you excluded yourself from that part of my life." She reaches out to touch Dina's hand. "And I couldn't exclude them, they needed me."

"My father needed you too," Dina snaps.

"Seeing my parents didn't take anything away from him."

"He loved you."

"And I loved him," Gabriella replies quickly, "and we both loved you. The marriage fell apart for other reasons that had nothing to do with my family or my work for that matter."

"Did you want the divorce?"

"In the end I did."

"He was alone for so long, alone and miserable afterward," Dina says quietly.

"He had Adrienne almost immediately, which was good."

"That didn't count, he was alone in other ways," Dina repeats stubbornly.

"He wasn't alone," Gabriella repeats just as stubbornly. "He had Adrienne." And then the error. "I was the one who was alone, I had no one."

As if on cue, the girl leaps. "You had a succession of no ones."

By then Gabriella is no longer thinking rationally. "And he had a succession of no ones while we were still married," she rejoins, silently berating herself for sinking to this level.

Dina's expression is cagey. "Do you think that having one no one is any better than having a lot of no ones?"

"Why are you making this some kind of a contest that I seem to be losing?"

"Because that's why you got divorced."

"Oh, I see, it was all right for him to do it but not me."

"It didn't affect my life when he did," she says angrily. "When you did it, it screwed everything up."

"So it was a moral issue with you, is that it?"

"Yes, that's exactly it. I went to live with Daddy because I had no respect for you any more."

Gabriella's gaze is steady as she makes the instant decision to push it right over the edge. "What I really think, Dina, is that you're trying to dredge up all kinds of excuses to justify what the reality is, the reason that you went to live with your father."

"What's the reason, if you're so smart?"

"No," Gabriella says sadly, "I'm not so smart at all, in fact I'm pretty dumb, but I think the reason you went to live with him was because it was easier both financially and socially. I think you went to the highest bidder." What amazes Gabriella is that what began as a ploy to induce a reaction has become a basic truth.

"That's what you want to believe because it makes it easier than admitting what a good father he was and what a lousy mother you were."

In a manner that is strangely detached and with a tone of neutrality that Gabriella has never before displayed, she answers, "No, I don't want to believe that because it's not true. The truth is that neither of us were so extreme, either good or bad, each of us had good qualities and made mistakes."

"I went to live with my father," Dina says, floundering, "because he was all I had." There is hysteria in the reasoning.

"You had me."

Flinging her sandwich aside, Dina challenges. "You want to hear the truth? Well, I'll tell you the truth, why I left you and went to live with him and there was only one reason and that was to hurt you, that's why!"

Gabriella's voice trembles. "And don't you regret that now, even a little, sweetheart?" Apparently the tone disarms the girl because she begins to weep. Or perhaps she weeps because it's the relief of not having to come up with bogus sentiments any more or lame excuses, or maybe it's because both of them have finally reached the end of the line or at least one of them has. "You couldn't possibly mean all those things," Gabriella says, tears in her own eyes, "because somewhere inside you know how much I love you." She pauses to catch her breath. "So don't you regret everything just a little bit?"

As an apostate who finds a better way, Dina allows her mother to gather her in her arms. "Yes," she admits tearfully, "of course I regret it."

"I love you," Gabriella consoles, holding her child against her breast, "and it's all going to get better, I promise you!" For she has been waiting for this for almost half her life, eighteen years, to hold Dina when Dina had a choice. Not when she was a needy and demanding infant, although it is suddenly clear that at one time or another she was also that needy and demanding infant. "You're right about so many things," Gabriella whispers, the tears streaming down her cheeks. "I never really knew how to be a good mother because I was so afraid of losing you. I wouldn't run away from you, though, because I loved you so much. Maybe I made you run away from me."

"You weren't that bad," Dina manages to say, the sobs having subsided.

"Thanks," Gabriella croaks, her lips pressed against the girl's hair, "but it doesn't excuse what I did either, and it's got nothing to do with what your father did. I should have known better."

Dina picks up her head. "You both should have known better," she says wisely. And when all the crying ceases and both women blow their noses and wipe their eyes, Gabriella draws her daughter close again. "I know about the letter and I know you know about the baby I gave up for adoption."

Dina gasps and withdraws suddenly. "How?" she asks, inching away more and more, digging her toes into the sand as she stares numbly out across the ocean.

Gabriella treads more prudently now. "Claire asked me to go to your father's house to clean out a few files and gather some papers that she needed and the letter happened to be among them."

"I can't deal with this," Dina yells, standing up and running toward the water. "This wasn't supposed to be part of it!" And the seagulls that had been in peaceful repose on that buoy several yards out flap their wings and screech in response to the shrieks that are now coming from the beach.

"How could it not be part of it when that was the real reason that you stopped speaking to me?" Gabriella cries, jumping up to follow Dina to the edge of the surf. "I hurt you, for God's sake, so why can't we talk about it!'' She chases Dina back and forth as the girl stomps around.

"It was between us,'' Dina screams, "Daddy and me.''

Gabriella clutches her shoulder but Dina twists away. "Please, Dina,'' she pleads, "can't you see how it affected all of us?''

"Then you shouldn't have done it,'' she yells as she sinks down onto the sand on her knees, brutally digging up chunks of mud and flinging them in the direction of her mother.

"I can't undo it,'' Gabriella cries, sinking down in front of her. "Do you want me to just go away and stop trying to talk to you? What do you want?'' Trembling, she reaches out for Dina.

"Don't threaten me!''

"I'm not threatening.''

"Then what do you call it?''

"I call it hurt and guilty and not knowing what else to do and maybe just giving up.''

"That's a joke!''

"What's a joke, that I don't know what to do any more?''

"You betrayed me!''

"You betrayed me,'' Gabriella says passionately, "by not talking about it when you found out.''

"It's too late now,'' Dina says, scrambling to her feet to head toward the water once again.

"Then let's settle it,'' Gabriella shouts, jumping up to follow her.

"There's nothing to settle,'' the girl yells, a clump of hair in her mouth. "You gave away a baby. So what? What am I supposed to do about it—it wasn't my baby.'' But the tears belie her pragmatism on the subject.

Gabriella is upon her, both of her hands holding her child's, forcing her to listen. "Talk about it now,'' she implores. "Tell me how shocked you were when you found out." Dina's efforts to extricate herself are not quite as fierce as before. "Tell me how angry or disappointed you were," Gabriella says, not letting up. "Ask me why I did it or what I was thinking about, scream, yell, for God's sake, Dina, hate me for it, but don't let it build up and build up and then tell me that you don't care because you're all I care about and if I hurt you I want to make it up and explain it to you."

"He never would've married you if he knew," she sobs, backing away slightly, a terrified look on her face.

"He knew," Gabriella says sadly, moving forward. "He knew before we got married because I told him."

She wipes her eyes and nose with the back of her hand. "You're a liar!"

"No, I'm not," Gabriella shouts angrily. "There's been enough lies and dishonesty around here. I'm telling you the truth."

There is no concealing that Italian girl now for she has overwhelmed all of those other pretend nationalities and personalities that she has practiced and affected for so long. "Dina Marie Molloy, I swear to you he knew, and I swear to you I don't care what he told you, I'm not even mad, I just want you back." She holds her ground then, the tears running into her mouth as she waits for the verdict. Collapsing in a heap of emotion against her mother, Dina presses her head against her shoulder.

"Why did he die?" she cries. "Why did he have to go and die?" Gabriella registers the words, she knows the rest of the sentence that will perhaps go unsaid forever: Why did he die and leave us with this mess?

"It's going to be all right," the mother soothes.

"How do you know?" the child whimpers.

"Because we have each other," Gabriella says, reaching down to produce a tattered and partially used Kleenex from her pocket to wipe Dina's nose and eyes.

"It could have been me," the child laments.

"No, I could never have parted with you, you're mine!"

"So was the other baby," Dina says, sniffling. "What's the difference?" But the difference has less to do with ties of blood and biological recognition than it does with a cerebral process, that same process that allows people like the Kelleys to love Daria as their own.

"The difference," Gabriella says, trying to reason, "is emotional." She smiles slightly, touching Dina's face. "Come with me, I've got an idea."

They walk over the hard mud and up to where the smooth grains of sand abut the sea wall in front of the row of houses. Finally Gabriella points to a spot on the beach, somewhere between the fine granules and the wet ridge when the tide is out. Dina follows her mother's example and sits down, the two of them side by side on the beach until Gabriella springs up onto her knees. "Lie back," she instructs with a twinkle in her eye. Dina obeys, a memory flashing across her face as Gabriella begins heaping sand over her legs. "This is one of the good memories," she says, "burying you in the sand when you were little."

The girl's face softens into a funny grin, a touching expression of contentment and security, up up Mommy up, when there were no limits, no boundaries on their love, no pretenses at being independent, no commitment to dredge up old wounds. They had their entire lives before them, endless possibilities for their relationship to grow, a bond that was as yet unspoiled by restlessness or resentment, each of them posed somewhere between acceptance and expectation of what the other would become. And Gabriella had always considered this child to be hers alone, not the result of something that might have transpired once or ten times or a hundred or a thousand times between herself and Pete that had something to do with her creation.

Under the best of circumstances, she viewed her

daughter as a peace offering to Pete when things seemed to be irretrievable, and out of desperation she would offer the child as a reminder of their joint obligation. Perhaps later on after the divorce, she viewed her as a cradle for her own instability or perhaps even her own irrationality when there was nothing else around to get her through crisis after crisis. Yet never throughout any of the years could she ever imagine life without her, for Dina was styled miraculously after her, anxious to emulate everything she did, her favorite words in a childlike or grown-up form had always been "Me too, Mommy!"

"You missed a spot," Dina says, pointing to a patch of bare flesh right above one knee.

Working quickly, Gabriella piles sand upon more sand until the spot is covered completely, everything is covered, right up to the chin, the little body grown into adult size but still the same flesh and blood. "So what do you think?" Gabriella asks after she pats the final mound of sand on Dina's chest before rolling over on her stomach, her head resting on her arms.

"About what?"

"About starting over—you and me from square one?"

"I'm not sure."

"What do you have to lose."

"Nothing any more, I guess."

"Should we try, then?"

Dina squirms a bit, the granules spilling over to one side.

"I thought I'd take off for Europe when school is over. Adrienne and I talked about it when I was in the hospital, and she said she'd like to go too."

Gabriella feels a peculiar sinking feeling but only for an instant. "That sounds like fun," she says brightly.

"You should have told me, you know," Dina says, suddenly reverting back. "You should have realized after the separation that he'd do anything he could to hurt you because he was so hurt.'' Her voice catches in her throat. ''We were close enough, Mom, for you to have trusted me.''

Gabriella looks at Dina, tears again. ''It never occurred to me,'' she answers honestly.

''You made a mistake.''

''I know that now.''

''It just would've been better if we all could've been honest with each other.''

''You're right,'' Gabriella says, determined not to berate herself, though, for what once was, ''but I never believed he'd tell you.''

A silence then as both lie very still, a warm breeze beginning to rustle the trees near the houses and blow the top layer of sand from Dina's legs. ''Nick's a nice guy!''

''Yes, he is,'' Gabriella says nonchalantly.

''Are you in love with him?'' Dina presses.

''Of course not!'' she replies automatically and then smiles. ''Honest, right, we're going to be honest?''

Dina nods.

''All right, yes, I'm in love with him.''

''Then why are you going back?''

Gabriella sighs as she turns over onto her back, propping herself up on her elbows, her face tilted toward the sun. ''Because first things first, and I needed to work things out with you and then I need to work things out about myself, since I never did it after the marriage broke up.'' She pauses. ''And then who knows?''

''Did you love her?'' Dina switches lanes.

''Who?''

''The baby?''

''I never knew her.''

''Did you love me when I was born?''

''Instantly,'' she responds without the slightest hesitation, ''before you were born, I loved you.''

''You know, Mom,'' Dina says thoughtfully, ''I felt sorry for her in the beginning when I first found out, and then I didn't because she was the only one who didn't have to live in our crazy family!'' She laughs briefly. ''I mean, it wasn't easy being a Molloy, was it? We were all trying to be what we weren't. Daddy wanted to be governor, you wanting to be anything other than what you were, and me thinking I was some kind of debutante—what a bunch of lunatics we all were.''

''Not lunatics,'' Gabriella says gently, ''just different. But every family thinks they're different I guess, and every family has something wrong with them. In that way we certainly weren't unique.'' Gabriella sighs. ''Will you let me know where you'll be and what you're doing?'' And suddenly she finds herself prepared to let go of this child that she has just rediscovered.

''Sure, and maybe I'll even come to visit you someday in Paris.''

A sense of resignation envelops Gabriella then, for there is suddenly no other choice but to join in. ''Anytime, Dina.'' She touches the girl's face tenderly. ''And in the meantime, I'm going to miss you.''

''It's different this time,'' she says pragmatically.

Tears spring into Gabriella's eyes.

''I need time,'' Dina falters.

''Will you finish Brampton or transfer?'' Gabriella asks.

''Finish,'' she replies with conviction, ''despite everything.''

''Does it bother you that I've chosen to go back to Paris?''

''Nope, but you won't be there forever.'' A shrewd look follows.

''Maybe not forever but right now it's the place for me to be because the work is so good.''

''There're other things that count too,'' Dina replies in a knowing tone, ''and you're not getting any younger, you know.''

A smile then.

Silently they decide the time has come to leave the beach and make their way back up to the house. Arm in arm they walk the several yards back down to the water's edge to retrieve their things before slowly making their way up the incline of the dunes, out onto the road to tredge the half mile to Egypt Lane.

When they arrive at the house and while Dina is busy rinsing the sand from her feet, Gabriella studies her daughter. Struck by an indefinable transition that has occurred from bewildered child to forgiving adult, she hugs her impulsively. Embarrassed, Dina twists away. "I'm going upstairs to take a shower and wash my hair."

And Gabriella wants to add something, anything, about not getting the stitches wet over her eye or that a nap might not be such a bad idea considering that they talked of going to a movie after dinner. Instead she controls herself, afraid of sounding too motherly or too possessive. She bites her lip, keeping silent as Dina proceeds up to the second level to disappear into her room, the door clicking shut behind her.

A screen of light passes before Gabriella's eyes, a reflection from the afternoon sun that streams in from the living room window. Somehow she feels both euphoric and depressed, aware that once again there is an adjustment to be made, different this time than the others and certainly less painful, but a separation to manage nonetheless.

Strange how she still tends to view herself as a girl although these past few weeks have certainly forced her to face some very adult realities. She realizes that nothing is forever, not for having to face Pete's death or for having to make concessions and adjustments to recapture Dina but because of Nick, who has left her feeling so empty.

"Do you think you're going to be able to fit everything into the trunk?" Gabriella asks as she places several plants down on the gravel next to the car.

Adrienne laughs. "I think so but the car's going to ride heavy on one side, that's for sure!"

Dina is heading toward them, carrying a pile of freshly folded laundry. "How about putting this on the backseat since I can't seem to fit it into my suitcase?"

"That doesn't surprise me," Gabriella says, relieving her of the bundle. "What do you think, Adrienne, will it fit?"

Dina swats a fly from her arm. "How come I always end up going back with more stuff than I came with?"

"That's because you rethink all the clothes you discarded on the last trip home," Adrienne says and then adds, "You're just like your father, he couldn't throw anything away either."

Gabriella and Dina exchange a glance before each busies herself with arranging and rearranging several plants and shopping bags. "Well, I guess that's it," Dina announces when the last item is packed away.

The three women gather awkwardly around the car, the clothes and plants piled inside. There is nothing left to say then except good-bye. Gabriella, with a red scarf tied around her forehead, dirt streaks on her nose and cheeks, and beads of perspiration dotting her upper lip, wipes her hands on her white shorts before clasping one of Adrienne's hands.

"Are you sure you don't need me to drive up with the two of you?"

"We're fine," Dina answers for the woman. "And anyway you've got a lot to do—you're leaving tomorrow!"

"Don't worry about anything," Adrienne adds. "It's a nice drive, and if I'm tired I'll stay up there for the night."

Gabriella turns to embrace her daughter. "I'm going to miss you but I expect to hear from you while you're flying around Europe." She smiles almost shyly. "And maybe you'll even make it to Paris?"

"Maybe," Dina says and then snaps her finger. "I forgot all my books, my entire knapsack. Shows you how much I want to go back and study." She dashes toward the house. "Be back in a sec!"

"Do you have someone to take you to the airport?" Adrienne asks when Dina is almost to the door.

"The magazine arranged for a car." She appears ill at ease. "Adrienne, I don't know how to say this but you've helped me so much."

"You've helped me too," she says, "just by accepting my relationship with Dina."

"You mean a lot to her."

"So do you."

"Maybe I do," Gabriella says quietly, "at least I hope so."

"It's none of my business," Adrienne begins, "but she's grown up now." She pauses. "Look, it's time to make your own life, Gabriella."

"I have been."

"Then don't be stupid."

Gabriella blinks away the reference to what she already considers to be a terrible mistake; she says instead, "You'll have a wonderful time in Europe with Dina."

"I know, since I haven't been to half the places she wants to go."

"Neither has she." She chooses her words carefully. "I've learned something from you, or maybe I learned it from Dina, but I realize it's better to have a piece of something or someone than nothing."

"Then stop running away."

"What do you mean?"

"Come back here and be with him."

Gabriella blushes. "I thought we were talking about Dina."

"We were but I decided to change the subject."

"It seems so far away," Gabriella says vaguely.

"It is, so come home."

"No, I meant Thanksgiving. It seems so far away until I'll see you all again, since Dina probably won't come to Paris before."

"At this stage of the game, Gabriella, we don't get a lot of chances to start a new life."

"I'm not looking for another life. I'm just beginning to live this one." Gabriella's gaze is on Adrienne for another moment until she turns her attention to Dina who is coming in their direction.

"Here," Dina says as she thrusts several books at her mother, "please hold these while I make room for everything." Rummaging around on the backseat, she talks to her from over one shoulder. "Did you give Adrienne your address and telephone number?"

"Yes, but I thought you had it."

"I lost it," the girl says, straightening up.

"Well, Adrienne has it. Will you call?"

Dina's expression is stern. "This isn't a happy ending, Mom. I want you to understand that because there's still a lot of work to do to accept what my life has been."

"I know," Gabriella says, her expression loving, "for both of us."

Dina appears surprised. "Why you?"

"Only because I'm a person too," she responds with a vague smile.

Dina hugs her briefly before she climbs into the car, her profile perfect as she stares ahead. Adrienne walks over to her to embrace her as well. But Gabriella can't manage words right then—for either of them. She waves instead after Adrienne is seated behind the wheel, moving to one side of the driveway as the car heads down the road. Twisting her head from side to side to relieve the sudden tension in her neck, she remains unmoving for minutes more, considering how lucky she is to have gotten another chance.

□

"Do you wanna eat somethin' before you leave?" Sylvie asks, his shoulders slumped in defeat.

"No, I don't think so, Papa," she says. "They'll stuff me on the plane." She walks toward him. "Are you leaving for the restaurant soon?"

He nods miserably. "Yeah, soon. Rocco's already there, he said the two of you took a walk before."

"Around the block," she replies nervously. For she has chosen not to confront the issue of his interference in her life.

"What time's the car comin'?"

She glances at her watch. "In about an hour or so."

"You all packed?"

"Almost."

He shifts from one foot to the other while she studies her hands. "Gabriella," he begins, "what can I say except you're bein' a fool."

"How about saying that you'll miss me but that we'll see each other soon."

"Yeah, I could say that but this here arrangement stinks!"

"Where's Mama?" she says, shifting the subject. "Is she awake?"

He shrugs. "Awake, asleep, what's the difference?" Kissing her forehead, he hugs her a final time before hurrying out of the room. "Call Claire," he calls out in a voice choked with emotion. "She called before."

□

Gabriella sits on the floor in the foyer, her back against the banister, the phone cradled between her chin and shoulder. "Did you get everything that I dropped off?" she asks.

"Yeah, thanks, and it's been a nightmare going through everything, making sense out of things."

"We've all been trying to make sense out of things, I guess," Gabriella mutters.

"Well, have a good trip, and let's hope that the next time we see each other we won't be sharing another terrible loss."

"Let's hope," Gabriella replies before hanging up, although she doubts it. At least from her point of view.

Before the car arrives, Gabriella tends to every last detail fiercely, as if her rapid efficiency will mask this awful pain that she feels. For him. Packing quickly, she sometimes doesn't even bother to fold the last-minute things that she tosses into the suitcase. She showers only when the valises are closed and downstairs near the front door, dresses, and to the casual observer might appear as a woman who is actually anxious to leave. But it's only when the car arrives and is waiting for her that she breaks down.

"I'm not crying because of you, Mama," she says, on her knees at Audrey's chair, "because we're going to see each other soon and we're used to being apart, aren't we?" She wipes her face with the back of one hand. "And I know what you'd say, that I should do whatever makes me happy, but the truth is that it's not making me happy." She reaches up to hug her, to kiss her on either cheek. "Forget happy, forget unhappy, it's making me miserable!" Standing up, she bends over to take Audrey's hands in hers, pressing each of them to her lips, amazed right then at how quickly the years have passed and how many regrets she still harbors. "Good-bye, Mama," she says for the last time. "I'll see you soon." If she dwells on the past and on all the things she should have done or could have done differently, she could easily cause an enormous eruption inside her head that would obliterate all the good memories as well.

CHAPTER TEN

The Resolution

THE AIR FRANCE LOUNGE at Kennedy Airport is not terribly crowded this evening, several American families setting off on French holidays, several French families returning after American vacations, an assortment of obvious foreigners to both countries traveling abroad, and Gabriella Carlucci-Molloy looking disoriented, ill at ease, and miserable.

Huddled in one corner of a sofa, Gabriella observes the others carefully, struck by the fact that each cluster of people is a unit: a mother, a father, and children, a family that shares food, fear, hope, and life with one another, related and connected on one level by choice, on another by blood.

White nylon socks, buff-colored mesh oxfords, skimpy jackets, crumpled pants with pleated fronts, and anxious expressions around mouths that puff on foul-smelling cigarettes, French fathers watch with detached interest as French mothers nurse French infants. Ankle-length, flare-skirted, buttoned-up-to-the-front cotton sundresses, gold Repetto ballet slippers, their straight dark hair cut in boyish bobs and falling over untweezed brows, French mothers leaf nonchalantly through *Marie Claire* or *Elle* while their babies nurse. Older toddlers sit quietly on the floor at their feet, looking at picture books or their fathers' most recent Ton Ton comic. Bags of fresh fruit are produced after the infants are fed, knives also, to cut the apples and pears in those typically neat French sections to be offered as snacks before boarding, washed down with water from bottles of Evian or Volvic.

Reebok running shoes, designer blue jeans, crewneck cotton shirts, expressions of concentration around mouths that chomp on chewing gum, American fathers bottle feed their infants. Velour jogging suits with designer imprints on the pockets, names spelled out in gold on chains around their necks, hair frosted and permed in waves around their heads, American mothers meticulously arrange and rearrange the contents of plastic carry-on bags filled with baby provisions for the seven-hour journey while a papoose canvas sack is opened and ready to be attached to their backs before boarding. Toddlers cling to the hands of older children as they race around the waiting room, screeching and shrieking in delight each time that an airplane takes off or lands on the other side of the glass wall facing the runway. After infants are fed, bags of potato chips, peanuts, and chocolates are produced and offered around and are washed down by cans of soda—something light to calm and distract the children or stave off the fathers' hunger until that plastic food called dinner is served on board.

Each of them, Gabriella reflects, is about to embark upon a journey that will cover the same distance of time and space in miles or kilometers while she will make that same trip alone, measured for her in light years away from everything she loves and holds dear. So she tries not to dwell on this solitude that she feels, concentrating instead on the gestures and movements and voices of those around her, an exercise she has perfected since aircrafts became potential infernos and airports likely battle sites for Holy Wars. Leaning back, she tries to imagine these same faces attached to names that would appear on a casualty list in a newspaper. Only possible and valid if the combination of chemistries is just right, which is why she observes this collection of humanity so carefully, to see if perhaps they are all destined to share a final adventure.

Restless, she tires of watching everyone, feeling so alienated sitting there that this lounge could be a waiting room for a rocket ship to Mars, or a capsule that could beam her up to a distant planet. She turns her head and notices an airline hostess sitting on a chair, a concerned expression on the woman's face, not unlike a mother testifying before a Senate subcommittee on the dangers of insecticides in baby food. Or perhaps she knows something about an engine or the hydraulic system or perhaps Gabriella's level of paranoia is just unusually high this evening.

An African in colorful robes takes a seat on the sofa opposite Gabriella, nodding his head as a companion talks incessantly in his ear, a silly Dizzy Gillespie grin on his face. Fiddling with a brochure, Gabriella reads that the movie on board tonight will be something called *Frantic*—a title that could best describe her state of mind—about an American tourist who is kidnapped while visiting Paris. How she would love that to happen to her, but only if she was spirited right back on a plane and home. To Nick. Which is when she glances to her left and notices a man and woman leaning against each other near one wall and kissing. She turns away to see a small child being cuddled on his mother's lap and then looks to her right to witness a man resting his hand protectively on the belly of his very pregnant wife. She glances toward the exit to observe an elderly couple sitting very close together, hands clasped on his bony knee as each leafs through a magazine. Tears fill Gabriella's eyes as she realizes there comes a point in every woman's adulthood when loss is no longer limited to parents who have grown old or sick—a time in every woman's motherhood when sadness is no longer related to children who have grown up or away, when excuses for lousy childhoods are no longer valid and lousy offspring no longer seemly. Sometimes old wounds heal without anyone even trying to heal them and whether anyone wants them to heal or not. And for Gabriella Carlucci-Molloy, formerly unresolved daughter and guilt-ridden mother, nothing seems to be as crucial than to transcend those roles and become a woman. Now. Right here in this Air France lounge at Kennedy Airport. To shed that ridiculous veneer of cultural tolerance that continues to offer hope that she could find happiness and security in a foreign country. When in reality all she has been doing is ignoring all the bad memories so she can continue rationalizing her various Houdini escapes from life.

It is only forty-five minutes until the scheduled departure time, approximately fifteen minutes until boarding. Yet the moment has arrived when Gabriella is convinced that it would go against every fiber, vessel, instinct, and bone in her body to turn her back on this man whom she loves and wants more than anybody ever. Which is when she knows that she wants out of here and wants it now.

Jumping up and startling the African and his companion into silence, the first time the man has stopped jabbering into the other man's ear since they entered the room, Gabriella grabs her carry-on bag, briefcase, and trench coat and dashes up to the desk where an Air France hostess is seated.

"Excuse me," she begins pleasantly, although anyone who knew her well would detect a note of hysteria in her unnaturally high-pitched tone, "but I've changed my mind, I don't want to go to Paris tonight."

The hostess remains calm, at least outwardly. "Have you checked baggage through?" she asks, appraising Gabriella from head to toe and then back up again.

"Yes I have, but why?" Tense, she runs a hand through already disheveled hair.

"Because there're regulations about unaccompanied luggage on overseas flights." She shakes her head, purses her painted lips, and blinks her clear blue eyes. "I'm sorry but you'll have to board."

"Take my bags off the plane," Gabriella says, bursting into high gear.

"If we did that, there would be a huge delay."

At the word *delay,* several of those who have been milling about near the desk stop their conversations in mid-sentence to listen to what is transpiring between the two women.

"Look, if it's that complicated, then leave the bags on board and ship them back from Paris." She smiles, trying to keep the tremor in her voice in check.

"I don't think you understand," the woman replies with exaggerated patience. "There are rules to be followed and certain procedures that must be carried out and that includes not allowing any unaccompanied baggage to remain in the hold." She takes in a blast of air through one tapered nostril, which ends up sounding something like a snort.

"Then-take-it-off-the-plane," Gabriella says, separating each word just the slightest bit to make the meaning sharper.

"It would take two hours." The woman leans forward to hiss in Gabriella's face.

"Then let the suitcases go without me" is the immediate retort before she also leans forward to inquire, "Tell me, do I look like someone who would put a bomb in a suitcase?"

At the word *bomb* a sudden hush falls over the four sectional sofas and three armchairs positioned within hearing distance of the reception desk. The woman now looks at Gabriella as if she is brain-damaged.

"If we knew what people looked like who put bombs on airplanes, there'd never be a bomb on an airplane." A pause then while she glances around as if for approval, but there is only silence and several terrified expressions. Gabriella takes a breath.

"I really don't want to cause any problems and I understand about your regulations, but I've changed my mind. Don't I have the right to change my mind?"

"Why don't you tell me what the problem is and perhaps I can help you to solve it," the woman coaxes with what seems to be an entirely changed attitude. "Then we can all avoid a tremendous complication."

Gabriella considers her options only to conclude that she has none. "The problem is that I've changed my mind, that's all."

"Are you ill?" the hostess asks, barely able to mouth the words, her hands flat on the desk.

"Actually, I'm feeling a little weak but I think it's only anxiety."

"Shall I call a doctor?" she says, stalling.

Gabriella shakes her head, still leaning forward over the guest register and the flight schedule, one elbow resting on top of the computer. "No, it's all right, I'll be fine just as soon as I can go—either with or without my bags."

A ripple of conversation erupts around them, for a group has edged its way over, gathering at one side of the desk. "Are you sure you want to do this?" the woman asks, "because if you do, I've got to make an announcement." The tone is resigned. "We're supposed to be boarding in about ten minutes."

"I'm not boarding," Gabriella says tightly, suddenly fighting for everything that means anything in her whole life. Another buzz of conversation follows as she reaches down to collect her possessions, a motion that the Air France employee interprets as a sign to take immediate action.

"Wait a minute," she rushes. "At least wait until I can get someone from security here." A lock of hair has fallen from the neatly rolled chignon at the nape of her neck. "Please, just let me call the gate as well to tell them that we've got a delay."

A passenger, French from his accent and appearance, approaches the desk to inquire.

"Exactly how much of a delay will there be?" he asks, giving a scathing look in Gabriella's direction while he waits for a reply.

"We don't know yet, sir, but as soon as we do I'll make an announcement. Just take your seat please."

An American comes forward then, his stomach spilling over a turquoise-studded belt. "So what's the story? I've got an important business meeting in Paris tomorrow morning. Are we boarding or not?"

"Not yet, sir," the hostess answers, a smile frozen on her face, a muscle twitching at her jaw.

"Do I have time to make a phone call?" another passenger asks as the half dozen people who had been gathered around move over to make room for another half dozen people who have wandered over as well. Gabriella is slouched down in a chair, her head leaning against the palm of one hand, wishing that this wasn't happening, wondering why she let it go this far, disbelieving that she could have been this dumb to think she was capable of actually leaving him.

"Will everyone please move back and take seats so we can sort this out? Please, we'll get this settled a lot quicker if you just keep calm!" Her mouth twitching, she leans over to whisper to Gabriella. "Security's on the way!"

□

"God damn it," Nick swears, "how the hell did this whole thing happen anyway?" Standing in his front yard, he clips the same hedge in the same spot that he's been clipping for the last fifteen minutes so that it's a good six inches shorter than the other hedges that border his property with the main road. Not that the question nor the expletive has anything to do with his uneven landscaping efforts. He glances at his watch and sees that it is already ten minutes to four. Unless he leaves right now there isn't a prayer in hell that he'll get to the airport before six-thirty, when the plane is scheduled to take off.

It started as an idea this morning when he was in the shower, a scene that played in his head. He would arrive at the airport at the last minute, just as the steps were being rolled away from the plane's door, and only after frantic discussions, pleadings, and the sentimentality of one warm-hearted security guard would the steps be rolled back to the plane and the door opened so that Gabriella could tumble out to fall into his arms. Only the scene had little to do with reality on any level and more to do with the final moments in *Casablanca*, even if in his film there was a modern airport and an updated airplane.

There were other problems with the fantasy that included rules, regulations, and emotional reactions, like his not being able to get through the security area to reach the craft or Gabriella's anger as he attempted to remove her from the plane. Still, Nick seemed perfectly content to keep it as he played it in the shower instead of perhaps making an effort to reach the end of their story in a more realistic way, to work out all the mistakes and wrong decisions so they could live happily ever after. In real life. But like everyone who writes, directs, and stars in his own fantasy, Nick found himself left with only an image of that fabulous ending without any clue at all about how to make it really happen.

After his morning shower he finally threw on some clothes, with every intention of heading over to the construction site in Freeport. But at the last minute he decided that he was in no condition to surround himself with guys who expected him to take charge and solve problems. How could he when he couldn't even take charge and solve problems having to do with his own life? So he chose to be alone instead, to hole himself up in his office and catch up on the billings and other tedious paperwork even if he found, once there, that he kept adding the same column of figures and coming up with different totals each time.

At around eleven in the morning he gave up and jumped into his car, destined for that familiar stretch of beach in Montauk—a favorite spot since he was a kid to work out all the anger and frustration that sometimes over-whelmed him—where he did his usual three miles up to the old boathouse, where the Windsurfers and Sailfishes from Gurney's Hotel were dry-docked, and back to the edge of the property where the tennis courts first become visible from the beach.

Nothing seemed to help, not the sand nor the water nor the cloudless blue sky, nothing cooled him down or propelled him into taking some kind of action. All he could feel was the most incredible sense of failure, of loss and impotency, of excruciating pain and confusion whenever he thought of her. Which was constantly.

It was absolutely crazy that he couldn't pull himself together to stop her, demented that he hadn't realized be-fore today how miserable he would be. Already. And she was still in this hemisphere, on this side of the ocean, in this country. Which was when he climbed back into his car, after sloshing around in the surf for a couple of surprisingly chilly minutes, and headed home, which is when he picked up the hedge clippers and started mangling that hedge.

"Pure bullshit," he mutters disgustedly, as thoughts of getting caught in some kind of highly stringent security regulations at the airport flit in and out of his mind. Sud-denly, he flings aside the hedge clipper and sprints toward the house for the car keys. Clutching them in one hand, he races to the convertible, parked in the driveway, jumps over the door rather than bothering to open it, and starts the ignition.

A pair of filthy khaki cutoffs, a dirt-streaked T-shirt, and a two-day stubble certainly don't give the impression that he exactly dressed for the occasion or planned it, for that matter, even if the truth is that somewhere inside his head he had been planning this move since the first time they made love and she announced afterward that she would be leaving soon. Shaking his head, he grins slightly at the memory, so typical of her, always leaving, running somewhere, that bottom lip of hers trembling as she made those sweeping pronouncements of departure. "What a schmuck I was!" he mumbles now.

The car screeches down the driveway with Nick hunched over the wheel, nervously gnawing on his bottom lip as he negotiates the winding road that leads into town. Strangely though, he is suddenly filled with an all-encompassing optimism, as if from the moment he made this decision to bring her back, it was clear that it was the decision she wanted him to make. Not a thought about being rejected or rebuffed, for he is more sure of this than he has been of anything else before. Accelerating beyond the speed limit, he approaches the entrance to the expressway and gets on in the direction of Kennedy Airport. To bring her home. Wherever that is. But if she gives him a chance and he gives her one too, maybe they might be able to solve that problem too.

□

The voice crackles over the loudspeaker in a flat nondescript male twang. "May I have your attention, please. Air France Flight 2292 for Paris has been detained." Lightheaded, suddenly of the knowledge that she is the reason for the delay, a sense of dread envelops Gabriella that she has actually made this stand. But for the first time in her life or at least for the first time since life began dealing her a series of disappointments, she has decided to be optimistic and spontaneous—everything a woman was once supposed to be.

A murmur rushes through the group of passengers in the lounge after the microphone squeaks and hums into silence, not so much a reaction of surprise as one of resignation. Gabriella glances around furtively, sinking lower into the chair, trying not to make eye contact with anyone until a man with an official clip-on badge pinned to his shirt and a walkie-talkie in his hand approaches.

"May I have a word with you?" he asks, and without waiting for a response, pulls up a chair next to her. Her expression is enigmatic under the guise of serene, although if she were forced to express her feelings right then they would be of isolation and an awareness of a vastness of space that was hers alone.

"What seems to be the problem?" the man begins gently. "I understand you're refusing to board?"

Embarrassed, she replies, "There's no problem, it's just that I've changed my mind."

He studies her a moment. "You know that's going to cause a lot of chaos."

"Yes and I'm sorry."

"We're going to have to unload the entire baggage hold until we find your bags."

"I'm sorry," she repeats although as she listens to the security guard and his problems with the plane, she can't believe that she ever intended to leave Nick. It seems impossible that she could have thought of walking away from someone whom she loves as much as she loves him, especially with all the other heartbreak and confusion that has already touched her life.

"I really wish you'd reconsider," the man says.

Like an anemic let loose in a blood bank, she feels an enormous surge of strength and hope. "That's just what I've done," she says happily, "I've reconsidered."

"And?"

"And I'm not boarding."

But then a tug of war begins to wage inside her head or her heart, each side struggling to make known the pitfalls of this stand. What if Nick would be less than thrilled with her appearing on his doorstep claiming to have changed her mind about spending the rest of her life with him? After all, it's one thing for a man to ask those kinds of questions—about loving and living together forever—and another for a woman to call him on his good intentions by actually accepting.

"Look, these aren't our rules," the airline official is quick to add, "they're Federal Aviation regulations." Another boyish grin. "If it were up to us, you could just go and the heck with the bags." She appears to be paying attention to him, nodding in all the right places, but her thoughts are focused right now on a definition of what she has come to realize as real life. I trust, she thinks, pushing her innermost reserve of nerves to the hilt, I trust and I love, she repeats like a Buddhist chant, only to hear the anguished reply from the wounded child that still lurks within to contradict: I don't trust and I am not loved.

"Do you want to think about it for a few minutes?" the airline employee inquires tactfully. "I'll wait over there," he adds, pointing to the buffet table of coffee and tea and an assortment of soft drinks.

She shakes her head slightly, her eyes flickering up to meet his, her thoughts still in another solar system. Perhaps some of the best relationships and love affairs are dependent upon women being elusive. Perhaps Nick feels relieved that she left, and if she decided to stay, would suggest that she turn right around and board the plane as planned so both of them could mull things over for a while. Or worse, perhaps he was already with another woman either for solace or simply because he was a man and Gabriella had mentioned that she had plans for the rest of her life, which didn't include him.

The security guard wanders back, a container of coffee in hand. "Want some?" he offers.

"No, thanks."

Sitting down, he observes, "There're a lot of kids in here and pretty soon we're going to have a lot of screaming kids if we don't get moving."

She looks at him then with tears that threaten to spill from her eyes and shrugs.

"It's getting late," he presses, making a pretense of checking his wrist.

A voice screams inside her, berating her for living in the past or in the future, never in the present, never until now, until she met him. Logic has become her excuse and her escape from loving while abstractions have taken the place of concrete promises. Yet to put herself on the line like this without taking months or years or decades for him to prove himself, to convince her that this time would be different, is sheer lunacy. And she can suddenly feel herself slipping back into that familiar primordial pain that she can best define as loss, the kind of pain that displays all the hurts and fears like so many family heirlooms. "All right," she says in a voice so small and so meek that she has the impression he must lean forward to catch the words. "I'll board the plane."

□

Nick Tressa arrives at the Air France terminal at Kennedy Airport after parking his car so sloppily that it takes up two spaces in the short-term lot. Checking the departure screen when he enters the terminal, he sees to his sheer delight that the plane has been delayed. He races up to the place through which only those people holding valid tickets can pass, and breathless and agitated, blurts out, "I've got to get to someone who's about to board Air France Flight 2292 for Paris."

"I'm sorry," the bovine guard drones, "but only passengers with tickets can go beyond this point."

"Look, this is an emergency."

"What kind of an emergency?" the woman asks, taking in his appearance, including the gritty dirt caked on his hands, his unshaven face and tattered clothes.

"There's someone I've got to stop from leaving," he evades. A look of apprehension crosses the woman's face as she moves over to consult a colleague. But Nick is right behind her. "Guy says it's an emergency," she says as if he is invisible.

"Yeah, well, the plane's about to leave. They're boarding now."

"I've got to get through," Nick interrupts. "Please!"

"Too late."

"Call," Nick orders urgently.

"Where would you like me to call?" The sarcasm drips from the woman's voice.

"The plane, the runway, I don't care where you call, just call."

The airport personnel are clearly rattled. Obviously no amount of training has prepared them for what could possibly be the real thing—a lunatic trying to stop an airplane. "Take it easy," the man who had been manning the detection machine says in a deliberate tone. Several other airport guards gather around. And as Nick begins to explain, the woman has already picked up a telephone, her face flushed underneath the blue cap as she waits for someone to answer.

The boarding process has started, from the lounge through a side door, down a long corridor and then onto the aircraft. Elderly and unaccompanied children, women with infants and strollers, and families are ushered through before the others. Economy Class is called next, beginning with the very last rows of smokers and then down toward the front of that section. Gabriella has collected her belongings and is already standing in line before the door leading into the wind tunnel, waiting for the nonsmoking part of Business Class to be called—to get the first part of this nightmare over with so she can fall into a senseless sleep. As she moves, it is as if she moves in a trance, the world inside her head suddenly becoming more real than what is happening around her, her subconscious having taken over to spare her the remorse.

Several Air France officials, the man who tried to talk her into changing her mind, another man whom she doesn't recognize, and a woman, are walking alongside the line as if there is some kind of an inspection in progress. Gabriella turns around to watch, mildly curious if this is all routine or an aftermath of the earlier delay. Which is when she sees him in the distance, lingering at the door of the lounge, craning his head in the direction of the crowd waiting to board.

Tears half blind her as she relinquishes her place in the line, and for one horrifying moment she imagines it is all a mirage, that her tears and the setting sun that streams in through the huge window in the lounge make it impossible for her to focus, creating only an illusion that he is really there.

The airline employee who had the initial contact with her edges over now to inform her that there is someone who wants to talk to her. "An emergency," he says although his expression says something else. Barely nodding, she bends down to move her possessions over to one side.

"Will everyone please just stay put or take seats," the voice on the loudspeaker instructs. "Just a short delay, just take seats and we'll continue boarding in a very few minutes."

If Gabriella had to say right this moment what it was about Nicholas Tressa that she loves the most and why it ended up being him and not a hundred other possibilities or no possibility at all, she would have to say that it is partly the way he always draws himself up when he holds her, always slightly out of breath after they kiss, or the way he watches her when she speaks, or smiles in delight when she reacts to something she has just discovered for the first time, or his sheer enthusiasm for life. Or she would have to admit that she loves him for making her a wanted woman once again. For she had reached the end of her invention when she met him, of everything, every last game and dance, every last self. All of it. She might say all of those things or she might say that some things are simply impossible to explain.

Out of the corner of her eye she notices several uniforms conferring in low voices, voices that seem to be preparing for a procedure which she honestly didn't think would be the result of anything she did. "Unload the plane," she thinks she hears someone saying, "possibly we'll have to delay." She struggles not to break into a wild sprint toward him, because it seems suddenly paramount that she walk with grace and dignity. So he came to get me, she thinks, tears brimming in her eyes. Not bad for a beginning. Original, something that never happened before. But then he's something that never happened before either.

Gabriella touches Nick's hand first, pressing it to her face before she ends up in his arms. Trying desperately to think of something to say makes her fraught with confusion until she finally blurts out in a lame attempt at humor, "What took you so long?"

Tilting her chin so her lips are only breaths away from his, he replies perfectly seriously, "I got hung up in security."

She takes a step back, possibly to explore his motive or perhaps merely to seek a confirmation that it is as it appears. "I'm glad."

It's not quite over yet, not this interminable day nor this ability to absorb the positive aspects of this encounter. "There's been so much," she begins, her voice choked, her head pressed against his chest.

"The only way to make it work is to start again." He tilts up her chin. "With me."

To be loved unconditionally is like a gift of air, or better, to be loved despite the damage is like a gift of life. The conveyor belt in the distance is carrying the baggage from the belly of the craft while Gabriella and Nick stand in one corner of the crowded room in an embrace that overwhelms each of them from within. As a child she survived by being the caretaker, as an adult by false hopes and failed deeds. Now the journey is complete, for she has finally run out of excuses. She has finally come home.